THE QUESTING

A Medieval Romance

By Kathryn Le Veque

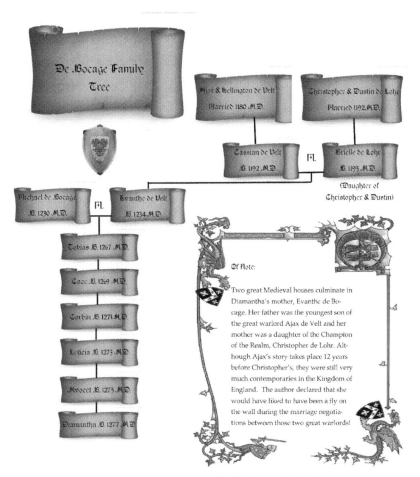

De Bocage Family Tree

Ajax & Kellington de Velt
Married 1180 A.D.

Christopher & Dustin de Lohr
Married 1192 A.D.

Cassian de Velt
B. 1192 A.D.

M.

Grielle de Lohr
B. 1195 A.D.

(Daughter of
Christopher & Dustin)

Michael de Bocage
B. 1230 A.D.

M.

Evanthe de Velt
B. 1234 A.D.

Tobias B. 1267 A.D.

Cace B. 1269 A.D.

Corbin B. 1271 A.D.

Leticia B. 1273 A.D.

Avocet B. 1275 A.D.

Diamantha B. 1277 A.D.

Of Note:

Two great Medieval houses culminate in
Diamantha's mother, Evanthe de Bocage. Her father was the youngest son of
the great warlord Ajax de Velt and her
mother was a daughter of the Champion
of the Realm, Christopher de Lohr. Although Ajax's story takes place 12 years
before Christopher's, they were still very
much contemporaries in the Kingdom of
England. The author declared that she
would have liked to have been a fly on
the wall during the marriage negotia-
tions between those two great warlords!

Ajax de Velt's story: The Dark Lord
Christopher de Lohr's story: Rise of the Defender
Michael de Bocage appeared in The Wolfe

To my Team – the best team an author could have:

Kris – who harped on me for a year and a half to finish this book (harped in a good way!). You have motivated and inspired me!

Scott – a kick-ass editor if there ever was one. Thank you for your feedback, your wit, and your friendship.

Also, to fellow authors Suzan Tisdale and Tanya Anne Crosby, who are a constant source of knowledge, camaraderie, and humor.

And finally, to my readers – you keep me striving with every click of the keyboard for a bigger, better novel. My deepest thanks for your support.

Love to all!

PROLOGUE

July 22, 1298 A.D.
Falkirk, Scotland

The skies had opened up sometime around mid-afternoon, pounding the gently rolling hills with a terrible onslaught of rain. It had rained the day before, too, soaking the already saturated ground to the point where it could no longer absorb the water that was now falling from the angry black clouds in buckets.

In a field to the south of what was known locally as Callendar Wood, a drastic scene was taking place; Scotsmen, led by William Wallace, were taking a pounding from the English who outnumbered them by more than two to one. Wallace, an excellent tactician, had his pikemen in four great armored groups, called "hedgehogs", making them difficult to penetrate by the English. The Scots archers hadn't fared so well. They were already mostly destroyed by a wave of Sassenach knights who had descended on them with all of the good manners of a horde of starving locusts. The battle between the mounted cavalry and the archers on foot had not lasted long.

Now, the English archers had been called in and the knights had fallen back, allowing the archers to bombard the hedgehogs with their spiny arrows in great falling clouds, more numerous than the raindrops falling from the sky. After a few rounds of well-aimed English arrows, the small number of Scots cavalry abandoned the battlefield, leaving the pikemen in their hedgehogs to face the barrage alone. Those men were now falling, too, and the English were sitting atop of a great victory. It was only a matter of time.

Near the east end of the field, there was still a bit of skirmish going on between Scottish cavalry and English knights that had blocked their escape. There were no more than thirty or forty mounted Scots against two dozen English knights, big men on big horses, well armored and well trained. The lesser trained Scots cavalry never stood a chance as the English knights swarmed them.

A big knight on a bay charger finished off two Scotsmen, toppling one off of his horse by punching him squarely in the chest and then using his broadsword on the other. It was brutal, and messy, but it was a job well done. He was still in combat mode when another knight came up behind him, startling him.

"Ease yourself, Edlington!" the man shouted, holding up his sword to fend off Edlington's powerful blow. The man flipped up his visor, a grin on his face. Dark eyes, as black as night, glimmered humorously. "You have them on the run, man. Ease down that vicious weapon."

Sir Robert Edlington grinned at his fellow knight, a friend, lifting his hinged visor and wiping the sweat that had trickled into his right eye. Edlington was a handsome man with blue eyes and dark blond hair, now plastered against his wet forehead.

"I think we all have them on the run," he said, turning to gaze off towards the west where the last remnants of the battle were occurring. "Edward's might once again rules the day."

The other knight nodded as he, too, looked off into the distance where the Scots were making their last stand. The stench of defeat was heavy in the air, leeching into the Scots soil upon which they stood.

"Indeed it does," the knight with the black eyes said. "Mayhap now we can finally return home."

Edlington glanced over at the man. "Until the next time," he said, almost begrudgingly. "We shall all end up in Wales next time, scaling those jagged mountains with a rope in one hand and a sword in the other. Edward would have us fighting like mountain goats."

The knight with the black eyes snorted. "He does not care how you fight for him, as long as you do," he muttered, watching the clash in the distance. "Mayhap we should join the others. This will go a lot faster if we help, you and I. I suspect they are waiting for us to deliver the death blow."

It was a humorous quip, one that set Edlington to laughing. Just as the man reached down to gather his reins and prepared to follow his friend back to the heart of the fighting, they both heard a high-pitched buzz overhead. Too late, they realized it was an arrow and before either one of them could move, Edlington was struck squarely in the chest. The blow of the arrow was so forceful that it knocked the man cleanly off his horse. Edlington went flying off backwards, hitting the mud behind him with a sickening thud.

His friend, his companion, was off his charger in a moment, falling to his knees beside Edlington.

"Sweet Jesus," the companion breathed as he realized that the arrow had struck Edlington cleanly in the middle of his torso. "Let me see, Rob. Let me get this out of you."

Edlington lay on his back, gazing up at the sky. He was stunned, that was true, but he was also rather bewildered.

"A... Scots arrow," he said with disgust. "I... I thought the Scot archers were all dead."

His companion was tearing at his tunic, pulling it back so he could get a look at the arrow where it had pierced the mail and entered Edlington's chest. But what he saw sickened him; the arrow had been what was called a "blunt". The head of it was sharpened but it didn't follow the usual shape of an arrowhead. It was meant to enter the body and tear great holes in its victim, which is what it had done to Edlington.

There was a big hole in him, sucking with air as the knight struggled to breathe, with the arrow buried several inches deep into his body. The companion could see that he was going to have to work quickly in order to save the man's life, if it was at all possible.

He didn't want to entertain the thought that there was no hope, not now. Not when they were so close to victory. But deep in his heart he knew that it was already over. Edlington was already dead.

"I must roll you onto your back, Rob," he said hurriedly. "Help me. Roll with me if you can."

Grunting as he tried to pull the man over from his right side, he realized that he couldn't because the arrow had gone all the way through. It had sliced directly through Edlington's spine and at least two inches of arrow protruded out of his back. His horror must have reflected in his eyes because Edlington suddenly grabbed his hands, squeezing tightly.

"Cortez, listen to me," Rob gasped as it became increasingly difficult to breathe. "You must promise me something."

Cortez de Bretagne stared at Rob, grief etching his features. "Let me help you," he pleaded softly. "If I can get this arrow out, I can...."

Edlington cut him off. "Nay, my friend," he whispered. "It is over. I cannot feel my legs. This is the last of me now and I must say what is in my heart before I die. Will you listen? Will you please?"

Over to the west, they could hear the sounds of fighting again as more Scots and more English came together. It was too close for comfort and Cortez stood up, grabbing Rob under the arms and dragging him away from the fighting, through a cluster of trees, slugging through knee-deep mud in places to reach what appeared to be a safe spot. There was a big oak tree to protect them from the rain even though the tree itself was surrounded by a sea of dark, clinging mud.

Grunting with effort, Cortez propped Edlington up against the tree trunk, falling to his knees beside the man. He grasped the spine of the arrow, preparing to remove it, but Edlington stopped him.

"Nay," he gasped. "Leave it. There is nothing you can do."

"But...!"

"Leave it," Edlington begged, grasping for Cortez's hands again. He found them and held them tightly, gazing into the face of his friend. "Please, Cortez... you must promise me something."

Cortez was verging on tears of sorrow, of rage. He knew this was the end for his friend and there was nothing he could do to stop it.

"Anything at all," he said hoarsely, squeezing Robert's hands tightly. "Whatever it is, I shall do it."

"Diamantha," Robert breathed. "My wife. This will be very hard on her, Cortez. She must be comforted. I ask that you tell her my last thoughts were of her and of Sophie, my daughter. You will tell her, won't you? You will tell her that I was very proud to be her husband."

Cortez nodded vigorously. "You know I will," he said, feeling tears sting his eyes. "But let me try to remove this arrow. Mayhap there is...."

"Cortez, listen to me," Robert interrupted him; he was having great difficulty breathing. "Diamantha... I want you to take care of her. Swear to me that you will. Since your own Helene is gone these past three years, you are free to marry Diamantha. I want you to, Cortez. Swear to me you will marry her and that you will be very good to her."

Cortez looked at the man in shock. "*Marry* her?" he repeated, stunned. "But... Rob, she may not want to...."

"Please!" Robert gasped with anguish.

Cortez couldn't refuse the man. He couldn't stand to see his pain, to see his life draining away. The anguish he felt was staggering.

"Of course," he assured the man quickly, to ease his mind. "I will do what you ask. Rest assured, my friend. I will take care of her. She will want for nothing."

Robert still had a grip on him. "Seek out her father," he muttered. "He is a great knight, living at Norham Castle. Seek him out and tell him what has happened. He will give you his blessing, I am sure."

"If that is your wish, I will do it."

Robert seemed to relax a great deal after that, slouching back against the tree trunk as the rain poured down around them. Off to the west, they could hear a horn sound, a call to arms. Cortez knew that it was Edward, summoning all of his available fighting men to deliver the death blow to the Scots. The day was growing late and he wanted to tie up his business. Cortez looked at Robert, collapsed against the tree, and squeezed the man's hands tightly.

"I will be back," he said determinedly. "Edward has need of his knights but I will return as soon as I can. Do you hear me? *I will be back.*"

Robert nodded faintly. "I am at peace, Cortez," he muttered. "Whatever happens now, I am at peace knowing my wife and daughter are in your hands. Pray be good to them. Love them as I do."

Cortez stared at him a moment as the man took a deep, ragged breath and closed his eyes. Filled with sorrow, Cortez leaned over Robert and kissed his exposed forehead.

"You are my brother," he whispered. "You are one of the finest knights I have ever known. Godspeed, Robert, wherever your path may take you."

Robert's eyes flickered, giving Cortez a sign that he had heard him, and with that, Cortez staggered wearily to his feet and chased down his charger as the animal grazed several feet away.

With a lingering glance at Edlington, propped up against the ancient oak with the split trunk, Cortez spurred his charger to action, avoiding the great swamps of mud as he headed towards the death throes of the battle of Falkirk, as the Scots fell beneath the English hammer. The end, at that point, was not long in coming and soon enough, it was finished. The English had triumphed.

Before the sun set, Cortez made it back to Robert but when he arrived at the split tree, all that met him was a sea of mud, so deep in places that it could have easily swallowed a man. Edlington was gone, returned to the earth as all men did when it was their time to meet God. A search for him the next day turned up no sign of the big, strapping knight who had been gored through the chest. Just like that, he was gone, and the battle of Falkirk faded into the annals of history.

But the quest to find Robert Edlington's body did not end that day. In fact, it had only begun.

For it was not into my ear you whispered, but into my heart.
It was not my lips you kissed, but my soul.
~ 13th Century Poet

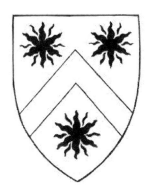

CHAPTER ONE

Corfe Castle, Dorset
October 1298 AD

"For the love of God, he has only been dead these three months. Why must you force my husband from my memory so quickly?"

A lone woman faced off against a man clad in pieces of mail and leather, her words of anguish filling the air between them. The question was infused with sorrow and curiosity. Yet, it was a legitimate query. In the lavish solar that was the heart of Corfe Castle's mighty stone keep, the emotions filling the room were as heady as the black smoke from the snapping fire.

The man with the silver hair tried to be stern with his reply but found he could not when he gazed into her agonized face. Her dual-toned eyes, a mesmerizing shade of bright green with a splash of brown around the iris of the right orb, slashed into him until he could no longer hold his gaze. He ended up rising from his chair and turning his back to her. It was the only way he could breathe.

"I am not attempting to erase his memory, Diamantha," he said quietly. "Robert was my son and my grief exceeds your own. However, the fact remains that he is no longer with us and it is your father's wish that you remarry as soon as possible. You are young and wealthy, and your father wants you to find a suitable husband."

The Lady Diamantha de Bocage Edlington changed moods as swiftly as a flash of lightning; she charged to her father-in-law, forcing the man to look her in the eye. When she spoke, it was through clenched teeth.

"My father," she seethed. "By all that is holy and right, I knew he was behind this. I *knew* it!"

Sir George Edlington was old; too old for what he was about to face. A dead son, a grieving daughter-in-law, and pain in his heart that was deeper than an ocean. No parent should ever have to bury a child. With a deep breath for courage, he grasped Diamantha by the arms as if to shake some sense into her.

"Your father wants his daughter to be taken care of," he said firmly. "Robert, God rest him, would want this also. He would not want you to spend your life reliving memories that are of no use to anyone. And he would want Sophie to know a father again."

Diamantha yanked away from him, her small body showing more strength than George had imagined it held.

"Sophie's father is dead," she half-hissed, half-wept. "She will never know another. And I do not want another husband."

"So you would let your daughter live her life without the guidance of a father?" George was growing agitated. "And you would rather live your life alone and bitter? That makes little sense."

She lost some of her fire. "It is my life. How I live it is none of your concern."

He cocked a dark, bushy eyebrow. "I wonder what Robert would say to that?"

She opened her mouth in preparation for a scathing retort but found herself unable to muster the energy. After a moment, she shook her head and turned away.

"He would say nothing to me," she said weakly, her brilliant gaze finding the lancet window and the lush green hills of Dorset beyond. The scent of early summer was warm upon the air and she inhaled deeply. "He would do what he always did. He would bow to my wishes and let me do as I please. Your son was far too much of a gentleman to contradict his wife, even when she was wrong."

George watched the slender curve of her back beneath the blue damask surcoat and the way her reddish-brown hair fell in a heavy, shimmering sheet past her buttocks. It was long and straight and silky and she always pulled it off her face in a pleasing style that Robert had liked. Though it was the custom for married women to cover their head, Robert could not bear to see his wife's luscious hair covered.

As George gazed at the woman his son had outright adored, the familiar pangs of grief began to claw at him again. With her, he saw the last memories of his son and he was loath to send her away as her father wished.

But what he wanted was of little consequence. Diamantha's father was a powerful warlord serving the Earl of Teviot in the north and George, as a servant of the king, would do as he was ordered. It was out of his hands. With a blustery sigh, he turned back to the chair that had once held his weary body.

"At least you will not go far," he said softly. "You can take comfort in that."

Diamantha looked at him. "What do you mean?"

George picked up the parchment that lay upon the table next to the chair. "You will go to Sherborne Castle," he replied, not looking at her. "Cortez de Bretagne is to be your new husband."

Diamantha looked at him as if she did not understand his words. Then, her eyes widened. "De Bretagne?" she repeated incredulously. "Is that the man my father has chosen?"

George nodded faintly, re-reading the missive had had received several hours earlier. It had taken him that long to summon the courage to tell Diamantha of its contents. He still did not have the nerve to tell her that her proposed fiancé was waiting in the outer bailey, far removed from the view of the main keep, for an introduction. It was, in fact, de Bretagne who had delivered the missive written by the lady's father.

"Sir Cortez de Bretagne, garrison commander for King Edward's holding of Sherborne Castle," he said as he read the words again.

15

"You have known Cortez for years so it is not as if you will be marrying someone you have never met."

Diamantha could not keep the shocked look off her face. "Of course I know him," she muttered, looking away as she struggled to digest the news. "His wife was my friend until she died three years ago, around the time Sophie was born. Helene died in childbirth and I remember Robert telling me how grief-stricken Cortez was. The man could hardly function."

George dared to look at her to see if he could register any manner of acceptance with the arrangement. "Then this does not displease you?" he asked softly.

Diamantha was still caught up in the memories of Helene de Bretagne and her dark, handsome husband. She ignored her father-in-law's question. "I wonder how my father came to this agreement," she pondered, wandering back towards the window. "How would he know of Cortez? How would he have...?"

"Perhaps Cortez went to him," George interrupted with a shrug. "He was there when Robert was killed. He knew that you were widowed. Perhaps he went to your father with a proposal."

Her head snapped to George. "Do you think that is true?" she suddenly sounded angry again. "Why would he have done this? I have barely spoken ten words to the man the entire time I have known him. Why would he go to my father and demand my hand?"

George put up a hand to stop any building rage. "I do not know if that is the case," he insisted. "It was merely a suggestion. Your father is a great warlord for Edward and so is Cortez. It would not have been difficult for him to arrange an audience with your father, as they are of the same social standing."

She thought on that a moment before refocusing on George. There was resignation in her manner when she spoke.

"Being the youngest of three daughters, I am sure my father was most receptive to Cortez's offer," she said ironically. "My father was always so protective of me and my sisters. He was probably thrilled with the thought of marrying off a widowed daughter purely for the security it would provide."

"Your father loves you a great deal."

"He means well."

George wasn't sure how to respond. He wasn't any good at gauging her mood; he never had been and neither had his son. So he set the parchment back to the table and faced her.

"Cortez delivered the missive," he said, hoping she would not explode at him. "He is waiting to take you back to Sherborne."

Her only reaction was to stare, rather dazed, at him. "Is this true?"

"Indeed it is."

The reply came from the door. Both George and Diamantha whirled in the direction of the entry. Standing in the archway was a tall man with enormous shoulders, partially shrouded by the shadows. They could see his silhouette in the darkness. When he saw that their attention was upon him, he stepped forward into the light.

Cortez de Bretagne was a big, muscular man with cropped black hair and onyx-colored eyes. He was Spaniard on mother's side, Welsh on his father's, giving him a dark and sultry countenance. There was something about the man that oozed strength and seductiveness, far more charisma than most pale and fair Englishmen.

More than that, there was something about him that was unsettling in a giddy sort of way; Diamantha remembered that from the first time she had met him. Every woman in Dorset knew of the gorgeously handsome Cortez and Helene had quietly weathered the female attention to her husband. She remained composed and gracious even as flighty women would challenge her for her husband's affection. It was a quality that Diamantha had appreciated in the woman, her friend gone these three years. Now, the handsome husband was to become hers. She could hardly believe it.

Cortez glanced at George but his focus returned to Diamantha. His attractive, chiseled face smiled timidly as he bowed in her general direction.

"Lady Edlington," he greeted in a soft baritone voice.

"I thought I told you to stay in the bailey until I sent for you," George was the least bit perturbed.

"I was in the bailey," Cortez cast him a long glance, his tone no longer soft. "Now I am here. I think a six hour wait was sufficient."

17

Diamantha stood there gaping at him, shocked by his appearance and not at all certain she was able to grasp what was going on. Not a moment before she was a young widow with a young daughter, looking forward to a lonely future. Now she was betrothed and heading for Sherborne Castle. Rather than become confrontational about it, she turned away and sank into the nearest chair.

"God's Blood," she breathed. "This has all happened so quickly."

George opened his mouth to reply but was cut off by a stern look from Cortez. The younger, more powerful man was not one to be trifled with. George knew that; he had seen the man in battle and he was absolutely ferocious. And he had the reputation of having quite a temper when aroused, something attributed to his mother's Spanish blood. Therefore, when Cortez jerked his head in the direction of the door, George took the hint and left. It was out of his hands, anyway.

Diamantha didn't see George quit the solar. She was turned in the direction of the fire, watching the flames as they licked against the stone. And she didn't see Cortez kneel beside her chair until it was too late. By the time she caught a glimpse of him, he was nearly upon her and she started at his nearness.

"Forgive me," he said, his voice soft once more as he addressed her. "I did not mean to alarm you. But I must speak with you."

Diamantha was leaning against the opposite arm of the chair, as far as she could get from Cortez without actually leaving the chair. She studied his face, reacquainting herself with the man she remembered from distant memories.

At Robert's funeral mass, she had seen him at the church of Corfe's village but she hadn't given him any thought. There had been many knights there to pay homage to the memory of Robert Edlington and Cortez had been one of the many. It had been a memorial service and nothing more. They did not have a body to bury. Robert had been left, like so many others, at Falkirk where he had fallen.

As she studied Cortez's square jaw and dimpled chin, she noticed that he was studying her in return. He was smiling faintly while she was clearly not returning the gesture. It didn't seem to deter him, however. His smile grew the longer she stared at him.

"I realize this is something of a shock to you, my lady," he said in his deep, almost gentle voice. "I wanted to be present when the missive was delivered to you but George thought it best that I wait. But I could not and I do apologize if that seems rash."

Diamantha's brow furrowed slightly as she watched his full lips form words, spewing forth information that was puzzling and slightly urgent-sounding.

"Rash?" she repeated. "Rash that you wanted to be present? Or rash that you burst into the solar in the midst of a private conversation?"

He seemed somewhat chagrined. "Both," he admitted. His black eyes lingered on her. "May I speak plainly, my lady?"

Her brow furrowed even more. She didn't like the way he was looking at her, eagerly, as if he was preparing to swoop down upon her. She did rise from the chair, then, to put some distance between them. He was making her uncomfortable.

"I... I am not sure...," she stammered.

"Please," Cortez rose to his considerable height, watching her as she moved away from him. "I realize that all of this is unexpected and I find that I must explain myself so there will be no misunderstanding."

She paused several feet away to look at him, her hand on her forehead as if shoving back the headache that threatened. There wasn't much she could say to deny him. She was feeling very resigned at the moment.

"Very well," she said. "Speak if you find it necessary although I am not sure there is much that either of us can say given the contents of the missive. What is done is done."

He nodded in concession. "Indeed it is," he replied. "However, there is something I would make clear to you. I was present when your husband was cut down by archers. In fact, it was I who pulled him out of the line of fire once he was struck. Given the fighting going on around us and the severity of his wounds, we both knew it was of no use to attempt to save him."

Diamantha's features paled and the hand came away from her head, moving to her chest as if to hold in her heart. "Why must you tell me such things?" she demanded in a hushed tone. "I do not wish to hear of it."

"I realize that," he said honestly. "But you must. You must understand why you find me standing here tonight."

She realized she was blinking back tears but she fought them. "Speak, then. But know this conversation gives me no pleasure."

"Nor I," he insisted softly. "Still, it must be said." He paused, choosing his words carefully as he continued. "When Robert realized his time was growing short, he swore me to an oath. He spoke of his beautiful wife and daughter and how he worried for them. He made me promise that I would see to their safety and to their future, and since I lacked the courage to deny a dying man, I agreed. I promised him that I would take care of you both and although I was inclined at first to forget my pledge, in my heart I know that I cannot. Robert was my friend, my lady. He was a good man. And I would be forever guilty if I did not hold true to my promise to him and that is why you find me standing before you this night. I am here because I promised him that I would come."

By now, the tears were streaming down Diamantha's cheeks. As his words sunk in, she hastily wiped at her face and sniffled delicately, struggling not to fall apart. But she found that she could not take her eyes off of the man. As he spoke those gentle words, something inside of her had changed. Her opinion of him had changed. She now saw him through different eyes, as if the man before her held some semblance of honor. He could have well forgotten a promise to a dying man and no one would have known. But he had not forgotten.

"But why you?" she asked hoarsely. "It is not as if you were as close as brothers. You were friends, that is true, but there were men he was closer to. Why *you*?"

"Because I was the only one there," he replied quietly. "While everyone else was laying waste to the fields of Falkirk, I was near your husband when he was struck. It just happened to be me, my lady; it could have been anyone. But it was me."

Diamantha understood a great deal in that softly-uttered explanation. But it also deepened her sense of despair. It was what

Robert had wanted and she would be forced to comply with his wishes. Her bright gaze was intense.

"How did my father become a part of this pact?" she asked. "Did you seek him out?"

Cortez nodded slowly. "I did," he replied. "I explained the situation to him and he was more than happy to comply."

So it was as she thought; or, at least, partially so. But the fact remained that she was betrothed to Cortez and there was nothing she could do about it. Resigned, she turned away from him. She realized that she found it difficult to look at him, difficult to realize that she was gazing at her next husband. She needed to acclimate herself to the idea. But there was still something else, something that had been gnawing at her since the day she had received news of her husband's death. It was something that was difficult to think on and not look at Cortez with a great deal of resentment.

"But you left him there," she murmured. "You left my husband on the battlefield. You did not bring him home so that he could be properly buried."

Cortez knew that subject would arise and he was prepared. He had been prepared for three months. But now, gazing at the lady's lovely profile, he resisted the urge to plead for her forgiveness.

"It was not by choice, I assure you," he responded quietly. "I explained the circumstances to your husband's father at the time we delivered the news of Robert's passing. I assumed he had told you."

Her head came up again and he was struck by the anguish in those beautiful dual-colored eyes. "I was told that the circumstances for bringing him home were impossible," her voice was soft and hoarse. "Beyond that, I was not given the courtesy to know the details."

Cortez sighed softly, wondering if he should tell her the truth. As he gazed into her distressed features, he found himself telling her, whether or not it was a wise idea. He felt a good deal of pity for the woman.

"It had been raining for weeks, my lady," he spoke softly, deeply. "The ground surrounding Falkirk was a marsh. It was thick, black mud we found ourselves fighting in. A massive storm hit just as we were beginning our siege. Robert was struck in the midst of a horrible storm. As I tried to help him, Edward was making a final charge against the Scots and I was forced to leave him to answer the call of the charge."

She looked at him, not comprehending what he was saying. He exhaled sharply, running his fingers through his short black hair.

"My lady, I cannot think of a way to delicately phrase what I must tell you so I will simply be truthful," he fixed her in the eye. "I was not able to return to the place where I left Robert until the next morning. By then, the rains had stopped and the ground had begun to dry. There were literally hundreds of bodies that had been caught in the horrific mud. When the ground dried, it dried over and around them. There were many we could not recover simply because they were buried in the muck. Your husband was one of them."

She had no outward reaction other than to stare at him. It took several seconds for his words to sink deep. When they did, Cortez watched the magnificent eyes fill with tears and spill over. Like a waterfall, they coursed down her cheeks.

"Then you left him buried in the muck with the others," she whispered.

"There was no way to find him."

"But surely you remembered where you left him?"

He eyed her, nodding after a long pause. "I remembered."

"Did you at least return?" she wiped at her cheeks furiously, smearing tears. "Did you at least try to find him or did you simply discard him as one would a pile of rubbish?"

Cortez kept his cool in what could be interpreted as an accusation. He knew she was distraught. "I returned to the area where I left him," he said patiently. "The mud had partially dried over the entire area. There were no bodies."

"Then you assumed he was under the mud?"

"There was nowhere else he could be."

She sniffled, wiping at her eyes as she contemplated his words. But there was something brewing in the brilliant green-brown depths, something he could plainly see. She took a deep breath, laboring for composure, when she met his gaze again.

"Was my husband dead when you left him to return to the battle?" she asked.

He stared at her. That was a question he had not expected. He did not want to lie to her but he wondered what manner of grief he was opening himself up for with his honest reply. "Nay, lady, he was not," he whispered. "He was still alive."

Her eyes flickered, growing intense. "Then it is possible he did not die at all."

He shook his head. "There was no way for the man to survive the wound," he was beginning to lose his calm demeanor. Even on the best of days, he was not a normally patient man. "Even if he had crawled away, he would not have made it very far and we covered that entire area with men. Someone would have found him."

She shook her head, hard. "Nay," she said firmly. "Robert was a strong man. It is possible that he simply crawled away to hide. Perhaps he survived somehow and even now is waiting for someone to come and find him. 'Tis possible that...."

"Nay, Lady Edlington," Cortez reached out and grabbed her arms, gently but firmly. She seemed to be losing grip with the reality of the situation. "You will understand me when I say that there was no way for the man to survive."

She took exception to his hands on her arms. Startled by his touch, she struggled to pull away.

"But...!"

"Listen to me," he cut her off with a shake, their struggles increasing as she fought to pull away. "There was no way for Robert to survive. He had a great sucking chest wound that was oozing blood and innards. You could see his lungs inflating through the hole and the arrow had penetrated so far into his torso that it nearly cut his spine in half. He could not feel his legs, my lady. There was no way for the man to move much less crawl away. Trust me when I say he did not survive."

His words came out forcefully and brutally, trying to snap some sense into her. Diamantha's struggles came to a halt and she stared at him, horrified, as the last few words came spilling from his lips.

Cortez regretted the words before they even left his mouth. From the way Diamantha was staring at him, he knew it had been a mistake to tell her but his determination to make her understand that her husband could not have survived had put a noose around his common sense and severed it. Split, his tactless words had slipped through the gap. So he stared at Diamantha, wondering what damage he had just created.

"I am sorry," he whispered when he realized what he had done. "I was attempting... my lady, you must not hold out false hope that Robert survived. There was no way he could have. I am sorry to have explained it to you so harshly. I am sorry if I upset you."

Diamantha was in shock. Beyond tears, her mind muddled with distress, she had no other course of action than to pull from his grip, gently but firmly. Then she turned her back on him. She found that she could no longer look at the man.

"I release you from your promise," she murmured, moving away from him in a rather staggering gait. "I understand you made the promise to marry me because you had no other choice. It was unfair of Robert to ask it of you. I therefore release you from your promise to take care of me and Sophie."

Cortez watched her as she came to an unsteady halt next to the lancet window that overlooked the Dorset countryside to the south. Big gray clouds were blowing in from the sea and he could smell rain upon the wind. But his attention was riveted to the small woman with the miraculous brown hair and brilliant two-toned eyes. She was a truly ravishing creature; he'd always thought so. She was as unique and beautiful as her unusual name, *Dee-a-MON-tha*. He felt rather disappointed with her statement but knew why she said it. He had offended her. His disappointment grew.

"Although I understand that you are attempting to be gracious, please understand that I gave my word," he said quietly. "I cannot go back on my word nor would I. I made your husband a promise that I intend to fulfill."

"But I do not want to marry you."

"What you want is of no matter. I promised Robert that I would take care of you and your father has consented."

"I will not go."

"You have no choice."

She turned to look at him. Cortez watched her carefully, studying her expression, wondering how she was going to react. He'd hoped to take her back to Sherborne Castle this day but knew, in reality, that it was probably an unrealistic hope. Especially now. As he watched, she silently moved away from the window, walked past him, and left the solar. With a heavy sigh, he followed. Something told him not to let her out of his sight.

It was a hunch too late.

CHAPTER TWO

It was dawn on the second day of Cortez's visit to Corfe Castle. He had originally come to collect his bride; now it had turned into a standoff. When Diamantha had left the solar yesterday afternoon, she had retreated to her bower and locked the door. Nothing anyone could do or say could coerce or convince her to open it.

Cortez had been up all night trying to determine the best course of action. As the sun rose in the eastern sky, Cortez found himself wandering the grounds of the mighty castle. His men were camped in the lower bailey, a massive thing that was well removed from the upper bailey and keep. The lower bailey was separated from the upper by an enormous gatehouse and drawbridge, cut into the steep hillside upon which Corfe resided.

The day dawned lovely and clear in spite of the rain that had fallen during the night. There was no chill in the air, even at this early hour, and it promised to be a brilliant day. Cortez stood in the upper bailey facing west, gazing out over the rolling green hills of Dorset and contemplating his next move. He truly could not fathom the woman's resistance. Any well-bred lady would have been thrilled at the opportunity for another husband willing to marry her, especially given that she had already been married and had a young child. Cortez simply didn't understand the reluctance.

Or perhaps it was that he was simply over-eager. Cortez had distantly known Lady Edlington for years, as she had been a friend of his wife's. The most prevalent memory of her was that she was clearly the most beautiful woman in the county, if not the whole of England. She had pale skin, pink cheeks, shiny reddish-brown hair and the most amazing eyes he had ever seen. Robert Edlington had been mad for the woman, proud and honored to have been her husband. When Rob had been dying of the nasty chest wound and had asked Cortez to take care of his wife, all Cortez could think of was the woman of unearthly beauty. When he saw her for the first time in several years the night before, he was struck not only by the fact that she had gotten more beautiful, but by her delicious body outlined in the dark blue damask. He hadn't remembered *that* part. Everything he saw pleased him immensely.

But she wanted nothing to do with him. He had been widowed three years and she had been widowed three months. She'd not yet come to terms with what he was already accustomed to. He knew he should give her time but he also knew he was unwilling to wait. He wanted her now and he wanted to return to Sherborne. He knew that once she came to know him, she would no longer be resistant, but they could not come to know each other if she locked herself away.

He grunted with frustration, shifting on his big legs, when he caught a glimpse of something beside him. Looking to his left, he noticed a very small girl standing next to him. She was an astonishingly beautiful child, gazing up at him with bright blue eyes and long honey-colored hair. It took Cortez a moment to realize he was gazing into Rob Edlington's face. The little girl was his spitting image. Slightly startled, not to mention curious, Cortez smiled faintly.

"Greetings," he said.

The little girl gazed innocently up at him. "Greetings," she repeated.

"Who are you?"

"Sophie Amalia Teodora Edlington," she spit out the long name with a charming lisp in her speech. "Who are you?"

Cortez's smile grew. "My name is Cortez." He looked around to see if there was a nurse around. Seeing no one, he peered at her. "Are you alone?"

She nodded, holding up a poppet made of rags. "This is Rosie."

Cortez pretended to greet the doll. "My lady," he refocused on Sophie. "Did you come outside by yourself?"

Sophie cuddled the doll. "Aye."

"Where is your nurse?"

She shrugged disinterestedly. "I have a pony," she announced. "Would you like to see him?"

Cortez gazed down at her, feeling his heart warm to the child. She was absolutely adorable. "Mayhap later. You should go back inside where it is safe."

She reached out and took his hand, tugging. He couldn't help but follow as she began to pull him across the small upper bailey.

"My pony's name is General," she told him as they headed for the gatehouse that led into the lower bailey. "He came from France. My grandfather bought him for me."

The ground sloped sharply towards the rocky and uneven path of the gatehouse. More than once Sophie nearly slipped but managed to keep her footing with Cortez's substantial help. Cortez followed her, or was rather pulled, to the gatehouse where several Edlington soldiers were stationed. They watched curiously as little Lady Sophie pulled the large figure of Cortez de Bretagne through the gatehouse and onto the drawbridge that covered the gap between the upper and lower baileys. One of the soldiers came forward as the pair passed through.

"Is there a problem, my lord?" he asked, his gaze moving between them.

Cortez lifted his free hand helplessly as Sophie tugged. "I fear I've been abducted."

"Shall I send for her mother?"

Cortez looked at the man, an inkling of an idea coming to him. The more he thought on it, the more he settled on the thought. "Aye," he said slowly. "Send for her mother. Tell her that de Bretagne and her daughter are in the lower bailey and await her."

The soldier nodded swiftly and went on the run. Meanwhile, Sophie had pulled him down into the lower bailey where one hundred of the king's troops were housed, men that served de Bretagne. The stables were lodged against the eastern wall and

Sophie took Cortez in that direction. He passed his men along the way, smiling wanly at the collection of confused and amused faces. It was a rather comical sight but no one would dare laugh. Their large and powerful liege was being led around by a toddler, and going quite willingly. As Cortez followed Sophie through a muddy patch, he was joined by a senior sergeant.

"Am I to assume you are being taken against your will, my lord?" Sergeant Peter Merlin was an older man with a calm, wise manner about him and had served de Bretagne for four years. He nodded his head in Sophie's direction. "The young lady has you well in hand."

Cortez wriggled his dark eyebrows. "She is cutting the circulation off in my fingers," he said in a low voice. "She is determined to show me her pony."

"Ah," Merlin lifted his eyebrows in understanding.

Sophie looked up at the tall, pale, red-haired sergeant that had joined them. "Do you want to see my pony, too?" she asked.

Merlin grinned. "It would be my pleasure, my lady."

Pleased, Sophie now had two people willing to view her pony. As the sun rose, so did the temperature and the horse flies were out in force. The smell of the stables grew stronger. Cortez leaned in Merlin's direction and lowered his tone as they passed into the shadow of the wall.

"Send my knights to me and prepare the men to leave," he said. "If all works as it should, we should be heading home within the hour."

"But I must see a pony, my lord."

"As soon as you see the damnable thing, be gone."

"Aye, my lord."

Neither man said another word as they entered the stable yards. Sophie confidently pulled Cortez towards the stalls on the north end of the stable. Cortez could see a couple of small gray palfreys and in one of the stalls, a small black and white pony. Sophie let go of his hand long enough to unlatch the stall door and shove it open as much as her little hands would allow.

"See?" she turned to the men proudly. "This is General."

Cortez smiled faintly as he leaned up against the open stall door, gazing down at the fat pony. The pony was eating its morning meal, crunching the grain and nuzzling Sophie with dusty lips. She rubbed the pony's velvety nose, laughing loudly when his big lips nibbled at her.

"He is a fine animal," Cortez said, eyeing Merlin. The man received the silent message and quit the stables as Cortez continued. "Did you give him his name?"

Sophie nodded; she was no more than a toddler but very bright. She spoke quite well for such a young child. "My Dada calls me Little General. So I named him General." She looked up at him with those great blue eyes. "Do you know my Dada?"

Cortez nodded slowly. "I did."

She cocked her head thoughtfully and Cortez could literally see the thoughts rolling through her young mind. "He's been gone a long time," she said sadly. "Do you know where he is? My mother says he is away. She does not know where."

Cortez's smile faded as he stared down at the little girl. He began to see how Lady Edlington's grief had spilled over onto her child, unable or unwilling to tell the little girl the truth of her father's absence. Initially, Cortez felt some irritation about that, but then he simply felt pity. It was obvious that the child missed her father. At that moment, something inside Cortez began to feel the slightest bit of concern and protectiveness over the girl. His own child, had she lived, would have been the same age. It occurred to him that when he married Lady Edlington, he would gain the child he had lost. The realization brought an oddly pleasurable moment.

He gazed down at her over the top of the stall. "Your father is far away, little one," he said softly. "He has gone to a place where we cannot go."

She stopped petting the pony and walked towards him across the crunchy rushes on the bottom of the stall. "Why not?" she wanted to know. "I want to go where my father is."

He reached down and picked her up, holding her against his broad chest. They gazed at each other a moment as if sizing one another up, onyx eyes against brilliant blue. He thought she might actually demand to be set down by the way she was looking at him but, strangely, she did not. She simply stared at him.

"Your father is in a wonderful place of light and joy," Cortez said quietly. "He is living with the angels. They are taking great care of him and someday, if you are a very good girl, you will be able to see him again."

She stared at him with her bottomless eyes. "Where do the angels live?"

"In Heaven with God, our Holy Father. Have you not been told this in church?"

She blinked, thinking. "I do not like church."

"You do not like it? Why not?"

Her brow furrowed. "It is a scary place."

He turned away from the pony's stall and began to move out into the morning sunshine. "Why is it scary?"

She put her little arms around his neck to hold on. He was very tall, much taller than her father, and Sophie felt as if she were on top of a very high tree, looking down at everything. But she missed her father so much that she rather liked being held by this strange man who had been very kind to her. It made her feel safe and comforted.

"Because the priest yells," she said frankly. "He sings scary songs."

Cortez laughed softly and patted her chubby little leg. "Aye, they do yell. I think church is a scary place, too."

She looked at him, grinning. Cortez winked at her, becoming more enamored with her by the moment. "Now, tell me the truth," he said gently. "Where is your nurse?"

She scrunched her nose up, making him laugh again. "I do not know."

"You do not know?"

"Nay."

"Hmmm," he wriggled his eyebrows as they emerged into the sunlight. "Do you think that she is looking for you?"

Sophie shrugged, averting her gaze by pretending to look at his tunic, and he dipped his head to try and look her in the eye. "Do you think she is frightened that you are missing?" he asked gently.

Sophie twitched her nose and pursed her lips, torn between guilt and not caring. Cortez didn't push her. He patted her leg again and passed from the stables into the enormous lower bailey. To the south, he could see his men beginning to break down their encampment; fires were being doused and horses wrangled. Above, white clouds scattered across the sky in the sea breeze blowing in from the south. He could hear the scream of gulls riding the drafts.

Glancing to his right, he could see the Corfe's mighty keep soaring to the sky, knowing that somewhere inside, Lady Edlington was being informed that her daughter was with de Bretagne and more than likely having fits over it. He fully expected to see her any moment. But first, he knew it was imperative that he gain Sophie's cooperation. If he was to accomplish his task, then having the child on his side would be paramount. He didn't want to create a scene with a terrified mother and child, demanding they accompany him back to Sherborne. What he had to do needed to be done with foresight and care. He had to be sly.

"Lady Sophie," he slowed his steps, watching his men efficiently break camp. "Would you like to go on an adventure?"

She stared at him curiously. "An ad... ad...?"

"Adventure," he finished for her. He pretended to think. "Let me see; an adventure is something fun, like a journey or mayhap a visit somewhere. Have you ever been away from your home?"

Sophie shook her head. "Nay," she said. "I have always been here or to church."

"Where it is scary."

"Aye."

He wriggled his eyebrows. "I live in a place called Sherborne Castle. My castle is a big place with many ponies and dogs and rabbits. It is surrounded by a big lake. But it is a sad place."

He had her interest; she was focused on his words. "Why is it sad?"

"There is no princess there."

"No princess?"

He nodded. "I need a princess so that my home will not be sad. Would you like to be the princess of my castle?"

Sophie's big eyes glittered with the possibilities. Before she could reply, Cortez caught sight of people spilling forth from the upper bailey. He was not surprised to see Lady Edlington leading the pack. Clad in a dual-colored surcoat of deep blue and pale green, like the colors of her eyes, she approached with a stricken look on her face.

The sea breeze had picked up, streaming her beautiful hair behind her like a banner. It also plastered her garment against her body, affording Cortez and any other man who happened to notice her, an unobstructed view of her magnificent figure. She had large breasts, more than likely due to child bearing, and a tiny waist. Cortez was torn between absorbing the lines of her spectacular body and gazing into her magnificent face. There was nothing about the woman that was imperfect.

But he forced himself away from thoughts of her body, realizing he had been correct in using her daughter to coerce her to leave her chamber. He could have laid siege to the keep for days and never achieved what one tiny girl had managed to accomplish in a matter of minutes. Lady Edlington came straight at him and held out her arms.

"Give me my baby," she demanded quietly.

Cortez's gaze was cool. He looked at Sophie, who was staring down at her mother. Surprisingly, the little girl didn't immediately reach for her mother. Cortez ignored the demand.

"Lady Sophie and I have been visiting her pony," he said casually. "She is a delightful child."

Diamantha was beginning to lose her calm demeanor. "Give her back to me, de Bretagne," she lowered her voice. "She is of no use to you."

He lifted his eyebrows at her. "I beg to differ, madam," he said. "She is of great use. She released you from your chamber, did she not?"

Diamantha dropped her arms, looking at Cortez as if he were the most contemptible creature on earth. She struggled not to lose her temper, knowing it would only work against her. She cursed herself for being stupid enough to let Sophie out of her sight, although she had let the child go with her nurse early that morning to feed and dress her. She had no idea that Sophie would escape the older woman although she should have guessed. Sophie was always desperate to see her pony first thing in the morning. Diamantha's gaze moved to her daughter.

"Hello, sweetheart," she purred. She had a sweet and low voice. "How is General this morning?"

33

Sophie had her arms wrapped around Cortez's neck. "He is eating," she said. "Mummy, I am hungry. Can I have porridge and honey?"

"Of course," Diamantha lifted an expectant eyebrow at Cortez as she held her arms out to her daughter. "We shall go inside and break our fast."

Cortez met her gaze, his dark eyes glittering. But instead of handing over the child, he began to walk towards the upper bailey with the girl snugly in his arms. "I rather like porridge and honey," he told Sophie. "May I have porridge, too?"

She nodded. "Annie says it is mush."

"Who is Annie?"

Sophie pointed to an older woman standing behind Diamantha, wringing her hands worriedly. "My nurse."

Cortez grinned at her, patted her leg, and continued on to the keep. Frustrated and the least bit furious, Diamantha collected her skirts and stomped after the pair. She caught up to them in short order, sticking close to her daughter as the enormous knight held her. She couldn't help but notice that Sophie didn't seem the least bit distressed. The little girl had been inordinately attached to her father and the man's absence had rocked her deeply. Diamantha hadn't the heart to tell her daughter that her beloved father was never coming home. At some point she knew she would have to, especially in light of her betrothal to Cortez, but she simply wasn't ready to yet.

As Cortez and her daughter moved to the path that led through the gatehouse that protected the upper ward, Diamantha fell back slightly and eyed Cortez as the man walked ahead of her. He was keeping up a running conversation with Sophie, smiling at the child as he spoke. Little Sophie held on to his neck, nodding her head on occasion and even speaking once in a while. But Cortez seemed to be doing all of the talking and he had Sophie completely enthralled.

At first, Diamantha had naturally been irritated and fearful that the big knight had physical possession of her daughter, but as they walked up the hill and into the gatehouse that led to the upper bailey, she was beginning to feel something else. In spite of her resistance to everything Cortez represented, she couldn't help but be softened by his manner with Sophie. It was almost enough to ease her, but not quite.

Darker thoughts filled her head. Seeing Cortez again reminded her of their last conversation, of the discussion of Robert's death. Cortez had not couched his delivery of the details. In fact, he seemed to have been rather forceful in the way he had spoken, as if to emphasize the fact that there had been no chance for Robert's survival. Diamantha had spent the better part of the evening weeping about that, so very shattered at the description of her husband's mortal wounds.

She had fallen asleep with visions of Robert's broken body languishing in the mud and she had awoken to mental images of great sucking chest wounds, as de Bretagne had so inelegantly phrased it. She felt as if she was living Robert's death all over again now with the exact knowledge of his final moments. She almost wished de Bretagne hadn't told her. It had been such a horrible way to die for a man she had dearly loved. Now, instead of her last memories of him being those of a sound and strong husband departing for battle, she had thoughts of a broken shell of a man who had suffered a terrible death, and she had de Bretagne to blame for it. She was trying very hard not to hate him.

Therefore, it was a struggle not to snap as they made their way into the upper bailey. The new day was dawning and the fog and clouds that had drifted in from the sea were starting to clear out. Her gaze was fixed to the massive form in front of her, this bear of a man carrying her precious child in his arms. As they neared the tall keep, with stonework like rib bones stretching up the walls, Sophie squirmed down from Cortez's arms and grabbed his hand.

"Come," she said, rather firmly.

Once again, Cortez found himself being dragged along by a toddler. Diamantha followed close behind, watching her daughter lug the big knight after her. Cortez seemed to be taking it all in stride, allowing the child to lead him around. He was showing a remarkable amount of patience and understanding, which she'd heard were not his finer attributes. The man had fire all about him, or so Helene once told her. But with her daughter, he seemed to be mushy like clay.

Corfe's enormous keep soared in front of them as they neared the entry. The big, heavy entry door, more iron than wood, opened wide and they were ushered into the cool innards. They passed directly into a corridor that opened up into a smaller hall where a hearth tall enough for a man to stand in was spitting out smoke and flame. Servants bustled around, carrying plates of bread and bowls of butter, as Cortez took Sophie to a heavy feasting table and carefully sat her down on the bench.

"There you are, my lady," he said to her. "Delivered safely for your meal."

Sophie was on her knees on the bench. A small fat hand patted the seat next to her. "Sit down," she commanded. "You sit here."

Cortez obliged, grinning as he sat down next to her. "My thanks, my lady."

By this time, Sophie was completely enamored with him. It was clear that anyone who had so willingly visited her pony and had spoken so kindly to her naturally had her attention. When Cortez took a hunk of white bread off a plate and began to slather it with butter, she ran her finger along the butter and licked it. He took the dulled knife and smeared butter on her hand, causing her to laugh loudly. It was an enchanting exchange.

Diamantha stood at the end of the table, watching the interaction between them grow. It was increasingly difficult to hate a man who was so easily charming her daughter but she knew why he was doing it; she was no fool. He was using Sophie to get to her, or at least manipulate her. Any man who would do that was a beast indeed, but on the other hand, he was certainly making her daughter happy regardless of his reasons behind it. Torn and confused by the man, his actions, and her own feelings towards him, she made her way down the table and sat on her daughter's other side.

In silence, she began to prepare her daughter's meal as Sophie played with Cortez. Now, he was pretending to bite the buttered fingers and she was squealing happily. Diamantha eyed her child as the nurse handed her the girl's porridge and Diamantha put the right amount of honey on it. She even put in a few raisins and dried currants before putting it in front of Sophie.

"There, now," she said in her soft, sultry voice. "Eat your porridge, sweetheart."

Sophie happily picked up a wooden spoon and began shoveling. She was on her knees on the bench, leaning forward with one hand on the table and the other hand spooning the sweet porridge into her mouth. She pushed about four spoonfuls in before turning to Cortez and tried to feed him some of her mush. Cortez begged off politely.

"That is *your* meal, little one," he told her. "Eat all of it so that you may grow up strong."

Sophie grinned at him, mouth full of porridge, and he snorted. It was really quite sweet and quite comical. As the little girl turned back to her bowl, Cortez's eyes locked with Diamantha's over the top of her daughter's head.

The woman was watching him, appraising him, still uncertain of his motives. But it was more than that; he could see fire there, lingering in the depths. A jolt ran through him, one of warmth and mild excitement. He couldn't help it. The woman seemed to have an effect on him like he had never before experienced. Not even his sweet Helene had breathed such fire into his heart, making it flutter with a mere glance. It was a wholly odd but entirely delicious sensation and for lack of a better response, he simply smiled.

"My mother, being Spanish, used to feed my brother and I rice with very dark sweet-salt sprinkled on it," he told her. "Our cook used to make cakes from the same grain and sweet-salt. It is still my favorite thing to eat."

Diamantha just stared at the man. She wasn't in any mood for small talk but she was in the midst of an increasing dilemma. It was obvious that Sophie liked the man and Cortez seemed to feel the same way towards her. His gentleness and patience with her little girl made her look at the man through new eyes and she struggling not to. She knew it was all an act for her benefit; he had ulterior motives. Bewildered, and resistant, she lowered her gaze.

Cortez's smile faded as he watched Diamantha's lowered head. He was trying very hard not to feel discouraged but her lack of response to him, any response at all, had him fighting off depression. Aye, he had used the girl to get to the mother and he didn't regret it. He had to get to her somehow. He was fairly certain that Lady Diamantha thought of him as a cad, a scoundrel, but he supposed that in a small way he was. She hadn't wanted him since the beginning of their renewed association and he knew it. She had been very clear with her wants, just as he had been. But in this case, his wants would win out over hers. He would make sure of it.

As he sat next to Sophie and pondered his next move, George entered the hall. He didn't seem surprised to see Cortez seated at the table but his gaze appeared to be mostly on Diamantha. When Sophie saw her grandfather, she crowed.

"Grandpere!" she cried. "I have porridge!"

It all came out as a mumbled bit of fluff because her mouth was full. No one had any idea what she had said. George, however, smiled sweetly as he sat down across the table from her. Sophie swallowed the big bite in her mouth as her mother wiped the mess on her lips away with a linen napkin.

"Grandpere, I am going on an ad-ad-adventure!" she stumbled over the word. She pointed her messy spoon at Cortez, flicking porridge onto his leather breeches. "He has a castle with ponies and dogs. I want to go there."

George's smile turned into a grimace. "Is that so?" he said, trying to be pleasant as he thought of losing his only grandchild and his last link to his beloved son. "It would be nice to visit, would it not?"

Cortez's dark eyes fixed on George as he wiped the spilled porridge off his breeches. "It would be lovely to *live* there," he said plainly, daring Edlington's father to debate it. "I told her that my castle is sad because there is no princess. She has graciously agreed to become my princess."

George's smile vanished completely. "I see," he muttered, looking at Diamantha. "When is this happy event to take place?"

Diamantha was clearly as unhappy as her father-in-law. "That has not yet been discussed," she said. "I believe that...."

Cortez cut her off. "Then let us discuss it now," he said. It was another ploy at manipulation, knowing that neither Diamantha nor George would become too angry with Sophie in their midst, and he was wise enough to take advantage of the situation. He was, if nothing else, cunning. "The ride to Sherborne is a half day at the very most. Therefore, I will give you the day to pack your belongings, and those of Lady Sophie, and we will leave first thing on the morrow. We will be married at Sherborne Abbey once we arrive. I have already made the necessary arrangements."

Diamantha looked at him in shock. "A day?" she repeated, aghast. "You are asking me to pack my entire life away in one day? It cannot be done. I need more time."

Cortez had to take the upper hand; he had no choice. He was afraid if he gave in to her requests, or rather her demands, that he would lose control of the situation. He had no desire to lose his grip on that which he so badly wanted. He *needed* it. God help him, he needed Diamantha and her sweet daughter. He had been so lonely for three years. He didn't want to be lonely anymore.

"Pack what you can," he said steadily. "We will take it with us and you may leave behind servants to pack and then send along the rest."

It was not a request. Diamantha and George both saw that. De Bretagne was very good at giving commands that were not intended to be refuted. Furious, Diamantha lowered her gaze and stared at the table as Sophie continued to sit between her and Cortez and happily eat. To the child, all was joyful in her world with a new friend and her mother seated beside her. But to the adults, the hall was filled with brittle discord, fragile enough to shatter at any moment. It was a horrible, tense ambiance.

But Cortez ignored it. He wanted his own desires fulfilled above all else and to the devil with George and Diamantha's resistance. They had already put up too much of a fight and he was at the end of his patience. He wasn't in the mood for any further games. He could feel his irritation rising and since he had little control over his anger at times, he made the decision to leave before he said something he would regret later. Abruptly, he stood.

"I will be in the lower ward preparing my men to depart on the morrow," he said evenly. "Have your men bring your trunks down so that we may pack them onto the provisions wagons. You will also give me an accounting of the servants you intend to bring with you. Is this clear, madam?"

Diamantha was near tears. She was incredibly frustrated, feeling as if she were being yanked from her home by a man with no heart or soul. The shock from the marriage proposal was wearing off, leaving in its place a sense of desolation and sorrow. Her inclination not to hate the man was weakening. She was starting to hate him a great deal.

"Madam?" he said again, more firmly. "I require an answer."

Diamantha was still staring at the table. She wouldn't give him the courtesy of looking at him. "I understand," she said.

Cortez didn't say another word, even when Sophie turned to him and begged him to stay. He smiled at the child and patted her fat little hand before quitting the hall, leaving behind him one oblivious little girl and a whole host of distressed adults. But he didn't care. He would have his way in all things.

Damn Lady Edlington for resisting him in the first place. She was instigating a battle she had no chance of winning. But he suspected he could butt heads with her all night and she would never retreat. She was prideful and she was stubborn, two qualities he happened to share with her. He understood them. Therefore, he knew he would have to win her over another way.

He thought perhaps that honey would attract her better than vinegar would. He intended to give it a try.

CHAPTER THREE

Diamantha could hear Sophie in the next room, playing with her poppet. She had a toy cradle that Robert had made for her and she liked to put her doll to bed repeatedly. Sometimes the poppet was naughty and needed to be spanked, like now. Diamantha couldn't help the grin as she listened to her daughter scold the doll because it didn't want to go to sleep. The joy of the simple pleasure helped lighten her heavy and sorrowful heart.

It was late, well after the evening meal that saw Cortez demand that she be ready to depart for Sherborne on the morrow. She'd had her trunks brought around and gave the servants basic instructions, but beyond that, she was incapable of doing much more. Her fury, her outrage, at de Bretagne's order had died down, leaving grief in its wake. He was removing her from the chamber she had shared with Robert and from everything that was important to her. She felt as if she were living her husband's death a second time as de Bretagne tried to bully him from her memory.

George had tried to come and see her, twice, but she would not see him. Every time she looked at him she could see Robert's face and it was tearing her apart, great claws of sorrow ripping at her heart. Now, everything was changing and she was loath to accept it. She didn't think her heart could be any heavier as she thought of her tall, handsome husband with the dark blond hair, of his ready smile and that roaring laughter he had. She could still hear it echoing in her memory.

She could still see him as he bid her a farewell before leaving for the north, his gentle smile as she had gazed at him with tears in her eyes. He had promised to return but he had not kept that promise. It wasn't a surprise to realize that not only did she hate de Bretagne for his role in all of this, but she was angry with Robert as well. She was angry with him for putting duty over his family, for leaving her to raise their child alone. Damn the man; she should have never let him go.

Breaking from her morose train of thought, she went into Sophie's chamber and put the little girl, and her naughty poppet, to bed. Neither wanted to go to sleep, however, so Diamantha spent a few minutes with her child, telling her a made-up story of a rabbit and a fox that were friends, and giving her at least two drinks of water because Sophie swore she was very thirsty. Sophie went down to sleep resisting all the way but finally, she drifted off and Diamantha snuffed the taper by the bed and quietly crept from the room.

Back in her own adjoining chamber, she was in the midst of servants packing her things. Trunks full of clothing, accessories, plate, valuables… everything that reminded her of her life with Robert was being neatly stored away in cold and unfeeling trunks. Struggling against the horrible sorrow of her life reduced to trunks and cases, she sat on her bed and collected a piece of embroidery she had been working on. She needed something to distract her and to pass the time and, hopefully, she would eventually be tired enough to sleep. Right now, she didn't want to waste any time on it because these were to be her last hours within Corfe's walls, walls that breathed and spoke of her husband. She could hear the reflections softly, like the gentle patter of rain in her heart and mind. She wanted to live these last few moments and speak to Robert, if only in prayer.

A knock on the chamber door distracted her and she set the embroidery aside to open the panel. A male servant was standing there, an old man who usually tended the lower floors of the keep, and he was holding a small painted box in his hands. When Diamantha looked at him curiously, he thrust the box at her.

"One of de Bretagne's men brought this, my lady," he said. "He told me to tell you that de Bretagne has sent this to you as a gift. It used to belong to his wife."

Diamantha stared at the old man a moment, her brow furrowed in both curiosity and displeasure, but because her dear friend Helene had been mentioned, she reluctantly took the box.

"Is that all he said?" she asked, eyeing the pretty box colored in shades of pink.

The old servant nodded. "Aye, my lady."

With that, Diamantha dismissed the man and softly shut the door. Her serving women had paused in their packing to watch the exchange, curious about the gift, but when their lady turned around and glanced at the gaggle, they quickly went back to work and pretended they weren't the least bit interested. Diamantha had known the women a very long time, including Sophie's nurse Annie, so she smirked at their seeming disinterest. They were all liars, the lot of them.

"Very well, you nosy hens," she said, pretending to scold them. "You may come and see what the man has sent me."

The women, all five of them, immediately dropped what they were doing and rushed over to the great bed. Diamantha sat on the edge of the feather and straw mattress and carefully opened the lid on the box.

The serving women strained to see the treasure inside, gasping with awe when Diamantha lifted the jewelry out. It was a spectacular necklace comprised of a great silver collar, intricately woven, with a massive silver cross hanging from it. As she inspected it, she noticed that the shape of a heart was interwoven into the fine silver chains at the head of the collar and the cross hung just below the heart. It was an absolute masterpiece of craftsmanship. Diamantha was impressed with it as she gazed at the truly spectacular piece.

As she continued inspecting it, she seemed to recall seeing Helene wear the piece at one time. Helene was a little woman and something this big and fabulous clearly overwhelmed her small frame, so it was indeed memorable. She also recalled that Helene told her that her husband had given it to her for their wedding. Now, he was giving it again to seal another marriage.

Something in that knowledge irritated her. Irritation turned to anger, and anger to outrage. So he was purchasing another wife, was he? Did he actually think to buy her with pretty gifts? She could think of no other reason for the offering. She certainly hadn't done anything to earn it. *The man was trying to barter for her!* Putting the jewelry back in the box, she slapped the lid closed and charged from the chamber.

The serving women watched her go with some dismay. Lord only knew what their mistress was going to do. Anger like that usually came to no good end in their world.

Clad in only a dark gray linen surcoat with a soft wool sheathe underneath, Diamantha ignored the cold of the keep as she took the narrow spiral stairs down to the entry level. Throwing open the heavy entry door, she gathered her skirts and marched out into the damp night. Fog had rolled in from the sea and the kiss of moisture was on everything. Visibility was greatly reduced, leaving everything cloaked and eerie. As she walked, she realized that she only had soft doeskin slippers on and they were already soaked and slick. She ended up sliding in the wet earth as she made her way towards the lower bailey. As she approached the upper gatehouse that separated the upper from the lower ward, she was met by two of her husband's sentries.

"Lady Edlington," one soldier said as he rushed to her side and grasped her arm to keep her from slipping further on the wet incline. "How may we be of service?"

Diamantha pointed to the enormous gates, lit by torches that struggled against the mist. "Open the gates, please."

The sentries looked rather surprised by the request but dutifully yelled to the men inside the gatehouse. Lady Edlington's orders were not meant to be questioned or disobeyed. Men appeared and threw the big iron bolt that secured the panels. Diamantha moved towards the gates as the men lugged them open, slipping through the gap when it was big enough for her to pass through. As she charged towards de Bretagne's encampment, shoved down into the far south section of Corfe's massive bailey, the pair of sentries that had greeted her filtered out after her. They weren't entirely sure about Lady Edlington being alone in a camp full of strangers, so their sergeant sent them after her.

It was a fast walk, however, for Lady Edlington was evidently very determined. Her skirts were hiked up almost to her knees, keeping the linen free of the wet earth as she moved, but her shoes were soaked through and starting to come apart. She ignored the shoes that were only meant for delicate travel, however. She was clearly on a mission. On and on down the wet, misty bailey they went until she barked at the first of de Bretagne's men that she came across.

"Where is your liege?" she demanded.

The men were slow to move, looking rather puzzled that a beautiful woman had emerged from the darkness and was now demanding audience with de Bretagne. While one man openly leered over her, another went for his superior officer, who immediately recognized Lady Edlington. Peter Merlin happened to be the superior officer and, jolted by the surprise appearance, he made haste to her side.

"My lady," he greeted pleasantly though it was with a hint of concern. "How may I be of service to you?"

Diamantha was in no mood to be kind or sociable. "Where is de Bretagne?"

Peter could hear the edge in her tone. "In his quarters, I would assume," he said, increasingly concerned by her manner. "May I escort you?"

Diamantha merely nodded and followed the red-haired soldier deep into the cluster of tents, men, and animals. It smelled heavily of smoke and urine, the smell of a camp that was now saturating the ground of the lower ward. She hated it. In fact, she hated everything about de Bretagne and his men. She had been building a righteous fury all the way from the keep and by the time Merlin announced her to de Bretagne, she was fairly steaming with it. The rather smug look on de Bretagne's face when he realized she had come to visit him only threw more fuel on the fire.

"Dismiss your man," she told him.

Cortez's smile faded somewhat as he caught the growl in her tone. Quietly, he dismissed Peter and the man quit the tent, closing the flap behind him. Alone with Diamantha in his dimly lit shelter, Cortez set aside the dagger he had been sharpening. Something in the expression of her face told him this was not a social call.

"How may I be of service, Lady Edlington?" he asked politely.

Diamantha was literally quivering with rage. She thrust the painted box containing the jewelry in his direction.

"You can take this back," she said, her voice tight with fury. "I do not want it."

Cortez's smile vanished completely. "My lady, I assure you that it is a gift," he said. "It used to belong to my wife but I am sure she would not mind if you have it."

Diamantha tossed it onto the pallet nearby because he would not take it and it landed harmlessly. Both hands free, she faced Cortez with all of the ire and emotion she had been feeling since the moment he had entered George's solar with news of their betrothal. The events of the day had only stoked the blaze of indignation and rebellion. She had reached her limit and everything was about to come bursting out.

"Nay, I am sure Helene would not mind, for she was a sweet and gentle creature, and I miss her very much," Diamantha said. "But I do not want it. In fact, I do not want you, either. You burst into my home, tell me I am to marry you, present gifts with which to purchase my compliance, and show kindness to my daughter so that I may soften towards you. Well, I will not soften. I do not wish to marry you. I wish to remain here with my daughter and I wish to live out my life in the same room that my husband and I shared, sleeping on a bed that still smells of him, and dreaming of the hopes and wishes we shared together. You are not a part of that life. I want you to return to Sherborne and leave me alone."

Cortez kept his cool in the face of her angry words. He wasn't surprised by them but he was very disappointed. In hindsight, he supposed he had been expecting this reaction all along no matter how hard he had tried to diffuse it. With a sigh, he reached over and picked up the painted box, turning it over his hands as he inspected it. His manner was pensive, his mood somber.

"I cannot say I blame you for what you feel," he said quietly. "I have been widowed for three years and you have been widowed for a mere three months. I understand how you feel."

Diamantha had expected him to fly at her. She had been geared for a battle. Instead, his quiet response had her off balance because she wasn't sure how to counter it. Was he trying to manipulate her again?

"Then why do you push?" she insisted. "If you understand my feelings, why in God's name do you push?"

Cortez was still staring at the box. He sighed sharply. "Because I see something I want very badly," he murmured. "I see something I am ready for – marriage and a family. But you... you are not ready. You only see someone who seeks to erase your life with Robert and that is not my intent."

"What *is* your intent?"

"To create a new life with you," he replied, lifting his head to look at her. She was so hauntingly beautiful in the weak firelight from the open brazier and he felt a strange tugging at his heart as he gazed at her. "When... when Helene died, I was much like you. I was filled with grief because not only had I lost my wife, but my daughter as well. I was so torn with sorrow that I would not allow them to be buried. For three days, I stayed with my wife, holding the baby, cursing God for his cruelty. I was drunk beyond measure. My knights finally put something in my wine to drug me so they could take my wife and daughter away for burial. I was so distressed that I refused to go to the mass. I stayed in our chamber, the chamber she died in, and drank myself into oblivion. It took me months to pull myself together enough to function like a normal man. So, indeed, I do understand your pain. I understand it all too well."

By this time, Diamantha's rage was nearly gone. His sorrowful words were like water on a fire and she stared at him, her hand unconsciously moving to her chest as if to cover her broken heart. She couldn't help it.

"I can still feel pain from you," she confirmed as if surprised by the realization. "I can feel it in your words. I remember attending Helene's funeral and you were nowhere to be found. Robert went looking for you, do you recall? When he returned to me, he said that he had found you and that you were mad with grief."

Cortez nodded, not particularly wanting to relive those horrible memories. For the first time since his arrival at Corfe, he was genuinely not trying to be controlling of the situation. He was trying to show some understanding.

"I was," he agreed. "I still cannot go into the church where her body lies. I was to go into it for the first time since her burial when I married you. I thought... I thought that mayhap Helene would like to see our wedding for herself."

Diamantha completely lost her anger. It was sucked right out of her by Cortez's lingering grief, something that was still with him after all of this time. It was something they shared, a common ground they both understood. A common ground that left them both empty and hollow. At that moment, her strength seemed to leave her and she pitched forward onto her knees. She simply hadn't the power to stand any longer because all of the fight had left her. Cortez rushed to help her but she waved him off. Not unkindly, but she waved him off just the same. She wasn't angry with him any longer but she didn't want him touching her; not yet, anyway. She tried to speak but there was a lump in her throat. Before she could stop herself, the tears began to come.

"I miss her," she wept quietly. "I miss her and I miss Robert. But at least you know where your wife is. You know she is safely buried with your daughter in her great stone crypt in Sherborne's abbey, but I have no such comfort. I do not know where my husband's body is and every night when I go to sleep, I pray for his soul. I am so afraid that it is restless, that *he* is restless, and I pray that God comforts him. I ask God to tell Robert that I am sorry that his body is lost and his soul has no rest. I pray that same prayer every night and feel so helpless that there is nothing I can do for him. For a man who was so loved, it destroys me to think that he was lost and abandoned in death."

Cortez eased himself down onto his bum next to her, watching her weep with pain. It was heartbreaking. This woman, who had lost so much, with grief that was still raw and agonizing. In that realization came a great deal of guilt for him even though she hadn't meant to cause it. He had been with Robert in his last moments. He had allowed the man to fade into oblivion, to die alone and abandoned. It was his fault.

"I wish I could have done more," he insisted softly. "I remained with him as long as I could. I swear to you that I did not intentionally abandon him."

Diamantha nodded, wiping at her nose. "I understand that now," she said. "But he is missing all the same. I will never have my husband to bury as you had your wife to bury. I cannot visit his grave and know that his remains are safe. The only place I can see him now is in my dreams."

There was a huge amount of anguish in that statement and Cortez turned away as she wiped the stray tears from her cheeks. He was coming to realize that his inaction of bringing Robert home for burial had caused a great deal of her pain. The woman had no closure. With no body to bury, she was still expecting a miracle and hoping that Robert would return home someday. But Cortez seemed to be the only one who knew that was not to be.

Furthermore, he was beginning to understand something else - even if he married the woman, Robert Edlington would always come between them because in her mind, he wasn't truly dead. No body, no death. Cortez had to right that wrong, if for no other reason than to pave the way for a new life and a new marriage with Diamantha. He wanted the woman's adoration but if not that, at least her respect. He was coming to see he was going to have to earn it. He couldn't bully her into submission. She had made that clear. He was going to work for it.

"My lady," he finally said. "May... may I make a proposal to you?"

Diamantha sniffled, swallowing the last of her tears. "You already did last night."

There was a surprising tinge of humor to the statement and he looked at her with a glimmer in his eye. "Not *that* kind of proposal," he said, "although I would like to make one that would mayhap see both of us satisfied. May I continue?"

Diamantha looked at him dubiously for a moment before reluctantly nodding. "You may."

He smiled faintly. "During the course of this conversation, it has become evident to me that I hold a good deal of responsibility for your grief," he said. "I was with Robert in his final hours and I should have been more diligent in my care of him. I know that you do not understand the dynamics of battle so I will not bore you with them. The reasons behind my perceived carelessness do not matter. All that matters is that I am a knight of noble character and to leave a comrade behind was inexcusable. I should have done everything in my power to locate him. That being said, it is therefore my duty to return for the man and bring him home."

An expression of shock crossed Diamantha's face. "*Return* for him?" she repeated. "What do you mean?"

He lifted his eyebrows in a resigned gesture. "I mean exactly what I said," he replied quietly. "My proposal is this... if I bring Robert's body home for burial, will you consent to marrying me without reservation upon completion of this task?"

Diamantha's astonishment deepened. "But... but you told me last night that my father had already given you permission to marry me," she said, although she genuinely wasn't trying to be combative. "What does it matter if you have my consent or not? You told me this morning that you were going to take me back to Sherborne and marry me immediately."

He nodded, appearing rather contrite. "I was doing the only thing I knew to do," he said. "I was issuing a command. My lady, I have nearly twelve hundred men at my disposal and I am not accustomed to asking permission from anyone. I see now that my approach to you has been incorrect. I should not have made such demands. I should have at least tried to gain your agreement in a more polite manner but I fear I am very out of practice with such things."

She was genuinely surprised to see that he seemed like a man who had realized his arrogance had overwhelmed his better judgment. It was quite astonishing given all she'd ever heard about Cortez de Bretagne. The man she had heard tale of never backed down from anything, or anyone. Inevitably, she could feel herself softening towards him just the slightest but more than that, he had offered to bring Robert home. That fact alone had her very interested in what he was saying.

If agreeing to a betrothal would bring her husband's body home for good, then perhaps she should consider it. Perhaps she should use de Bretagne for that purpose alone and if she ended up married to the man then at least it was for a good cause. She wanted Robert home and Cortez had offered to do it. As much as she professed to pray to God for Robert's soul, the truth was that she was willing to make a deal with the devil if it would see her husband returned to her. Aye, she was willing to do anything. She studied the man a moment, his dark beauty and glittering eyes, before replying.

"When will you do this?" she asked.

He was hopeful that she hadn't refused him outright. "Immediately," he told her. "I will go tomorrow morning."

"All the way to Scotland?"

"All the way to Scotland."

She pondered that a moment. "It will take weeks at the very least," she said. "Probably months."

"Probably."

She fell silent a moment, contemplating. "What happens if you cannot find him?"

His gaze was intense. "I will find him," he assured her. "I will bring him back to you."

"But you said he was lost in the mud. You said it was impossible."

He cocked his head. "It was impossible at the time," he replied. "The situation was far too volatile to recover the dead. It is not too volatile now and I can take the time to search without fearing for my life."

She looked at him, hard. "And you truly believe you can find him?"

"I swear I will do my very best."

She had no idea why she believed him completely, but she did. There was something in his tone, in his manner, that gave her that confidence. Cortez de Bretagne was a great knight with a golden reputation and if he said he would return Robert to her, then he would. She very much wanted to have faith. It was the first time in three months that she had felt any hope at all and she was desperate to cling to it.

"As you say," she whispered as she nodded her head, her gaze locked with his. "When you bring Robert home, I will keep my part of the bargain. I will marry you without reservation."

Cortez's expression remained earnest yet serious. "Thank you," he muttered. "But we must also address the possibility that my best may not be good enough. If the worst happens and I am unable to bring him home, then I would like to know that my effort alone will also warrant your agreement. It is a sincere man who would go on such a quest for a woman he wishes to marry."

He was correct in that observation. It would be a sincere man, indeed. Diamantha couldn't help the shadow of a smile upon her lips.

"If you cannot return Robert home, then I will agree that your effort alone is worthy of my agreement," she said softly. "You have my vow that I will still marry you."

Cortez's dark eyes glimmered at her, she thought, with some warmth. It was a magnetic expression, one that set her heart to racing. It was an entirely new sensation to experience with the man who had, until this moment, only brought about feelings of frustration and rage. The warmth was something completely new, something that bolted through her and took her breath away. As she sat there and struggled to process it, he extended a hand to her.

"When a bargain is struck between two honorable individuals," he added, "it is usual to seal the deal with a shake of the hand."

Hesitantly, Diamantha extended her right hand and he took it within is massive mitt, shaking it gently. His smile grew.

"Very well, Lady Edlington," he said. "We have an agreement. I shall endeavor to fulfill my end of it."

It took Diamantha a moment to realize that he had stopped shaking her hand. Now, he was just holding it, his warmth enveloping her small fingers. There was something very powerful and heated and stimulating about his touch. She could feel the bolts of excitement shooting up her arm. Jolted, uncertain, she pulled her hand away.

"And I shall endeavor to fulfill mine," she said. She was still disturbed by the thrill of the man's touch and struggled to her feet. "For now, I will make sure you are well supplied for your journey to find my husband. I must return to the keep and make arrangements for your provisions."

Cortez stood up next to her, his hand politely on her elbow as she steadied herself. Even though it was just her elbow, he could feel the same jolts of excitement he had felt when he had been holding her hand. He was fairly certain she had felt them as well judging by her rather bewildered expression. He was beyond delighted. He hadn't felt such emotion in years. He had wondered if he ever would again.

"That is a kind offer but unnecessary," he said. "I will stop at Sherborne before heading north and gather supplies."

Diamantha shook her head firmly as she struggled on her freezing wet slippers. "I must insist," she said. "You are going in search of my husband, are you not? Therefore, I must make sure you are amply supplied. It is my duty."

He wasn't going to argue with her about it; she seemed determined. "Then whatever you can provide would be much appreciated," he said as she stumbled her way towards the tent flap. He couldn't help but notice she was walking rather oddly. "Forgive me for prying, but is something the matter?"

She looked at him innocently. "What do you mean?"

He suspected she was evading him. "You walk strangely," he said. "Is something the matter with your feet? Have you hurt yourself?"

Diamantha's pride was a great and terrible thing. She was prepared to fend him off but realized she couldn't. She didn't want him to know she had come to do battle with him so ill prepared but she supposed in hindsight that none of it mattered any longer. With a wry expression, she lifted up her skirt to show him her ruined slippers.

"They are not meant to become wet or walk over rocks and soil," she pointed to her shoes. "I ruined them on my way to berate you. I should have put on more durable shoes but I suppose my anger would not wait."

He looked at the wet, torn slippers. "It is a good thing you did not stop to put on more durable shoes," he said. "You might have tried to kick me with them."

She couldn't help but crack a grin. "You are too big to engage in a kicking fight," she said. "I would have lost."

He smiled broadly, displaying his straight, white teeth. "I would have let you win."

She eyed him with doubt. "Somehow, I do not think so," she said. "You are not a man, I suspect, that would easily surrender."

He shrugged. "I surrendered to your daughter when she abducted me and forced me to visit her pony."

Diamantha couldn't help it; she laughed softly and Cortez was entranced. She had the most beautiful smile had had ever seen, one that positively lit up the heavens. His heart began to flutter strangely at the sight and limbs seemed to tingle oddly. It was a strange but wonderful sensation and it took him a moment to realize that he was actually giddy. *The woman makes me giddy!*

"You were not so unwilling," Diamantha said skeptically. "When I saw you, you seemed quite complacent."

"Only because I did not want to upset your daughter."

He was being stubborn but it was all for show. "Then I appreciate your sensitivity," she said, mocking him with good humor. "Now, if you will excuse me, I will see to your needs for the morrow."

He couldn't seem to let go of her elbow. "You will never make it in those shoes."

"I have little choice."

His dark eyes smoldered at her. "Aye, you do." Bending over, he swept her into his arms. "Will you allow your betrothed to carry you back to the keep? It will save your feet."

Diamantha's first instinct was to slap his face but she couldn't bring herself to do it. Then, her next thought was to push herself from his arms but she couldn't seem to manage that, either. There was something about his big, muscular arms and warm body that destroyed every last shred of resistance she had against the man. The last time she had been held by a man... oh, God, it seemed so very long ago. Robert had warm and powerful arms that had made her feel so very safe and cherished. She had missed that terribly. Now, she was in Cortez's arms and not entirely surprised that she liked it very much. His arms were bigger than Robert's had been and she found them very safe and wonderful. She thought herself weak for liking it so much. Aye, she was weak, indeed.

"So we are betrothed?" she asked, trying not to sound breathless and excited. "I thought we were not betrothed until you returned with Robert's body."

He cocked an eyebrow. "For now, we are betrothed," he informed her in that commanding tone she had heard before. "When I return, I plan to marry you that very day. I will not wait."

Diamantha didn't have anything to say to that. They had made their bargain and the terms were accepted. At the moment, she was struggling to process the course the night had taken. De Bretagne was no longer her enemy or a man to be hated. He was going to bring Robert back to her to give her peace and closure.

Aye, it was a sincere man who would do that for the woman he planned to marry. She suspected that he was doing it to gain her compliance more than he was doing it to make her happy, although she supposed in a small way he did want to make her happy. He had no idea just how happy he had made her, but along with that happiness came something else. It was a feeling of curiosity, of emptiness, and of longing.

As Cortez carried her across the outer ward and towards the great gatehouse, Diamantha couldn't help feeling as if something was missing. It was the oddest sensation, truly. There was a feeling of anxiety and impatience as it began to occur to her that she would have to wait for Cortez to return from his questing and that could take months. It might even take years. If he lost interest in the project, then he might never return at all. Nay, she couldn't stand it if that happened. It would surely kill her.

By the time Cortez politely dropped her off on the steps to the great keep, Diamantha was deep in thought, mulling over plans for the future and weighing her options. She pretended to go inside when Cortez left her off, but in truth, she stood just inside the door, watching the big man disappear into the misty night. Her thoughts, her ideas, centered around him entirely; if he truly wanted to make her happy, and if he truly wanted her commitment to his marriage proposal, then she was about to put that desire to the test.

She was going to go with him.

CHAPTER FOUR

An hour before dawn, she was back.

Cortez had just managed to fall into a fitful sleep when Merlin was back in his tent, telling him that Lady Edlington was asking to see him again. Afraid that something was amiss, or perhaps she had even decided to go against their bargain once she'd had time to reflect, Cortez was just sitting up as Diamantha entered. It was very dark in the tent since the fire in the brazier had been reduced to glowing embers, making it difficult to see clearly. Merlin went to hunt down a taper as Diamantha approached Cortez.

"I am sorry to wake you," she said, sounding anxious, "but I must speak with you. It is very important."

Exhausted but alert, Cortez was concerned by the tone of her voice. Rising wearily to his feet, he reached out and gently grasped her shoulders.

"What is it?" he demanded softly. "What has happened?"

His grip burned her tender flesh like red-hot irons. His hands were enormous and powerful, nearly causing her to forget what she needed to say. But not quite; with her last shred of reasoning before his heated grasp burned holes through her sanity, she pulled back, out of his reach.

"Nothing has happened," she said, trying to shake off the memory of his touch. "I have come to tell you that I have made an important decision."

He blinked at her, wondering what she could possibly mean. "What decision?"

I had much more courage when I practiced this speech in front of my serving women, Diamantha thought ironically as she gazed into his dark eyes. But she had come this far and would not back down. With a deep breath, she continued.

"I have done a good deal of thinking since last we spoke," she said. "I fear I have bestowed upon you a heavy burden by asking you to locate Robert's body and return him home. Mayhap it will be a burden that, in time, you decide is too great to bear. Mayhap you will decide you no longer wish to bear it."

He listened to her carefully although he did not quite understand what point she was attempting to convey. He rested his hands on his slender hips as he eyed her.

"Are you afraid I will give up the search?" he finally asked. "Lady, I can assure you that I will not. I told you that I would find Robert and return him to you, and I meant it."

Diamantha nodded shortly as if she believed him, but by her sheer expression, it was clear that she was uncertain. She began to wring her hands. "Sir, I am trying desperately not to offend you, for that is certainly not my intention," she said. "I know you understand how important this is to me and because it is so important, I fear that I cannot allow you alone to bear the burden. I must bear it with you. I must ensure that Robert's body is located and properly buried. This is *my* task. In hindsight, I should not have delegated it to you. I should not have made you feel responsible for it. I suppose it was my grief that prompted me to do so. Therefore, I was hoping... nay, I am *asking* that you escort me to the fields of Falkirk where I may find my husband's body and ensure he has a property burial."

Cortez stared at her. It was then he noticed that she was wearing what looked like traveling clothes. He hadn't noticed right away because the tent had been so dim, but now, he could clearly see that she was wearing a heavy woolen dress, dark blue in color, with a matching cloak. She had gloves on her small hands and her hair, that glorious mass of color, was secured in a braid that was pinned to the nape of her neck. He'd been so stupid not to notice before, but now he could see everything. The woman was dressed for travel. So she wanted to go with him? He could feel his outrage rise.

"Absolutely not," he said flatly. "You will remain here. I will bring Robert's body to you. I told you I would. Do you doubt my word of honor, Lady Edlington?"

Diamantha shook her head. She could tell by his manner that she had indeed offended him. "Of course not," she assured him. "I told you that it was not my intention to insult your word, but you must understand… I cannot wait here for the months or years it might take for you to return with Robert. I would go mad with the worry, wondering if or when you were going to return. What if you are set upon by bandits? What if you somehow die in this great questing to find Robert's body? What if you never returned? Do you not understand, sir? I would be wracked with guilt and anxiety wondering what happened. I would go to my grave as restless as my husband's spirit. Surely I could never rest in peace."

He was looking at her with a furrowed brow. "Is that what this is all about?" he demanded. "You would feel guilty if I never returned? If that is the case, then I absolve you of this guilt. It is my choice to go. You did not force me into it."

She averted her gaze. "I did, in a sense," she said softly. "I… I have been resistant to your proposal of marriage. I believe you made this bargain so that I would agree to marry you in the end. 'Tis a sincere man who will go on such a quest for a woman he wishes to marry."

Cortez eyed her, hearing his own words reflected in her statement. His irritation was cooling. "I made the bargain to show you that I was indeed sincere," he said. "Never did you push me into it."

Diamantha watched him as he turned for a small, portable table that contained a wooden basin upon it. He splashed icy water on his face and neck as she stood behind him, watching his big form in the weak light. When Merlin emerged from the dim recess of the tent with a small lit taper, hardly enough light against the darkness of the tent, she lowered her gaze and kept silent until the red-headed sergeant quit the tent and shut the flap. Not knowing the sergeant, she was afraid she had already said too much in front of the man.

She did not want her business with Cortez to become fodder for soldier's gossip.

"I am afraid I must make an amendment to our bargain," she said quietly after Merlin had left the tent.

Cortez stood up, drying his neck with a linen rag. "You may *not*," he told her. "The bargain has been struck. I leave for the north this morning."

Diamantha watched him as he moved to a small leather satchel and began pulling items out of it. "Will you not even hear me before you deny me?" she asked.

He looked at her, then, but there was impatience in his expression. "What is it, then?"

She cocked her head. "Sir, you must learn to be more patient when dealing with me," she said as if she was scolding him. "I do not react well to harsh tones or annoyed manners."

He lifted her eyebrows at her and his impatience increased. "You woke me out of a sound sleep to tell me that you are coming with me to Scotland and expect me not to become irritated?" When she nodded once, firmly, he shook his head with exasperation and returned to his satchel. "Once you make a bargain, lady, you keep to it. I know that Robert was a man of great patience but unfortunately, I am not. Mayhap he allowed you to go back on your word, but I will not. I do not tolerate foolishness."

Diamantha's brow furrowed. "It is not foolishness I give you," she said, feeling her ire rise. "I came to speak to you on a matter of great importance to me but mayhap the only importance you will allow is a matter of your own. If that is the case, then I suppose we are in for a turbulent marriage because any matter of importance to me should be a matter of importance to you as well. As my husband, you should be greatly concerned for anything I deem significant."

Cortez had seen this agitated manner from her once before in George's solar and he was coming to quickly realize that he didn't like to see her upset. It made him feel anxious and edgy. Nay, he didn't like that feeling at all, especially when he was trying to establish a relationship with her. They didn't need this kind of disruption to their already tenuous association but he knew that she was reacting to his agitation. Evidently, his irritation didn't force her into submission as it used to do with Helene. It only seemed to aggravate her. Therefore, he took a deep breath and struggled to calm himself because it wouldn't do either one of them any good if they were both angry.

"Anything that is of great importance to you is naturally of great importance to me," he said, sounding much more patient than he had moments earlier. "You came to discuss your thoughts with me and I rudely cut you short. Forgive me. Please tell me everything that is concerning you."

She crossed her arms stubbornly. "You do not care to hear it."

"I do, I swear."

She scowled. "Tell me you are sorry for saying I was foolish."

His irritation threatened to return but he fought it. She was, if nothing else, a plucky creature. "I never said you were foolish," he said steadily. "I simply said I do not tolerate foolishness. Now, will you please tell me what you wished to discuss? I would very much like to hear it."

She wasn't ready to forgive him yet but softened out of necessity. They hadn't much time. "I will tell you, but you must swear to me that you will not become angry with me."

He grunted, resisting the urge to roll his eyes. "I swear."

Diamantha eyed him as if she did not believe him but dutifully continued. "Very well," she said. "As I was saying, I fear I have placed a terrible burden on you by making you responsible for returning Robert to me for a proper burial. It was wrong of me to do that and since we are to be married, it is a burden you should not assume alone. I must assume it with you. Therefore, I will be riding with you to Falkirk to help you retrieve Robert's body and I thought... well, as a show of good faith, I thought that we should be wed before we go."

Cortez stared at her a moment, struggling not to openly react. "Before we go?"

She nodded. "We cannot travel together as an unmarried couple," she said as if it was a terrible thing. "Therefore, we must marry out of necessity."

She made it sound rather cold, but he didn't care. He could hardly believe what he was hearing. "*Before* we go?" he said again, just to make sure he heard right. "Today?"

Diamantha nodded again, even before the words had completely left his mouth. "We can be married at St. Edward's," she said. "It is the church in the town. The priests will be happy to conduct the ceremony."

Cortez wasn't hard pressed to admit that he was stunned. This was something he had not expected to hear, not in the least. He tried not to sound too excited or enthusiastic about it, fearful that it might frighten or upset her. He didn't want her to see the joy of victory in his eyes. Truthfully, all he could think of was marrying her quickly so she could never refuse or deny him again because it meant that once they were married, she would have to do what he said and he could tell her that she could not accompany him north. It was an outlandish idea, anyway. As her husband, he would demand she remain behind and she would be forced to obey. Or so he thought.

"When did you think to do this?" he asked, rather neutrally.

Diamantha fidgeted with her hands as if she wasn't fully convinced her decision was sound. Still, she was determined.

"Now, I would think," she said. "The priests are preparing for Matins, so I am sure they would not be opposed to performing the marriage mass afterwards. That way, we can be on our way this morning without too much delay."

Cortez didn't delay another second. He quickly tossed the rag aside and went about dressing in a heavy woolen tunic over the lighter one he already wore. "Very well, Lady Edlington," he said, rushed, as he pulled the tunic over his head. "I accept your proposal. We shall be married immediately. Is there anything else you wished to speak to me about?"

Diamantha opened her mouth but was cut short as the tent flap suddenly snapped back and a tall young man entered. She stepped back, out of the lad's way, as he fell to his knees next to Cortez and began collecting pieces of armor that had been stacked next to the cot. As Cortez's squire went to work, interrupting a rather personal conversation, she frowned.

"Even if there was, I could not speak of it now," she said, eyeing the big red-haired youth on the ground. "I will wait for you outside."

Cortez held out a hand to her to prevent her from leaving. "Nay," he said quickly. "Remain where you are. My squire will be finished in a moment and we can go together to the church. Please do not leave."

Diamantha pulled her cloak more tightly about her in the chill of the tent but she said nothing, easing back into the shadows and watching the squire work quickly and efficiently. The lad couldn't have been more than fifteen or sixteen years of age, with a crown of glorious red hair and very big hands, and when he stood up he was taller than Cortez. He moved like lightning, confident in the knowledge of his job. When he moved to collect the mail coat, which was strung over a frame that was behind Diamantha, she quickly moved out of the lad's way to give him a wide berth.

Cortez was alternately watching her movements and his tasks as he dressed. She seemed very quiet now and he knew she was irritated with him. She'd had more to say but his squire had prevented it, which he was fairly certain was a good thing. All he wanted to do now was get the woman to the church and legally marry her. Then, whatever came after that would be dealt with, including her unreasonable demands. In all things, and especially this marriage, his wants would take precedence. In their brief association he could already see that she was a spoiled creature and used to getting her own way. It was a lesson she would have to quickly learn.

"I will introduce you to my men today, men who will be serving you," he said, simply to make conversation so they weren't hanging about in awkward silence. "I may as well start with my squire. Peter Summerlin is from a fine family in Norfolk. His father is Sir Alec Summerlin, who was known in his youth as The Legend. No finer swordsman has ever existed and his son seems to have taken after him. Although Peter is young, I expect to knight him myself next year."

Diamantha looked at the big youth when the young man eyed her with some embarrassment. He cheeks were nearly as ruddy as his hair. He bowed swiftly to her even as he finished pulling the mail coat over Cortez's head.

"He seems very efficient," she commented, her attention returning to Cortez. "I have not seen any other de Bretagne knights since you have been here."

Cortez lifted his arms as Peter began to secure his heavy leather scabbard, crafted in Rouen by a master tanner. The de Bretagne crest was emblazoned upon it, discreetly, a three-point shield with a bird of prey upon it, and the tip of the scabbard was protected by a riveted steel tip. Cortez glanced down at his beloved scabbard as Peter gave it a final adjustment.

"That is because they have remained in camp," he told her. "I only brought two with me. The others are at Sherborne Castle, including my brother."

Peter swept from the tent and they were alone again. Diamantha could hear the camp outside as men began to rouse and go about their tasks, but she found herself somewhat interested in her conversation with Cortez. She was still irritated with him for his attitude towards her concerns, that was true, but she could feel the mood of the conversation shifting to something casual and she was willing to go with it.

"I was not aware you had a brother," she said. "Helene never mentioned him."

Cortez strapped his purse onto his scabbard. "That is because my brother has been in the north, serving with my father," he replied. "My father is the garrison commander at Sandal Castle for the Earl of Surrey, and Andres is two years younger than I am. He came to serve with me at Sherborne right after Helene died. My father sent him to tend me, I suspect, fearful of what I might do in my grief, but instead, Andres has given me something else to focus on because I am constantly having to bail the man out of trouble."

Diamantha cocked her head. "Trouble?" she repeated. "What kind of trouble?"

Cortez fidgeted with the collar of his tunic where it chaffed him. "The man has an eye for women and a taste for alcohol, and the two do not often mix well," he said before he could think about who he was speaking to. "In fact, there have been times when I have had to pull my brother out of the gutter and drown him in the nearest trough to… forgive me, but I probably should not be telling you this, should I?"

He appeared rather chagrined and Diamantha fought off a smile. "Probably not," she said. "But tell me anyway. I would know what character of new brother awaits me."

Cortez could see that she was trying very hard not to smile and he grinned. "Andres is a good man and an excellent knight," he told her firmly. "But there will be times that you may have to throw a bucket of water on him to revive him."

"Or drown him."

He laughed softly. "Truer words were never spoken," he said, his gaze lingering on her and seeing a flicker of a lovely smile. It was glorious. "I would imagine that my brother will not be able to get away with his usual foolery with you around. I suspect you would not tolerate it."

"You would suspect correctly."

His warm gaze lingered on her, hoping against hope that they were overcoming their turmoil and soon to embark on a new chapter in their association. Nay, *relationship*. He wanted more than an association with her. He wanted the same thing he'd had with Helene, a warm and gentle relationship that gave him comfort. He prayed Diamantha would see reason and understand that her role in his life would be one of thoughtfulness and obedience. With a faint sigh, perhaps one to summon his courage, he approached her.

"May I be honest with you, Lady Edlington?" he asked softly.

There was something in the expression on his face that made Diamantha feel weak in the knees. It was a warm and giddy sensation, something she had experienced with Robert back when they had been courting, but it wasn't something she'd been familiar with much since that time. This was an incredibly electrifying sensation, as if invisible rivers were flowing from his dark eyes and enveloping her in their liquid exhilaration. It was enough to cause her some unsteadiness.

"Aye," she replied after a moment.

His smile grew. "I realize that we have not had the most pleasant of associations up until now," he said quietly. "I suppose I am to blame for some of that, but there is something I wish to say to you. Even though I promised Robert I would take care of you, please know that I do not view this marriage as an inconvenience. I view it as a new hope. Please know that I will do everything in my power to make you happy and comfortable and safe, and I swear that I shall be faithful only unto you. You will be my wife and my loyalty, both emotionally and physically, shall belong to you. I hope that you will treat it with respect."

They were surprisingly deep words but Diamantha was torn by them. She and Robert had been exceedingly faithful to each other so she knew of no other way. She was glad to hear that Cortez, too, shared that view. Given the women in the past that she knew of who had thrown themselves at him, she was relieved by it. Still, it sounded to her as if he was perhaps asking for something more than that, something she wasn't yet ready to give. It seemed to her that he was also asking for her affection. She found she couldn't look into that hopeful, eager face.

"Of course I will," she replied, averting her gaze. "You will have my loyalty as well, in all things. But... but this marriage is simply an agreement between us. It is something I am being told to do and I shall do it. When you speak of new hope, I do not know how to answer you. What is it that you hope for?"

Cortez had to remind himself yet again that she was still grieving. Her loss was so new; his was years old. Still, his impatience had the better of him. "I would hope for a pleasant marriage," he said. "I would hope that someday you will cease to view me as a contract and begin viewing me as your husband. I would hope that someday we will grow to like each other, mayhap even enjoy one another. I would also hope that you shall bear me strong sons one day, sons we will both be proud of. I hope that one day you shall be able to refer to me as your husband and be pleased with the fact. These are the things I hope for, my lady. I do not believe they are too unreasonable."

Diamantha lifted her eyes to look at him, seeing that the eagerness, so prevalent in his expression earlier, was now restrained because she was so reserved. She realized that he could sense her hesitation and was reacting accordingly. Everything was still so uncertain in her heart and mind, and she simply couldn't bring herself to agree with him. Every time she closed her eyes or drew a breath, all she could see was Robert. It was like a stab to the gut.

"It is not unreasonable," she said, feeling her composure slip, "but until my husband is located and until I have reconciled myself to the fact he is truly dead and in his grave, I cannot... I simply cannot...."

She trailed off, hanging her head and biting her lip to keep from weeping. Cortez watched her lowered head, feeling a tug at his heart. "You loved him," he whispered.

It was a statement, not a question. Diamantha nodded firmly. "I did," she murmured tightly. "I do. I still do."

Cortez sighed faintly. "I know how you feel."

Her head came up, the mesmerizing eyes swimming with tears. "You loved Helene?"

He nodded. "I did," he said softly. "As you said, she was a sweet and gentle creature. There was much to love."

Diamantha's lower lip trembled and the tears spilled over. "How... how long before you did not wake up every morning with the pangs of grief twisting your stomach?"

His gaze lingered on her a moment before he moved, slowly, in her direction. "It took some time," he said honestly. "But I can promise you that one day you will wake up and the pain will be less. Every day will see it diminish slightly until all that is left is a warm and bittersweet memory."

She wiped furiously at her eyes. "I am not sure I want it to ever go away," she said. "I do not want it taken from me. It is mine, a reminder of the love we shared."

He came to within a foot or so, pausing as he studied her intently. "No one wants to take it from you, Lady Edlington, least of all me."

Her head came up, her eyes accusing. "Aye, you do," she said. "You have come to marry me and wipe the man from my memory."

He shook his head. "I never said that," he insisted softly. "I would never try to erase the man's memory."

Diamantha studied his sincere expression. "Your actions versus your words tell me differently," she said, somewhat bitterly. "Tell me something, de Bretagne; if the situation was reversed and it was Helene dead only three months, how would you feel if someone had come to marry you so soon after your wife had died? How would you have felt?"

He locked gazes with her, feeling on the defensive with the question because he knew what his answer would be. But he could not lie to her; it was not in his nature. Furthermore, if he wished to establish a trusting relationship with her, it had to start somewhere. Let it start here.

"Three months after my wife's death, I was barely able to function," he said truthfully. "Therefore, I would not have been receptive to a marriage proposal. I more than likely would have run the messenger through."

His honestly was gratifying. "I will not run you through, but you must understand that this is simply something I am not ready for," she told him, her tears fading because the subject was growing seriously. She could see that Cortez was coming to understand her position completely. "I have heard you say that I am not ready but I do not think you truly believe it. I will still marry you this morning but you must give me time to come to terms with everything. You cannot force me into acceptance, de Bretagne. Much like you after the death of Helene, I am still very much grieving Robert's loss. It is my right to be allowed to do so. Do you understand what I am saying?"

After a moment, he nodded faintly. "I do," he confirmed. "I am sorry if you have felt forced into this situation before you were ready, but I know of no other way. You are to be my wife and I see no reason to wait."

He only sees his wants, Diamantha thought. It occurred to her that whether or not he truly understood her position, what he wanted mattered more. But she could also see something else; it wasn't that he was being selfish about it. It was simply the way his mind worked. His desires came before anything else. De Bretagne was a spoiled man. With a sigh, perhaps one of resignation, she turned away.

"As I said, I will marry you this morning," she said. "As for the rest... you must be patient, sir. Anything else might result in something neither of us would like."

He watched her as she moved away from him, putting space between them. "I will be as patient as is reasonably expected."

Diamantha came to a halt and faced him. She sensed something stubborn in that statement and it was time to return the volley and establish lines. He had to know that she wasn't going to let him push her around because it wasn't in her nature to be pushed.

"As I have seen, your ability to be patient leaves something to be desired," she said. "You will listen to me now so there is no mistake. I will marry you this morning and then we shall proceed north. If you try, in any way, to prevent me from going with you, know that I shall follow you. I shall hire guides and escorts, in any matter I deem necessary, to follow your path into Scotland. You cannot stop me short of locking me in the vault, and even if you do that, know that I will escape and I will continue my pursuit of you. This is *my* quest too, de Bretagne. You cannot take that from me."

He believed every word she said, causing him to quickly re-think his strategy of marrying her and ordering her to remain behind. He had no doubt she would do what she said so he made the decision at that moment. Would it be worth a lifetime of a hate-filled marriage for him to force her to remain behind, a battle with no end, or would it be better for them all if he would simply allow her to go with him on his quest north? If he did, it would be a journey that could hopefully build trust and even the fondness he spoke of earlier. It would be something they could do together and therefore build together. As much as he didn't want her along, he was coming to think it was the wiser choice, for certainly, the alternative was bleak. After several pensive moments, he finally nodded his head.

"Very well," he said. "If you truly wish to accompany me, I will not stop you. But we will come to an agreement here and now. You will do everything I tell you. You will not argue with me and you will not disobey. If any of these terms are not met, I will leave you at the nearest castle and tell them to lock you in the vault until I return for you. Know that I do not threaten and I do not jest. I am as serious as death and twice as final. Is this in any way unclear?"

Diamantha only cared about the fact that he had agreed to let her go. She would have agreed to anything at that point. "It is perfectly clear."

His gaze lingered on her. Something told him that it wasn't as clear to her as it was to him. Time would tell. He broke away from her and moved to the small table beside his cot that held the water bowl. It also contained the pretty painted box with the silver collar inside, the one Diamantha had thrown so angrily onto the mattress earlier that evening. Picking it up, he opened the box and pulled forth the heavy silver necklace as he turned in her direction.

"I apologize that I am unprepared with a wedding ring, as I did not expect to marry you so soon," he said, holding out the necklace to her as if making an offering to an angry god. "Would you please accept this necklace as a token of my respect for the event of our marriage? I will purchase a ring for you as soon as I can, but until then, I would be very pleased if you would accept the necklace. Please, my lady?"

Diamantha eyed the beautiful piece. Her initial reaction was that she still thought he was trying to buy a bride with such a gift, but it didn't matter any longer. She'd already agreed to marry him so her refusal was baseless. Reluctantly, she reached out to take it and in silence, she put it around her neck. It was so big and cumbersome that she needed help fastening it, which Cortez gladly did. As it settled against her chest, she couldn't help but admire it.

"It is a very lovely piece," she said. "I remember seeing Helene wear it."

Cortez watched the glittering silver cross against her breast, mesmerized. "It was her favorite piece," he said. "Before her, it had belonged to my mother. It has been much loved."

"Then I shall handle it with the greatest of care."

He pulled his gaze from the stones, looking her in the eye. "You would treat her jewelry with the greatest of care," he said softly. "But I wonder how you would treat her husband?"

Diamantha held his gaze. "I suppose we shall soon find out."

Cortez didn't take much comfort from that statement.

CHAPTER FIVE

In the swirling mists of the early morning, Cortez and Diamantha made their way to the church directly across from the gatehouse of Corfe, alone. He wanted to get it over with and she didn't want any close witnesses, so they journeyed to the church without any entourage or retainers. It was just the two of them, traipsing through the fog and damp.

The village of Corfe was crowded around the southern end of the castle, waddle and daub huts that were clustered tightly together like a herd of lonely sheep. St. Edward the Martyr's church was literally across the road from the main entrance to the castle, a rather large cathedral that had been there in some form long before the Normans came.

It was into this cavernous church that Cortez and Diamantha had proceeded. It smelled like wet earth and incense, a strange and acrid smell. Cortez remembered the church from Robert's funeral mass, when it had been packed with knights who had fought with Robert Edlington at one time or another. The man had been well-liked. In a massive hall that had once intoned the utterings of Edlington's death, now it was witness to the marriage of Edlington's widow to the man who had left Edlington to die. At least, that's how Cortez viewed it in ironic reflection. Those were the facts.

He wondered if the priests knew the facts, too, from the way they looked at him. They had been more than happy to perform the marriage sacrament at Diamantha's request and, because they knew her, three of them shared the duties of the liturgy. They also eyed Cortez with some suspicion, not knowing who he was and seemingly protective over the lady of their castle. Cortez took it all in stride but the wariness of his presence lingered, even when the priest made the last sacrament and bade Cortez to kiss his bride. Cortez did, on the cheek, only because he swore those priests were shooting daggers at him with their eyes. After that, he was impatient to leave.

The priests carefully recorded the marriage in their big book of events, much as they recorded the births and deaths of the town as well. Anything of note that happened at Corfe was recorded. Since the mass had been witnessed by three priests, all three signed the book with their marks and presented Cortez with a stamped sheet of vellum that legitimized the marriage. Once Cortez had that certificate in his hand, he paid the priests well, took Diamantha by the hand, and practically pulled her out of the church. He had a mission to accomplish and he was ready to get on with it. He was ready to move forward with his new wife and get away from the church where the priests were eyeing him as if he were stealing the lady away from them. He was coming to feel like a thief.

Diamantha had been oddly silent throughout the event; at that point, Cortez was grateful for small mercies. At least she wasn't weeping, which had had expected. She seemed rather stunned by it all and had lapsed into uncharacteristic silence. He wondered how long it was going to last. By the time they entered the gatehouse of Corfe and headed into the massive lower bailey, the fog was lifting somewhat as the sun began to rise. Cortez could see his men gathered for travel, with tents packed and fires doused. His two knights were on horseback, spurring their heavy-boned coursers along the group and making sure everyone was prepared to depart. Cortez's hand was still on Diamantha's arm as they headed towards his men.

"Since you are already in traveling clothes, I will assume you are packed and ready to depart," he said. "Where are your possessions?"

Diamantha seemed to be staring off into the distance, as if seeing things that were no longer there. Perhaps she was seeing her life past, with Robert, something that was now gone. There was a new, uncertain life in its place. In any case, she snapped out of whatever trance she was in when Cortez spoke to her.

"Everything is in the keep," she told him. "Will you have my horse brought forth while I go inside to retrieve my belongings?"

Cortez's hand dropped from her arm. "It would be my pleasure," he said. "Do you require any other assistance?"

She shook her head. "Nay," she said. "I would suppose we are traveling lightly so I am not bringing anything heavier than what can be carried upon the back of a horse."

He was rather pleased by that statement. *A sensible woman*, he thought. If she was forcing him to take her, then at least she was being reasonable about it.

"Very well," he said. "I will await you by the upper gatehouse."

Diamantha nodded her head and moved away from him, heading up the wet incline of Corfe's enormous outer ward on her way to the inner gatehouse. Cortez couldn't help but notice that she hadn't made eye contact with him in any fashion since they'd left the church, not even in this brief conversation. She seemed preoccupied and sad. Not that he blamed her, but he couldn't worry about that now. What was done was done, and she would have to accept it. They were now married.

Turning for his men, now grouped and prepared to leave, he went about final preparations as he awaited his wife to rejoin him. With a lingering glance over his shoulder at Diamantha's dark blue form as she disappeared through the upper gatehouse, he wondered if he shouldn't go with her. He was rather wary of letting her out of his sight considering what had gone on between them in the past. The last thing he needed was her changing her mind and barricading herself inside the castle.

He hoped it didn't come to that, but he couldn't be sure. At this point, he was praying he wasn't going to have to lay siege to get his wife back.

Diamantha could feel Cortez's eyes on her back as she made her way up to the keep, but she ignored it. She was trying not to think of the fact that this could very well be the last time she ever saw her beloved Corfe. The marriage, the mass... all of it had passed in a blur. All she could think when they had entered the church was of Robert and the last time she had attended church with him. It had been right before he'd left for the north and she recalled how he'd held her hand the entire time. There had been such comfort and strength there. God, she couldn't think of it anymore. It was making her mad with grief. Now, she was no longer Lady Edlington but Lady de Bretagne, a title once held by her dear friend. Helene had looked upon her position in life with such honor. At the moment, all Diamantha could manage to feel for it was sorrow.

By the time she reached the gatehouse, the soldiers were opening the great panels for her and she walked through, trying not to slip on the rather steep slope as the path ascended into the upper ward. She was struggling to focus on what tasks lay ahead of her and not the distress she was feeling. The course took a steep turn to the right and the stairs to the keep lay before her. She took the steps as she had taken them a thousand times before, already missing the comfort they brought her, knowing that the keep she called home would soon be swallowing her up. She was barely through the massive oak and iron panel that comprised the front door before her women were upon her.

They had been lying in wait for their mistress. It was dark and cold in the entry, shielding them in the shadows, but Diamantha grinned at the group, wearily, as they began to fuss over her. Someone was trying to pull off her damp cloak while someone else was trying to hand her a cup of warmed mead. She put up her hands to stop all of the tugging and fussing.

"Cease, my little goats," she said softly but firmly. "I am not removing my cloak and I plan to leave just as soon as my bags are retrieved. Where are they?"

One of the women, a very tall female with a big white wimple pulled tight around her head, motioned to the wall near the entry door. Diamantha noted the two rather large leather satchels and she nodded, satisfied.

"Excellent," she said. "Where is my daughter?"

One of the women hustled over to the narrow spiral stairs and disappeared up the well. The woman with the white wimple spoke in a nervous voice.

"Do you truly plan to leave, m'lady?" she asked.

Diamantha nodded. "I do," she said, glancing to the group. She spoke with more bravery than she felt. "I became Lady de Bretagne this morning. I plan to travel now with my husband to retrieve Robert's body, as I told you I would. You listened to me as I reasoned out my plan before presenting it to de Bretagne. I *must* do this, ladies. I told you as much, so worrying over it will not change the way of things. It is done."

One of the women teared up, wiping at her nose as she turned away and went to stand in the shadows to shield her loss of composure. Diamantha was struggling not to become weepy as well. If she were to cry, then her women would become positively hysterical and she couldn't deal with it. So she squared her shoulders and went to check her bags. Crouching down, she tossed her cloak back to remove the magnificent silver collar. She didn't want to wear it while traveling and ended up tucking it carefully into one of her satchels.

"I am not entirely sure how long it will take us to travel to Scotland," she said as she finished packing the necklace into the larger of the satchels. "I can only imagine it will take us several weeks at the very least. I will even ask to visit my father in Northumberland. He is at Norham Castle, you know, and it is along the path we will take. My mother wrote me several months ago and told me that Papa no longer lifts a sword. He leaves it to my brothers to guard the border. She says Papa is feeling his age, I suppose. He has knots in his hands, so severe that he can hardly hold anything at all. I miss him."

Diamantha reflected on her father, the tallest man she had ever seen, who had once been a very fine knight. Sir Michael de Bocage had served under the illustrious William de Wolfe for many years and earned himself a fine reputation in the process. But those days of glory along the Scots border were long gone for her father. Now, he relied on his sons and the sons of other great knights to keep the

Scots at bay. De Wolfe, de Norville, Hage, de Bocage, and de Longley were great names along the border from Berwick to Kelso. They kept watch for the Crown and no one dared challenge them, not even the Scots. Diamantha had grown up in the shadow of England's greatest knights.

She was therefore eager to return to the north where she had been born. As much as she loved Corfe and the town's folk, she was a northern lass at heart. As she re-secured the ties on Robert's satchel, Annie emerged from the stairwell with Sophie in her arms. Diamantha smiled broadly at her child and reached out to take her from her nurse.

"Greetings, sweetheart," she said softly, kissing her little girl's cheek. "Have you eaten this morning?"

Sophie was tired, rubbing her eyes wearily. "Aye," she said. "Annie gave me mush. Mama, can I see General?"

Diamantha's smile faded. "Of course, my love," she said, setting the little girl to her feet. She noted, per her instructions when she had left the keep in search of Cortez that morning, that the child was dressed heavily in gray wool for travel. She had a little cap on her head to keep it warm, snuggly tied. "Would you like to go see him now?"

Sophie nodded eagerly, dragging her poppet along the ground as her mother guided her towards the door. Diamantha paused a moment, her gaze moving along the dark entry to the stairwell to the hall beyond. It would be perhaps her last glimpse of it. She could still hear Robert within the walls, his laughter echoing. The memories tugged at her heart but she fought them. It would do no good to make herself miserable. *It is done*, she reminded herself. *You cannot look back, not now*. She had to bring Robert home and marrying de Bretagne had been the only way to accomplish it.

Asking one of her women to collect the two satchels and follow her out of the keep, she was just opening the door when George appeared, coming off the stairwell. He looked as if he had just rolled out of bed. In fact, George was a poor sleeper and usually did most of his sleeping in the early morning hours, so it was difficult for him to rise early. Diamantha had counted on that. But she could see the man was alert, and he appeared stricken. He headed right for her.

"Where are you going?" he demanded. "De Bretagne's army is prepared to depart. I could see them from my window. God's Blood, Diamantha... you are not really going with him, are you?"

Diamantha tried not to look too remorseful. She had purposely kept her plans from George. The last he'd seen of her interaction with Cortez had been the night before in the feasting hall. He had no idea what had transpired since then. But she could see now that she needed to tell the man something, anything at all, for he was about to lose his entire family. First his son, and now his granddaughter. Like a coward, she'd hoped to depart before he awoke but that was not to be the case. She didn't want to listen to him tell her what a bad decision she was making. Turning Sophie over to Annie, she grasped George by the elbow and pulled him into the vacant hall beyond.

When they were well away from the ears in the entry and on into the dark, cold hall, she turned to the man.

"Listen to me, George," she whispered, somewhat sorrowfully. "Much has happened since last night. You must listen and remain calm for I swear upon our Holy Mother that I cannot take any more emotion this day. I've had quite enough of it already."

George looked traumatized but he nodded. "I will listen calmly," he assured her, though he wasn't sure if he meant it. "What has happened?"

Diamantha sighed faintly. "It is quite simple, truly," she said quietly. "De Bretagne has agreed to return to Scotland to find Robert's body and bring him back for a proper burial. I am going with him to make sure he finds the right corpse and Sophie is going with me."

George's eyes widened. "De Bretagne is... he is going to find Robert?"

"Aye."

The old man was having a difficult time controlling himself. "But *why*?" he hissed. "Did you ask him to do this?"

Diamantha was patient. "I told him I would marry him if he did," she said. "In fact, I have already married him. We were wed this morning. We are going to Scotland and I swear to you that I will bring Robert back. He will be buried at St. Edward's next to his mother. Does this please you, George?"

George was looking both horrified and relieved. It was an odd expression, truly. He tried to speak but no words would come forth. Finally, he reached out and grasped her by the arms.

"Oh, my dearest lass," he breathed in one big sigh. "You would do this simply to bring Robert home? You would make a deal with the devil?"

Diamantha shrugged. "I had no real choice in the matter," she said truthfully. "But de Bretagne wanted to marry me now. He did not wish to wait. I used his impatience to my advantage. I told him I would marry him this day if he would escort me to Scotland to bring Robert home. It is a great questing he and I will undertake, George. This is something I think we both must do."

George was still struggling to come to terms with it. "Why is it something de Bretagne must do?"

Diamantha's expression turned distant. "He was the last man with Robert before he died," she murmured. "He left him on the field of battle to die alone. I believe he feels the need to right that sin and return him home to those who love him."

George's gaze lingered on her. "Are you certain of this?" he asked softly. "Or did he simply agree to do it because you promised to marry him if he did? He could go back on his word, you know."

Diamantha met his gaze. "He will not go back on his word," she said. "Do you truly believe I would let him? We made a bargain and he has what he wants; he has married me. Now, we will go to Scotland and find Robert, and that is all I care about."

George was calmer now, absorbing the reality of the situation. He had to admit that he was relieved to the point of tears to know that Robert would soon be returning home for a proper burial, but the cost seemed to be Diamantha herself. It was an overwhelming realization. He let go of the woman's arms, now feeling suddenly weak and defeated. He sank down on the nearest bench.

"So you have already married him?" he asked.

Diamantha nodded. "Aye."

George pondered that, raking his fingers through his graying hair. "And Sophie?" he ventured. "You are taking her with you?"

Diamantha nodded firmly. "I will not be away from my child for the amount of time it takes to go to Scotland and back," she said. "Moreover, this will be Sophie's questing also. Robert was her father. Let her be a part of the mission to bring him home. Let her know that the man rests in peace. It may not mean anything to her now, but it will in time."

George wasn't in full agreement but he didn't argue. He simply sat there like a man who had just had all of the life sucked out of him.

"Are you sure of this?" he begged softly.

"I am."

There was nothing more to say. George fought back the tears. "Very well," he finally muttered. "May I at least bid Sophie farewell?"

Diamantha nodded. "Of course you can," she said, turning towards the archway that led into the keep entry and calling out. "Annie? Will you please bring Sophie to me?"

There was some hissing and Diamantha swore she heard a screech. Annie suddenly appeared in the doorway, wringing her hands nervously as she always did. The woman had wrung her hands into blisters at times.

"I turned my back for a moment, my lady," she wept. "She was there one moment and gone the next!"

Diamantha stared at the woman a moment before bolting past her. "She has gone to see General," she hissed. "God's Blood, she has escaped us again!"

Diamantha fled the keep with her women. In the mists of the early morning, they knew exactly where one little girl would be.

George, however, remained behind. He found that he couldn't muster the strength to follow; everything that was dear to him was either dead or departing. It was a difficult thing to reconcile. All he could think of was that he was now alone, so very alone. He had nothing left to live for except the hope that his son would indeed be returned to him for a proper burial. He would live for that day but when that day had come and gone, he wasn't sure he wanted to remain in the land of the living after that.

He seriously wondered if he could go on with nothing left to him but memories.

Cortez wasn't sure he was seeing correctly.

In the white mists that were lingering so close to the ground, he swore he saw a ghost near the massive wall of the inner bailey. It was a tiny white wisp, moving through the fog, and he focused on it, trying to make it out. He could see legs and little feet. When a patch of fog lifted slightly, he could see that it was Lady Sophie heading straight for the stables and she was quite alone. *Another escape*, he thought. Swiftly, he went in pursuit.

Cortez caught up to the child just as she reached the stable yard, enclosed with its big oak fence and smatterings of dried grass strewn about. The smell of animals was heavy in the dense fog. He reached out to gently grasp her, stopping her momentum.

"Good morn to you, little one," he said. "Where do you go in such a hurry?"

Sophie turned to look at him, her sweet little face framed by the woolen cap. "To see General," she told him what he already knew. "He is waiting for me."

Cortez held out his hand to her, which she immediately snatched. "Where is your mother?"

Sophie shrugged and yanked on his hand, pulling him with her as she made her way towards the stables. Cortez, however, slowed his pace and gently but firmly pulled her to a stop.

"Sophie," he said, more plainly. "*Where* is your mother?"

Sophie looked up at him. "Inside," she told him. "She is speaking with Grandfather."

Cortez wasn't particularly concerned about a conversation between Diamantha and George, but he was unwilling to delay too much longer before departing. Already, the day was here and time was passing quickly. He tugged on the little girl's hand.

"Let us go inside and get your mother," he said. "I am sure she would like to see General, too."

Sophie's brow furrowed as she looked between Cortez and the stalls several feet away. She was far too close to General to be willingly taken away from him. After a moment, she shook her head.

"I want to see General *now*," she told him.

Cortez could see a battle with a three-year-old coming on and, to be frank, nothing could intimidate him more. He didn't want to be on the child's bad side now when he was just coming to know her, and perhaps love her just a little. He didn't want her to view him as anything other than a kind man who took interest in her pony. It was selfish, he knew, but let the mother be the one she viewed as the disciplinarian. He didn't want any part of that role in her eyes.

"If I take you to see General first will you then go with me to retrieve your mother?" he bargained.

Sophie's features brightened. "Aye."

Resigned to the will of a toddler, and the fact that he was a coward, Cortez allowed her to lead him into the stable where the horses were being fed their morning meal by the stable servants. The air smelled of dust and grass, and Sophie let go of Cortez's hand as she scurried over to the stall where General was munching his grain. She slipped right into the stall and began petting the pony as it ate.

Cortez leaned against the stall door, a faint smile on his lips as he watched the child hug and pet the pony, who was more interested in his food. His thoughts turned from those of his cowardice to those of warmth and contentment. *This child belongs to me now,* he thought as he watched her giggle. It was an odd but wonderful sensation and one that made him feel whole in a manner he couldn't begin to describe. For the past three years he had been so alone, and now he had a wife and a child. He was a knight, and an excellent one, and the true mark of a male by any standard. But now... now, he felt like a *man*. He had dependents. He had a family. He had what he had lost three years ago, something he had always wanted. He couldn't describe it any better than that.

As he stood there and pondered the course that his future had taken, he heard a soft voice come up beside him.

"So she dragged you in here, did she? I thought as much."

Cortez turned to see Diamantha standing next to him, her gaze on her child as the girl fussed over her pony. "Indeed she did," he replied. "Truth be told, I found *her* as she was running to the stables. Can I surmise that she escaped you again?"

Diamantha's attention was still on her daughter. "You can," she said. "She has always been that way, as soon as she learned to walk. If you turn your back on her, she will disappear before you know it."

Cortez grinned. "Mayhap you should tie a bell around her neck so you will always be able to find her."

Diamantha couldn't help but smile. "I can just see her running around with a big bell around her neck, dragging her down. I do not think she would be a very happy child."

Cortez laughed softly, watching Diamantha as she, in turn, watched her daughter. She was such an exquisite creature and the infatuation he had felt for her since nearly the moment he first saw her in George's solar seemed to be growing by the second. It made his heart skip a beat, the queasy, giddy feeling he was coming to associate with her.

Diamantha could feel Cortez's eyes on her. The liquid heat was palpable, reaching out to caress her with invisible fingers. It made her uncomfortable and interested at the same time, this magnetism that she seemed to be unable to resist. After a moment, she turned to look at him, feeling a jolt when their eyes met.

"Actually, I am glad she found you," she said quietly. "We must have the pony saddled for her."

Cortez lifted a curious eyebrow. "Why?"

Diamantha made sure to look him in the eye when she spoke. "Because he is going with us," she said. "So is Sophie."

The warmth in Cortez's eyes vanished. "What do you mean?"

Diamantha didn't back down; truthfully, this was the best possible atmosphere in which to tell him something he would undoubtedly not want to hear. She suspected he wouldn't raise his voice or become too angry with Sophie just a few feet away. It was all very calculated on her part. She saw the opportunity and she took it.

"I mean exactly what I just said," she explained, her voice soft. "Sophie is coming with us on our quest north and since I know she will not leave General behind, he is coming with us, too."

Cortez's jaw flexed dangerously and the onyx eyes flashed. "Are you mad?" he hissed. "I am not taking a child over hundreds of miles of road, through situations that could possibly be dangerous or even deadly. I cannot believe I am hearing this from you, her own mother!"

He was doing a good job at keeping his voice down but Diamantha could see that he was positively furious and it was a struggle not to become intimidated by it. She looked back over at her daughter.

"Let me state this to you quite plainly," she said evenly. "As I am going with you to retrieve Robert's body, I do not plan to be separated from my daughter for an unknown length of time. It could be weeks or even months before I see her again, and I will not be kept from her for that long. Therefore, it is the logical solution that she goes with us. You will be able to protect both of us quite ably. I have faith in you. Besides, Robert is her father – this is as much her questing as it is yours or mine. In time, she will appreciate that we allowed her to go. It is her right."

His cheeks were starting to turn red. "This is utter and complete lunacy," he growled. "I forbid it."

"You cannot. It is my decision, as she is my daughter."

Cortez just looked at her. His eyes seemed to widen and his mouth worked as if he wanted to say something. In truth, there was a good deal he wanted to say. But instead, he abruptly turned and walked out of the stable. Diamantha stood there a moment, wondering if she should follow, when she suddenly heard a loud and angry yell. It reverberated off the stone walls and caused the animals to start, including General. Even Diamantha jumped when she heard it, for it was most angry and primal. But as soon as it ended, Cortez was back in the stable, taking a deep breath and looking a little more in control of himself. He resumed his place against the stall door as he faced Diamantha. It took her a moment to realize that he had been the one to release the furious roar.

"That," he said quietly, "is the most ridiculous thing I have ever heard in my life. Are you that careless of a mother that you would actually expose your child to such danger?"

Diamantha could have become incensed over what was a slanderous comment against her abilities as a parent but she did not. She remained calm.

"I am not careless at all," she said. "I am thinking only of her. She was very close to her father and I feel strongly that she must go."

"Your daughter is *not* going with us."

Diamantha could have done one of two things at that point; she could have gone head to head with him, or she could try to soften him with a little honey. She thought to attempt the latter just to see how well it would work. It was manipulative, she knew, but she wasn't beyond being a little manipulative to gain her wants. Besides, she had married the man. It was time to find out just how far she could push him because, so far, his bark seemed to be worse than his bite. Well, except for that primal roar, which had been quite frightening. But it was time to find out if the man was *all* bark and no bite at all. Reaching out, she put a soft hand on his arm.

"Please," she begged softly. "It means so much to me. I could not be away from her for so long. And I feel as if this is her calling, too. Robert was her father, after all. Please let her go with us. I promise she will not be any trouble."

She even threw a little sniffle in, as if she was verging on tears. Cortez, however, was focused entirely on her warm hand against his flesh. It was by far the most marvelous sensation he had ever experienced in his life. He could feel himself folding like an idiot, without a fight, and he struggled not to.

"You do not understand," he said, his tone considerably more gentle than it had been moments before. "It is not that I do not wish to take her. She is a sweet and beautiful girl, and I would like nothing better. But if something happened to her on our journey, I would never forgive myself. I have already lost one daughter. I could not bear to lose another."

He was beating Diamantha at her own manipulative game. The last several words were like a dagger to her heart and suddenly, she was the one in danger of folding. She could see the pain in his eyes as he spoke and it touched her. But she held her ground.

"You would not lose her," she whispered. "But I cannot be without her. She must come with me or I cannot go."

"Good," he said with great relief. "Remain here and I will return as soon as I can. That is the way I prefer it."

Diamantha could see that he had called her bluff, turning her own scheme of manipulation around on her until he was now the one verging on his wants. She removed her hand from his arm.

"Nay," she said, now sounding hard where only moments before she had been soft. "If you do not allow us both to go, I will commit both myself and my daughter to a convent and you will never see us again. If we cannot go together, then I will not wait for you to return. You will lose us."

The game of gentle persuasion had suddenly turned cold and serious. Fact was, Cortez believed her; she was a determined and head-strong woman, and he believed her implicitly. Uncertain, he knew he couldn't leave with that threat hanging over his head. He couldn't trust that he wouldn't return to find both his wife and daughter barricaded in a cloister. Nay, he couldn't stomach that at all. Now he was backed into a corner and he couldn't see any way out. He had no choice.

She had him.

"Very well," he muttered, sighing with great regret. "If that is the way you feel, then Sophie may come. But know I will be against it every step of the way. If you wanted to start this marriage off with resentment and bitterness, then you are well on your way, lady."

Diamantha's brief flash of victory was quickly doused. She could see he was genuinely resentful. "That is not my intention," she said. "But I cannot leave my daughter behind and I must go on this quest with you. Therefore, she must go with me. If you had a child of your own, you would understand."

He took it as a low blow. With a lingering gaze on the woman, he moved away from her and headed out of the stable. She could hear him giving orders to the grooms to have the pony saddled as he went. There was hazard and discouragement in his tone.

Diamantha didn't follow him. She had won the battle and that was all she cared about at the moment. So what if the man was bitter and resentful? She hadn't wanted to marry him, anyway. What did she care what he thought? If he wanted her, then he was going to have to take everything about her – the good and the bad. The man deserved everything coming to him for being so unfeeling and forcing her into a marriage she did not want.

Without another thought to de Bretagne, Diamantha remained with her daughter in the stable, waiting as the grooms prepared the pony before lifting her daughter onto the animal's back. The tiny saddle had a strap that went around Sophie's waist to keep her from falling out, and she secured the little strap and led the pony from the stable.

Outside, the fog had lifted and patches of blue sky could be seen overhead. Cortez had his army gathered down by the main gatehouse, waiting for her, and as her own palfrey was brought around, Merlin broke off from the army and made his way towards her. She glanced up at the red-haired sergeant as he came alongside, reaching down to take the pony's reins.

"My lady," he greeted. "Sir Cortez has asked me to ride with you from Corfe Castle. I am to be your shadow, my lady, and your daughter's. I hope this is acceptable."

Diamantha's stance against Cortez began to waver. So he was to assign a soldier to escort her, was he? It was indicative of his anger, and perhaps even his regret that he had married her in the first place. Cortez was furious with her and, if she was honest with herself, perhaps it was rightfully so. She was willing to admit that she had been aggressive and cruel. She was also willing to admit that she had been punishing him for forcing her into the marriage, but the fact remained that she had what she wanted out of the situation. In fact, she had everything she wanted and Cortez, other than marrying her, had virtually nothing. He had made all of the concessions and she had done nothing but bully the man.

With a sigh, coming to think that she had behaved badly, she gathered her reins and nodded at Merlin.

"It is acceptable," she said. "Have my satchels been secured somewhere?"

Merlin nodded. "Your maids brought them down to the provisions wagon."

"Good," Diamantha said. "In that case, we are ready to depart."

Merlin simply nodded as he spurred his horse back towards the cluster of troops, pulling Sophie and General along with him. Diamantha followed, her gaze moving over Corfe for the last time. Her beloved Corfe. There was a lump in her throat at the thought of leaving, but she comforted herself with the fact that she was heading out on a mission of great importance. It was utterly vital to locate Robert's body and bring the man home. It was all she was concerned with. Now, the great Questing had begun.

Her life was about to change forever.

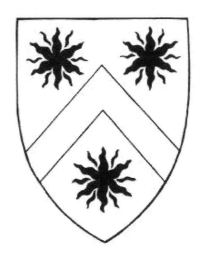

CHAPTER SIX

Sherborne Castle
Dorset

Diamantha's first glimpse of Sherborne Castle was through sheets of driving rain. Coming over the hill on the road leading in from the south, she could see the mighty castle of the Bishop of Salisbury in the distance like a great gray sentinel planted in the middle of the green Dorset countryside. It was shaped rather like a crown, she thought, with soaring walls and towers, and an enormous gatehouse at the front. But the rain pounded and the thunder rolled, distracting her from the impressive sight as she was eager to be under a dry roof.

Everyone else in the party was eager, too. After leaving Corfe Castle, which was only a day's ride under good circumstances, Sophie grew weary of riding General about an hour into the journey and Merlin had brought her to her mother. Snuggled under her mother's warm cloak, Sophie had slept most of the trip away and when she did awaken, it was to pop her head out from underneath the cloak and point at the scenery.

The little girl saw rabbits and deer, and it thrilled her tremendously. She even tried to talk Merlin into going off and catching a baby bunny, but Merlin was very regretful that he could not break rank to do so. Sophie wasn't entirely disappointed and found other things to corner her interest. Mostly, she found Merlin to corner her interest and it was a running conversation between a very talkative little girl and a rather quiet sergeant. It had been rather sweet to watch, leaving smiles on the faces of those within earshot.

In truth, it had been a pleasant trip once the fog lifted and the sun came out. The rolling hills of Dorset were green and lush, and the smell of foliage was heavy in the air. Diamantha and Sophie were midway in the group, well protected by de Bretagne's men, while Cortez rode up at the front of the column with two of his knights. He hadn't said anything to Diamantha since leaving Corfe, and the journey in general was rather quiet except for Sophie and her chatter with Merlin.

Diamantha could see him, however, up at the front on his big black and white charger with the hairy legs. He was hard to miss, being as big as he was, and he rode without his helm. She could see his black head clearly. With him in her line of sight a good deal of the time, she had spent the entire trip north pondering their acquaintance since the moment he had appeared in George's solar and told her of her destiny. It had been rough, no doubt, and she couldn't help but compare it to her courtship with Robert, which had been very sweet and pleasant. Robert had been a very amiable man and Cortez was not. He was arrogant and aggressive, and she didn't like it one bit. She wondered what hell she was in for with this marriage. If she had any courage, she'd take her daughter and run off to the nearest convent right now and be done with it.

As she contemplated life in a nunnery versus life as the wife of Cortez de Bretagne, the sky had clouded over and very quickly a storm set upon them. The road, well-traveled and rather rocky, had soon become a muddy swamp of dark brown soup. Diamantha's palfrey was a durable creature and plodded through it without much fuss, but the men on foot were having an increasingly difficult time. More than once they'd had to push the provisions wagon out of the heavy ruts. By the time they reached the crest of the hill overlooking Sherborne, everyone in the party, with the exception of Sophie, was a fairly soggy mess.

Once de Bretagne's castle was in sight, they made haste for it. Sherborne Castle, much like Corfe Castle, covered a lot of ground, and the ground Sherborne sat atop of was flat. As they drew closer, Diamantha could see the towering gatehouse, three stories tall, and enormous curtain walls with a massive ditch below them. As big as Corfe Castle was, and it was enormously big, Sherborne could compete with it on that scale. The soaring walls had to be twenty feet high and the depth of the very large moat was unfathomable. It was filled with muck and rot, and as the party passed over the drawbridge and into the great yawning gatehouse, Diamantha tried not to look at the moat. She was positive it would make her ill.

Once inside the gatehouse, the passageway was surprisingly narrow until it spilled them out into a massive bailey beyond. In the center of the bailey was a complex of buildings, not unlike the complex of buildings at Corfe, only these seemed tightly clustered together by comparison. A four-storied, gray-stoned keep was part of the complex. As the rain poured and the thunder rolled, men ran out to greet the incoming party, taking the horses away and moving the provisions wagon off to the south where the stables were stationed. As Diamantha sat on top of her palfrey, looking rather lost as efficient chaos went on around her, a very tall and very blond young knight was suddenly at her side.

"Lady de Bretagne?" he greeted though the pouring rain. "My name is James. I am to take you out of this weather."

Diamantha was wet and exhausted. As Merlin rushed up to help, she opened her cloak and allowed her daughter to slide down into Merlin's waiting arms. The young knight reached up and politely lifted her from the palfrey, swiftly escorting her towards what seemed to be the keep of Sherborne. It was four stories, rather big and block-like, and there was a massive oak and iron door that opened up to the bailey. It was now open, waiting for them to enter.

As James escorted her through the door, she noticed that the walls were very thick because the door itself had a small portcullis, partially raised. The door opened up into a corridor of sorts. There was a darkened passageway to the right and stairs leading up to the left. He took her up the steps with Merlin and Sophie following. The keep was cold and dark, and Diamantha kept turning around to glance at her daughter as Merlin carried her up the stairs. Sophie's eyes were wide at the new, scary place and this time, it was Merlin keeping up the patter of small talk. In truth, he was very gentle with Sophie, which pleased Diamantha greatly.

The stairs opened up into a first floor chamber, a rather large room with a massive fireplace that servants were tending. Smoke billowed out into the room, rising to the ceiling, which had a round, wheel-like chandelier that was lit with several fat tallow tapers. A rope connected the chandelier to a nearby wall for easy lowering and lifting in order to light the tapers. There was a table in the middle of the chamber, near the hearth, and as Diamantha approached, she could see that there was food upon it.

There were many servants rushing about. As James moved to help her remove her cloak, a round female servant with a tight kerchief around her head hustled up and collected it.

"I'll go shake this out, m'lady," the woman told her. "Sit by the fire and dry out. The poppet, too."

Diamantha turned to acknowledge the woman, seeing that she was helping Sophie remove her little woolen cloak. Sophie was still in Merlin's arms and seemed disinclined to let go of the man at the moment. The expression on her face told Diamantha that her daughter was sufficiently intimidated by their new surroundings. She held her arms out to the little girl.

"Thank you, sergeant," she said softly. "I will take her now."

Merlin handed the little girl over, who immediately clung to her mother as Diamantha moved over by the fire. More servants rushed up to put a stool next to the fire for her to sit on, which she accepted gratefully. Sophie wasn't wet, but Diamantha was; she held out a wet, freezing hand to the warmth of the blaze, relishing the heat it delivered. As she dried out her wet flesh, she noticed that James and Merlin were still standing over by the table, more than likely on Cortez's order not to leave her. They were watching her with both curiosity and uncertainty. Diamantha looked around the chamber which seemed to run from one side of the keep to the other.

"Is this your feasting hall?" she asked, simply to break the ice.

James shook his head. "Nay, Lady de Bretagne," he replied in his deep, smooth voice. "This is a secondary hall. It is mostly where we eat. The great hall is only used when the bishop is in residence or when Cortez is conducting court."

Diamantha had flinched at the sound of her new title, fighting down the sorrow it provoked. She knew she had to get used to it and even though she understood very well that she had married the man, still, a greater part of her didn't want to hear the confirmation. She wasn't ready to, not yet. But rather than dwell on it at the moment, as it could not be helped, something the knight said caught her attention. She turned to look at him.

"Court?" she repeated. "What does he do?"

James came around the table so she wouldn't have to crane her neck. There was a hint of a grin on his face. "It is rather complicated, but it goes something like this," he said. "Sherborne Castle belongs to the Bishop of Salisbury, who is Simon of Ghent. The man is also the Chancellor of the University of Oxford and the Archdeacon of Oxford, and spends most of his time there. Being that he is allied with our king, he has allowed Edward to station Cortez here as a garrison commander. We are stocked with a mixture of the bishop's men and crown troops. In the bishop's absence, Cortez is also the law for both the king and the church. He hears cases every month and dispenses justice."

Diamantha hadn't known that. It was rather impressive if she thought about it. "What is Cortez to Edward, then? Has he been granted special powers by the king?"

James nodded. "He is acting Sheriff of the Shire, my lady," the knight replied. "In reward for his exemplary service at Falkirk, Edward has bestowed much wealth and power on Sir Cortez."

Diamantha's interested expression faded. *Exemplary service at Falkirk*, she thought bitterly. *He left my husband to die at Falkirk*. It wasn't exactly the truth and she knew it, but it didn't stop her resentful thoughts. Not wanting to speak her mind, however, because such a thing could only cause confusion and bitterness, she shifted the subject.

"And you, Sir James?" she glanced at him as she began to untie the little cap from Sophie's head. "Where are you from?"

James was very polite and professional in his answer. "I was born at Lioncross Abbey on the Welsh Marches," he replied. "I have been in the service of Sir Cortez for two years come September."

Diamantha looked at him curiously. "Lioncross Abbey?" she repeated. "The seat of the House of de Lohr?"

James nodded. "Aye," he said. "My name is de Lohr."

Diamantha smiled faintly. "My grandmother was a daughter of the great Christopher de Lohr," she said. "How are you related to him?"

James seemed surprised at her declaration at first, then pleased. "Christopher de Lohr is my great-grandfather," he said, warming to the conversation as he shifted out of professional mode. "My father was a son of Christopher's eldest son, Curtis. Who is your grandmother?"

"Brielle," Diamantha replied. "She was Christopher de Lohr's second daughter."

James smiled brightly. "She was only three years older than my grandfather," he said. "They are brother and sister. I met her, once, when I was very small. She is still alive, is she not?"

Diamantha was thrilled to find a relative here amongst strangers. "Indeed she is," she replied. "She lives far to the north with my grandfather, who is still alive also. He is a son of the great warlord, Ajax de Velt."

James, in his comfort, sat down on the bench that was situated next to Diamantha's stool. He, too, was very happy to discover a new relative.

"Ah, yes, de Velt," he said, pondering that information. "A great warlord, indeed. Ruthless and savage in his younger years."

Diamantha nodded. "You know of him, do you?" she asked. "Well, I suppose most people in England do. His legends are quite frightening but he eventually settled down, thankfully."

James lifted his eyebrows to agree. "Thankfully, indeed," he agreed. "I heard tale that the man used to... well, I suppose that is not a story for female company. Suffice it to say that I am honored to know that I am related to Sir Cortez's new wife. I must write my grandfather to tell him of this happenstance. He will be quite thrilled by it."

Diamantha grinned, pulling the cap off of Sophie's head and allowing the little girl to slip from her lap. She held on to the back of her dress, however, so the child couldn't wander too near the flames of the hearth.

"What a small world this is," she said, studying James and seeing that he had the very blond de Lohr hair and sky-blue eyes. He was perhaps five or more years older than she was; not too terribly old. "Since our great-grandfather had seven children, I knew there were many cousins that I have not met yet. Imagine finding one here at Sherborne."

James nodded. "Indeed," he agreed. "I remember my father telling me that there were at least a hundred of us descended from Christopher, possibly more. And, of course, Christopher's brother, David, had many children as well. There is an entire branch of the de Lohr family in Canterbury that I've not yet met, although I did come across a cousin at Falkirk by the name of Macsen du Bois. His mother is descended from David de Lohr, but Macsen must look like his father's side of the family because he was an enormous man with black hair. He looked like a big, shaggy bear."

Diamantha giggled. "Mayhap someday we will be able to visit our family in Canterbury," she said. "Honestly, I have spent most of my life in Northumberland. Only when I married did I move south to Dorset. Robert kept me at Corfe Castle most of the time. He said there was not much worth seeing outside of the beauty of Dorset."

James' smile faded at the mention of Robert Edlington. "I knew your first husband," he said softly. "Rob was a good man. His was a great loss."

Diamantha sobered quickly. She thought perhaps that she could see something in James' expression, something more than just general sympathy. There was grief there, too.

"You knew him well?" she ventured softly. "Was he a friend?"

James nodded. "He was," he said. "We slept in the same shelter the night before the battle at Falkirk. He sat up all night... well, it was only soldier's talk. He was unable to sleep and kept us all awake because of it."

Diamantha was very interested. "What talk?" she wanted to know. "What did he say?"

James wasn't sure he should say any more, but he was cornered. He'd already broached the subject and could not refuse her question. "He spoke of you and he spoke of his mother a great deal," he said quietly. "He said that his daughter looked just like his mother. He said that he missed her very much. But you... he said the longing for you was unfathomable."

Tears sprang to Diamantha's eyes and she lowered her head, unwilling to let the man see her agony. She was trying so very desperately to be strong through all of this but other than Cortez's story about Robert's death, this was the first she'd heard about him in those final hours. The tears popped out onto her cheeks and she wiped them away quickly.

"I miss him," she whispered. "Thank you for telling me that."

James watched her lowered head. "I am sorry to have upset you," he said quietly. "That was not my intention."

She nodded quickly and patted his hand to let him know that she wasn't angry with him. "I very much appreciate that you told me," she said, struggling to be brave. "Mayhap someday you will tell me a little more about your night with him before the battle."

James nodded, although he wasn't sure that was such a good idea. He had been at Corfe Castle when Cortez had gone to collect his bride so he knew there was some animosity between them. Certainly it was no love match and rumor had it that it was because Lady Edlington, or now Lady de Bretagne, was still in mourning for her husband. He felt very badly for the situation in general, but he knew something Diamantha did not – he knew Cortez. He knew the man and his character. As he watched her lowered head, he thought to reassure her somehow.

"My lady," he said softly. "Forgive me for speaking on a subject that is none of my affair, but I would like to say... I would like to tell you that although I am very saddened for your loss of Robert, please know that Cortez is a very fine man also. I realize he can be... abrupt. And quick to temper. But no finer knight has ever walked this earth, and he has a true and solid sense of honor. He is also generous and emotional to a fault. I have seen it myself. Do not... what I mean to say is that he will be good to you and to your daughter. You must not despair. He will be kind to you if you will let him."

95

By the time he was finished speaking, Diamantha was looking at him with an expression between hope and doubt. It was rather strange, but very powerful. It was clear that she wasn't quite sure what to say to him.

"I am not in despair," she assured him, although it was a lie. "But I am grateful for your concern."

James opened his mouth to reply when boot falls suddenly filled the chamber. They were harsh and loud against the dusty wood floor, creaking the joists with their power. James stood up from the bench, swiftly, to see that Cortez had entered the room. He was soaking wet from head to toe, his black hair plastered against his head, but he had a basket in his hand that was somewhat dry. It was covered by a cloth and the man's gaze seemed to be on Sophie as he approached. He didn't look at Diamantha and he barely looked at James.

"My lord," James greeted. "Your lady wife and her daughter are settled in and tended. They were just drying out."

Cortez's gaze was mostly on Sophie. "Very well," he acknowledged. "You may see to your other duties, de Lohr. I will send for you if I need you."

James nodded smartly and, with a brief smile to Diamantha, quit the room and took Merlin, who had been lingering in the shadows, with him. He also motioned to the servants to stay out of the room, and quickly, those remaining in the chamber cleared out. The mood of the chamber had changed the moment Cortez had entered and no one wanted to be a part of it. Very shortly, it was only Cortez, Diamantha, and Sophie, clustered near the hearth. The only sounds filling the cold, stone-walled room were those of the rain outside and the snapping fire.

Diamantha was watching Cortez closely but he seemed exclusively focused on Sophie, who had somehow managed to find a small straw broom and was pretending to sweep the hearth. She swept up clouds of ash dust as Cortez sank down onto the bench formerly occupied by James. He set the basket down beside him.

"Lady Sophie," he said. "I thought you would like to know that General is in his own stall now eating his supper. He is well."

Sophie stopped sweeping and turned to him. "Where is he?" she wanted to know. "I want to see him."

Cortez pointed to the windows and the rain that was dripping down on the inside of the walls from the open sills.

"It is raining very badly," he told her. "General is warm and safe right now. I will take you to see him when the rain stops. Meanwhile, I found something in the stables that I think you and your mother might like."

Sophie let the broom fall to the ground and made her way over to him just as he pulled the cloth off the basket. Inside were two small kittens, a multi-colored one and a white one with black spots. Sophie squealed with delight as Cortez lifted the multi-colored kitten out and handed it to her.

"I brought you a kitten because I thought you might like to take care of him," he said. "I did not want you to be lonely without a pet since General cannot come inside."

Sophie was thrilled beyond words. She was surprisingly gentle with the kitten, cuddling it and cooing to it. Diamantha watched her daughter with a smile on her lips until Cortez reached in and grasped the other kitten, handing it over to her.

"And this," he said softly, "is for you. I did not want you to be jealous that I gave your daughter a gift and I did not bring one for you."

Diamantha looked at him, their eyes meeting, and feeling that familiar jolt of excitement. She took the kitten, the sweet little thing, and cuddled it against her breast. "I would not have been jealous," she said softly, averting her gaze. "But I thank you for the gifts, for both of us."

Cortez looked at her, then, because she was looking away, down at the kitten in her hands. Over near the hearth, Sophie sat down and put the kitten on the ground between her legs, teasing it with a piece of straw from the broom. As the little girl giggled and played, Cortez focused on Diamantha.

It had been difficult to ride for an entire day away from her, ignoring her for the most part, at least outwardly. But inside, his attention, his focus, was on her as it had never been on anyone in his life. The woman filled his thoughts and mind like nothing he had ever known, and he felt so very badly that things had not gone well between them. He knew he was to blame, at least for most of it, but he was at a loss as to how to handle it. He'd never known animosity like this before with a woman he was fond of. Or, at least, powerfully attracted to. Aye, he was fond of her, too. He'd caught glimpse of much to be fond of.

"Have you been made comfortable?" he asked softly. "Have you eaten?"

Diamantha nodded. "James and Merlin have been very attentive and we have been well taken care of," she replied. "But we've not yet eaten. There is food on the table. We simply haven't gotten to it yet and I do not know if we ever will. We have been interrupted by kittens."

Cortez grinned at her unexpected touch of humor. It gave him hope that perhaps things were not as bad as he thought, that sense of dread in the pit of his stomach that made him wonder if he'd ruined two lives in the course of his impatience. In fact, he sighed heavily, unwilling to continue with the polite but tense conversation. He was a man of many words. If something was wrong, he righted it. He wanted to right this in the worst way.

"My lady, I must say something," he said quietly. "I realize that the past three days have been quite difficult between us but when the difficulty eased, I saw moments of such brilliance. It was as if the sun had emerged from the clouds, so bright and hopeful this vision. I will take responsibility for much of the animosity between us because I know you believe I have pushed my way into everything. I have been demanding and impatient. But it is only because I believe that what I am doing is right. Robert asked me to take care of you and it took me three months to do it. I did not want to delay any longer."

Diamantha's head shot up and she looked at him with big eyes. She opened her mouth to dispute him but thought better of it because she remembered James' words, *he is a good man.* Perhaps he was, but she was still uncertain, about everything. She grunted softly and looked away.

"I would like to believe that," she said quietly. "But I would also believe that there was some selfishness in your actions. You said yourself that you have been widowed these three years. Were you not just the least bit eager to be widowed no longer?"

He knew she was right. He nodded his head after a moment. "Aye," he said honestly. "You are correct. I wanted a family and I did not want to wait any longer. I am sorry if that caused you to resent me."

She glanced at him. "I do not resent you," she said. "In fact, I suppose I should apologize for my demands which you consider unreasonable. I know you believe so, but they are not unreasonable to me."

Cortez was caught off-guard by the apology. It softened him greatly. All of the resentment he had been feeling since they had departed Corfe seemed to slip away. He didn't want to stay angry with her; he didn't want to be bitter. He had a new wife and in spite of everything, he was genuinely thrilled. He just wished she felt the same way. With a sigh, he raked his fingers through his dark hair.

"I know it is because you do not want to be separated from your daughter," he said softly. "I understand. I am sure there aren't many young ladies who have traveled the length of England. Sophie will have something to tell her grandchildren about, if she even remembers the journey."

Diamantha was starting to feel very badly for manipulating the man so. He was being rather acquiescent about the entire circumstance, as if they'd never had bitter words. As she looked at him, she knew that it was time to clear the air between them. She didn't like unspoken forgiveness, or allowing time to dissolve harsh words spoken in haste. She sighed heavily and looked at him.

"I thank you for understanding my position," she said, "but there is something more I must say to you. Please understand that I hold nothing against you personally for this marriage. I know you were doing what you told Robert you would do. I suppose my hus... that is, I suppose Robert was really only thinking of me in the end. He wanted to make sure I was taken care of and I will honor his wish. I want you to know that I will try very hard to accept this situation but I am sure there will be times when I falter. You must forgive me for those lapses. My world has changed so drastically over the past few months that I am still overwhelmed by it all."

He was gazing at her, into those miraculous dual-toned eyes that were so haunting yet so lovely. "I understand," he said. "And you will forgive me for charging in and creating the chaos of a rutting bull. When one has lived alone as I have for the last three years, one thinks very selfishly."

Diamantha smiled faintly, stroking her purring kitten. "I have no such excuse for being selfish other than Robert always let me have my way in everything," she said, shrugging with resignation. "It is what I am used to."

Cortez grinned. "I will also try to let you have your way in everything, too," he said. "But there will be times, very few I am sure, when I would like to have my own way. Will you allow this?"

She cast him a long glance, her grin broadening in a rather coy gesture. "It would depend on what it is."

He laughed softly. "I will plead to your good graces, madam," he said. "Actually, this is one of those times when I would like to have my own way."

She looked at him, a smile still playing on her lips. "What would that be?"

His expression sobered as the black eyes grew intense. "I would like for you to call me Cortez," he said softly. "And mayhap when you are comfortable enough, you will call me 'husband'. I can think of no greater honor."

It was a sweet request and one she could hardly refuse. Graciously, she nodded. "Of course," she replied. "The honor would be mine. You may call me Diamantha if you wish. I will not protest."

His smile was back. "I would like to, very much," he said, thrilled the conversation was growing pleasant. He was very curious about her and took the opportunity to find out more about the woman he had married. Pleasant times like this had been very rare. "It is an unusual name. How did your parents come by it?"

Diamantha shrugged. "My sisters all have unusual names," she said. "I have two older sisters, Leticia and Avocet. My mother's name is Evanthe. They are all old family names. I am named for a grandmother, generations back, whose name was Diamanda. My father changed it to Diamantha just because he liked it."

"I like it, too," Cortez concurred. "Do you have brothers?"

She nodded. "Three older brothers," she replied. "Tobias, Cace, and Corbin. They are all great knights."

"And you are the youngest of the family?"

"Aye," she replied, eyeing him with some curiosity. The conversation was flowing well and just as he had asked about her, she would ask about him. "And you? What of your family? Helene told me once that your mother was Spanish."

Cortez nodded. "Indeed she was," he said. "She married my father, Gorsedd, who is from a very old Welsh family. I have a younger brother, Andres. There are just the two of us, as my mother died when Andres was about two years of age. My father never remarried."

Diamantha looked at the man with some sympathy. "I am sorry to hear that," she said. "What was her name?"

His grin broadened. "Allegria de Montoya y la Rosa," he said in a very fluid Spanish accent. "Her family is very old and very wealthy. I have spent time with my grandfather, her father, in Spain. I fostered for some years in Spain before returning to England. Many years ago, King Edward thought it would be an excellent exchange to send me to foster in the house of my grandfather while my grandfather sent a few of his Spanish grandsons to foster in England. My father, Gorsedd, was a retainer for Edward when he was young. It was Edward who helped broker the marriage between my parents."

Her brow furrowed slightly. "The king brokered a marriage for a mere knight? That is strange, is it not?"

Cortez shook his head. "My father is related to the ap Gruffydd family," he said quietly. "We descend from the Princes of Powys, so Edward sought to make an alliance somewhat with the Spanish house of Rosa, hereditary rulers of the ancient Spanish kingdom of Zaragosa. It's all very complicated, but suffice it to say that it was a political match, although my father did love my mother a great deal. He was devastated to lose her."

Diamantha was quite fascinated by his family lineage. "How sorrowful," she said. "Where is your father now?"

"In Shropshire along the Marches," he replied. "He inherited a castle from the de Bretagne side of the family, Coven Castle, and he has lived there for quite some time. Edward keeps men stationed there and my father keeps peace on that section of the border."

She cocked her head. "But your father is Welsh."

Cortez lifted his eyebrows thoughtfully. "He is Welsh on his mother's side and English on his father's," he said. "He is mostly English. The only thing Welsh about him is the name. Edward made sure of that; he has conditioned my father well."

Diamantha digested the information. "I would say that you have a very complex family history," she said. "Mine is not so complex. I come from a long line of English, back to the time of the Conqueror. In fact, I just discovered that I am related by blood to your knight, James de Lohr. Our grandparents were siblings, children of the great Christopher de Lohr."

Cortez bobbed his head with interest. "Is that so?" he said. "He has served me for a couple of years. He lives here with his wife and three small boys."

Diamantha smiled. "I should like to meet them," she said. "Mayhap they can be playmates for Sophie."

Cortez looked over at the little girl playing happily with the kitten. "It is possible," he said, then turned his attention to Diamantha. "But I plan to leave tomorrow morning for the north. If you want Sophie to come, she will not be here long enough to need playmates. In fact, the first thing I did when we reached Sherborne was hand-pick an escort to accompany us to Falkirk. I cannot make this trip with a big army and it is too dangerous for just the three of us to go, as my wife and daughter must have protection. Therefore, the escort is currently preparing and before dawn tomorrow, we depart. I would suggest that you and your daughter eat and rest as much as possible tonight because it is going to be a very long and very exhausting journey."

He said it in a way that was rather serious, hoping she might actually back down from wanting to accompany him. He was hoping against hope that, after a day's long and rainy ride, she might reconsider her desire to ride all the way to Falkirk with her young daughter in tow. The reality of being on the road with a small child was much different than merely talking about it. Practicality might win out. Or, at least he hoped it would.

Unfortunately for him, Diamantha didn't back down. She didn't even hint at backing down. Instead, she nodded obediently. "We will get as much rest as we can tonight," she said. "How many men will be coming with us?"

His lips twisted wryly when he realized she wasn't going to reconsider her position. Thwarted for the moment, he scratched his head pensively.

"We do not want to be so big that we attract attention," he said, "but if we encounter trouble, I want to be sure we can defend ourselves. I have selected twenty-five men to accompany us, including a wagon with which to carry Robert's remains, and four knights including my brother. That should be sufficient. But I may have to arm you as well because the open road can be a deadly place. Dangers abound everywhere. There's no telling when a crazed assassin might come flying out at you. Can you use a dagger?"

It was a question he once again hoped would deter her. He was trying to make it all sound so terrible. Instead, she nodded bravely. "I can," she said. "My father taught me."

He sat back and rolled his eyes, defeated. So much for her changing her mind. After a moment, he nodded in resignation.

"Good," he muttered. "I will give you a dagger, then. But God help the man who truly tangles with you."

Diamantha wasn't quite sure what had him so discouraged, but she thought it was perhaps because it was costing him a great deal of money to make this trek north. It was the only reason she could think of. The quest was turning into a rather large production that would undoubtedly be expensive. All of those men would need to be fed and housed, and their horses fed and housed. Aye, it was coming to be expensive. But no matter; she had some wealth of her own. She would make it up to Cortez somehow. This trip was her idea, after all. She needed to take some financial responsibility for it. She needed to show Cortez that she wasn't a complete and utter burden, making demands and expecting him to make all of the sacrifices.

"Then Sophie and I should eat and retire," she said softly. "If you would show us where we are to sleep, I would be grateful."

Sleep. Cortez looked at her with only one thought on his mind; *it is our wedding night, lady.* Marrying her was one thing, and that had been difficult enough, but consummating the marriage... he knew she wasn't ready for that. If he were to try, the consequences could be disastrous. He could take her body, but her mind was something completely different. He didn't want their first intimate encounter to be wretched and painful for them both. He wanted it to be the most beautiful thing they'd ever experienced.

God, he was so impatient. He didn't like waiting for anything, and especially not something that rightfully belonged to him. So much of this situation was unpalatable to him and had been from the start. Had he known then what he knew now, he might not have agreed to Robert Edlington's deathbed plea. He might have told the man to take a flying leap.

But no, he thought to himself. Looking at Diamantha as she turned her kitten over to her daughter, and then watching Sophie's utter joy, he knew his answer would have still been the same. Once the turbulence settled and once they came to know one another, and became comfortable with one another, the situation would improve. At least, that's what he hoped for. He had to keep telling himself that, 'else the temptation would have been great for him to march back to St. Edward's Church and demand an annulment. He had to have faith that this would all work out in the end.

But he was positive the wait was going to kill him.

CHAPTER SEVEN

It was raining when twenty five men-at-arms, five knights, and two ladies departed a water-logged Sherborne Castle in the early pre-dawn hours. After a night that saw her getting very little sleep, Diamantha was introduced to the knights who would be escorting her north; Sir Andres de Bretagne, Sir James de Lohr, Sir Drake de Winter, and Sir Oliver St. John.

De Winter was a big man with big hands, very handsome, while St. John was tall and sinewy and blond. Andres looked a good deal like his brother except he was taller and thinner, and he seemed to have a perpetual smile on his face. He had winked at her a couple of times, too. He thought he was being quite flirtatious but she thought he was being a fool and already she wasn't sure if she liked him. She wondered if Cortez had even noticed.

She politely acknowledged these men clad in full armor, with rain dripping off their faces, looking as if they were heading into battle. They were well armed and well supplied with their massive war horses, animals that were muzzled in the bailey because they were so ferocious. Diamantha would learn later that each man personally owned several horses, from palfreys to the more durable coursers or rounceys, but they had, in fact, chosen to take the expensive destriers on the trip north. Being a long and perhaps dangerous journey, they wanted the stability and viciousness of the destriers. Diamantha thought it felt a bit like a battle march.

After Diamantha and Sophie had retired the night before in Cortez's rather large and comfortable chamber, Cortez had spent most of the night making sure all of the details were settled for their journey on the morrow. Men were prepared, horses were readied, and he had taken a section of one of the provisions wagons and turned it into a comfortable little nest for Sophie. He figured the girl wouldn't want to ride all of the time, so he and James had fashioned a padded pallet. He had even put some pillows around the sides, pillows that James' wife had given them.

Suspecting that Sophie might also want to take her kittens along, Cortez confiscated one of the wooden cages in the kitchen yard used for the chicks and put straw at the bottom of it, putting it next to Sophie's pallet. He made sure to put a small wooden bowl in it for water, and part of an old horse blanket for warmth. When he was finished primping the entire section of the wagon for the child, he had his quartermaster sling oiled cloth over the back of the wagon for protection, making a cozy little hovel. When all was said and done, he was rather proud of it. It was a nice little place for his new daughter.

It was into this warm haven that Cortez deposited Sophie, who was thrilled with her comfortable little space. Bundled up against the weather, she had her two kittens underneath her cloak and happily put them into their little cage. She was also still rather sleepy so after her mother bundled her up in a heavy blanket beneath the oiled tarp, Sophie lay down on her pillows and promptly fell asleep. In the pre-dawn hours, she wasn't ready yet to face the world.

But Diamantha was. After tending her daughter, she allowed Cortez to escort her to her palfrey, a rather big-boned mare that Robert had given her. It was a gray horse, with black speckles, and she mounted silently, gathering her reins as Cortez and one of his knights covered her with an oiled cloth to protect her from the rain. Cortez was polite, as he had been the night before, and Diamantha again felt a jolt when their eyes met. He smiled faintly at her, which made her heart leap strangely. He was, indeed, a devilishly handsome man, and perhaps for the first time since he appeared in George's solar, she allowed herself to feel it. She didn't try to chase it away or talk herself out of it. For once, she allowed herself to feel the thrill of his smile. Even if she didn't want to admit it, the man was starting to grow on her.

Diamantha watched him make his way to his big black and white charger. When he mounted, someone gave a shout and the entire party began to move. The great gatehouse of Sherborne Castle was open and men on horseback began to trickle out, heading out into the land that was brilliant green and wet with rain. Diamantha rode beside the wagon where her daughter was sleeping peacefully, hardly believing that they were finally on their way. It seemed dream-like and surreal.

The great Questing to locate Robert Edlington's body had begun.

No glory, no great triumph. No inspiring thoughts or words. No great shouts of encouragement or great blessings from God.

In all, the trek north out of Sherborne was nothing that Diamantha thought it would be. It was, in truth, a monotonous march through horrible weather, sloppy roads, and whipping winds. The storm that had crept upon them yesterday as they'd made their way from Corfe was now part of their very fabric, a constant travel companion with seemingly no end. It was wretched and vicious as the thunder rolled and the lightning flashed. Everyone in the party was beyond miserable but had the sense not to show it. It was simply the way of things and the men were used to it. The only person that was seemingly comfortable was Sophie.

As the procession moved north through the small and flooded village of Kington, the fields were so saturated with water that the soldiers were coming across groups of wet rabbits and foxes who had been flooded out of their dens. Most of them ran off when the troops moved through, but a tiny little bunny and a small fox kit didn't move fast enough and were picked up by a couple of the men so they wouldn't get stepped on. They were too small to eat so the men took them back to the little girl in the wagon.

Sophie, of course, was thrilled with a baby bunny and a fox kit, and she put them in her little cage where they could dry off and warm up. The kittens were too young to care that there were intruders in their cage, and after the rabbit and the fox dried off, they snuggled up with the kittens and fell asleep. Sophie was very proud to show off her growing collection to anyone who came near the wagon, including Cortez. He had been riding at the head of the column but had come back to see how Sophie and Diamantha were faring in the terrible weather. One look at the four small animals cuddled up in the cage, and Sophie's joyous features, and the rain and storm suddenly didn't seem so bad. There was sun, somewhere, and he had found it unexpectedly in the back of his provisions wagon. It was enough to make him forget his misery.

As Sophie fed her animals with some apples and jerky procured from the quartermaster, Cortez walked alongside the wagon, watching her tend the hungry creatures. He was surprised by how gentle she was with them, considering most children her age didn't have a strong concept of being gentle with smaller creatures. It was sweet to watch, inevitably reminding him of the little girl he lost and wondering if she would have been like Sophie. He would have liked to have believed so. As he observed the child, he very much wanted to look at Diamantha but kept his eyes away from her deliberately. He was, in fact, working on a theory.

For the past hour, riding alone up at the head of the column, he was starting to wonder if backing away from her might do some good. After all, he'd chased her relentlessly so he thought perhaps backing off might make her more receptive to him. He really didn't know what else to do because nothing he'd done up to this point had worked. Women who were chased usually ran, but women who were quietly wooed were usually much more amenable. It went against his nature to do anything quietly, but he had to admit that in this case, he might have to. Therefore, he essentially ignored her. It wasn't long before he heard a softly voice behind him.

"How far do you plan to travel today?"

Diamantha had reined her horse up behind him and he turned to see her beautiful face gazing down at him from beneath the hood of her cloak. As he'd hoped, limiting his attention to her had garnered a positive reaction. She had approached him instead of the other way around. He wiped water out of his eyes before replying.

"Shaftesbury, I hope," he said, glancing up at the sky. "Even at this pace, we should reach it by sundown. I have sent some men ahead to secure rooms at the first available inn."

Diamantha cocked her head. "Why?" she said, indicating the second provisions wagon behind them that was stuffed with rolled canvas. "You have brought shelter. Why the expense of an inn when we can stay in your shelters?"

He looked at her. "Because these shelters are damp at best and it would not do for you or your daughter to become ill this early on in the journey," he said. "It is worth the cost to pay for a dry chamber and a warm meal. Wouldn't you rather see your daughter in a dry bed as opposed to a damp tent?"

She was forced to agree. "I would," she said. "Sophie is usually a very healthy child and I would like to keep it that way."

Cortez nodded to agree with her, glancing at Sophie and her pets one last time before politely excusing himself and making his way back to the front of the column. He'd decided that he wasn't going to say anything more to Diamantha since ignoring the woman had seemed to make her marginally more sociable. Perhaps that was the way to handle her and he had been doing it wrong all along. In any case, he was willing to make an experiment out of it. He left the woman without so much as a hind glance.

Diamantha watched him go, her gaze lingering on the man who was now her husband. The more she reminded herself of the fact, the more accustomed she was becoming to it. As he walked away, she found her attention lingering on his rather large form. For such a big man, he moved quite gracefully and had an easy gait about him. As he moved through his men, he gave them a word here and there. She could see that his men were pleased with the attention. That was an important attribute of a knight as far as she was concerned, whether or not he showed interest in those he commanded. Compassion was a rare and valuable trait in a fighting man.

He's a good man. James' words ran through her head again as she lost sight of Cortez in a group of soldiers up towards the front of the column. She was coming to think that perhaps James might be right.

For all she'd put Cortez through, his attitude towards her hadn't changed. He was still polite, and still very kind to Sophie. A good man, indeed.

As she plodded along next to the wagon, lost in thoughts of Cortez, her horse suddenly slipped on the soft shoulder of the road and tumbled down a small incline, sending Diamantha flying. She went face-first into the wet grass, landing heavily on her left wrist. She could hear the shouts of the men on the road and as she was shaking off the ringing in her ears, hands were reaching down to help her.

"I am fine, truly," she insisted to those trying to assist her.

"Stay down, lady," someone said to her. "Do not try to rise. Just sit a moment and gain your bearings."

Diamantha lifted her right hand to wipe the wet and grass from her eyes, looking up into the concerned faces of two of Cortez's knights. She recognized Drake de Winter first.

"My horse?" she asked, straining to look about. "Is she well?"

Drake, crouched down beside her in full armor, looked over to see someone tending to the now standing horse. "She looks well enough for the most part," he said, returning his attention to her. "And you? Did you hit your head?"

Diamantha lifted her left arm, moving to put a hand to her head, but she winced when pain shot through her wrist. Instinctively, she gasped and grabbed it. "God's Bones," she hissed, realizing she had hurt her arm. "Now, that is not a good sign, is it?"

It was a rhetorical question. But there was a second knight with de Winter and he, too, crouched down next to her. Oliver St. John was a very tall man with piercing blue eyes. He had heard her comment and his expression was one of concern.

"May I see, my lady?" he asked, holding out a hand. "Mayhap it is not broken."

Timidly, Diamantha extended her hand about the time Cortez came thundering up on his big hairy war horse. The entire column had come to a halt by now and he bailed off his charger as he hurried to her side. St. John was just starting to examine the wrist when he came up.

"What happened?" he demanded, looking rather frightened. "My lady, are you well? Did you hurt yourself?"

She opened her mouth to answer but winced when St. John touched a tender spot. "I am well enough," she said, sounding disgusted. "It was stupid of me, really. I was not watching where my horse was going and she slipped down the embankment. Is she truly well?"

De Winter stood up and went to check on the horse himself for the lady's peace of mind. Cortez took his place beside her, realizing when he looked at her face that it was covered with pieces of grass. It was in her beautiful hair. Before he could comment, St. John looked at him.

"We must wrap this wrist," he said. "She must have used it to catch her fall and it is already swelling."

Cortez was concerned. "Is it broken?"

St. John shook his head. "I do not believe so," he said. "But we must wrap it just the same."

Between Cortez and Oliver, they managed to pull Diamantha to her feet as the rain pounded down upon them. She turned to walk back up to the road but Cortez was already in motion. He swept her into his big arms and carried her up to the wagon where Sophie was trying to catch a glimpse of her mother. When she saw Cortez carrying the woman in the direction of the wagon, she popped out from beneath the oiled tarp.

"Mama!" she called. "Mama, what 'tis wrong?"

Cortez set Diamantha carefully down on the end of the wagon bed. "Nothing is wrong," Diamantha assured her child. "My horse slipped, 'tis all."

As St. John and Cortez moved to wrap Diamantha's wrist with items brought around by Cortez's quartermaster, Sophie plopped herself onto her mother's wet lap. Diamantha shrieked softly.

"Sophie, nay," she said, trying to hold her child back with one good hand. "I am all wet!"

Cortez intercepted the little girl and picked her up, taking her away from her mother and tucking her back beneath the oiled tarp where it was dry. When the little girl started to whine, he pointed to her caged pets.

"Have you named them, yet?" he asked, trying to distract her. "I should think you would have thought up many names by now. What have you named the kittens?"

His ruse was working. Sophie turned to look at her little pets, who were sleeping contentedly after their feeding. As Cortez had hoped, she crawled back beneath the tarp and went to the cage, hovering over it and pointing.

"This kitten's name is General," she told him.

Cortez shook his head. "You already have a pony named General," he said. "The kitten deserves his own name. What else have you thought of?"

Sophie's brow furrowed as she thought on his question. "I do not know," she said. "I do not know any other names."

Cortez cocked his head, mulling over the situation. "Well," he said slowly, "when I was young, my mother had two cats named Edward and Eleanor, after the king and queen."

Sophie's expression brightened. "I will name my kittens Edward and Eleanor, too!"

Cortez grinned. "What about the rabbit?" he asked. "Rabbits like grass and clover. Why not name him Clover?"

Sophie squealed happily and nodded her head. "What about the fox?" she wanted to know. "I want to name him after my father!"

Cortez patted her little leg. "I believe he would like that," he said softly. "The fox shall be called Robert."

Sophie's face fell. "But I want to call him *Father*."

Cortez bit off a chuckle. He was trying to prepare a reply she would not only understand, but agree with, when Diamantha spoke.

"Sweetheart, your father's name is Robert," she told her. "You know that is his name. You cannot name a fox Father."

Sophie was moving into a pout. "Why not?"

Cortez and Diamantha looked at each other. Why not, indeed? With a shrug, and fighting off a grin, Diamantha replied.

"Very well," she said. "If that is what you wish, my little love."

Sophie was back to being happy again and Cortez's gaze lingered on the little girl for a moment before returning his attention to Diamantha, whose wrist was very nearly wrapped by now. St. John, who usually tended the wounded because it was a great skill he had acquired in the Holy Land, had wrapped it quite neatly. The knight tightened up the bindings to the point of Diamantha wincing.

"There," he said, inspecting his work. "That should do for now. I will take a look at it tonight to see how it fares. Meanwhile, we should keep it cold. The cold will help with the swelling. Keep the wrist exposed to the rain and let it soak. The temperature is so cold that it will keep it chilled."

Diamantha had never heard of such a thing but she didn't argue with him; she simply nodded. "May I ride my horse?"

St. John and Cortez glanced over their shoulder as a soldier brought Diamantha's mount up onto the road. The horse had bloodied knees. Cortez went over to the animal and ran his hand up both front legs, feeling for injury. After a moment, he turned to Diamantha.

"I feel some swelling in the left front leg," he told her. "Mayhap you should ride in the wagon with Sophie until we stop for the night. You do not want to put undue strain on your horse right now."

Diamantha had no choice but to agree. As they tied her horse to the back of the second provisions wagon, next to General, Diamantha moved beneath the oiled tarp where her daughter was. Sophie was excited for her mother's company and happily pointed out her bunny and fox kit. Diamantha showed interest in her daughter's pets as she removed her wet cloak, using it as a blanket to better cover her from the rain coming in off of the oiled tarp.

Even as she listened to her daughter speak of Clover and Father, her attention seemed to drift back to Cortez, who was speaking with one of his men about Diamantha's horse. They were both watching the horse as it walked, making sure nothing else was wrong with it. Diamantha thought it was rather kind of the man to take such an interested in her palfrey. And sweet, aye, it was sweet. He was showing an inordinate amount of kindness and concern towards her.

When he had picked her up and carried her back to the wagon, the power of his arms hadn't gone unnoticed by her. In fact, she rather liked the hard bulk of the man, his strength radiating out from behind the armor. It was hard to miss. She realized that in those brief few seconds that she felt safe and protected. She hadn't had that feeling in a very long time. She wasn't hard pressed to admit that she liked it.

Perhaps she was coming to like *him*, just a little.

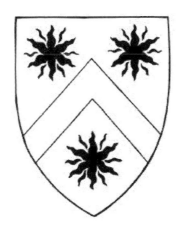

CHAPTER EIGHT

"What do you think of de Bretagne's new wife?"

The question came from Drake de Winter, proposing the query to either of his two companions. Oliver St. John and James de Lohr were standing just inside the front door of an inn in the city of Shaftesbury, watching Cortez and Andres from across the room. The brothers were negotiating with the fat innkeeper, a man with a great pot belly and big scabs on his knees. They could see them through his torn breeches. Before Oliver could answer the question, James put up a hand.

"Before you say anything, you both should know that I am a cousin of the lady," he said, watching their surprised expressions. "We discovered that my grandfather and her grandmother were siblings, both children of Christopher de Lohr. So keep that in mind when offering your opinion of the new Lady de Bretagne."

Oliver grinned faintly. "I was not going to say anything to the negative," he said. "In fact, she seems rather pleasant. Quiet, but pleasant."

Drake lifted his dark eyebrows. He was the son of Davyss de Winter, who had been a major player in the wars against Simon de Montfort thirty years earlier. He had his father's legendary arrogance and his mother's legendary compassion, a paradoxical combination. He was conceited to the core but a brilliant commander and a deeply loyal friend. He was very loyal to Cortez and, at the moment, he didn't seem convinced of Oliver's opinion.

"I was at Corfe when Cortez went to retrieve her," he said. "Those two have not had an easy start. Rumor has it that George Edlington was very much opposed to the marriage. In any case, she did not make it simple for Cortez. She fought him every step of the way."

James looked over his shoulder at Cortez and Andres as they continued to barter with the innkeeper. "That is because she is still in mourning, I am sure," he said quietly. "God's Bones, Rob Edlington has only been gone three months. The woman has not yet had time to grieve."

"She's had three months," Oliver muttered. "The man is not coming back."

James looked at him, pointedly. "Aye, he *is* coming back," he said. "Why do you think we are heading to Falkirk? Cortez told me that she wants Rob home for a proper burial, and that is exactly what we are going to do. You all knew Rob Edlington. You know what kind of man he was. It is the least we can do."

Oliver St. John was another legacy knight from a long line of great knights. His father, Christian St. John, was Lord of Eden, a castle far to the north in Cumbria. Oliver had his father's blond good looks and a rather ironic way of viewing the world. He was pragmatic to the bone and he saw this entire venture north to retrieve Edlington's body as a folly. He shook his head to James' statement.

"We will never find him," he said quietly, looking between James and Drake. "The man has rotted under several feet of mud and we will never find him. Cortez is doing this just to make the woman happy but it is only going to cause her more heartache when she realizes that Rob is lost to the ages. What are we supposed to do? Dig up the entire battlefield? That is madness!"

Drake waved a hand at him to keep his voice down. "Madness or not, that is what we've been ordered to do and we shall do it," he said, grunting with the same disapproval Oliver had expressed. "But I must say it is bad enough to bring the woman along much less her daughter. Lady de Bretagne has no idea how difficult this is going to be. To drag her child along is stupid at best."

James eyed his friends. "Be that as it may, keep that opinion between us," he mumbled. "You do not want Cortez to catch hint of that rumor. He'll have your head."

Oliver and Drake nodded reluctantly. The trio fell silent as Cortez and Andres, evidently finished with the barkeep, made their way back over to them. The main room of the inn was moderately full of people and extremely smoky from a malfunctioning chimney. It also smelled like raw sewage, a most unpleasant smell. Andres shoved an old drunkard out of his way as he and Cortez reached the rest of the knights.

"Idiots and drunkards," Andres sniffed, looking at the rabble in the room. "Could we not have found a more appropriate place to spend the night, brother? Why this dog-hole?"

Cortez gave him a disdainful look. "Because they are all full," he snapped without force. "I told you that already. This is the only place with availability and we are going to take it. If you do not like it, sleep out in the rain with your horse. I care not."

Andres was obviously displeased. "We deserve better accommodations than this."

Cortez didn't want to hear his brother's complaining. "Then you are welcome to go and find them," he said. "I have secured three rooms in this establishment and I'm sure the other knights will not mind if you drag your carcass somewhere else. If you do not, then shut your mouth because I do not want to hear your grumbling."

Andres simply made a face and looked away, smart enough not to engage his brother in more of a verbal battle. Cortez would win anyway, and if he didn't, the argument could very well end with the man throwing a punch, and Andres didn't want a bloodied nose this night. He was exhausted and hungry, as they all were.

Cortez waited for his brother to throw a tantrum but the man wisely remained silent. Andres was unpredictable sometimes, and spoiled, but he wasn't foolish. He knew when his brother was at his limit. When Cortez was sure there would be no more argument, he turned to his three knights.

"The barkeep tells me there are two barns in the back," he said, "one for the animals and one that is used for storage with hay and other things. Tell the men they are welcome to sleep in the storage barn if they do not wish to raise their shelters. They are not to have a fire in it, however, for obvious reasons. Whatever they decide, make sure the men are assembled by dawn. I plan to make it to Warminster by tomorrow night and I want to stay on schedule. I will not tolerate late risers."

The knights nodded and moved out, heading into the rainy night as they began to bellow instructions to the men who were standing out in the elements. When Cortez's escort began to move, he headed outside to the provisions wagon where Diamantha and Sophie were. Lightning flashed overhead as he walked through the ankle-deep mud, crossing the road and ending up next to the saturated wagon.

Peering inside, he could see Diamantha sitting far back on the pallet with a sleeping Sophie in her arms. She was dry for the most part but he could tell by the color of her face that she was cold and exhausted. Her pert little nose was red and her face pale, indicative of the cold. Turning around in search for some help, he spied his brother and whistled the man over. Unhappy, Andres sloshed through the mud as Cortez turned back to Diamantha.

"Give me Sophie," he said softly, holding out his arms. "I have a nice, warm bed waiting for her."

Diamantha shifted, carefully handing over Sophie to Cortez, who took her gently. Diamantha then took her cloak and covered the child with it so the rain would not soak her. As careful as if he were holding the Baby Jesus, Cortez took Sophie and then handed her over to his brother.

"Take her inside immediately," he whispered to Andres. "We have the room at the top of the stairs, last door on the left. Take her there and try not to get her wet."

Andres, surprisingly, was very careful with Sophie in spite of his surly attitude. He cradled her as Cortez fixed the cloak so the child would not get wet, and soon he was making haste towards the inn. Cortez watched him go, making sure his brother was well on his way, before turning to Diamantha. He smiled politely.

"Now it is your turn, my lady," he said, holding out his hands. "Come along, now. Let us get you inside where it is warm and dry."

Diamantha shifted along the wagon bed but not before she reached out to grab the cage with the animals in it. She tried to hold on to them with her wrapped hand while pushing herself along with the other. Cortez took the cage from her and set it aside as he lifted her out of the wagon bed. Snug in his arms, Diamantha reached over and picked up the cage, and away they went towards the inn.

By the time Cortez got her inside, they were both fairly wet from the downpour, as were the animals, who were now awake and restless. The kittens were crying and Cortez set Diamantha to her feet, politely grasping her arm to escort her up the rickety stairs that led to the darkened second floor above. She moved slowly, seemingly very interested in the room, a smelly, smoky hovel of men and women seeking shelter from the storm.

"Will we be eating down here?" she wanted to know.

Cortez was trying to urge her to move more quickly up the steps. "Nay," he said. "We will take our meal in our room."

Her head snapped around to him. "*Our* room?"

He met her eyes. "Aye," he said steadily. "There were three rooms available and my knights will occupy two of them. You, me, and Sophie will have one for ourselves."

Diamantha pondered that with some uncertainty but she didn't say anything. She didn't have a right to say anything, after all, she was the man's wife and it was perfectly acceptable to share a room with him. She continued to follow him to the second floor where a slightly tilted corridor led them to their chamber at the end of it. Even the door was leaning as Cortez shoved it open. Andres was inside, just laying Sophie upon a very small bed pushed over near a hearth that had a bit of heat to it. Diamantha smiled politely at the man as he pushed past her on his way to leave the chamber.

"My thanks," she said.

Andres was back to his smiling, flirtatious self in an instant. "For you, dear lady, anything at all," he said, then his smile vanished unnaturally fast as he eyed his brother. "Will there be anything else, Cortez?"

Cortez hung the wet cloak, the one used to cover Sophie, up on a peg next to the hearth. "Make sure my wife's cases are brought in," he told him. "Then you are free for the evening."

Andres nodded and headed out of the door, winking at Diamantha as he left. Diamantha shook her head reproachfully, disapproving that he would be so flirtatious with his brother's new wife. She began to unwind the scarf from around her neck with her good hand, thinking on Cortez's bold brother.

"Your brother is rather... friendly," she commented quietly.

Cortez moved to stoke the fire. "My brother is pushing the boundaries of my good graces," he muttered. "If he winks at you again, I am going to gouge his eyes out."

She turned to look at him, a half-smile on her lips. "So you've noticed, have you?"

Cortez pursed his lips irritably. "I would have to be blind not to notice," he mumbled, working the wood and peat up into a flame. "If you slap him for his liberties, I will not blame you."

Diamantha burst into soft laughter. "I am sure it will not come to that," she said, pulling the scarf free and hanging it on the peg next to the cloak. "I am sure he will behave himself."

Cortez grunted. "If he does, it will be the first time," he said, reaching over to grasp the cage with the wet animals and moving them near the fire. He peered at the little collection. "This should be warm enough for them. I'll see if the barkeep has any milk."

Diamantha looked at the man, thinking that he must be rather soft-hearted if he was worried about little animals. "That would be lovely, thank you," she said softly. "I am sure Sophie will appreciate that. In fact... thank you for all you've done for us. You have gone out of your way to make this as pleasant a trip as possible and I am grateful."

He stood up, his black eyes lingering on her. "You are welcome."

Diamantha smiled at him, the first time she'd done so without prompting. It was a genuine smile and one that went straight to his heart like an arrow, piercing it. In fact, he was a bit dumbfounded by it and as he thought of something more to say, she indicated his wet armor and clothing.

"Mayhap you should change out of your wet things," she said. "I... I would be happy to help you unless you are expecting your squire to come."

God's Bones, it was an offer he couldn't refuse. He still had some things to attend to but nothing short of a command from God was going to move him out of this room and away from her lovely hands.

She was offering to help him, the first such overture he'd ever had from her, and there was no way he was going to refuse. He looked down at himself and, seeing how wet and disheveled he really was, nodded wearily.

"That would be appreciated," he said softly.

Diamantha moved to stand in front of him. "Tell me where you wish for me to start," she said. "Robert liked to start at his feet and work his way up but you may do it differently."

Cortez looked down at himself again. "It would be easiest, in my estimation, to start from the top," he said, indicating the tunic. "If you help me remove this, the rest will easily follow."

Diamantha gestured with her hands. "Arms up, then."

Cortez swiftly unstrapped his broadsword from his waist and thigh and propped it up against the wall. Then he lifted his arms and bent forward while she pulled the drenched tunic over his head. It was a dark gray in color, wool, with the de Bretagne bird of prey carefully stitched in white thread upon the front. He watched her take the tunic over to the hearth and spread it out over a broken wooden frame that was there just for that purpose. It took her a few tries to get the frame to stand as she positioned the tunic next to the fire so it would dry.

Turning around, Diamantha could see that Cortez had remained bent over so she could help remove his mail coat. It was a heavy thing, and tricky to remove, so she started at the bottom and basically worked it over his head. But it was extremely heavy for her, and wet, so it was a messy job. By the time she pulled it off completely, the front of her surcoat was utterly soaked. He saw the mess.

"I am sorry," he said, indicating the enormous wet stain on the front of her garment. "I should have had my squire do this."

She gave him a reproachful expression. "I am already soaked," she said. "Let me help you remove the rest of your wet things so that my soaking will not have been in vain."

He smirked. "No need, madam," he said. "From this point, my squire can take over. The rest of this will be very cumbersome and nasty for you to deal with."

She cocked a doubtful eyebrow. "Are you sure? Your padded tunic should be spread out to dry immediately."

Beneath the mail coat, which was the length from his shoulders to his knees, he wore a padded tunic that was damp and stained, as well as leather breeches and very fine, well-used leather boots that had been heavily oiled in order to make them resistant to water. At her prompting about the padded tunic, he shrugged, held his arms out, and bent over at the waist again. Diamantha gave a good yank and pulled the heavily padded tunic right off.

Holding the tunic at arm's length because it was wet and smelly, she hung it up on a peg above the hearth to dry it. Helping Cortez undress reminded her of how she used to assist Robert. Rather than use squires like he should have, Robert liked to have his wife tend him. More often than not, when clothes were coming off, he would make a point of taking everything off and then trying to bed her, and most of the time she would play his game. She smiled faintly at the memories of the times when she would not permit him to bed her after such undressings, listening to his cries of utter disappointment and the pathetic pleadings of a madman. Robert could be dramatic at times, humorously so. She missed those moments.

But she didn't dwell on it. It was of no use, especially now. She was sure that she and Cortez would make their own special moments, although she wasn't sure what those would be. Things were still very uncertain. Lost in thought, she turned around to face him again and was confronted by a half-naked man.

But it wasn't just *any* man. It was her new husband in an unexpected display of flesh and raw allure. Diamantha's eyes fell on Cortez, nude but for his breeches and boots, and her breathing began coming in strange, giddy gasps. She'd never seen anything to magnificent in her life.

Startled, she tore her eyes away and pretended to look at something else, *anything* else, but his muscular chest, big shoulders, and powerful arms. There was perfection there as God had intended the male form to be but, as a mere mortal, she wasn't meant to look upon it. She couldn't because, like a man gazing upon the face of Medusa, the sight seemed to want to suck every rational thought out of her head and turn her into stone. For certain, she felt frozen in awe. Struggling to focus on something other than Cortez's beauty, she ended up looking at the animals in their cage.

"Were you...?" she began, swallowed, and then started again. "Were you going to find some milk for the animals?"

Completely unaware of Diamantha's flustered state, Cortez was in the process of inspecting his breeches, which were very wet around the waistline.

"Aye," he replied, loosening the lacings on his breeches. "As soon as my squire arrives with my saddlebags so I can put on a dry tunic."

Diamantha still wouldn't look at him. Trying to keep herself busy, she took the small wooden bowl out of the animals' cage and put some water in it from the pitcher in the room. She put it back in the cage, petting the kittens who very much wanted to come out and play. She ended up picking them both up, cuddling the little creatures who were purring like mad, when there was a sharp knock on the door. As Diamantha moved to put the kittens back into the cage, Cortez in all of his nude, manly glory opened the door.

James and Oliver were standing in the corridor, their young faces grim. "Sorry to disturb you, my lord," James said. "But you'd better come. The town's sheriff is in the room downstairs, wanting to know your business. He is bellowing something about too many soldiers about. He is demanding answers."

Cortez glanced down the corridor, towards the stairs that led into the common room. He could hear raised voices. "Who is the man?" he asked. "Did he give a name?"

James shook his head. "He simply said he was the sheriff and demanded we bring you to him."

Cortez cocked an eyebrow as he looked at his knights. There was hardness in his expression. "Demanded, did he?"

James nodded, giving him a rather concerned look. "Aye, he did," he said, lowering his voice. "He could be trouble."

Cortez pondered that statement for a brief moment. "Where are Andres and Drake?"

"In the common room, watching him."

"Are they armed?"

"Indeed, my lord."

"Is this sheriff armed?"

"He is."

"How many men does he have with him?"

"At least ten."

"Knights?"

"No, my lord. Ruffians, it looks like. They have clubs but no real swords that we could see."

That was enough for Cortez. Swiftly, he turned back into the room, going to the peg where his padded tunic was hanging. He snatched it as James and Oliver came into the chamber, collecting Cortez's mail and assisting the man in dressing. They had him completely dressed in under a minute as James collected Cortez's broadsword and handed it to him. Cortez was strapping it on when he glanced up and saw Diamantha's worried face.

The expression on her features startled him. She actually appeared... concerned, as if she cared what happened to him. His manner immediately softened.

"I shall return shortly," he told her. "Bolt the door after I've gone. Do not open it for anyone but me or my knights. Is that clear?"

She nodded, fear swelling in her breast. "What are you going to do?"

Cortez could see how concerned she was and it touched him deeply. It gave him hope, hope that all of the animosity they had experienced hadn't irrevocably damaged their relationship. God, it made him so very happy. He reached out to gently touch her cheek in a calming and reassuring gesture. He simply couldn't help himself.

"The man wants to speak with me," he said rather casually as he turned for the door. "Let him speak."

"But...!"

He interrupted her, gently done. "Not to worry, my beauty," he assured her. "There are more of me than there are of him. This will be a short conversation."

With that, he left the room, shutting the door softly behind him. Diamantha ran to the panel and threw the big iron bolt, her heart thumping fearfully against her ribs. As she leaned against the door, listening, her hand came up to finger the spot where Cortez had touched her. She could still feel his warmth. He'd branded her with his fire.

God's Bones, she thought, straining to hear through the crooked door. *I've already lost one husband. I don't want to lose another, not when we are only coming to know one another.* For a moment, she thought about her life should Cortez be killed. Her trip north to reclaim Robert's body would end this very day and she would more than likely return to Corfe, to George and his melancholy, to grieve not one but two husbands. If she thought very hard about it, her grief for Robert had eased these past few weeks. She still missed him terribly, but the gut-wracking pain wasn't there any longer. Now, she simply felt sad.

But the idea of losing Cortez already had her stomach in knots. She couldn't stand the thought. Damn the man for attending this "conversation". Damn the man for not thinking of her first, knowing how terrified she would be at the thought of losing another husband. Well, maybe he didn't know at all. She'd never given him a reason to think that she might actually be concerned for him. For all he knew, she was just as resistant to this marriage as she'd ever been. But Diamantha was forced to admit that it was no longer the truth. She realized that she wasn't particularly averse any longer.

With a heavy sigh, she moved away from the door, her gaze falling upon her sleeping daughter. Sophie had shown Cortez acceptance from the very beginning, something Diamantha still couldn't openly do. But perhaps that needed to change. Perhaps she needed to show the man that she was indeed resigned to being his wife.

Nay... not resigned... *accepting.*

If he made it through this "conversation", she would be sure to tell him.

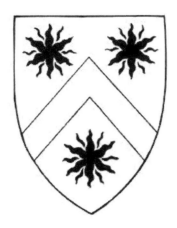

CHAPTER NINE

Forcing thoughts of Diamantha's worried expression out of his mind, Cortez focused on the situation at hand. Making his way down the leaning corridor with James and Oliver flanking him, he paused at the top of the stairs and observed the situation in the common room below.

Somehow, the room was smokier than he had remembered and it was filled to the rafters with people seeking shelter from the storm. There was a good deal of eating going on and laughter could be heard on occasion. The fat innkeeper was moving amongst the crowded tables with a pitcher in his hands, delivering his cheap wine into the cups of those who would pay for the privilege of drinking it.

Above the smoke and conversation, Cortez could see his brother and Drake near the entry, back in the shadows. He made eye contact with them and Andres pointed over near the hearth. Cortez followed his brother's pointed direction but he noticed nothing special or unusual in the area his brother was indicating. There were several people dressed in what looked like rags, drinking heavily and pulling apart a knuckle of sheep. There was also a couple that looked relatively well dressed, a man and woman who appeared to be travelers seeking shelter for the night. They kept to themselves, nearly huddled, seemingly fearful of the rabble around them. Cortez couldn't blame them.

Then, he spied a man who was very well dressed sitting at a table that was directly in front of the hearth. It was difficult to see clearly through the smoke, but he was sitting at a table with five men who were dressed in shabby mail. At the table next to them, there were at least seven men, all armed with nasty-looking clubs. Cortez could see at least three clubs on the table where the sheriff sat, branches of wood wrapped in leather and studded with nails. These were not weapons of honor. They were crude weapons meant to inflict as much damage as possible. He leaned towards James.

"Is that the man?" he asked, pointing down to the table with the clubs on it.

James nodded. "That's him."

Cortez's gaze lingered on the table. "Go rouse some of the men," he muttered. "Tell them to come here in a hurry."

James nodded and descended the steps, heading for the front entry and the wild rain outside. As Cortez began to descend the stairs, slowly, Andres and Drake came out of the shadows to meet him at the base of the steps. All the while, Cortez's eyes never left the table with the sheriff and his henchmen. Already, he could smell blood. He knew they hadn't come here to socialize.

Once Cortez and his knights grouped at the bottom of the rickety stairs, Andres bellowed over to the sheriff.

"You, there," he called. "Turn around and face me."

The sheriff jerked around and his men immediately stood up, clubs in hand. When the knights saw the clubs, the broadswords came out. The sounds of tempered steel grating against leather scabbards pierced the air and tension filled the room. The rest of the eating, drinking occupants of the inn began to scatter. It was never a good thing when two armed groups made themselves known. Even the innkeeper scurried back into the kitchen, away from the situation. His fat head peered out from the doorway, watching and waiting like the rest of his patron. Watching to see who drew the first blood.

"Who are you?" the sheriff stood up from his chair, pointing at Cortez. "By what right do you bring your army into my town?"

Cortez gazed at the man unemotionally. "Tell me your name or I will have nothing to say to you."

The sheriff's brow furrowed. "Not until you tell me yours first!"

"Then we are at a standoff already."

The sheriff sighed unhappily. He put his meaty hands on his big hips. "Dornauld," he told him through clenched teeth. "This is *my* town. Now tell me your name and be quick about it."

Cortez remained calm. "I am Sir Cortez de Bretagne," he told him. "I am garrison commander at Sherborne Castle, servant to our King Edward, and Sheriff of the Shire. I am passing through your town in my travel north. Is there anything else you wish to know?"

Dornauld faltered somewhat. He hadn't expected a man of high standing. It made him nervous. "I have heard of you," he said with some reluctance, eyeing Cortez. "How do I know you are truly de Bretagne?"

Cortez held up his broadsword with the de Bretagne crest etched on the hilt. "I would be more than happy to show you."

It was a threat and they all knew it, and upon knowing who this man was, Dornauld wasn't so sure he wanted to engage him.

"That is not necessary," he said, trying to maintain control of the conversation. "Why are you traveling north?"

"That is my business."

Dornauld faltered heavily this time. He glanced at the men around him, men holding studded clubs. He didn't want to lose face with them, especially since he promised them a fight and the possessions of the losers. Swallowing hard, he struggled to appear as if he wasn't intimidated. He had to make good to his men somehow.

"All great parties passing through my town must pay tribute," he demanded. "You have many men. It will cost you twenty gold crowns to pass through my town."

Cortez could see the man was a weakling. He sheathed his broadsword. "I will not pay," he said, putting his hands on his hips in a rather sassy gesture. "What are you going to do about it?"

Dornauld's face began to turn red. "If you do not pay, I will set my men upon you."

Cortez's mouth twitched with a smile just as several of his men began to pour in through the front and back doors. Soon, the inn was full of men in armor, heavily armed, and Dornauld and his men were visibly unsettled. Those holding the studded clubs lifted their weapons threateningly as Cortez's men fanned out through the room.

"Beware, de Bretagne," Dornauld said furiously. "I can summon hundreds of men to overwhelm your paltry troops. Beware your next move!"

Cortez was finished arguing with the idiot. He made his way over to Dornauld with his knights flanking him. Andres and Drake shoved a couple of Dornauld's men out of the way when they crowded too close. Once Cortez reached Dornauld, he slapped the man across the face so hard that Dornauld fell back on the tabletop. Cortez was on top of him in an instant, his onyx eyes blazing.

"You are either the stupidest man I have ever come across or you truly have no idea that there are men with armies that can crush you like a spider," he snarled. "I have fifteen hundred men at Sherborne Castle who can be here within hours. I can give them orders to torch your dirty little town and everything you hold dear will be gone. Anger me and I may just do it. Anger me further and I will send to London for more of Edward's men, and we will wipe your village and your family from the face of the earth. Is this in any way unclear?"

Dornauld knew the man wasn't bluffing. He could tell by his expression. But he was used to controlling this town and everyone in it. He wasn't used to someone dominating him. Angry, he tried to push Cortez away.

"You have no power here," he growled. "You have...."

Cortez cut him off by another slap to the face. It was a humiliating gesture, for only women were slapped. "I have more power here than you do," he exclaimed. "Allow me to tell you what is going to happen now."

"You cannot...!"

Another slap shut Dornauld up. Cortez had the man around the neck. "You and your men are going to go far, far away," he said, his voice low. "If I see just a hint of you, ever again, I will order my men to torch the town and I will set out after you as a hound tracks a fox. When I find you... well, you will not like it. You must trust me on that. Do you comprehend me?"

Before Dornauld could say a word, Cortez caught sight of something in his periphery that was moving towards his head and he dropped to his knees in the blink of an eye. Dornauld, however, was not so fast. One of the sheriff's men had evidently decided to take it upon himself to kill Cortez and the studded club that had been meant for Cortez's skull missed Cortez completely and sailed right into Dornauld's face.

Dornauld howled as nails pierced his forehead and eyes, and immediately the entire room deteriorated into a massive brawl. Cortez's men rushed in from the perimeter of the room as the knights in the center of the room began swinging their massive broadswords. Cortez was trapped beneath his brother fighting with one of Dornauld's men. He crawled underneath the table to get free, unsheathing his broadsword in the same movement.

When Cortez finally came up on the opposite side of the table, it was into a skirmish between his men and a few of Dornauld's. The massive blade with the de Bretagne crest entered into the fray. What Cortez didn't see, however, was one of Dornauld's men making a break for the stairs. Only when James yelled at him did he realize there was a man at the top of the stairs, heading back towards the sleeping rooms.

Diamantha and Sophie were back there. Cortez had never moved so fast in his entire life.

Diamantha was in the process of laying out her wet hose in front of the hearth to dry when she began to hear heavy footfalls. Thinking that Cortez might be returning, she was moving towards the door when she heard a massive crash against one of the other doors out in the corridor.

Startled, she jumped back, heart in her throat, as she heard another enormous blow. It shook the very walls. Then another blow on the door across the hall, now accompanied by bellows she couldn't make out. Someone was yelling angrily. Terrified, she snatched Sophie from her small bed near the entry door and took the little girl with her to the opposite side of the room near one of the cloth-covered windows.

Yanking the cloth away, she could see that they were several feet off the ground and there was nothing between her and the mud below. If she had to jump, there was nothing to break her fall, but there was something going on in the corridor and she would not wait for it to come to her. She had to get out of the chamber.

A loud bang crashed against her door and she screamed with fright, holding Sophie tightly as she sat on the windowsill, putting a leg out of the opening. The door, being poorly constructed, gave way in spite of the iron bolt and a shabby man with a big club burst through. Wood and debris went flying all over the chamber. Diamantha slung her other leg over the windowsill and prepared to jump but was stopped short when Cortez came charging into the chamber.

Like an avenging angel, he arrived just in time and he went after the intruder with a vengeance. Cortez pounced on the man and they both went sailing onto the bigger of the two beds in the room, collapsing it in a violent crash. The man had an enormous club, studded with wicked-looking spikes, and he tried to swing it at Cortez, who had him in a headlock. The man couldn't get a good swing at Cortez, who had a big arm across the man's throat and was squeezing as hard as he could.

Within several seconds of Cortez's strangulation, the man stopped trying to swing the club. He was losing air and losing consciousness, but he fought for all he was worth. It was a life and death struggle until eventually, he couldn't fight any longer. Everything within him was fading. He went limp as his life drained away.

But Cortez didn't let go. He held the man tightly around the neck and when he finally stopped fighting back, he loosened one arm long enough to smash it against the side of the man's skull, twisting his neck grotesquely. The sound of a dull snap filled the room as the spine fractured, breaking in half. As fast as it had started, it was over with deadly finality.

Cortez didn't stop to rest or regroup, or even offer words of comfort to Diamantha. He was still in battle mode. Breathing heavily, he stood up and pulled the man out of the room by his feet, dragging him back down the corridor and throwing him down the rickety stairs. The man landed in a heap down in the common room, dead for all to see. Such was the penalty for anyone attempting to harm Lady de Bretagne. Cortez wanted that message made abundantly clear.

Still breathing heavily, Cortez staggered back to the room where Diamantha was still sitting on the windowsill with Sophie clutched tightly against her breast. She was becoming soaked from the rain pouring in through the opening but still, she sat there, her eyes wide with terror. It looked as if she was still contemplating jumping. Cortez went into the room, his arms reaching out for her.

"Come out of the window, sweetheart," he told her. "I am very sorry you had to see that. He did not harm you, did he?"

Diamantha let him pull her out of the window. She even let him take Sophie from her and set the girl back on her bed. But the moment he turned to Diamantha for an answer to his question, she burst into tears and collapsed onto her knees. Cortez was next to her in an instant.

"Oh, God," he groaned, his hands on her arms, trying to see if she was, indeed, injured. "Where are you hurt?"

Diamantha couldn't speak. She was overwhelmed with terror. She shook her head, sobbing loudly, before throwing her arms around his neck. It was a gesture of both terror and relief, the actions of a woman who had been too close to disaster before fate in the form of Cortez de Bretagne intervened. She squeezed so tightly that she nearly strangled him.

"I am fine," Diamantha gasped repeatedly, sounding hysterical. "I am fine, I am fine."

Stunned by her gesture, by the feel of her against him, Cortez was nearly moved to tears. He hugged her tightly.

"Are you sure?" he asked hoarsely, his face in the side of her head.

Diamantha was close to swooning. She nodded her head furiously and released her hold on him, her hand to her mouth to try to stifle her hysteria. "I thought I was going to have to jump to escape him, but you...." She put her hands on his face, inspecting him for damage. "Are you well? Did he hurt you?"

Cortez smiled faintly as she ran her hands all over his face and head, looking for injury. "He did not hurt me," he murmured softly, loving the feel of her flesh against his. "I am well, truly."

Diamantha couldn't stop crying. She was absolutely terrified. "Good," she wept. "I am glad. But what happened? Who was that man?"

Cortez shook his head, his arms still around her, trying his best to comfort her. He glanced over his shoulder at the destroyed door, wondering what would have happened if he had been a few seconds too slow. He couldn't even think about it. It made him feel sick to his stomach. Standing up, he pulled Diamantha will him.

"It does not matter who he was," he said. "He is no longer any concern, but it looks as if he broke our door. We will move across the hall for tonight."

Diamantha was shaking so badly that she could barely walk. Cortez collected her, sleepy Sophie, and the animals, and moved them across the hall into a smaller room with two small beds. He put Sophie down on one, Diamantha down on the other, and set the cage down next to the hearth. All the while, Diamantha could hear the sounds of fighting going on in the common room. It sounded like a war.

"What is happening out there?" she asked, her voice sounding exhausted and weak. "I thought you said you were only going to speak to the man?"

Cortez poked at the smoldering peat, throwing a few sticks of wood on it to get a blaze going. "He demanded money in exchange for allowing us to pass through his town," he replied. "I was not going to pay him. He was then inclined to demonstrate his unhappiness at my refusal."

Diamantha's tears were fading but she was still rightly upset. Wiping at her eyes, she stood up on unsteady legs and made her way over to her daughter, who was lying down on her little bed. In fact, the girl hadn't uttered a sound through the entire event and even now, she was nearly back asleep. Diamantha stroked her daughter's forehead, pulling the covers over her. Seeing that her daughter was well, and calm, helped Diamantha to relax. Things were well now. Taking a deep breath, she turned for Cortez.

"What will we do now?" she asked quietly, making her way over to him. "Will we still remain here tonight?"

Cortez finished with the fire and stood up. "We will," he said. "I will go now and see how the situation is faring. I'll have the innkeeper bring you some food so that you may eat and get some rest. We will leave before dawn."

He started to move past her but she grasped his arm. "What about you?" she asked softly. "Will you not eat and sleep, also?"

He nodded, gazing down into her beautiful face. Her hand was still on his arm and he could feel the heat of her touch through his mail, making his heart race.

"I will eat and sleep eventually," he said.

He gave her a weary smile and continued to the door, but she stopped him one last time. "Where will you sleep?" she asked.

He sighed heavily, looking at the two small beds. There was hardly room for two adults and one small child. "I will find someplace, I suppose."

Diamantha moved towards him, her expression sincere. "Please...," she said. "Please come back here. You may sleep with us."

To Cortez, it seemed like an open invitation. He could hardly believe his ears. "If that is your wish," he said gently. "It might be a bit... crowded."

Diamantha shook her head. "We will make do," she said. "Please return to us when you have finished. I... I believe I would feel much safer if you did."

Cortez didn't have to be asked twice. Impulsively, he reached out to touch her on the cheek. "I will return, then," he promised. "Rest assured."

Diamantha shut the door behind him after he left but she didn't bolt it. Her thoughts lingered on the man, on his heroics, and she realized she was starting to see something different about him. This night had been full of revelations for her regarding Cortez de Bretagne. Her first impressions of him had been that of a spoiled, forceful man, but the past several hours had seen that opinion drastically change. There was more to Cortez de Bretagne than his good looks and arrogant manner. *He is a good man*, James had said. More and more, she could see that James had been correct.

After a meal had been delivered by the harried barkeep and her satchels had eventually been brought up to her by one of Cortez's men, Diamantha was sufficiently calm enough to prepare for bed. She had brought soap and other toiletries with her, all carefully wrapped in a soft pouch, and she washed her face with rose-scented hard soap and brushed her teeth with a frayed reed and a mixture of ashes of burnt rosemary and mint. She was still in her traveling clothes, the heavy blue woolen ensemble that had seen her through rough weather, and she happily peeled it off, stripping down to her shift, and hanging the clothing up on one of the pegs near the hearth to dry out.

In the darkness of the room, she took her rag and soap and washed herself as best she could, drying off with a small piece of linen she had packed just for that purpose. Her long hair, braided for travel, was unbraided and brushed vigorously with a horsehair brush before being braided again for sleep. All the while, Diamantha's thoughts lingered on Cortez and on the events of the night. It was only their first day of travel. She could only pray the rest of the journey was easier.

The little animals were stirring in their cage so right before she went to sleep, she poured some of the milk the barkeep had brought up for Sophie into the small wooden bowl, watching the babies drink hungrily. Even the rabbit sipped at it. She put a few bread crusts, part of an apple, and a few pieces of meat into the cage as well, sealing it up for the night. When she finally laid down to rest, sleep was nearly instant.

When Cortez returned to her well after midnight, it was with great anticipation and a bit of nervousness. He was a bridegroom, after all, and he wanted their first night together to be something pleasant and memorable. Given the rocky nature of their entire association, he could only pray for the best.

Posting guards in the corridor so he and his knights could sleep without fear of reprisal from Dornauld and his men, he entered the small room with the two small beds, looking forward to the night to come. His thoughts were already heated, thinking of her soft flesh against his, and when his eyes grew accustomed to the weak light in the chamber, what he saw sent his lustful thoughts into ironic disappointment.

Diamantha had asked him to return to sleep with them, but now he saw that she hadn't meant what he'd hoped she had meant. Diamantha was snuggled into one of the small beds with Sophie, leaving the other small bed for Cortez to sleep alone. He was sleeping with her, all right, all by himself in another bed.

He fell asleep watching Diamantha's slumbering form from across the darkened room.

CHAPTER TEN

Cortez awoke to movement in his bed.

It was dark in the room and he could feel something up against his belly, something warm and soft. He could also hear a whispering voice, too. Without moving his head, he opened his eyes to little slits and looked down at the midsection of his bed, just in time to see Sophie standing there.

She had something in her hands and as he struggled to focus in the darkness, he could see two kittens and a baby rabbit up against his torso. Sophie had the fox kit in her hands, telling it that it would be safe now as she put it next to the others. Then, she took hold of Cortez's blanket and covered him back up with the baby animals nestled against his belly. Like any good mother, she was tucking them all in.

"Sophie?" Cortez whispered. "What are you doing?"

Sophie turned to Cortez and, seeing that he was awake, went over to stand next to his head. "I am putting them to bed with you," she told him.

"Why?"

"Because they were afraid."

"I see," he replied, looking at her sleepy little face. "How do you know they are afraid?"

She turned and pointed to the cage, now open, nestled next to the nearly dark hearth. There was hardly any fire at all. "They were shivering," she said. "They were afraid."

It was very cold in the room with the fire out and he suspected the animals weren't afraid as much as they were simply cold. He thought he should get up and stoke the fire but didn't want to move too much with four small animals tucked against his torso. He opened his mouth to say something but the stabs of tiny claws as the kittens happily kneaded the skin of his belly had him wincing. Cortez's deep, dark secret was that he was ticklish as hell, and the baby claws were about to send him into fits.

"Ugh," he grunted as tiny stabs poked at him. He tossed the covers back and went straight for the scratching kittens, picking up the entire menagerie in one big hand. "Sophie, sweet, can you please bring the cage over here? We should put them back so I may rise."

Sophie obediently padded over to the cage on the floor and picked it up, bringing it over to him. Cortez took the cage, gently putting the animals back inside. Then he closed the door, sitting up on the bed. Both he and Sophie hovered over the cage, inspecting the little animals.

"I will find them clean straw before we leave," Cortez told her, looking at her little blond head. "Have you fed them yet this morning?"

Sophie shook her head and Cortez patted her on the top of her soft hair, rising from the bed. His bare feet met with a very cold floor and he headed over to the fireplace to stir the embers a bit. As he moved, he happened to glance at the other bed only to realize that it was empty. Diamantha was missing. Fear gripped him.

"Sophie," he tried not to sound panicked. "Where is your mother?"

Sophie shrugged. She was more interested in the animals. "She left."

Cortez was already yanking on his boots. "Where did she go?" he asked, fear in his tone. "Did she say where she was going, sweet?"

Sophie shook her head again, her hands in the cage as she petted her kittens. Cortez didn't linger. He secured his last boot and bolted to the door. He paused, however briefly, before exiting as he looked pointedly at Sophie.

"You will say here," he told the little girl. "Do you understand me? Stay in this room and do not leave."

Sophie nodded again and even looked at him, her big eyes staring straight at Cortez. He could only pray she understood what he was telling her, so he rushed out of the room and shut the door. As he seemed to recall, the child had a habit of slipping away. He didn't want to have to turn the town upside-down looking for an errant little girl.

There were soldiers in the small corridor and he headed straight for them. "Where did Lady de Bretagne go?" he demanded.

The soldiers, three of them, pointed towards the stairs. "She went that way, my lord," one of them said.

Cortez was already moving to the rickety old stairs. "The little girl is still in the chamber," he told them. "Make sure she stays there. In fact, one of you go into the room and sit with her. Keep her in your sight and keep her safe at all costs."

The soldiers nodded but Cortez didn't stick around to confirm the understanding of his orders. He was already flying down the steps, his gaze searching out every corner of the common room looking for Diamantha. It was full of people sleeping on the floors, on the tables, but no sign of his wife. *His wife.* It still seemed odd to think that way. He had a wife again and it was the best feeling in the world. It was also the most vulnerable. He would have been devastated if something happened to her before he got the chance to truly know her. When she was out of his sight, he felt frantic. *Vulnerable.* As he charged towards the entry, he heard hissing behind him.

Whirling around, he saw Diamantha coming in through the rear entrance to the tavern. She was gesturing at him, trying to get his attention. Relief such as he had never before experienced washed over him, rendering him weak. After a deep breath and a hard swallow to regain his composure, he went to her.

"Where did you go?" he asked, trying not to sound demanding or accusing. "I woke up and you were gone."

Diamantha was back in her traveling clothes, the heavy dark blue woolen dress and cloak. In fact, she appeared refreshed and lovely in this early hour. She pointed to the door she had just come through.

"The privy is outside," she said softly. "Why? Where did you think I went?"

He should have assumed it was something so simple. He knew she would never have run away, leaving her daughter behind, and felt rather foolish that he had reacted so. He put a hand on her elbow to escort her back to their chamber.

"I thought a gang of savages had abducted you," he said, trying to cover for his lack of faith. "I was coming to save you."

She smiled at him, an astonishingly beautiful gesture in the weak light of dawn. "Like you did last night?"

He returned her smile. "For you, my lady, I would do that and more."

Her smile broadened at his rather gallant reply. "I did not thank you for your chivalry," she said. Then, her smile faded. "I was a bit upset, I suppose. I have never had anything like that happen before."

His smile faded as well as he lifted his eyebrows, perhaps in resignation of a world full of dangers. "Hopefully you never will again," he said as the reached the steps leading to the upper floor. "Which brings me to my next point, for your own safety, you should never go anywhere unescorted, even if it is to only find the privy."

She paused on the steps and looked at him. "Oh," she said thoughtfully. "You are correct, I suppose. I did not think of it that way."

He nodded as he urged her up the stairs. "You said yourself that you'd not been out of Corfe much," he said. "Traveling as we are, the road is wrought with dangers. You must trust that I know best in these things."

They reached the top of the stairs and she glanced at him. "After last night, I would say that you know a great deal more than I do about the world in general."

"It can be an unpredictable place."

"That is putting it mildly," she agreed. "But I seem to be traveling with my own guardian angel and for that, I am truly grateful. You are a sight to behold in times of need."

He didn't know what to say to that. It was a sweet compliment and one that made him nearly bashful... *him, bashful?* He didn't think it was in his arrogant nature to be bashful, but evidently it was. Lady de Bretagne had brought that out in him with her gentle accolade. Therefore, for lack of a better reaction, he merely smiled at her as he took her back to the room where her daughter had let the animals out of their cage and they were now running wild in the room.

As Diamantha dressed Sophie for the day, Cortez found himself wrangling baby animals and putting them back in their cage. But he didn't really mind. Seeing Sophie's happy smile when all of her animals were safe and sound somehow made it all worthwhile. In fact, waking up to her sweet little face had been one of the best things he'd ever done. He knew he could get used to it; he could grow to depend on it. That, and waking up to Diamantha every morning. There was something about that thought that seemed to make his entire life complete.

As the sun began to break the eastern horizon to reveal a rather clear and bright day following an evening of a massive storm, Cortez and his party were on the road again, heading to points north.

After the wild rains from the previous day, the brilliant blue day of travel seemed rather surreal. Everything was crisp and green, and more than once they saw fallow deer grazing in the meadows. The road, however, was rutted and still very muddy, making it difficult for the wagons to pass. Cortez's soldiers had to keep breaking rank to get in behind the wagon carrying Sophie to push it out of a hole.

Eventually, Sophie wanted to ride General, who had been growing very fat and lazy being led around and constantly fed by the soldier in charge of the horse provisions. About three hours since their departure from Shaftesbury, Cortez put Sophie on General and strapped her onto her little saddle. But Sophie wanted to ride with her cage of baby animals and Diamantha had to convince her daughter that it was best to let them remain in the wagon. Sophie wasn't happy about it but she did as her mother instructed. After that, Diamantha took General's reins and led the pony next to her.

Unfortunately, horseback travel wasn't particularly exciting for a three year old. Less than an hour after Cortez put her on General's back, Sophie was growing restless. Diamantha tried to distract her daughter with butterfly or bird sightings, and that worked for a while, but then the little girl would grow restless again and ask for something to eat. She seemed to be growing increasingly restless until one of Cortez's soldiers came to the rescue.

Luckily, the quartermaster was nearby and, having two young boys of his own, understood how to handle a small child. He presented Sophie with a small bag of dried apples, which she happily ate. She wanted the quartermaster to give General some, and the man did. The pony ate them eagerly. All the while, the quartermaster walked next to Sophie and listened to the little girl's chatter. Sophie seemed to like to chat with any man that would listen to her, as she had with Merlin on their trip from Corfe, and Diamantha knew it was because Sophie had been used to having her father and grandfather around. It gave the little girl comfort to have a man to talk to, a man who reminded her of her father. It was a bittersweet thing to watch.

The day continued on and they stopped briefly for a meal around mid-day. The party paused by a rather large stream that fed into a crystalline lake, and as Diamantha stretched her legs, Sophie played contentedly with her cage of baby animals. Cortez lingered near them both, vigilantly watching over their personal safety, as his knights checked on the men, and inspected the soundness of all of the animals, before finally settling down to wolf down a quick meal.

Diamantha watched how Cortez was with his knights. The man had a calm manner about him in both command and service, and it was clear how much his men respected him. As she sat back against a tree with the remnants of a nooning meal spread out next to her, she found herself watching Cortez as he interacted with his men, seeing flashes of humor or bouts with seriousness as they engaged in conversation. At one point, Sir Drake even provoked loud laughter, which was charming to see. The more Diamantha watched Cortez, the more charming she found him. Aye, that rude and aggressive man who had come to Corfe to claim her was changing before her eyes and she didn't mind one bit. She was even coming to like it. But that was her last pleasant thought before a grimy hand went over her mouth.

Startled, Diamantha yanked away from the hands that were grabbing her from behind the tree, screaming as loud as she could. Cortez and his men bolted, running in her direction, as the copse of trees behind her came alive with men wielding studded clubs. As they ran towards the knights, Diamantha managed to escape the hands that were clutching at her and ran straight for her daughter.

Fortunately, Sophie was just a few feet away and she grabbed the girl, and her cage of baby animals, and made haste for the wagons upon the road. The quartermaster, being an older man who didn't involve himself much in fighting unless absolutely necessary, bolted from his wagons and rushed forward to help her. As men with weapons began to clash violently near the tree line, the quartermaster took the cage of animals from Diamantha, grabbed her by the elbow, and helped her up to the road where the wagons were.

As Diamantha and Sophie sought shelter in the wagon, the quartermaster grabbed a sword he usually kept hidden for events just like this one. He stood next to the wagon, next to Diamantha and Sophie, with the sword in a defensive position as he watched the battle in the distance. And what a battle it was.

Dornauld followed us. It didn't take a genius to figure that out. Cortez knew it the instant he heard Diamantha scream and saw men with clubs emerging from the trees. Unfortunately, the shifty sheriff had delivered on one of his promises. He had brought at least a hundred men with him, men who were armed with those spiked clubs, and although Cortez and his men had very sharp and serious weapons, he knew they would be overwhelmed by sheer number.

But it wasn't in his nature to run. Cortez knew he had to beat Dornauld once and for all if they were ever going to have any peace. Therefore, he aimed for the sheriff as the man sat just inside the trees astride a fat white horse. But he didn't make a move before shouting to the soldier nearest him.

"Go back to the wagons and tell Bean to get the wagons moving," he said. "Tell him to get the lady and her daughter out of here and head to Warminster. We will catch up once we've taken care of this fool and his men. And you go with them!"

The soldier nodded sharply and was gone, running at top speed back to the wagons. When Cortez was certain the wagons were starting to move, thus removing them from danger, he turned back for Dornauld.

Cortez had to fight his way through groups of battling men as he made his way towards the man on the round white horse. Around him, his knights were making short work of Dornauld's less-experienced men, cutting off limbs and heads with skill and ease. Very shortly, the battle had turned into a blood bath, and all of it spilled by Dornauld's men. Cortez was growing more furious with each successive step that the fool sheriff was bold enough to attack them on the road. *Damn the idiot*! He intended to make the man pay.

As Cortez drew near the trees, he ducked back into the tree line, using it for camouflage. He didn't want to give Dornauld an open shot at him. Using foliage and tree trunks as shields to hide him as he moved, he made his way very quietly to Dornauld, who had limited vision since his sight had been damaged the night before by one of his own men's clubs. In fact, most of the top of his head was wrapped up, including his right eye. Since Cortez came up on the man's right side, Dornauld never stood a chance.

Using the small, razor-sharp dagger he always carried on his body, Cortez plunged it into Dornauld's back and yanked the man off his horse in the same smooth motion. As Dornauld screamed, Cortez withdrew the knife and used it to slit the man's throat. As Dornauld lay there, drowning in his own blood, Cortez stood over him.

"Let that be a lesson to all who threaten me," he growled. "I hope you rot in hell, you whoreson."

Dornauld's wide-eyed, terrified expression glazed over and Cortez knew that he was dead. Without another glance to the corpse, he leapt onto the fat, very expensive white courser and spurred the animal out of the trees and into the skirmish beyond.

"Your leader is dead!" he bellowed as he went. "Drop your weapons and flee, and I may show mercy. Keep fighting and I will kill you all!"

Dornauld's men, seeing Cortez astride the sheriff's horse, quickly realized that what the man said must have been true. Dornauld was fanatical about the horse and would not have willingly relinquished it. Death was the only answer to such a thing. Therefore, they began dropping their clubs and running for the woods where Dornauld's body lay. Some men ran without dropping their clubs, but Cortez didn't particularly care. They were running away and that was all that mattered to him. He watched the gang of them disappear into the trees.

"My lord?"

Cortez turned to the source of the question, seeing James standing there. The young knight was somewhat winded but unharmed.

"Was anyone badly hurt?" he asked de Lohr.

James shook his head. "Nay, my lord," he replied. "There seem to be a few with puncture wounds from those clubs, but nothing that will not heal."

Cortez nodded, satisfied. "Then get the men moving," he said. "We must catch up to the wagons, which surely could not have gotten far with the condition of this road."

James nodded in agreement. "Should I send a few men after that rabble to make sure they do not come after us again?"

Cortez was forced to agree with that possibility. "Aye," he said. "I did not think that the sheriff was stupid enough to follow us after last night, but now with the man dead, we must discourage his followers from seeking vengeance. Send ten men to follow with orders to observe the group and then catch up to us in Warminster tonight with a report."

James saluted smartly and was gone. Cortez made his way back up to the road, taking a moment to inspect his latest acquisition. The fat courser was a beauty, healthy and strong, and he was quite a specimen. Cortez considered the prize almost to be worth the trouble. Almost... but not quite. He made a mental note to stop in Shaftesbury once they had returned from retrieving Rob Edlington's body just to make sure Dornauld's men were behaving themselves. Hatred and evil like that was not easily quelled.

They caught up to the quartermaster and the wagons less than a half hour later, stuck deep in road rut.

CHAPTER ELEVEN

The stop in Warminster had been thankfully uneventful. Since the weather was good, rather than sleep at an inn – and also being rather wary of the town after what happened in Shaftesbury – Cortez set up camp to the north of Warminster to rest for the night. The men had hunted at sundown and brought down two wild boars, which provided them with an abundance of meat for sup.

Underneath the black night sky with its carpet of diamond-stars, Cortez and his men stuffed themselves on wild boar and told great stories of valor around the fires. It had been a pleasant evening for the most part, with Diamantha and Sophie sleeping in the wagon bed to keep them off the damp ground. Cortez slept on the road next to the wagon, just to be near them. It was his duty as well as his desire.

The next morning dawned clear and bright again, and the roads were nearly dried up completely of their copious mud. It made travel easier as the party set out from Warminster and headed north once again. Their destination for that night was the ancient city with the great Roman baths, something Diamantha had heard of but never seen, so she was rather like an eager child as the group plodded their way from the relatively flat lands surrounding Warminster and into the softly rolling hills that made up the landscape around Bath. She was excited to reach their destination.

Once into the hills where the ancient Romans used to mine lead and other metals, the road grew narrower and heavy foliage surrounded it. There were big ruts to one side of the path so the party, and both wagons, stayed over to the left side to keep out of the holes. It was peaceful travel and one that Diamantha, after the hectic nature of the past two days, was enjoying immensely. So was Sophie. The girl was taking a nap in the wagon bed, her arms around the cage with her pets in it, and Diamantha grinned every time she glanced into the wagon to check on her child.

Diamantha must have been in a smiling mood because she also smiled at Cortez every time the man, at the head of the column, turned around to look at her. He would smile in return, making the morning full of smiles between them, gentle gestures that had been polite at first but were now gaining in warmth. Something had changed between them yesterday, as two people who experienced danger and triumph together. It had somehow brought them closer. At least, that's what Cortez thought. He'd never seen Diamantha behave so friendly towards him and at first he had been wary of it. He wondered why she kept smiling at him. Then, as the day went on, she continued to smile at him and his doubt turned to hope. Was it possible that things between them were truly improving? He could only hope so.

What was it he had thought to himself the day before? *A woman who is chased will run*? As hard as it had been to back off his aggressive pursuit of her, maybe in some small way, it was working. Giving her some time to acclimate and having some patience seemed to have paid off. As the village of Bath became visible in the distance, Cortez had Andres and Drake take point while he reined his charger back into the column to speak with Diamantha.

She had been looking in the wagon again when he approached and brought his charger alongside her leggy palfrey. When she saw that it was Cortez, she broke into one of those lovely smiled he had been seeing all morning.

"Look at her," she said, indicating Sophie. "She has not released that cage all morning. I told her she could not take them out, so she is doing her best to keep them close."

Cortez peered over the side of the wagon, seeing the little girl with her arms around the cage. He grinned. "She can take them out tonight," he told Diamantha. "I plan to sleep in a structure with a solid roof over my head and we shall get Sophie her very own room where she can take the animals out and play with them to her heart's content."

Diamantha wasn't oblivious to the deeper implications of that statement. *We shall get Sophie her own room.* In other words, Diamantha and Cortez would also have their own room. Gazing at the man, she realized she wasn't entirely opposed to that arrangement. She was his wife, after all. At some point, their marriage would have to be consummated. She couldn't hold the man off forever. Now, she wasn't entirely sure she wanted to.

"I am sure she would like that," Diamantha said quietly. "Do you have a place already in mind?"

Cortez looked away from Sophie and to the head of the road where Bath was becoming more visible. "I was here, once, with Helene," he said. "It was on our wedding trip and we stayed in a hostel called The Crystal Palace. It is near the ancient Roman baths, which I thought you might like to visit."

Diamantha was very intrigued. "I would love to see them," she said. "I have only heard tale of them. My father went there, once. He said it smelled terrible and the water was very warm."

Cortez chuckled. "I remember that it did smell strongly," he said. "There is something in the water, some kind of growth that turns it green and causes it to smell badly. You do not want to bathe in those ancient waters, I assure you."

Diamantha nodded her head, rather horrified by the thought of foul-smelling bath water. "I will admit that I would rather bathe in water without green growth," she said. "In fact, do you think it would be too much trouble to arrange a bath tonight? I should bathe

Sophie and I would also like to bathe. *If* it is not too much trouble, of course."

He looked at her, seeing that she was being exceptionally polite about requesting a bath. He shook his head. "It will not be too much trouble," he said, glancing over in the wagon that held her meager possessions. "In fact, I thought to arrange a shopping trip if we do not arrive into town too late. Mayhap the merchants will still be open. This is our wedding trip as well and I should like to buy you something."

Diamantha shrugged faintly. "That is not necessary," she told him. "You gave me that lovely necklace that belonged to both Helene and your mother. That is enough."

He shook his head, looking away as his gaze moved out over the city looming closer. "That is *not* enough," he said firmly, casting her a long glance. "I should like to give you something that no one else has owned before. I should... well, I should like to buy you a wedding ring if you will wear one."

There was a rather gentle and appreciative expression on Diamantha's face. He had expected her to resist outright but she didn't. In fact, she seemed receptive.

"If it would please you, I will wear one," she said softly.

He turned to look at her simply to see if she was being truthful. He still could hardly believe how much more accepting and pleasant she had become over the past day or two. This woman was nothing like the rebellious one he had first met at Corfe. She was kind and gracious and... beautiful. She was most definitely beautiful. Thrilled that she would agree to wear a wedding ring, he winked at her.

"It would please me if you would wear my ring," he said, then leaned into her and lowered his voice. "If only to let anyone who might have a notion to steal you away know that you belong to me. That goes for my foolish brother as well. Has he stopped flirting with you?"

Diamantha laughed, spying Andres up at the head of the column. "Truthfully, he's not spoken to me since yesterday," she said. "I would tell you if he was being bold and terrible, but he is not."

"Swear it?"

"I do."

149

"Even to protect him because he is now your brother as well?"

She giggled and lifted her hand in a vowing gesture. "I swear to you, my lord, that he has not taken liberties with me," she said, then lowered her hand and grew serious. "You will know when that happens without me having to tell you."

He cocked his head thoughtfully. "How will I know?"

She gave him a wry expression. "Because he will be sporting a black eye the size of a melon," she said, watching him grin. "You do not think I would let him get away with it, do you?"

Cortez shook his head, hard. "I do not," he replied frankly. "I have said it once before, God help the man who truly tangles with you."

Diamantha laughed again, lowering her gaze in a rather coy gesture that Cortez found utterly captivating. He would have liked to have chatted with her, and flirted with her, for the rest of the day had a call from the front of the column not interrupted him. Frustrated at the intrusion, he excused himself and charged back up to the front of the group, just as they were descending a hill that led straight to the south gate of Bath's city walls.

There were many people on the road at that point, crowding into the south gates as the bishop of Bath's men inspected the flow entering the city. Cortez could see the soldiers in their green tunics, scrutinizing all who passed. He nudged his brother.

"Ride up and announce us," he told Andres. "Tell the bishop's men that we simply wish to stay in town for the night and be on our way in the morning. You make sure to tell him that I am the garrison commander for Simon of Ghent. They cannot refuse us in that case."

Andres, like the other knights, wore closed-faced helmets with a hinged visor on it so they could lift the faceplate for better field of vision. At his brother's instruction, he closed his lifted visor and charged down the road towards the south gate of Bath. It was usually a battle-ready position but in this case, he meant it to be one of command. The bishop's men would think twice before denying a heavily-armed knight entry to the town. It was meant to intimidate, which was what Cortez required of all of his men. It was important to him, in any case, to have the upper hand.

As Andres charged towards the gates, Cortez had his knights close their visors and sling shields over their left knee for quick access. It was a battle stance. His foot soldiers, with their "kettle helmets", packed weapons but kept them sheathed. They weren't heading for war but they wanted to be prepared entering the rather busy and cultural city of Bath.

Diamantha, to the rear of the column, watched the preparations around her. They hadn't prepared this much heading into Shaftesbury, but they had definitely prepared heading into Warminster. It seemed to her that after their experiences in Shaftesbury, Cortez wasn't going to be caught unprepared again. The man would make his presence known as only de Bretagne could.

It had evidently worked. Cortez's party never even had to stop. The soldiers at the south gate of Bath motioned them in and even bowed politely to the lady as she passed by. Once through the big gatehouse, an entirely new world opened up on the other side.

It was a world of awe.

Sophie awoke the moment she heard the busy sounds of the town, standing up in the wagon bed to a sight she'd never really seen. An entire world of people spread out before her, merchants and vendors, visitors and beggars, all of them bustling about on the busy street that was literally crowded to the seams.

The child rubbed her eyes, blinking sleepily as the wagon moved down the main avenue of the town. She looked at the vendors, the people, but there wasn't much that would interest a three year old girl. It was mostly the noise that had awoken her. However, the moment she saw a vendor with trained dogs, performing tricks for the few coins he could collect, she nearly jumped over the side of the wagon.

"Mama!" she cried, pointing to the man with the four small dogs. "Look! Dogs!"

Riding just behind the wagon, Diamantha looked to see what had her daughter so excited. Indeed, there was a man with four small dogs and when he saw Sophie, he purposely made the dogs jump around to entice her. Sophie began screaming.

"Mama!" she yelled. "I want to see the dogs!"

She was jumping up and down, practically hanging over the side of the wagon, and the closest person to her was Drake de Winter. From the angle of his helm, he was looking down at Sophie as the child nearly came apart with delight. Diamantha was afraid her child was going to launch herself out of the wagon so she called out to Drake.

"Sir Drake?" she said politely. "Would you please grasp my child before she falls out of the wagon and is run over?"

Drake immediately reached down and picked the child up, who happily clung to him, thinking he was going to take her to the dogs. Diamantha reined her horse next to his and reached out for her child, taking her onto the saddle in front of her. Sophie was squealing happily as Diamantha reined her horse around.

"Please tell Cortez that we are visiting the dogs," she said. "He may want to stop and wait for us."

Drake knew that Lady de Bretagne was never to be without a knight for protection, which is why the knights took turns riding in close proximity to her. All except Andres, of course. Cortez kept his brother away from his new wife and they all knew why - the man was fond of women and more than likely not to be trusted. Therefore, Drake quickly told the nearest soldier to carry the message to Cortez while he followed Lady de Bretagne to the man with the dogs. It seemed that's where all of the excitement was happening.

By the time Diamantha reached the dogs, Sophie was nearly mad with enthusiasm. She held her arms out to the dogs as if to hug them as Diamantha dismounted her palfrey and pulled her daughter off. Setting the little girl to her feet, she admonished the child as she tried to run at the canines.

"Careful, now," Diamantha said cautiously. "They do not know you, Sophie. Do not scare them. Let them show you their tricks."

Sophie didn't go any closer but it was very difficult for her. She jumped up and down happily, clapping her hands as the dogs jumped over each other and then onto little wooden blocks the man had for them. They even jumped through a circular piece of wood.

All the while, Sophie laughed happily. She was so very thrilled at something so simple and sweet.

Diamantha stood back, watching her daughter and the dogs, with Drake hovering just behind her. She could feel the man's big presence. She also noticed that Cortez's column had come to a halt and she expected Cortez to show himself any minute. He was never far away, no matter where they were, and the thought brought her comfort. Meanwhile, she looked back at her ecstatic daughter.

"Do you have any children, Sir Drake?" she asked.

Drake flipped up his visor. "Nay, my lady," he said. "I am not married."

Diamantha turned to look at him, surprised. "Not yet?" she repeated. "Surely you are old enough."

He grinned, flashing big white teeth. "I am old enough, my lady," he said. "But, alas, I have not come across what I would consider worthy prospects. Certainly, my father has tried his best to marry me off. I am the last of my brothers to still be unwed."

She grinned as she watched her daughter dance around in circles because the dogs were dancing in circles. "I find that shocking," she said to him. "How many brothers do you have?"

Drake, too, was watching the little girl turn circles. "I have a twin brother, Devon, who is married and has four children," he replied. "I also have a younger brother, Denys, who recently married, and still another brother, Declan, who was recently betrothed."

Diamantha cocked an eyebrow thoughtfully. "I see," she said. "And what does your mother think about the fact that you are not yet married?"

Drake shrugged. "I would not know," he said. "I am afraid to go home and face her."

Diamantha laughed kindly, turning to look at the man just as Cortez walked up. He started to open his mouth, more than likely to ask Diamantha why they had to stop in the middle of a busy street, but she pointed to her dancing daughter before the man could get the words out of his mouth. When Cortez saw Sophie, dancing in circles because the dogs were dancing, he grinned broadly.

"I understand completely now," he said, resting his big fists on his hips as he watched. "We had to stop for dancing."

"Of course we did."

Cortez's gaze lingered on the twirling little girl before turning to Drake. "Ride ahead to The Crystal Palace and secure four rooms," he told him. "After that, see if you can track down a hostel or a dormitory for the rest of the men. If you cannot find either, tell them to sleep at the livery wherever we stable the horses. There should be one near The Crystal Palace. Locate it and make arrangements."

Drake nodded smartly. "Aye, my lord."

The man turned on his heel and disappeared. Sophie had stopped dancing at this point and was now hugging the little dogs, who were jumping happily on her. One pup in particular was licking her face and pushed her down in his excitement. The man who owned the dogs pulled the pup off of her as Cortez reached down and picked her up. Sophie wiped doggy lick off her face.

"Mama?" she said, looking at her mother. "Can I have that dog?"

She could have meant any one of the four but Diamantha shook her head. "Nay, sweetheart," she said. "The dog must stay with his master. Those other dogs are his family. We would not want to take him from his family, would we?"

That seemed to make sense to the three year old mind, at least enough so that she didn't try to argue. Cortez gave the man a few pences for entertaining Sophie and the three of them began to head back towards Cortez's caravan, now stopped along the avenue. His soldiers were starting to wander, particularly because there was tavern up near the end of the street and wenches were lingering near the door, calling out to them. Like sirens calling to sailors, they were luring the men to their doom.

Doom in the form of Cortez's wrath. When he saw what had his men's attention, he helped Diamantha mount her palfrey, handed Sophie up to the woman, and then turned in the direction of his men. As Diamantha gathered her reins, Cortez emitted the loudest whistle she had ever heard, a burst that came out right between his teeth.

It was a piercing, shocking sound, but he had done it with a purpose. The reaction from his men was instantaneous. They all turned to their lord as if he had just shouted commands at them. The men who had been wandering in the direction of the wenches quickly regrouped in the column. As Diamantha calmed her startled horse, Cortez mounted his hairy charger and, motioning for Diamantha to follow, headed up to the front of the column. She took up pace behind him, now at the head of the group.

They reached a crossroads shortly and Cortez turned right. Immediately before them was a massive cathedral, with soaring walls of sand-colored stone and flying buttresses that looked like the rib bones of a great beast. It was an intimidating structure, one that did not radiate the comfort that a church should. Diamantha felt coldness from it, perhaps judgment. She didn't like it in the least. Her astonished gaze moved over the structure.

"God's Blood," she breathed. "That is a very large church."

Cortez looked it over as well. It was nearing Matins and the pilgrims were beginning to flock into the church. He acknowledged her comment with a smile but they continued past the enormous structure and onto a street that was rather narrow compared to the others they had been on. It was also well-worn in the middle and higher on the sides, as a great gutter ran down the center of it. Just as the party entered the avenue, they came across Drake heading towards them astride his red charger. Cortez threw up an arm and brought the entire column to halt as he met up with Drake.

"My lord," Drake greeted. "The Crystal Palace is full but they referred me to lodgings across the street, a place called Lausanne. The rooms are small but clean and I secured four of them. They have a stable out back, a livery shared by some of the other businesses, and I am told we may store our horses in it. Any of our men who wish to sleep in it may do so."

Cortez was satisfied. ""Very well," he said. "Lead the way, de Winter."

Drake turned around and took the group down the street, almost to the end where a rather sad-looking, two-storied stone and timber building sat nestled up against other waddle and daub houses. It was painted white, even the stone was white, and there was a sign hinged to the front of it that was painted with green and red, announcing *Lausanne* to all who passed.

Cortez reined his charger up to the front door and dismounted, turning his horse over to a soldier as he went to take Sophie from Diamantha. As he held the little girl, Drake helped Diamantha off her horse. The street was an odd, up-sloped angle and Diamantha gathered her heavy skirts as she struggled to gain her footing. Just as they moved for the entry, Sophie pointed back to the wagons.

"I want my kittens," she said.

Cortez sent a solder back to collect the cage in the wagon, bringing forth the two kittens, rabbit, and fox kit that were becoming rather fat with all of the eating they'd been doing over the past couple of days. But Sophie was thrilled to see her menagerie and Diamantha took the cage from the soldier. As Cortez went to enter the structure, he turned to Drake.

"I will settle Lady de Bretagne and her daughter in our rooms," he said. "Find my brother and send him to me. Meanwhile, you and the other knights settle the men and wagons. Be prepared to leave at dawn on the morrow."

Drake acknowledged the orders and went about his business. Meanwhile, Cortez led his new wife and new daughter into the crowded hostel that smelled strongly of rosemary. The innkeeper had it burning in every room. Not an unpleasant smell, in fact, but it was rather potent. The innkeeper was a round woman with missing teeth and a pristine white apron, which Diamantha took to mean the hostel was also clean. She hoped so, at any rate. The corridor was narrow and the stairs made for dwarves, but somehow, they managed to make it to the second floor.

The innkeeper showed them their two rooms, adjoining, and although they were indeed clean, Diamantha thought that perhaps the entire hostel was made for dwarves because it was so very tiny. The beds, rooms, everything was small. Entering their connected rooms, Cortez took Sophie in the smaller of the chambers and set the little girl down on her feet. Sophie immediately jumped onto the bed and demanded her animals.

The moment Diamantha set the cage of pets down in Sophie's room, the little girl opened the door to the cage and began taking the creatures out, putting them upon the bed. She petted them and cuddled them, so happy to be with her friends again. Diamantha stood in the adjoining doorway and watched her child as soldiers moved in and out of her room, bringing in satchels and other possessions, which quickly filled the small room to bursting. Cortez's red-headed squire, Peter, made an appearance with items for his master but quickly disappeared. When Cortez finally shut the door behind his men and began organizing the bags against the wall, Diamantha turned to him.

"Now what shall we do?" she asked. "Is it too late to shop?"

Cortez shook his head. "It is never too late," he said. "We will go now."

"But the merchants will be closed to attend Matins."

Cortez gave her a wink. "Then I shall storm their citadels and demand entry," he said, glancing to the door when Andres finally made an appearance. He motioned his brother in. "Ah, Andres. I have a very important task for you."

Andres stepped into the room, his gaze mostly on Diamantha. "I can hardly wait to hear it," he said, his eyes lingering on his brother's lovely wife. "Pray, brother, what would you have of me?"

Cortez's good humor fled as he watched his brother mentally undress Diamantha. His quick temper flared.

"If you do not take your eyes off my wife, you will not live long enough to find out," he said, moving to put himself between his brother and Diamantha as the mood of the room suddenly grew dark. "I have spent the past two days watching you flirt with my wife and I will tell you now that it will stop. The disrespect you show for me with your roguish behavior is shocking, even for you. Do you truly think so little of me so that you would try to engage in some manner of inappropriate conduct with my wife?"

Andres was taken aback at the accusations, true though they might be. He was incensed. "I have done no such thing," he said hotly. "What gives you the right to accuse me of such things?"

Cortez sighed heavily. "Did you not just walk in here and size my wife up as if she was another one of your conquests?"

Andres blinked, unable to think of a swift reply. "I did not...."

"And have you not been constantly and lewdly winking at the woman every chance you get?"

Andres took a step back from his brother, fearful of what was going to happen. He knew the accusations were true and was wary of his brother's legendary temper. He had no desire to come face to face with the physical repercussions.

"I mean no harm, brother, truly," he insisted.

Cortez put up a hand to wave off Andres' usual volume of excuses. "I grow weary of your denials," he snapped. "One more wink, one more lascivious comment, and I will make it so that no woman finds you attractive ever again. Do I make myself clear? Lady Diamantha is *my* wife, Andres, and you will show her all due respect. She is not a trollop for you to toy with."

Humiliated, and angry, Andres nodded his head once, sharply. He wouldn't look at his brother. Cortez's gaze lingered on him a moment, hoping he wouldn't have to make good on his threat to maim him. Not that he would, but he would certainly give him a beating he would not soon forget. Wanting off the uncomfortable subject, Cortez turned in the direction of the adjoining room where Sophie was playing with her pets. He pointed at the little girl.

"You will remain with Lady Sophie while her mother and I go into town to purchase a few items," he said. "Order a meal and feed her sup. We will return shortly."

Andres was stricken. "*Watch* the little girl?" he repeated. "I know nothing of little girls!"

Diamantha wasn't so sure she wanted to leave her daughter with Andres given the conversation Cortez had just had with the man. She put her hand on Cortez's arm.

"We do not have to shop, truly," she assured him. "I will be just as happy remaining here, eating sup, and going to bed early. I am quite weary."

Cortez looked at her, appearing a bit crestfallen. "Are you certain?" he sounded as if he was pleading. "We will not be too long. Andres is perfectly trustworthy to watch over the child."

Diamantha simply shook her head and went back into the room where her daughter was. Disappointed, Cortez's gaze lingered on her for a moment, quite certain her response was because of Andres' behavior. She didn't trust the man and he didn't blame her, not in the least. Knowing that there was probably no way to convince her otherwise, he snapped his finger at his brother and pointed to the chamber door. Andres gladly took the hint and quit the room. As the man fled down the narrow hall, Cortez turned to Diamantha.

"I will have food sent up to you," he said. "I will post a guard outside should you need anything."

Diamantha, sitting on the bed beside her daughter, looked up at him. "Where are you going?"

Cortez jerked his head in the direction of the street outside. "To hell, more than likely, but that is a discussion for another time," he quipped, watching her smirk. "I will return, Lady de Bretagne."

Before Diamantha could press him, he fled, leaving her in the two tiny rooms with her daughter's pets running wild around the floor. When the meal was brought up a short while later, it was a feast of shredded pork, brown rye bread, beans and mushrooms stewed together, small green apples, pears, and figs with honey. Diamantha and the kittens ate the pork, the rabbit had a pear, the fox kit enjoyed both the pork and the apples, while Sophie exclusively ate the figs and honey until she was close to bursting.

There was a bath after supper as well. A big, burly man who wore a patch over one eye brought up a tub that was the bottom half of a barrel, lined with linen. There were three soldiers guarding the room and they helped the innkeeper and the burly man fill the tub with steaming water. Once the tub was filled and everyone had cleared the room, Diamantha went to her satchel and pulled out clean clothing and toiletries for her and her daughter.

Stripping Sophie of her little dress, her shift, her under clothing and hose, she plopped the girl into the warm bath, stripped down herself, and climbed in with her. Hair piled on top of her head to keep it out of the bathwater, Diamantha soaped her daughter's skin and hair as the little girl played in the bath, rinsing everything clean in the soothing and warm water.

With the small, flickering hearth as a backdrop, Diamantha used the hard rose-scented soap to wash away two days of travel, her thoughts lingering on everything that had happened since they had started their great questing to find Robert's body. It was odd how her existence at Corfe seemed like a lifetime ago. She found herself wondering how George was faring. She thought on the servants she'd left behind, women who had been with her for years. She missed them and their gossipy ways.

It was beginning to occur to her that this trip was going to take a very long time, much longer than she had conceived of in her own mind. Truth, she had traveled a great way once, those years ago when she left Northumberland and traveled to Dorset for her wedding. It had been a very long journey, but this time, things were different. She had such trepidation in her heart, trepidation that they wouldn't find Robert... and even more that they would. She was coming to wonder what she had gotten herself into, but there was no turning back. She had to push on.

The water eventually cooled and she pulled Sophie out of the tub, drying the now-sleeping little girl. Sophie whined as her mother dried her hair vigorously next to the fire, combing it out and braiding it tightly for sleep. She put the child in a heavy woolen sleeping shift and by the time she put the girl in bed, Sophie was nearly asleep. But not quite, her animals were on the bed, sleeping in a pile, and she wanted them to sleep with her, so Diamantha moved the pile of baby animals next to Sophie and covered everyone up. Soon enough, Sophie was fast asleep with her menagerie snuggled up against her.

Diamantha moved back into the other room to prepare for her own sleep. She had donned a heavy linen sleeping shift with great belled sleeves and a hood and put a pair of soft doeskin slippers on her feet. She opened the door and asked the soldiers to remove the now-cold bath, standing aside as they moved in to collect it. When they had left, she shut the door but didn't bolt it, knowing Cortez would soon return. She found that she was anticipating it as nervously as a virgin bride.

Seated on the floor in front of the hearth, she unbraided her hair and began to brush it, all the while staring dreamily into the flames. Visions of Corfe passed before her eyes, of Robert, and of the last day she ever saw him alive. It had been so hard to let him go. It was still hard to let him go, but let him go she must. It was time for her to move on because lingering on Robert's memory was damaging her somehow, weakening her, and she could not do that to herself. Cortez was her husband now and he was offering her a new life, a good life, if she would only accept it and stop acting foolishly.

Now, she knew she had to accept it. She could no longer dwell in the sad halls of grief. When Cortez returned tonight, she would give herself over to him as a wife should, and she would allow Cortez to wipe away Robert's memory from her body and replace it with his own. The scent of Robert would be washed away by Cortez, the feel of his flesh upon hers, the feel of his body within hers. It had been so long since she'd felt a man between her legs that the mere thought made her shudder. Robert had been capable of bringing a scream to her lips. She wondered if Cortez could do the same.

As she sat there on the floor, gazing into the mesmerizing flames, the hairbrush came to a halt as she thought of Robert's great manhood as it plunged into the folds of her body. The man had been very fond of her breasts, suckling her nipples hungrily when they made love, and her free hand came up to touch her breast, toying with a nipple as Robert used to do. But somehow, as she touched herself, Robert's face became Cortez. She pinched her nipple, closing her eyes in lust and ecstasy as she imagined what it would be like for Cortez to suckle her nipples. She wondered what it would be like for him to gently push her legs apart and impale her with his big, powerful body. She was so caught up in her fantasy that she nearly jumped out of her skin when someone knocked softly on the chamber door.

Diamantha jerked her hand away from her breast as Cortez quietly opened the chamber door, shutting it gently behind him and bolting it. Standing up to face him, she hoped he wouldn't see how breathless she was.

"Greetings," he said as his face came into the light. "Have you eaten?"

Diamantha nodded, struggling to calm her racing heart. "I have," she answered. "I ate with Sophie. She is sleeping now."

Cortez nodded, sticking his head into the smaller chamber to see that Sophie was, indeed, sleeping the sleep of the dead. He also noticed the empty cage.

"Where are her pets?" he asked.

"In bed, with her."

Satisfied that the girl was safe and warm, and the pets were also, he turned back to Diamantha.

"I am sorry it took so long to return," he said. "Were you waiting up for me?"

Diamantha grinned. "Who else would I be waiting for?"

Cortez returned her grin, rather flattered by her teasing answer. "Me, I had hoped," he confirmed. Then, he pointed at the bed. "Please, be seated. I have a story to tell you."

Obediently, Diamantha sat on the small bed, hardly big enough for the two people who were going to soon be sleeping on it. She looked up expectantly at Cortez, who seemed strangely nervous. He was dressed for travel, in his mail coat, tunic and breeches, with his big broadsword strapped to his side. He began to fidget with his broadsword, unfastening it from his waist.

"As you know, I wanted to purchase a wedding ring for you," he said as he pulled at the sword. "When I went back into the town tonight, most of the merchants were closing down as Matins approached. However, I found one merchant who seemed willing to do business, even in the face of sin. Of course, it helped when I put a gold crown into his hand simply as an incentive to let me look his wares over."

Diamantha giggled. "You bribed the man to risk his immortal soul?"

Cortez nodded. "It was either bribe him or beat him," he said, a twinkle in the dark eyes. "He took the bribe."

Diamantha couldn't fault the man his determination. "I see," she said. "Continue with your story. I am growing intrigued."

He could see the mirth in her eyes as he went on. "The man had any and all manner of goods," he said. "I looked at his cookware and jars, but thought that would not be a good wedding gift. Nothing says 'thank you for becoming my wife' better than an iron pot and, by the way, go cook my supper, you silly wench."

Diamantha's giggles increased. He was a very animated and humorous story teller. "You didn't get one for me, did you?"

Cortez was starting to chuckle, laughing because she was. She had such charming laughter.

"Nay, I did not, but I will admit I was tempted," he pretended to warn her as he continued. "I looked at fabric, wooden dogs, and small houses for birds. Then, I finally told him why I was there and he pulled out a vast array of jewelry. It would seem the man has family in Rome, and they send him valuable things to sell. He had a great array of Roman jewelry, things I had never seen before. When I told him I wanted to purchase a wedding ring, he presented me with what the Romans used to call a Posey Ring. It was odd, truly. The moment he showed the ring to me, I knew it was meant for you. It looked like something you should wear. In fact, I told him I would take it before I looked at anything else, so strongly did I feel about it. But then he showed me the inscription on the inside of the band. And that is when I knew... it was divine providence, my lady. That ring spoke to me and told me that it belonged to you. To *us.* So I bought it."

By now, Diamantha's giggles had faded because he seemed so serious. He seemed almost philosophical and mystical about the ring and she was growing increasingly eager to see it. Before she could ask, he dug into his scabbard and pulled forth a tiny silk pouch. Opening the pouch, he pulled out a band of dark gold. Then he sat on the bed beside her, holding the ring up in the dim light.

"You see this?" he asked, pointing to the exterior of the rather wide band. "There are flowers worked all around the band. That is why it is called a Posey Ring; it was an engagement ring of sorts, when young Roman men would purchase these rings for the women they loved in the hopes that the women would marry them. Posey Rings were meant for young women who loved flowers, considered a very feminine and fertile symbol. But this ring has something more, it has an inscription on the inside. The young man who had this ring made for his ladylove was a determined young man, indeed."

Diamantha was fascinated by the wide gold band with its array of intricate flowers all around it. It was truly a lovely piece. "Why?" she asked, gazing at the band. "What does the inscription say?"

Cortez turned it sideways, pointing at the Latin writing on the inside of the band. "It says *quaerenti tibi est.*"

"What does that mean?"

He took her left hand and sliding the ring down over her third finger. It was a snug fit, but not too snug. In fact, it was rather perfect. Then he looked up, gazing into her miraculous dual-colored eyes.

"It means *my quest is you*," he said softly. "The young man who had this ring made must have been pursuing his young lady rather strongly, much as I have been pursing you. *My quest is you.* But more than that, you and I are on a quest to find Robert. It could also mean that your quest *is* Robert. But I like to look at it from my perspective. My quest is you, Lady Diamantha. Now do you see why I had to have it?"

Diamantha was astonished. She held the ring up, looking so lovely on her slender finger, her wide-eyed gaze moving between the ring and Cortez. "It truly says that?"

"Truly."

She looked at the ring again, admiring the craftsmanship. "That is truly one of the most remarkable stories I have ever heard," she said, duly impressed. "What a story it will be to tell our children."

He just sat there, watching her as she looked at the ring. Then, he scratched his neck rather awkwardly. "As things stand, the event of children would be something of a miracle."

She looked up at him curiously. "What do you mean?"

He cocked an eyebrow. "Children are not born when two people merely sit on a bed as we are," he said, somewhat ironically. "There has to be a little more to it."

Diamantha should have been embarrassed by his inference of the lack of intimacy between them but she wasn't. He was correct. With a grin, she looked back at her ring.

"Ah, yes," she said, nodding knowingly. "We may have to actually make more of an effort."

"My thoughts exactly."

"It is also true that this is not a legitimate marriage until we consummate it."

"That is my feeling as well."

"Then mayhap we should get on with it."

Cortez was careful in his reply. "I do not want to force you to do something you are not ready to do," he said quietly. "We have only been married for two days, and we have only been re-acquainted with each other for three."

She looked at him as if scrutinizing him. "Is this the same Cortez de Bretagne who charged into George's solar to inform me that I was to be his bride?"

"The same."

"Yet your forcefulness has significantly diminished," she noted, feigning suspicion. "Why?"

He sighed faintly and looked away. "You are my wife now," he said, trying to explain something he didn't quite understand himself. "I suppose in my own way I am trying to be considerate of you. It is not easy for me, I assure you. It is my desire to have my way in all things. I have already forced you into a marriage you did not want. I do not want to push you into other things to the point that you would hate me for it. That is not how I wish for our marriage to be."

Diamantha studied his masculine profile, his comely good looks. She was starting to see much more to the man than just his handsome features. She was coming to see that beneath that selfish exterior lay a man of feeling and of compassion. A truly selfish man would not have backed away from his pursuit, leading her to understand that perhaps Cortez was not as selfish as he believed himself to be. He had the capacity to put others first, which was a rare commodity.

"How do you wish it to be?" she asked softly.

He shrugged, looking at his hands as he leaned forward, elbows resting on his knees. "My parents were quite fond of each other," he said. "Helene and I were quite fond of each other. I was hoping you and I would be the same."

Diamantha watched the man for a moment before reaching out and grasping his hand gently. Startled by the gesture, Cortez immediately clasped her hand, sitting up to look at the woman, wondering why she had impulsively touched him. He had hope that it was because she wanted to and when he saw her expression, gentle and kind, optimism burst in his chest. Could it be possible that she had finally accepted him, that he had finally overcome some sort of barrier between them? Had his patience come to fruition? God's Bones, he hoped so. He fervently hoped so. Then, he did the only thing he could think to do. He leaned forward and slanted his warm lips hungrily over hers.

My quest is you.

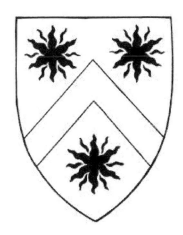

CHAPTER TWELVE

Diamantha could only feel unadulterated lust and passion as Cortez kissed her deeply. Being that she was not a maiden, his attentions did not frighten her. In fact, they seemed to kindle something deep within her, something hot and liquid that seemed to be begging to be unleashed. For the first few moments of Cortez's kiss, she didn't respond. She simply sat there and let him take the lead, allowing herself to become accustomed to his taste and scent. But once she'd experienced the first few moments of the man, she knew she had to have more.

Her hands came up, timidly touching his face, and that seemed to further ignite her. When she realized that Cortez had a wildly intoxicating taste, she began to take the offensive, snaking her tongue into the man's mouth and listening to him groan with pleasure. They were losing themselves in each other, one becoming bonded to the other as they had never experience with anyone else. It was lust beyond lust, and hunger beyond hunger. Just as Diamantha began to immerse herself in all that was Cortez, he suddenly leapt to his feet.

"My armor," he breathed heavily. "Help me with it, please."

Nodding unsteadily, for she was fairly breathless herself, Diamantha stood up next to him and helped him remove his tunic, mail coat, and padded undertunic. When the latter came off, exposing his muscular chest, Diamantha could feel the heat of desire flushing her veins. It made her knees feel weak. She stood back and watched him as he sat on the bed and practically ripped his boots free from his feet and then finally pulled free his breeches.

The man was quickly naked, standing before her in all of his smoldering glory. Diamantha could see that he was already aroused, his male member thick and large. She could only imagine what it would feel like within her and with that thought, it was as if she had no control over her actions. Something wild and uninhibited took over, and she let it. She no longer harbored resistance or reluctance towards Cortez. Now, she wanted him. She wanted him very badly and there was nothing left to stop her.

Dropping to her knees in front of him, she took his throbbing maleness into her hands and fondled it gently. It was soft and warm and stiff. As Cortez groaned and wound his fingers into her hair, she took his member into her mouth, suckling on it as she used to do with Robert, only this time, there was something more to it. She had to admit that there was something much more to this tasting than there had ever been with Robert. Perhaps it was lust alone, perhaps not. In any case, she was drunk with it. Using her mouth, she plunged down on Cortez's manhood, suckling it enough to cause the man to tremble. She continued to suckle him even as he pulled the shift from her body, leaving her naked and on her knees in front of him. But she didn't care, all that mattered was the wildfire of passion raging out of control within her.

Diamantha manipulated Cortez until the man couldn't take it anymore. Swiftly, he picked her up and put her on the bed, but she ended up on her belly. It didn't matter to Cortez. He fell on top of her, sinking his teeth into the soft flesh of her shoulder as his hands snaked underneath her, fondling her soft, full breasts. Using a free hand, he reached down and pulled her thighs apart, wedging his big body in between them. The same hand moved to the fluff of dark curls between her legs and he began to stroke her, realizing she was already wet and ready to receive him. Waiting no longer, he thrust into her, long and hard, from behind.

Diamantha groaned with utter pleasure, stifling her cries in the pillow as Cortez thrust deep. His heated body was all round her, his hands on her breasts, as he plunged repeatedly into her quivering body. She could feel his fullness as it built up that exquisite friction that would culminate in a burst of ecstasy rolling through her body, tremors without end, pleasure personified. She'd never known lovemaking like this in her life, something so emotionally and physically powerful that it literally consumed her. As Cortez drove his body into hers, she had to put her hands out to brace herself, preventing him from ramming her head into the wall next to the bed.

Cortez's powerful rhythm was unstoppable and it threatened to bring Diamantha to her peak faster than she had ever achieved it. She could feel the glow beginning, that marvelous sunburst looming, but just as she neared the peak, Cortez swiftly withdrew and flipped her over onto her back. Settling himself between her legs, he thrust into her again as his powerful arms went around her.

Warmth. Comfort. Desire. Diamantha was incoherent with lust and pleasure as Cortez held her tightly. Her physical reaction to him was astounding but it was also her mind that was responding, accepting his domination without hesitation as her hands on his buttocks encouraging him to go deeper. Within the first few powerful strokes, the glow in her loins swelled to bursting and she cried out softly as her body convulsed with passion. Cortez, feeling her climax as it throbbed around his manhood, thrust himself as deeply as he could go into her sweet body and joined her in her pleasure.

But it didn't stop there. He continued to move within her, feeling his hot seed as it made her so very slick and wet. His hands were all over her, touching her silken flesh, as his lips moved along her jawline. After the lust and fire had died down, there was genuine warmth and tenderness now as Cortez shifted to take his body weight off of her, his arms still holding her close. Diamantha was so overwhelmed that it was difficult for her to catch her breath. She had no idea she could respond to a man, any man, as she had responded to Cortez. There was some fear there, perhaps. Cortez had a good deal of control over her and didn't even realize it.

As Diamantha stared up at the ceiling and struggled with her thoughts, a tender hand cupped her face and Cortez softly kissed her cheek.

"Are you well?" he whispered.

She nodded, turning her head to look at him. "Are you?"

He grinned, that glorious gesture that had sent many a female heart to swooning. "I believe I am," he murmured. "Are... are you sure you are well?"

She nodded again. "Why do you ask?"

He lifted his eyebrows, unsure how to put his thoughts into words. "Well...," he said, paused, then continued. "It was rather... and the bed is small. Did you hit your head?"

She smiled faintly. "I did not," she said. "But I thank you for asking."

"You are welcome."

"I believe our marriage is valid now."

"It most certainly is."

She laughed softly, as did he. But he sobered, gazing into her features, a thousand thoughts racing through his mind. But he would not voice them. He wasn't even sure where to start. All he knew was that somehow, someway, the act of intercourse with his new wife had changed him. He felt different inside as he looked at her, but it wasn't anything he could put his finger on. Therefore, it was best not to say anything or risk frightening her. He'd never forgive himself if he did that, delicate creature that she was.

Carefully, he shifted so he was off her completely, wedging his big body against the wall. Reaching down, he pulled up the coverlet, covering them both up in the chill of the room. His arms were still around her as he snuggled down into the bed, pulling her close. Her body, soft and supple, didn't resist. She moved in closer still against his warmth. Sleep eventually claimed them both in one of the best, most restful sleeps either one of them had ever had.

From that day forward, the situation between them was never the same again as the memory of Robert Edlington slipped further and further away. He was no longer the obstacle that had kept them apart. Now, he was that which had brought them together. Things were changing, indeed.

My quest is you.

ᵹ

Almondsbury, Berkeley, Gloucester.

It was a steady stream of interesting and bustling towns they passed through, especially Gloucester, which was very large and had a massive cathedral in the middle of it. Rather than skirt the city, as Cortez had done with Almondsbury and Berkeley, he took his party into Gloucester because they were running low on some supplies and needed to restock. He sent James and Oliver out to scout merchants willing to sell them large quantities of flour, salt, and ground oats while he found a place for the party to rest near Gloucester cathedral.

It had rained heavily the day before on their trip past Berkeley but this day was bright and sunny, with wispy clouds overhead. The wind had picked up and it was gusty at times, blowing things around the wagons that weren't tied down. One of the things it blew around was the oiled tarp that had been rigged over Sophie's play area, so eventually, Andres pulled it down. Sophie and her caged animals didn't seem to mind.

Sophie had been inordinately good to travel with. As long as she had her poppet, Rosie, her pets at arm's length, and a view of General as he plodded along behind the wagon, she was as happy as a lark. As the group waited for James and Oliver to return, Diamantha climbed off her palfrey and went to sit in the back of the wagon with her daughter. Sophie immediately climbed on her mother's lap, and the two of them sat together and petted the baby rabbit, who was growing steadily. Clover the bunny had quite a diet of greens along the road as the men would grasp great handfuls of grass and clover, and then hand it over to Sophie for her pets. As a result, the little bunny looked like a furry round ball.

So they lingered away the morning because it took a couple of hours for James and Oliver to return with great sacks of flour and salt tied across their saddles. Quickly, the soldiers moved in and began to untie them, shuttling everything over to the quartermaster so the man could take an inventory. Meanwhile, Sophie had grown restless so Diamantha put the rabbit back into the cage, put the cage beneath the wagon bench for some shade against the sun, and pulled her daughter out of the back of the wagon.

It was time for the child to stretch her legs before they continued along their way. However, the moment Diamantha put Sophie on her feet, the little girl ran off. Diamantha scurried after her with Andres following close behind.

Although Cortez's brother wasn't in charge of watching his brother's new wife, he happened to be the closest, so he followed. Even though he was still stinging from his brother's lecture back in Bath, he wasn't so stung that he was negligent. His knightly instincts were strong. He thought he should follow just to make sure the women didn't come to any harm and perhaps in that small action, he might win his brother's trust where it pertained to Diamantha. It was a thought he'd had, anyway. Even if his brother *had* been right about the flirting, still, Andres thought to redeem himself.

As Andres lagged behind, Sophie ran down the avenue, gleeful that she was free as Diamantha called after her to stop running. The commotion caught Cortez's attention, as he had been discussing supplies with the quartermaster, so he begged a moment from the man and followed his wife, daughter, and his brother as the three of them moved down the avenue towards the city's center.

It was a busy day with many people out and about, conducting business. Diamantha caught up to the giggling Sophie before she could reach the busy hive of the city center, and she swung the little girl around a couple of times, listening to her laugh. Diamantha nibbled on her daughter's cheek, teasing her sweetly, and was about to turn around and head back to the traveling party when she caught a glimpse of scaffolding on the eastern part of the square.

Holding Sophie on her hip, Diamantha shaded her eyes from the sun as she gazed across the crowds at the scaffold in the distance. There was also a good deal of smoke coming up from an area directly beside the scaffold, but she couldn't see the source. The crowd blocked her complete view. From the corner of her eye, she noticed Andres coming up beside her.

"What is that?" she asked Andres, pointing at the scaffold.

Andres strained to get a good look at it. His eyesight wasn't too terribly good at a distance so it took him a moment to discern the image.

"A scaffold, my lady," he said.

She looked at him. "A scaffold for what?"

"Punishment," Cortez said as he walked up on her other side. "Scaffolds are usually built for things like executions or public punishment."

Diamantha knew that, or at least the general theory. She'd never actually seen an execution or public punishment. She looked at Cortez.

"You are the Sheriff of the Shire in Sherborne," she said. "Have you used scaffolds like that?"

Cortez nodded. "I have."

Diamantha looked back at the scaffold thoughtfully. Then she pointed at the smoke rising from beside it. "What is the smoke from?"

Cortez could see partially see where the smoke was originating. "A fire."

"A fire for what?"

"It looks as if they have a large iron cauldron on to boil."

Diamantha fell silent, pondering his answer, but Cortez and Andres understood what the boiling cauldron meant. Cortez purposely didn't elaborate. In fact, he thought it would be best for them to leave the area and be along their way. Whatever was about to happen, he didn't want Diamantha witnessing it. He went to take her arm to lead her away, but she was distracted by men climbing onto the big wooden scaffold.

"Look," she said. "Men have mounted the scaffold. Do you think something is going to happen?"

Cortez and Andres looked around, noticing the increased crowd of people in the city center. In fact, people were wandering in from other avenues, converging on the center which was really nothing more than a well and a vast, muddy parcel. There were also several soldiers bearing the yellow and red colors of the Earl of Gloucester milling about. Indeed, something seemed to be stirring. They could feel it in the air.

"Mayhap," Cortez said, eyeing the crowd that seemed to be restless. He took hold of Diamantha's elbow, more firmly this time. "Come along. We should be on our way."

Diamantha didn't argue with him. In fact, she actually turned to follow him. But a roar from the crowd captured her attention and she instinctively looked to see what had everyone yelling.

Emerging from one of the wider avenues that joined to the city square was an open wagon being driven by two soldiers wearing Gloucester yellow and red. The wagon was also flanked by several soldiers as it began to make its way around the square. It was a slow and somber procession, and people were yelling at the passengers in the wagon, hollering most angrily.

It was a curious sight and as the wagon headed in their direction, making the rounds, James and Oliver came to stand beside Andres. They, too, had heard the yelling and came to see what the fuss was about. James shielded his eyes from the sun as he watched the wagon approach.

"We heard about this when we were purchasing stores," he muttered to Andres. "It was all anyone could speak of."

Diamantha heard him. She looked over at James. "What do you mean?" she asked. "What is happening?"

James looked at her but his gaze moved to Cortez for a moment, lingering on the man, before answering. It seemed as if he was reluctant to spill the information even though he had brought up the subject. He cleared his throat nervously as he looked at Diamantha.

"Well," he said hesitantly, scratching his neck. "It would seem that there is to be an execution."

Diamantha cocked her head. "Do you know who they are executing?"

By this time, the wagon bearing the Gloucester soldiers was nearly upon them and as it made a right turn for the scaffolding, Diamantha and the others could clearly see the passengers of the back of the wagon. A woman was weeping hysterically, dressed in tatters and chained to the side of the wagon, while beside her were two young girls, also in tatters and sobbing. Diamantha's brow furrowed, first in concern and then in outrage. She pointed to the wagon as it made its way towards the distant scaffold.

"*Who* is that?" she demanded to anyone who could answer her. "That was a woman and two children. What have they done?"

James had no choice but to tell her what he had heard. He knew he was going to get a tongue lashing from Cortez, however, simply by the way the man was looking at him.

"We heard that the woman in the wagon is a former governess for the Earl of Gloucester," he said. "Evidently, she had been engaged to tend the earl's new babies, twin boys. But the boys died and the woman was convicted of poisoning them. She is slated to die along with her two daughters."

Diamantha's mouth popped open in shock and outrage. "But why the daughters?" she wanted to know. "Surely they are not guilty of poisoning babies. They are but babies themselves!"

Cortez put his hands on her shoulders, trying to turn her around to leave the scene. "Who is to say what the evidence was?" he said calmly. "We do not know all of the facts. In any case, we must be on our way. There is nothing we can do here."

Diamantha, however, would not be pushed around, not after what she had just seen. She pulled away from Cortez and looked at him. "Those girls were not much older than Sophie," she said, rather heatedly. "I cannot imagine they are guilty of anything."

Cortez sighed faintly, regretful that she was working herself up over something they had no control over. "Mayhap not," he said. "But we cannot do anything for them. It would be best if we left."

That wasn't the answer Diamantha was looking for. With Sophie still on her hip, she began to march in the direction of the scaffolding to gain a better look. Cortez, shaking a balled fist at James for telling Lady de Bretagne what he had heard, followed swiftly. The knights trailed after him. Cortez caught up to Diamantha in short order and grasped her by the arm, halting her forward momentum.

"Diamantha, please," he said quietly. "There is nothing you can do and you are only going to get yourself more upset if you witness this. Please come with me now."

Diamantha was deeply upset. "But... but those babies surely could not have done anything wrong," she insisted. "Why must they die with their mother?"

Cortez had her with both hands as Andres, Oliver, and James crowed up around them. They were trying to herd her back in the direction they had come, trying to block her view. They didn't want the scene with her to grow out of control, at least not in public. They didn't want to attract attention.

"Because that is what the law has decided," Cortez told her the basic facts. "If the woman was found to have poisoned the sons of the earl, then her children must have been found guilty along with her. You cannot change this, sweetheart. Please come with me now."

Diamantha simply didn't understand. Her world, for so long, had been protected and safe at Corfe. It was all she had ever known. Now, the ugly truths of the world at large were at hand and it was difficult for her to comprehend.

"But...," she began, having difficulty grasping the situation. "But this cannot be possible. You should demand they stop this immediately and then we will speak with Gloucester to see what really happened. Mayhap he is mistaken and simply doesn't realize it."

She was so naïve. Cortez shook his head. "I cannot and will not interfere in the man's business," he said, his voice low. "Come with me, now. I beg you"

The sounds of the crowd were growing louder and everyone turned to see the woman and her two small daughters being brought up to the scaffold. The little girls were crying, trying to cling to their mother, but being pulled roughly away by Gloucester soldiers. It was then that Diamantha caught sight of the cauldron Cortez had mentioned. There was great flame all around it as it sat at the base of the scaffolding and steam poured from the cauldron itself.

There was something cooking in the cauldron, boiling rapidly and hotly. As her gaze absorbed the scene, a horrific thought occurred to her. Diamantha turned to Cortez with an expression of shocked realization. *Dear God... it couldn't be....*

"What is that cauldron for?" she asked, her voice oddly hoarse.

Cortez didn't want to tell her. He sighed heavily, running a weary hand over his forehead in a hesitant gesture.

"Diamantha, please," he begged. "Let us leave now, I implore you."

"*What* is it for?"

He paused another moment, reflecting on his options. He had none. When he spoke, it was with the greatest reluctance.

"It is the instrument of execution," he told her quietly. "Death by boiling is the usual sentence for those convicted of poisoning."

It was as she had suspected. Sickened, Diamantha opened her mouth to say something when a horrific scream filled the air. Startled, she turned just in time to see a Gloucester soldiers throw the smallest of the two girls into the boiling pot. The mother screamed, the other daughter did the same, but the little girl in the pot didn't die immediately. Her weak cries filled the air for a few seconds, eventually fading away as the crowd cheered wildly.

It was the most horrible sound imaginable and Diamantha staggered. She had Sophie in her arms still and she clasped her hand over her daughter's head, forcing the little head down onto her shoulder and covering her ears as best she could. When she turned to Cortez, it was with tears streaming down her face.

"Get me out of here," she hissed. "Get me out of here *now*."

Cortez didn't hesitate. He whisked her away, back towards the avenue that held their traveling party, with his knights closing ranks around them. They practically ran the entire way back to the wagons where Cortez helped Diamantha and Sophie up into Sophie's padded little corner. Diamantha crawled all the way to the front of the wagon bed, beneath the bench, and huddled up there with her child. She wouldn't even look at Cortez. As he turned away from the wagon to get the troops moving, he could hear her deep sobs.

The sound nearly broke his heart.

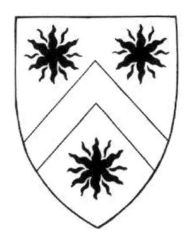

CHAPTER THIRTEEN

Norton. Droitwich. Bromgrove. Bloxwich. Penkridge.

They were just some of the towns Cortez's party had passed through, small bergs that were all beginning to look the same. After what happened in Gloucester, Diamantha wasn't so inclined to look upon any more towns with interest. In fact, her mood in general seemed to have dampened as the days passed and the party moved north.

It wasn't so much in her actions or words, because those seemed normal enough, but Cortez could see something in her eyes that had dimmed. It was difficult to describe any more than that. The battle with the sheriff in Shaftesbury followed by the execution in Gloucester had given the woman two instances of the brutalities of life that, thus far, she'd been relatively immune to sequestered and protected at Corfe as she had been. Now, she was starting to understand the hardships people faced, and the dangers, but it was only going to get worse.

It started innocently enough as they left the village of Penkridge on a gloomy morning. It was a morning like any other morning, with a hearty breakfast of porridge and dried figs and then everyone packing their bedrolls, heading out as the sun began to crest over the eastern horizon. Their destination that night was Cortez's father's castle just outside of the city of Stafford, and everyone was looking forward to a great feast and the warm hospitality that Gorsedd de Bretagne was known to provide.

Diamantha in particular was looking forward to the safety and comfort that a castle could provide. She'd never realized how much she missed it until she'd been forced to sleep in smelly hostels and in damp tents for the past several days. It was another part of this quest that she hadn't fully understood before the undertaking and she was coming to realize that she didn't like the world as a whole. It was frightening and brutal. It had to be experienced to be believed.

Bundled up against the mist and cold, Sophie had a bit of the sniffles this morning so Diamantha rode in the wagon bed with her daughter, keeping her warm and dry, entertaining her by putting pieces of straw through the cage and teasing the kittens with it. Just as the group moved to the city limit, a town sentry approached them with a lifted hand. Cortez brought his column to a halt.

"M'lord!" the man called. "M'lord, wait!"

Dressed in his usual armor, including a heavy tunic and gloves to ward off the cold, Cortez leaned forward on his saddle.

"What's amiss?" he asked.

The old man wiped at his running nose as he approached. Then, he pointed off to the north.

"The River Penk has been flooding its banks since last spring," he said. "It's flooded out several villages to the north, so be careful as you go. You'll run into those willing to do anything to steal your food."

Cortez glanced at Andres to his left, implying coming trouble with his mere expression. "Are we to expect great bands of starving villagers or just a few armed men?" he asked.

The old man nodded. "Both," he said. "Proceed with caution, m'lord, at least until you get to Stafford. That'll be a day's ride at least with the road as bad as it is."

"Noted," Cortez said. "Thank you for the warning."

The old man backed off and let them pass. Cortez and the party moved off, but not before Cortez instructed each one of his foot soldiers to arm themselves with crossbows. Knights went into battle mode, removing their shields from the provisions wagon and slinging them over their left knee for quick access. Leaving James and Andres at point, Cortez made his way back to the wagon containing Diamantha and Sophie.

The oiled tarp was back up, providing adequate protection from the mist. He leaned over, peering over the edge of the tarp and looking in at the women as they huddled together, covered by a warm traveling blanket. When Diamantha looked up and saw him, he smiled.

"You appear to be sweet and cozy in there," he said.

Diamantha grinned as Sophie answered. "I'm playing with my kittens," she announced.

Cortez laughed softly. "I can see that," he said. "Those must be the happiest pets in all the land. They eat more than I do, they certain sleep more than I do, and they get to play with you all day long."

Sophie sneezed, evidence of her sniffles, but it didn't dampen her enthusiasm. "Come and play!"

Cortez shook his head. "Alas, I cannot, little chick," he said, his gaze lingering on Diamantha. "I came to tell you and your mother to stay in the wagon for now. Do not leave its safety."

Diamantha's smile faded. "Why?" she asked. "Is there trouble?"

He shrugged faintly. "There could be," he said. "I want to make sure you ladies are safe. You'll stay in here until I tell you otherwise. Understood?"

Diamantha nodded. "We will."

"Promise?"

"I do."

Cortez winked at her. "Thank you," he replied. "I shall return later."

He was gone, leaving Diamantha with some anxiety in her chest. *There could be trouble.* She wondered what he meant but after what happened at Gloucester, when she had peppered him with questions and only learned a terrible truth, she thought perhaps not to bother him with silly questions. She was coming to think that ignorance was sometimes the better partner in all of this. If there was trouble, maybe she didn't want to know everything about it.

So the party trudged on in the misty morning, listening to sheep in the distance, bleating through the fog. The road was very muddy, terribly so, and every dozen feet or so the wagon would get stuck in the dark, rich mud and a few soldiers would have to throw their backs into shoving it out of the hole. But Diamantha stayed true to her promise to remain in the wagon. She didn't try to get out and help the men when the wagon stuck. She held on to her daughter as the wagon lurched forward, again and again.

The morning seemed to be passing with painful slowness and with degrees of apprehension felt by all. None felt it more than Cortez. He rode point with his brother, watching the landscape through the mists, waiting for the hordes of starving to appear, flying out at them. Not only did the fog hide the dangers, but there were great clusters of trees smothering the road in places which simply made it worse. It was a cloying, terrible feeling.

He kept focused on the city of Stafford, which was less than a day's ride ahead of them. His father's castle was five miles to the west of Stafford and he was looking forward to seeing the man he hadn't seen in three years, not since his father had come for Helene's funeral. He was anxious for the man to meet Diamantha and Sophie, for his father had dearly wanted grandchildren and heirs. Now, there was the hope for some, at least with Cortez, With Andres, there was no telling if the man would ever marry.

With thoughts of his brother and his wild ways, Cortez glanced over his shoulder to see Andres riding a few feet away astride his big yellow charger. Remarkably, the man had kept out of the bottle since departing Sherborne and Cortez hoped it would remain that way. He had enough on his mind without having to worry about dragging his brother out of a gutter somewhere.

Andres must have sensed his brother's attention because he turned to look at him, the visor down on his helm. When he realized Cortez was indeed gazing at him, he flipped the visor up.

"What is it?" he asked. "Why are you looking at me?"

Cortez shrugged, turning his attention back to the road. "I was simply wondering when, or if, you were ever going to marry," he said. "We will be seeing Father tonight and you know he will ask you that question. You had better have an answer that pleases him."

Andres sighed heavily. "No answer I will give him short of telling him I am already married will please him," he said, disgruntled. "I wish he would stop harassing me about it."

Cortez smirked. "He is your father," he pointed out. "It is his duty to harass you about marriage. What about that lord's daughter you met at Sherborne Abbey last month? What is her name? Adaline?"

Andres shook his head. "Adaliza," he corrected. "She is far too young and far too rich. Her father would never approve of the match."

Cortez cast him a long glance. "How do you know?" he demanded. "Have you asked? Have you even tried?"

Andres wouldn't look at him. "Leave me alone or I shall go ride at the rear," he said. "I will not let you bully me. You have had two perfect wives and I've not even had one."

Cortez grinned, his thoughts now lingering on Diamantha. The past few days had been quite pleasant between them and although they'd not made love again after that wildfire of a night back in Bath, the manner between them had definitely changed. She was much more polite and sweet to him, and he in turn looked upon her with nothing less than stars in his eyes. He couldn't help it. Even now, simply thinking on her, all he could feel was unadulterated giddiness. It was marvelous.

"My wife says she has two sisters," he told him. "Mayhap they are not spoken for. Would you like for me to find out?"

Andres shook his head. "I will find my own wife, thank you," he said. "If your wife wants husbands for her sisters, then talk to de Winter. His father wants him married so badly that he has threatened to beat him if he is not wed by next year."

Cortez turned in the saddle, seeing that de Winter was riding mid-pack, stationed by the wagons for protection. He wriggled his dark eyebrows and turned around.

"His father is going to have a task ahead of him," he said. "As much as I revere Davyss de Winter, Drake may be able to best his father. If I were Father de Winter, I would think of another tactic."

Andres nodded in agreement but he wanted off the subject of why he was not yet married. Opening his mouth to broach an entirely new line of conversation, he suddenly caught sight of something coming through the fog. The mist had lifted slightly, giving them a much greater range of vision, and he spied something on the road ahead, lingering by the edge of the trees. His good humor fled.

"Cortez," he snapped, unsheathing his broadsword. "Look, up ahead by the trees. Do you see it?"

Cortez was instantly on alert, his sword coming forth because Andres had drawn his. He could see people, ahead on the road, and he turned to de Lohr, who was riding several feet behind him.

"Protect the wagons," he ordered. "Tell the men to be on the defensive."

James nodded shortly and spun his charger around, riding back through the ranks and delivering orders. The pace of the travel slowed as the men went into defensive mode but, gradually, they came upon the cluster of people lingering by the roadside.

Cortez lowered his sword as soon as they came into clear view. It was mostly children, with a few adults intermingled, and he could hear a baby crying. Although his sword was lowered, he still had it in his hand in case this was a ruse. As the party drew nearer and he could see all of the women and children, he was positive it was a ruse. He turned to his brother.

"Ride up there and drive them off," he rumbled. "I'll not have them distracting the men so their husbands can attack while my soldiers are focused elsewhere."

Andres nodded sharply and charged forward, heading straight for the gathering of women and children. Most of them scattered with the big charger bearing down on them but one small boy didn't move fast enough. The charger bumped the child and the lad went flying, literally sailing into the mud a few feet away. He landed heavily but unhurt, screaming his lungs out. Andres, undeterred, pointed a finger at the fragmented group.

"Be gone, all of you," he bellowed. "Be gone before I turn my men loose on you!"

What had started as pathetic begging had now turned into frightened screaming with a big angry knight in their midst. The women were wailing and so were the children. The little boy who had been bumped by the charger scrambled to his feet and ran off towards one of the women who happened to be holding a baby.

Andres continued to yell at them, trying to intimidate them, but they did nothing more than scatter around. No one made a serious attempt to leave. As the column drew close, the beggars tried to migrate in their direction and away from the bellowing knight, but Andres kept them herded away from the road as one would have herded sheep. Weeping and pleas filled the air.

Diamantha could hear them from where she was safely insulated in the wagon bed. In fact, she had been hearing the cries for a couple of minutes now and they were growing stronger by the second. Pulling Sophie off her lap, she set the little girl down on the cushions beneath the wagon bench and crept over to the edge of the oiled cloth to take a peek. Cortez had told her not to leave the wagon, and she would not. But she would take a look and see what the commotion was about. It was natural curiosity, especially when she could hear children.

The mist had dissipated somewhat and yellow streams of light began to poke through the clouds, illuminating patches of ground below. Diamantha could see a group of people several feet away and a big knight positioned between them and the road. It was clear that he was trying to keep the group at bay. Diamantha could see many women and children, all of them dressed in layers of tattered clothing, feet bound with cloth and not shoes, and no one had proper protection against the cold morning. Increasingly concerned, Diamantha captured Drake's attention.

"Sir Drake?" she called over to him. "What do those people want?"

Drake, helm on and visor down, turned his armor-clad head in the direction of the women and children. "Beggars," he said. "They've come to beg for our food and whatever else they can wrangle from us. Andres is trying to run them off."

There were some very little children among the group and after what she had seen in Gloucester, Diamantha was rather sensitive to small children in general. Her brow furrowed with concern.

"They look so poor and hungry," she said. "Is there something we can do for them?"

Drake shook his head. "We would go hungry ourselves if we did," he said. "There is so much need here that it would drain us quickly."

The procession was passing by the group now and Diamantha, peering out from the wagon, was in clear view of the beggars. When they saw her, they ignored Andres completely and began to wail in her direction. One of the women, a round female with a mass of red hair wrapped around the top of her head, risked the angry knight and ran in Diamantha's direction.

"M'lady!" she screamed. "Please, m'lady, help us! We've no crops, no food to eat! The children are starving, m'lady, *please!*"

Diamantha wasn't sure what to say. As the lady of Corfe, she was often in the position of helping those less fortunate and she had indeed on many occasion. It was difficult for her to refuse those in need of assistance. But her region was rich and fertile, and those in need were usually those from whom sickness had taken its toll, or perhaps widows and orphans who simply needed help. She'd never seen starving, destitute people like this, not ever. It was an entirely new level of poverty. Before she could answer, however, Drake cautioned her.

"We were warned about these people, my lady," he said quietly. "They will do anything they can to steal from us. It would be best if you sat back in the wagon until we have passed through this stretch. These may not be the only people we meet along this road."

Diamantha looked up at him. "Why do you say that?"

Drake flipped up his visor and scanned the landscape. "Because we were told that the river has been overflowing its banks since last spring," he said. "This area has evidently been devastated and there has been much robbing and looting because of it."

The group was following Diamantha at a distance. As her wagon moved down the road, they followed like a herd of cattle following a source of food. She drew them to her with her beauty and health and radiance. In her, they must have seen hope. Perhaps they saw their only salvation. In any case, the group was following, begging her for help.

Cortez could hear the cries, of course, and he turned to see Diamantha looking out from her wagon at the people along the road. The least bit annoyed that she was not seated back in the wagon, sheltered from the outside world, he reined his charger around and

185

thundered back through the column. The charger kicked up mud clods as he reined the excited animal next to the moving wagon.

"Get back under the tarp," he told her quietly. "We have a few more hours of travel before we reach Stafford."

Diamantha looked at him seriously. "But these people," she said, indicating the wailing group. "They're starving, Cortez. I cannot look into the face of need and ignore it. Isn't there something we can do for them?"

Cortez shook his head firmly. "We do not have any to spare," he told her. "If we feed them, my men go hungry. Your daughter goes hungry. Who would you rather have hungry, those children out there or Sophie?"

It was a harsh way of putting it, but it was the truth. Diamantha's gaze moved over the group of beggars, hearing their sad cries. Particularly, she was looking at the children, skinny little waifs who were filthy and cold. She could see even from a distance that they had pale faces with even paler lips. They were the color of the mists, these children who were so hungry and so desperate. Greatly saddened, she turned back to Cortez.

"But those children...," she began, knowing he was more than likely going to deny her again. "They are starving. We picked up sacks of oats in Gloucester. Could we not cook a big pot for them to eat? It would be something and it would not drain all of our stores."

Cortez sighed heavily. "Diamantha, I realize you feel great compassion for them and it is an admirable quality, but we simply cannot spare anything," he said, trying to be patient with her. He thought pragmatically and she did not. "I would like nothing better than to feed the world's starving children, but not at the expense of my men and not at the expense of you. Can you understand that?"

She wasn't happy with his answer so she simply looked away. Cortez, seeing that he had damaged her fragile sensibilities, leaned down in her direction.

"Diamantha?" he said quietly. "Please do not be angry with me. I understand what you are saying, truly I do, but I must make the choice between feeding my men and feeding these people because it will not stop with this group, I promise you. Like mice, once you feed one, the entire nation will come running and soon enough, I will have nothing for our people. Do you understand that?"

She did but she still didn't agree with him. "We have two kittens, a rabbit, and a fox kit that you happily feed," she said. "They are fed small apples and other things, and you do not complain. Are you telling me that these animals are worth feeding more than these people are?"

He grunted, hoping they weren't heading for an argument. Things had been so wonderful the past few days that he was loath to take backward steps in this relationship, but in this case, he had to stand his ground.

"They are tiny little animals that hardly eat anything at all," he said, his voice low. "Are you truly going to argue with me about this? Do you truly want to give these people our food so we will have nothing?"

She didn't, but there had to be a way to help. An idea popped into her head. "We will be stopping at your father's castle tonight, will we not?"

Cortez nodded. "We will."

"If we need our stores replenished, can we not do it there? Your father should be able to resupply us most adequately if we give these people some of our food."

He rolled his eyes unhappily. "I cannot depend on that," he said. "I have no idea what my father will have. If he has nothing, we will be in a good deal of trouble and our quest to reach Falkirk might be seriously delayed. Is that what you want?"

Of course it wasn't. Reluctantly, she shook her head and let the subject die. Or so Cortez thought. Reaching out, he gently touched her cheek, smiling at her when she looked up at him. With a wink, he turned his charger around and cantered back to the front of the column.

Diamantha, however, wasn't finished, not in the least. There were children starving just a few feet away from her and she couldn't sit by and do nothing about it. No matter what Cortez said, she had to do something, however small. She couldn't live with herself if she didn't.

Eyes on Cortez, and on Drake, who happened to be closest to her, she sank back beneath the oiled tarp to hide from view, but the truth was that she was about to do some reconnaissance in the wagon. As Sophie sniffled beside her, she began to dig around in the wagon bed, coming across bags of walnuts, of almonds, of pears, and of little green apples. Heaving the bag of apples into her lap, she opened up the sack and was pleased to note that there were several dozen apples nestled in the bag. It was perfect for her needs.

Pulling a couple of the apples forth, she handed them over to Sophie, who was thrilled with more food for her animals. With the bag in hand, she dragged it along with her across the wagon bed until she was once again just outside of the oiled tarp. Drake was next to the wagon, riding slightly head of her position with his attention on the beggars. Diamantha eyed the big knight for a moment, planning out her covert operation.

"Sir Drake?" she asked politely, pointing off to the east. "Could that possibly be more starving people over there?"

Drake turned his attention away from the beggars, and from her, to gaze off into the distance. As soon as he turned his head, Diamantha grabbed several apples and hurled them towards the beggars. She had good aim because one, two, and then five apples sailed over Drake's head and into the field beyond as de Winter searched for something on the horizon, something Lady de Bretagne had asked about, that didn't exist.

But he heard the apples sailing over his head and by the time she launched the fourth and fifth apple, he was looking around to see where the sound had come from. When he looked curiously to Diamantha, sitting near the side of the wagon bed, she was the picture of innocence.

"Did you hear something?" he asked.

Diamantha shook her head. "Only the beggars," she said evenly. "What did you hear?"

Drake wasn't sure. He looked around and could see the beggars in the field as they evidently collected something off the ground. He couldn't see what it was, but suddenly, the beggars were running after the convoy, shouting their pleas. They were holding out their hands and crying for something, something he couldn't quite make out.

It was odd, truly. Intensely curious, he watched the beggars for a moment but the minute he looked away, towards the front of the column, he heard those strange noises over his head again. This time, he was faster, and he turned towards the starving folk in time to see small projectiles flying through the air. He wasn't sure what they were or where they were coming from, but he had a suspicion. He returned his attention to Diamantha, who was looking quite innocuous as she sat at the side of the wagon bed. She even smiled at him, brightly, which led him to believe that she was up to no good. No woman smiled that way unless she was trying to hide something.

With a heavy sigh, Drake simply faced forward, listening to projectiles sailing over his head. He turned a blind eye to it, at least for the time being, because he knew the lady was simply trying to do something kind. He also knew she was disobeying her husband, which put him in a very bad spot. Out of the corner of his eye, he saw it when she dropped one of the small green apples she had been throwing at the starving peasants. He could hear the beggars, off to his left, as they squealed excitedly over the thrown fruit.

Unfortunately, he had to do something about it. If he didn't, Cortez would have his head. He took the chance of leaving his post and spurring his charger to the front. He came up behind Cortez and cleared his throat loudly.

"My lord?" he said.

Cortez turned around abruptly, seeing that Drake was right behind him. His brow furrowed. "Why did you leave your post?"

Drake was clearly reluctant to say anything but he knew he didn't have a choice. "Lady de Bretagne...," he trailed off for a moment but then started again, stronger this time. "Lady de Bretagne is doing what you told her not to do. You must understand that by telling you, I am damaging any trust I might have with her, but if I do not tell you, then I am assuming responsibility for her actions and risking your wrath. I am in a bad position, either way."

Cortez's dark eyes flickered a moment before looking back through the column to the wagons in the middle. As he watched, two small projectiles sailed into the air and out into the field below. The starving people were swarming on whatever it was. Stricken, he pointed to another projectile as it went sailing.

"What in the name of Great Bleeding Jesus is *that*?" he demanded. "What is she doing?"

Drake watched the man's irate face. "She is throwing apples to them, I believe," he said sympathetically. "One of the many bags of apples we have on the provisions wagons."

"Apples?" Cortez repeated, outraged. "I told her not to feed them. She is deliberately disobeying me."

Drake put up a hand to stop the man before he went charging back to the wagon, quite possibly to spank his wife. In a small way, perhaps he was saving Cortez's marriage because, as new as it was, it certainly couldn't take a husbandly beating.

"My lord, if you please," he said quickly, "as you know, my mother runs a great charity, one of the biggest in all of England. As a young lad, I was raised in the halls of The House of Hope, so I well understand the conviction and self-sacrifice it takes to impart benefits to the poor. My father often chided my mother about it, but the fact remained that he admired her a great deal for her selfless and compassionate nature. Don't you see? The world needs people like my mother and Lady de Bretagne, for they see beyond the poverty to the human need beneath. Your wife will not give away all of our food, as you asked, but one bag of apples... to us, it is a small thing, but to those people, it is their life right now. Isn't this the England you fight for? All people, not just the rich? We are all God's creatures, after all."

Cortez gave Drake a rather wry expression before rolling his eyes, perhaps with some defeat. "Who taught you that, de Winter?" he wanted to know. "Your mother? She made a fine sap out of you."

Drake grinned. "Mayhap she did," he said. "But I understand the compassion your wife is demonstrating. Mayhap you should try to as well."

Cortez looked over Drake's shoulder, watching the last few apples fly into the air, into the hands of those who would look upon it as a gift from God. Much of what Drake said held true. The man was right, in many aspects, and the anger Cortez had been feeling vanished in a puff, much like the mist around them that was disappearing into the air. It vaporized and blew away. De Winter had wisdom about him, no doubt about it. After a moment, Cortez simply shook his head and jabbed a big finger at him.

"No more apples for you for the rest of this journey," he told him. "You just fed all of those Children of God your share of the fruit."

Drake fought of a grin. "Gladly, my lord. They were sour, anyway."

With that, he reined is horse around, leaving Cortez at the head of the column struggling not to smile. Compassionate wife, indeed. He still had much to learn about her, even her rebellious nature, which he frankly found rather charming. The woman had spirit and, in spite of everything, he rather liked it.

When Drake resumed his position next to the provisions wagon, Diamantha was finished throwing apples to the peasants and thanking God that de Winter had left his post and allowed her to dispense of the fruit as best she could. Oblivious to the fact that both Drake and Cortez knew of her own private rebellion, she settled back in the wagon and took her daughter in her arms again, making herself comfortable for the long ride ahead.

She couldn't do anything for those girls in Gloucester, but for the starving children of Stafford, she was able to contribute just a little and it gave her a satisfying moment in a trip that hadn't been full of many. In a trip that had been filled with it share of dark and light so far, Diamantha had been able to make a little difference in a few lives.

It wasn't much, but it was something.

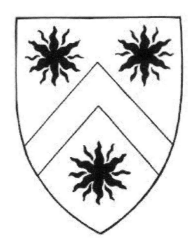

CHAPTER FOURTEEN

Coven Castle
Five miles northwest of Stafford

De Bretagne's party arrived at Coven Castle well after sunset, when the land was nearly pitch-black because of the sliver moon.

Diamantha had never seen darkness like this. It was so dark that one could literally not see the hand in front of their face, and Diamantha sat in the wagon with Sophie sleeping against her, both of them bundled up against the cold. The night was clear in direct contrast from the misty, wet morning, and there were a million stars strewn across the sky. It was a quiet night, too, the only sounds coming from an occasional night bird as the column made its way down the dark and lonely road.

About an hour into the trek from the point they had taken the western road from Stafford, a faint glow could be seen in the distance, a soft point of light against the inky blackness of night. Weary from the travel and lulled by the rocking of the wagon, Diamantha had placed her head back against the cushions with Sophie snuggled against her chest, and she had fallen asleep to the night sounds around her.

But her slumber soon ended when shouts could be heard, taken up by the soldiers. There were also shouts in the distance, shouts from Coven Castle as Cortez's party drew near. Cortez had sent two soldiers as messengers on ahead, so his father was expecting them. Men rode out from the castle to greet them, men bearing torches, and soon there were flickers of light everywhere, splashed against the blackness of the night.

Diamantha awoke to the shouts but Sophie did not, and she lay there with her arms around her daughter, listening to the chatter and seeing flickers of torches all around. The wagon picked up pace and soon the road became rather bumpy as she braced herself so she wouldn't bounce around. The oiled tarp that protected her from the rain also prevented her from seeing much of what was going on around her, but she saw clearly when they entered through a low, dark gatehouse and spilled out into a bailey. There were men all around with torches and as she tried to sit up, the oiled tarp was pulled back and Cortez appeared. He smiled wearily at her.

"We have arrived," he said, holding out his arms. "Give me Sophie, sweetheart."

Diamantha did, and Cortez handed her over to the waiting Merlin. Then Cortez reached into the wagon and pulled Diamantha out, holding her steady as she gained her footing after the long ride. Fearful of more hungry peasants, they had never stopped to rest and the nooning meal had been taken as they traveled. Now, they had stopped, and Diamantha was desperate to stretch her numb legs.

"Are you well enough?" Cortez asked her as she rubbed at her stiff legs.

Diamantha nodded. "I am," she said, sighing wearily as her gazed moved over the torch-lit bailey. "So this is Coven Castle? Is this where you were born?"

Cortez shook his head. "I was born in London at the home of my mother's uncle," he said. "Coven Castle is from my father's side of the family. Andres was born here, however."

As he tried to move her away from the wagon, she balked until he reached in and collected the cage with the animals in it. Diamantha clutched the cage as they made their way across the dark, rocky bailey towards the great hall on the north side of the complex.

Coven Castle had been built right after the Conquest by Sir Giles de Bretagne, using foundations from an old Roman fort upon which to construct his castle. Since the land around it was very flat for the most part, the Romans had built a mound and planted a watchtower atop it. The mound still remained but instead of a watchtower on the top, there was a box-shaped keep with three floors to it. There was one room on each floor, the top floor being Gorsedd de Bretagne's chamber.

Massive curtain walls surrounded the mound and keep, with a big gatehouse at the entry. The bailey, a flat piece of land that wasn't particularly large, housed a great hall and a secondary structure that held apartments on the top floor and a stable beneath it. There were a few outbuildings, too, mostly for horses and trades, and all of it crammed into a rather small space.

It was a very busy space now with Cortez's party settling down in the bailey. Horses were being tended and the wagons were being taken over to one of the outbuildings to be housed for the night. Holding the cage in her arms, Diamantha allowed Cortez to escort her towards the great hall but she kept glancing over her shoulder at Merlin, carrying the sleeping Sophie. As they neared the hall, a man in leather and furs emerged, throwing open his arms when he saw Cortez.

"My son!" he roared, moving swiftly for Cortez and throwing the man in a great embrace. He hugged him tightly before kissing his cheek. "Cortez, my shining star. I have missed you so very much."

Cortez was grinning at his father, a man he resembled a good deal. "Father," he said, as if reaffirming the man and the bonds. "You've not changed, not one bit."

Gorsedd laughed loudly. "You have," he said. "You have gotten older and...."

Suddenly, his gaze fell on Diamantha and he stopped himself mid-sentence. His eyes widened and his mouth seemed to pop open in surprise. Cortez, seeing where his father's attention lie, grasped Diamantha's hand and pulled her forward.

"Father," he said with satisfaction in his voice. "This is my wife, Lady Diamantha Edlington de Bretagne. I have brought her to meet you."

Gorsedd was beside himself. He went to Diamantha, his wide-eyed gaze devouring every line, every curve of her face, as if he could hardly believe what he was seeing.

"Your *wife*?" he repeated Cortez, just to make sure he had heard correctly. "You remarried and you did not think to send word to me?"

Cortez was grinning broadly as he put his big arm around Diamantha's shoulders. "We were married not quite two weeks ago," he said. "I am here to tell you in person. She is beautiful, is she not? I can hardly believe she belongs to me, but she does."

Gorsedd reached out to take Diamantha's hand, the one that wasn't holding the animal cage, and he brought it to his lips, kissing it gently. He appeared genuinely emotional.

"My lady," he greeted, his voice hoarse. "It is an honor and a privilege to meet you. Long have I prayed for this for my son. Long have I... well, it does not matter. You are his wife now and a part of our family. I am very glad you are here."

Diamantha smiled at the man, seeing Cortez reflected in the color of the man's black eyes and in the shape of his face. The resemblance was truly remarkable.

"Thank you," she said sincerely. "I am very happy to know you."

Gorsedd looked at Cortez as if surprised. "Not only does she look like an angel, but she speaks like one, too," he said, returning his attention to Diamantha. He still held her hand. "Dearest lady, will you kindly accompany me into the hall? We assumed Cortez had not yet eaten and have a feast prepared in his honor. Now it is in your honor as well."

Diamantha resisted slightly. "My lord, I would be more than happy to sup with you," she said. "But, at the moment, I believe my daughter and I could both use a few moments to rest and refresh ourselves. We have been traveling a very long time."

Gorsedd was nodding furiously even before the words left her mouth. "Of course," he said quickly, turning to Cortez. "Take her into the keep. You may both have my chamber. Do you remember where it is, Cortez?"

Cortez nodded. "At the top."

Gorsedd was still nodding, now gently pushing Diamantha in the direction of the keep. "Go now, my lady," he urged. "I will send servants with hot water so you may bathe if you wish. And your daughter? What a lovely child. I have another bed I can send up for her to sleep on. She will like her own bed, don't you think?"

Cortez took hold of Diamantha while his father began barking orders to the servants. A tiny man with a big torch moved in front of them, leading the way through the darkened bailey to the mound and its steep steps. Cortez took the animal cage as Diamantha collected her skirts and took the stairs carefully. Merlin, still behind them bearing Sophie, followed them up the steps and into the big, intimidating keep.

The ground floor was a solar of some kind with a big desk, a table, a roaring fire, and four very big dogs. When they saw the animal cage in Cortez's hand, he had to hold the thing over his head so the dogs would leave it alone. They smelled the cats. They were very interested in Diamantha, too, and she petted them timidly, but when they got to Merlin, he shoved the dogs out of the way with his feet.

There was a narrow spiral staircase that led to the first floor of the keep, which was used by the servants. It had all manner of chairs, beds propped against the wall, and a big bathtub. It was essentially a storage room and there were more dogs in there as well. Continuing up the stairs to the top of the keep, they found themselves in an extremely cluttered chamber.

An enormous bed was positioned near the hearth, which was spitting embers and smoke into the room. The bed itself was covered with mounds of furs, messily strewn about, and the mattress was lumpy and stained. A small table and leaning chair sat over near the lancet window, the only window in the entire room, and there was a wardrobe in the shadowed darkness with both doors open and piles of possessions spilling forth. There were clothes hanging on the open doors, boots kicked about, old cloaks, and bits of old food all over the floor. It was clear that whoever lived here was not fond of cleanliness or tidiness. It smelled like a sewer.

But Diamantha didn't say anything about it. Gorsedd had been generous to insist they sleep there, so she wasn't about to complain. As she tried not to look too horrified at their surroundings, she caught sight of Merlin standing behind her and she motioned him over to the bed.

"Please put Sophie on the bed," she said softly. "Thank you for carrying her."

He started to move but Cortez stopped him. "Hold," he said firmly, glancing apologetically at his wife. "There is no knowing what has been upon that bed. Let me at least send for something clean."

Diamantha wasn't going to argue with him. She was greatly relieved that he thought this room every bit as terrible as she did. Nodding gratefully, she took her daughter from Merlin so the man could go about his duties and went to the only chair in the room, easing herself down onto it. Merlin was headed for the stairs but he was pushed back as Gorsedd and Andres entered the room. The men were being quite loud, reveling in their reunion and happy to be together again, but Cortez shushed them both harshly.

"Are you a pack of wild animals?" he hissed. "Keep your voices down, for the child is sleeping!"

Gorsedd looked startled, then properly contrite as Andres slapped a hand over his mouth. Neither one of them were used to small children about. They both looked at Diamantha apologetically before returning their attention to Cortez.

"Andres tells me that you are only staying the night," Gorsedd said, massive disappointment in his tone as he tried to lower the volume of his voice. "Is this true? Why can you not stay longer?"

Cortez had hoped to speak to his father about the shortness of their visit well after pleasantries had been exchanged, but it seemed the subject was rearing itself now. As Merlin slipped from the room, Cortez held up his hands as if to ease his father's displeasure.

"Let us at least rest a moment before we launch into explanations," he said. Then he began to herd them both towards the chamber door. "Go to the hall and I will meet you there. I will tell you everything at that time."

Gorsedd clearly wasn't happy but he did as his son asked, apologizing once again for being loud around a sleeping child as he and Andres left the chamber. Cortez was about to shut the door when a pair of his soldiers appeared bearing satchels and saddlebags. They set them down just inside the door but Cortez grabbed the pair before they could leave.

"Find a servant and send them to me at once," he said, eyeing the state of the chaotic room. "Tell them that this room is unacceptable and that we require clean linens and a clean mattress."

The soldiers nodded swiftly and were gone. Once the room was quiet, Cortez shut the door, turning to his wife, sitting in the darkened corner near the window.

"Come over near the hearth, sweetheart," he directed. "It is warmer over here."

Diamantha stood up, allowing him to take the chair and move it next to the hearth. She sat down with the glow of heat in her face. It was a wonderful feeling, and one that made her realize just how exhausted she was. The warmer she became, the sleepier she grew, and she stifled a yawn. Cortez moved the animal cage near the hearth so the little animals wouldn't freeze, crouching down next to Diamantha's chair as they waited for the servants to appear.

"I am sorry for the state of this room," he said, looking around. "I shall have it cleaned up shortly."

Diamantha gazed at him, a faint smile on her face. "I am not worried," she said quietly. "You have done an excellent job of taking care of us so far. I am sure improving your father's hellish chamber will be no different."

Cortez laughed, running a weary hand through his black hair. "He is a good man, even if he does live like a pig," he said, watching her giggle. "He is very happy to see you in case you were not aware."

She shrugged. "Mayhap I was, just a bit," she said teasingly. "He seems very kind."

"He is," he replied. "And to him, family means everything. He speaks of his forefathers as if they are still living, breathing men. He holds our family honor dear."

"How lovely," Diamantha sighed, turning to the flames, enjoying the warmth on her body. "He seemed rather distraught that we were not planning to stay. What will you tell him?"

Cortez was looking at her, her beautiful profile in the soft light of the fire. "The truth," he said honestly. "We are on a quest, you and I. We will not be deterred, not even for him."

With that, he reached out and grasped her left hand, the one with the ring on it. *My quest is you.* He lifted it, gazing at the ring, before gently kissing it. It was such a tender gesture, and one that foretold of the fiery passion he was so capable of.

Diamantha's heart began to race as he held her hand, inspecting her fingers, fondling her soft flesh. She'd never known such raw excitement, anticipating every touch, every kiss. When he looked up and saw that she was gazing at him, something wild and exhilarating passed between them and he gently cupped her face, slanting his mouth sweetly over hers. It was a kiss like nothing else, wrought with awakening passion.

But a knock on the door shattered the spell and, startled, Cortez pulled away from her and bolted to his feet. Moving to the door, he opened it with more anger than he should have, frustrated that such a beautiful moment had been interrupted. They tiny old man who had led them into the keep with his trusty torch was standing in the darkened stairwell outside, hovering nervously.

"Ye wanted to see me, m'lord?" he asked. "Is the chamber not to your liking?"

Cortez shook his head, a wry expression on his lips. "It is *not*," he said. "My wife and I require fresh linens and, in the name of Christ, give us a new mattress. God only knows what my father has done to that one. It smells like a sewer. We also require hot water and a bathtub. I saw one on the floor below. Bring it up so my wife might bathe."

The old servant bobbed his head nervously and fled down the narrow stairs. Cortez turned to Diamantha.

"This will probably take some time," he said. "Mayhap we should join my father in the hall first so that by the time we return to this room, it will be moderately habitable."

It was a reasonable plan and Diamantha rose to her feet wearily. She would have liked nothing better than to crawl into bed and sleep for a week, but not in the state it was in. Indeed, they had to wait for the servants to properly clean it. As she turned for the chamber door, Sophie began to stir in her arms. The little girl rubbed her eyes and yawned, and Diamantha gave her a squeeze.

"Are you finally awake, sweetheart?" she purred. "Open your eyes and look at me."

Sophie did, her eyes popped up and she blinked, looking at her surroundings. She was immediately curious. Sophie was, if nothing else, unflappable. She was in a new place and, rather than be frightened, she was interested. She pushed herself out of her mother's arms and Diamantha set her gently on her feet.

"Mama?" Sophie looked around. "Are we here?"

Diamantha grinned at her daughter's confused question. "We are at Cortez's father's home," she told her. "We are going to go eat sup with him now. Are you hungry?"

Sophie nodded emphatically but as she did so, she spied her pets over near the fire. She ran to them, falling to her knees beside them. Diamantha went after her.

"Nay, sweet," she said, grasping her daughter's hand. "We will come back to them after we eat."

Sophie wasn't too sure. "But Eleanor and Edward and Father and Clover will be lonely."

Diamantha led her gently for the door. "They are warm and safe," she assured her. "We will bring food back for them."

Sophie still wasn't sure but let her mother lead her to the door where Diamantha paused, handing Sophie over to Cortez.

"A moment, please," she said. "Keep hold on her so she doesn't run back to her pets. If she does, I fear we will never make it to the hall."

Cortez held the little girl's hand tightly, dividing his time between smiling down at the sleepy little girl and watching Diamantha dig around in one of her satchels. She seemed to be searching for something. He waited patiently until she finally pulled forth a bundle of cloth. Carefully unwrapping it, she pulled forth the dramatic necklace Cortez had given her, the one that had belonged to Helene and to Cortez's mother before that. Rising, she brought it over to Cortez.

"I thought your father might like to see this," she said. "It belonged to your mother, after all. Will you please help me put it on?"

Obediently, Cortez let go of Sophie's hand and helped Diamantha secure the heavy silver collar. She was wearing her traveling clothes with the neckline that came all the way up to her throat, so the necklace lay against her with the backdrop of blue wool. It was truly stunning. Cortez watched her as she fussed with the necklace to make sure it hung correctly.

"He will be very happy to see it," he said confidently. "That piece meant a great deal to him."

"Did he commission it for her?"

He nodded his head. "Aye," he said, "for their wedding day."

"Then your father is sentimental like his son."

Cortez grinned. "I suppose so," he cooed, his dark eyes glittering at her. "You give us much to be sentimental about."

Diamantha smiled at him, a warm and genuine gesture, touching the necklace as she took Sophie's hand and led the little girl from the room, slowly navigating the stairs downward. Cortez was right behind them, closing the door to the chamber and following. When he came to the floor directly below, he saw the tiny old servant and a few others milling about as they prepared to take the tub up to the chamber. He cornered the old man.

"There is a cage up in that chamber with four small animals in it," he told the servant, pointing to the ceiling above to emphasize his point. "They belong to my daughter. I have seen dogs all around this place and you will not let them into that room, is that clear? If anything happens to those pets, I will have your head. Do you comprehend me?"

The old man nodded fearfully, watching Cortez as the man followed the woman and small girl out of the keep.

The first thing he did before he followed any of Cortez's other directives was find a small, sturdy table to place the animal cage on, just in case the many dogs milling about the keep wandered into the chamber. He made sure the cage was very safe, up high and away from the floor.

He didn't want to lose his life over two kittens, a rabbit, and a fox. It would have been a shameful way to go, but the fact was, he believed Cortez's threat implicitly. Being that the man was a de

Bretagne, they never gave idle threats, and everyone knew that Sir Cortez was the most frightening de Bretagne of all.

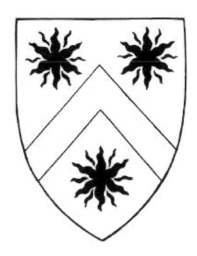

CHAPTER FIFTEEN

Gorsedd wept openly when he saw the great collar necklace on Diamantha. Water poured from his eyes, mucus from his nose, and he kept wiping it all on his sleeve. As everyone took a seat around the long feasting table in the cavernous hall of Coven Castle, it was several moments before Gorsedd could speak.

"Beautiful," he whispered tightly as Diamantha sat down between him and Cortez. "I have never seen the necklace look so lovely."

Diamantha was truly touched at the man's reaction. "As I told your son, I will treat this with the greatest of respect," she said. "It is a truly lovely piece."

Gorsedd sniffled away the last of his tears, loudly, as he motioned to the servants to start bringing forth the warmed trenchers of food.

"I am so pleased you like it," he said, sitting next to her and gazing intently between her and Sophie, who was seated on her lap. "And this is your daughter? What a lovely lass. What is your name, child?"

Sophie, who had already grabbed a chunk of soft white bread, spoke with her mouth full. "Sophie Amalia Teodora Edlington," she said in her rapid-fast delivery.

Gorsedd laughed uproariously at the adorable child, which startled Sophie. When he saw the fright he had given the little girl, he quickly sought to make amends.

"Such a beautiful name, truly," he assured her quickly. "I am sorry if I frightened you. I know I am a loud man."

Somewhat eased, Sophie went back to chewing her bread. "I have a pony," she told him. "His name is General. Would you like to see him?"

It was the same line she had given Cortez those weeks ago and Cortez laughed, reaching out to gently touch Sophie's arm.

"We will eat first," he told her. "Mayhap you can show him after."

Sophie wasn't particularly put off by the suggestion because her attention was diverted by all of the food they were bringing out. The bread, cheese, and fruit already on the table was now joined by other dishes – fish with apricots and peppercorns, pork with honey and cloves, and a variety of boiled vegetables. Great trenchers were placed before the diners and Cortez began filling Diamantha's trencher with the fish and the pork. Even as he spooned the items onto her trencher, Sophie was already sticking her fingers in it and eating. Gorsedd thought it was all great fun to watch and he even handed her his own spoon to use, but she wasn't interested. She was happier with her fingers.

Andres, Drake, Oliver, and James joined them in short order once their duties settling the men were complete. Andres sat across from his father, reaching for the pitcher of wine before he even looked at the food. As Cortez watched, his brother downed two large cups of wine quickly, and Cortez began to suspect that the sobriety his brother had adhered to for the past several days was about to come to an end.

Cortez's soldiers began filtering into the room, heading for the feasting tables closer to the door where food had been set out for them. Meanwhile the knights dug into the food with gusto, the finest spread that they'd had in days. There were even serving women about, which lured Cortez's men somewhat, particularly Andres, who by now was well into his third cup of wine and feeling the familiar flush of alcohol in his veins. When a busty young woman went to put more wine on the table next to him, he smiled leeringly at her and slapped her on her ample behind. She giggled while he laughed lewdly, pinching her arse as she scampered away.

"Andres," Cortez said, trying to distract his brother from his lecherous behavior. "Speak to the quartermaster before we leave and make sure we are well supplied. It has been four days since we last restocked and I heard today that we somehow lost a bag of apples. Puzzling. In any case, check with the quartermaster to make sure we haven't lost anything else. I do not want to set out tomorrow only half-supplied."

Diamantha heard his comment about the apples, keeping her head down as she fed Sophie some of the fish. She wasn't going to confess about tossing the apples to the starving peasants but she somehow suspected that he already knew. He was being tactful by not calling her out for it. Still, she thought it best to change the subject. She didn't want it known that she had openly disobeyed her husband.

"Sir Gorsedd," she said, turning to Cortez's father. "Cortez tells me that your heritage is Welsh and English. Do you have much interaction with your Welsh kin, living close to the Marches as you do?"

Gorsedd was sucking on a pork bone. "Not too much," he said, chewing. "My mother's family was part of the ap Gruffydd clan, you know. Did Cortez tell you that? At one time, the king thought he could use that to his advantage but my mother's family is all fairly destitute now. Once, they were very powerful, but the tides of fortune have not been kind."

Diamantha was listening with interest. "I am indeed sorry to hear that," she said. "I know that Edward has been quite active in Wales. It is all but conquered now."

Gorsedd nodded his head, perhaps thinking on the proud Welsh heritage that was now subjugated to an English king. "That is true," he replied. "But it cannot be helped, I suppose. The Welsh cannot rule Wales. All they do is fight, anyway, so mayhap Edward believes he can unite the country. He certainly cannot do any worse than generations of Welsh princes have done."

Diamantha watched the man carefully. "As a man who is part Welsh, I find your view somewhat surprising," she said. "Most Welshman I have heard of are fiercely patriotic of Welsh rule in Wales."

Gorsedd shrugged as he began to suck on another pork bone. "The only thing I am patriotic about is my family in general," he said. "Welsh *or* English, which puts me in an odd position at times. Still, I would give up my life for either side. My grandfather, in fact, did. He was killed in Wales defending his home many years ago. But enough about me, my lady. Tell me of your family, for I am eager to know."

Diamantha opened her mouth to speak but Sophie, finished with her fish, squirmed to get off her lap. Diamantha held her tightly.

"Nay, sweetheart," she said. "You cannot get down. Stay with me."

"She may wander the hall, my lady," Gorsedd said encouragingly. "The dogs in here will not hurt her. In fact, there is a litter of pups over near the hearth. See the pillar to the left of the fire? They are behind it."

"I will take her," Cortez said, wiping his mouth and standing. He held out a hand to the little girl. "Come along, my lady. Would you like to see puppies?"

Sophie nearly launched herself out of her mother's lap, thrilled at the prospect of baby dogs. Diamantha looked at Cortez with some hesitation in her expression.

"Are you sure?" she asked. "Surely you would like to stay here and speak with your father."

Cortez smiled, already being dragged away by Sophie. "I will return," he assured her. "You and my father become better acquainted."

Diamantha watched him go, with Sophie towing him along. She seemed to like to do that with him, leading around this big man who was sworn to do her bidding. It was rather sweet to watch, and it endeared her to Cortez that much more. If she didn't know better, she would swear the man was well on his way to stealing her heart. It was a surprising but not unpleasant prospect. Given their rough beginning, she wouldn't have believed that to have been possible.

"Do not bring a puppy back," she told Cortez. "Not even when she begs. Do you hear me?"

He was several feet away but waved an acknowledging hand. "I hear you."

"Promise me?"

He didn't respond and she didn't really expect him to. If Sophie asked for the moon, he would grant it if it was in his power. She was coming to realize that about him. With a smile on her lips and a shake of the head at the adorable picture of Sophie dragging Cortez along behind her, she turned back to Gorsedd.

"My family is rooted in England," she said. "My father serves at Norham Castle in Northumberland. He is still alive and in good health. On my mother's side, it is a bit more interesting. My maternal great-grandfather was Christopher de Lohr, who was King Richard's champion. Cortez's knight, James de Lohr, is also a descendent of the man once known as the Defender of the Realm."

The light of recognition went on in Gorsedd's eyes. "Truly?" he asked, looking across the table at James when Diamantha pointed at him. But his attention quickly returned to her. "De Lohr, you say? 'Tis a proud family, my lady. Most impressive."

Diamantha was warming to the conversation. "Thank you," she said. "My maternal grandfather was the son of another great warlord, although he did not have the pristine reputation that de Lohr had. My grandfather was the son of Ajax de Velt. Have you heard of him? He had a heavy presence in the north and also along the Welsh Marches for a time. His method was conquest and he accumulated quite a few castles in his younger years."

Something in Gorsedd's expression changed at that moment, as if a curtain was lowered, from top to bottom. The change started at Gorsedd's forehead and worked its way down his face. First, his brow furrowed, then, his eyes widened to astonishing proportions. Further down, his cheeks flushed a violent shade of red and his mouth began to work but no sound came forth. It worked and worked, and spittle began to form around his lips. As Diamantha looked at him with concern, she wondered if the man was having a spell. Gorsedd suddenly leapt to his feet and his chair toppled over.

"De Velt!" he roared. "Are you telling me that you sprang from that bastard's loins?"

Diamantha was taken aback at the tone, suddenly very uncertain of Gorsedd's behavior. "He was my grandfather's father," she said steadily. "My lord, if there is...."

Gorsedd cut her off by bellowing in her face as loud as he could. "Silence!" he screamed. "I never thought I would see the day when de Velt blood sullied the House of de Bretagne, but now you are here and de Velt's vile deeds have infiltrated those closest to me!"

Diamantha was seriously considering moving away from the man. She was hoping Cortez could hear what was going on and come to save her from whatever rage his father was suffering from.

"My lord, truly," she said, trying to remain calm, "I never knew my great-grandfather and although I know he committed terrible crimes, he...."

Gorsedd wouldn't hear her. He began shouting over her. "And now you pollute the memory of my wife by wearing her collar?" he pointed at her, suddenly fixed on the great necklace on her chest. "You are unfit and unworthy, de Velt spawn!"

Reaching out, he yanked the beautiful silver collar right off her neck, sending pieces of it flying in all directions. Terrified, Diamantha jumped out of her seat and scurried away from the man while across the table, James and Drake and Oliver were on their feet, moving to protect the lady from Gorsedd's wild demeanor. Even Andres, as drunk as he was, was focused on his father with concern and curiosity.

"Father!" he stood up, weaving dangerously as he leaned forward on the table. "What is the matter with you? Why are you...?"

Gorsedd stumbled away from the table, putting his hands up as if to block out the horrors rolling through is mind.

"*That*!" he screamed, pointing at Diamantha, who was now standing behind James and Drake. "That... that *whore*, that vile creature of de Velt blood, has bewitched your brother! Do you know what her great-grandsire did? He killed my grandfather! He put the man on a pole, driven up through his arse until it came out of his shoulder, and left him to die on a pike in the middle of the bailey of the castle where he was born! De Velt left the man to die a horrific death, squirming on the end of a pole as ravens plucked his eyeballs out! The blood that runs through her veins is the same blood that killed my grandfather!"

By now, the entire room was deadly silent except for Gorsedd's shouting. Cortez, who had been over by the hearth with Sophie, picked the little girl up and made haste back to the table in time to hear his father spout his terrible venom at Diamantha. Immediately, he handed the child over to Oliver.

"Get her out of here," he hissed. "Find Merlin and tell him to tend her. You will come back once you have delivered her to safety."

Oliver took the little girl, who was asking to see the puppies again. He fled the hall with the child in his arms as Cortez went to stand between his wife and father. All the while, the legendary de Bretagne temper was rising, like a cauldron about to boil, and by the time he faced his father, he was purely mad with rage. He simply couldn't believe all of the slander he was hearing, from his own father no less, shocking and uncalled for. It was difficult to remain in control.

"I could forgive you if you were drunk or insane, but you are neither," he growled. "You have insulted my wife in the worst possible way, for crimes committed almost one hundred years ago that she had nothing to do with. Have you lost your damn mind? What reasonable man would blame someone for the crimes of their ancestors?"

Gorsedd was enraged beyond control. He pointed a finger at Diamantha as she cowered behind Drake. "Look at her eyes," he hissed. "You can see that she has his eyes. She has his devil eyes. Everyone knew of de Velt's two-colored eyes, eyes through which Satan worked. And now you bring this... this horror into my home? She must be purged and you must be cleansed!"

Cortez snapped. He charged forward and grabbed his father around the neck. Andres, seeing the confrontation turning physical, leapt over the table and grabbed Cortez just as James ran forward to help pull the two men apart. But Cortez would not be deterred. He had his father tightly around the neck, squeezing as the man's face turned purple.

"Did you just threaten her, old man?" Cortez seethed. "Did I hear you threaten her life?"

Andres was struggling to no avail to pry Cortez off their father. "Cortez, stop!" he cried. "You will kill him!"

Cortez was in a haze of fury. "Answer me!" he roared at his father. "Did you just threaten her life?"

Gorsedd was starting to lose consciousness. "Her... family has committed heinous crimes against ours," he grunted, struggling to breathe. "How can you defend her?"

"Because she did not *do* anything!" Cortez bellowed. "She is innocent!"

Gorsedd was starting to fight back as his field of vision began to go black. "Get... get her out of my sight!" he yelled, trying to kick his powerful son. "Get her out of my sight or I will kill her! I will avenge my grandfather with her blood!"

Cortez squeezed so tightly that his father passed out but he was prevented from killing the man by James and Andres. Andres threw his arms around his brother and pulled him back, away from Gorsedd, who was lying limp on the floor.

"Nay, Cortez, *nay*!" Andres pleaded. "Come with me now. Let us leave tonight. We will get far away from here."

Cortez was blinded by rage, fighting his brother even as the man struggled to stop him. He was about to punch his brother squarely in the face but a soft, white hand on his arm stopped him. It was a gentle touch, but it did what no man could do. It instantly stopped his forward momentum. Diamantha pushed herself in between Cortez and Andres, a soft bit of ethereal love and hope where moments before, all that had existed in that space had been rage.

"Please," she begged, tears in her eyes. "Please do not fight any more. Just take me away of here."

Cortez wanted to fight. He wanted to fight in the worst way. Diamantha's life had been threatened, her heritage sullied, and all he wanted to do was destroy those who would hurt her, even his own father. He couldn't even describe the fury in his heart at the moment. All he knew was that he was mad enough to kill.

But that wouldn't solve the issue. It would make him guilty of patricide, and as he struggled to calm himself, he realized that he was not prepared to enter those heady waters. Something like that would damage him for the rest of his life and quite possibly damage his relationship with Diamantha. Who's to say that, at some point, he wouldn't blame her for his actions? Therefore, he took a deep breath and labored to ease his rage.

He looked at Andres. The man looked terrified. Drunk, but terrified. Then he looked at James and Drake, both of them poised to kill on his command. He knew they would, too, even if the command was to kill Gorsedd. Then, he looked at Diamantha. She was weeping and struggling not to. She was absolutely terrified. Taking a deep, calming breath, he put a hand on the back of her head and pulled her forehead to his lips for a sweet kiss.

"Andres," he said, his voice hoarse. "Take our father to the vault and lock him up for the night. It would be much easier to do that than pack up our entire party and flee into the dead of night. We will leave before dawn and give the servants instructions to release Father from the vault when we are well away."

Shaken, Andres nodded unsteadily and moved to his father, who was just starting to come around. He motioned to James, who helped Andres pick the man up and drag him out of the hall. Cortez waited until he was gone before turning back to the room full of men who were standing about uneasily. Taking his wife by the arm, he turned her back to the table.

"Now," he said with forced calm. "We can finish our meal in peace. Did Sophie get much to eat? I could not tell. Mayhap we should bring something to her."

Diamantha was choking back tears. "Where is my daughter?" she asked tightly. "Where did you take her?"

He shushed her gently. "Merlin has instructions to keep her safe," he assured her. "You know he will. The man will protect her with his life."

Diamantha broke into soft sobs. "I want my baby," she said. "I want to leave."

Cortez could see that the evening was ruined. Gathering her up, he told Drake to remain behind to make sure the men were adequately fed and that no one got too drunk so they would be ready to depart on time in the morning. He also told Drake to keep an eye on his father in the vault because he honestly couldn't trust that Andres wouldn't feel sorry for the man and release him.

Drake wanted to follow them, to take up a sentry position outside of the master chamber door for Diamantha's sake, but Cortez called him off. With Gorsedd in the vault, providing he remained there, such protection would not be necessary. Besides, Cortez had his broadsword with him. Just in case.

Leaving a great feast down in the hall, Cortez escorted his wife up to the chamber at the top of the keep. When they arrived, Diamantha was somewhat calmer, calmer still to see that Merlin had brought Sophie up to the chamber. When they came through the door, the first thing they saw was Merlin seated on the floor with a rabbit in his lap while Sophie, sitting on the floor next to him, held the kittens and the fox. Cortez walked up to his sergeant, shaking his head reproachfully at the man.

"You make a fine playmate, Merlin," he said.

Merlin shrugged, somewhat embarrassed. "She insisted," he said feebly. "I could not deny her."

Cortez pursed his lips wryly as he reached down and picked up the little rabbit, allowing Merlin to stand. As the sergeant bid Diamantha a good evening and left the chamber, Cortez bolted the door behind him. When he turned back around, he noticed the big tub over near the hearth, partially concealed in the shadows of the room, and on the small table there was a pitcher with cups and a platter of food. There also appeared to be a clean bed, mattress and all. They had all they needed for the evening and that helped his emotional state a good deal.

Already, Diamantha was telling Sophie to put the animals back in their cages so she could bathe the child and prepare her for bed. It was clear that she was trying to put the horror of the hall behind her. Cortez, with the little rabbit still clutched against his chest, went over to the cage and handed the rabbit to Diamantha, who put it back in the cage with its mates. He watched Diamantha's lowered head as she took Sophie over to the tub and began taking her clothes off, finally submerging the child in about eight inches of very warm water. As Sophie splashed about, Diamantha went over to their satchels and began pulling out clean clothing. Cortez followed her.

"I am sorry," he whispered, putting his hands on her arms and kissing the top of her dark head. "My father... I would have never imagined him capable of what I witnessed tonight. Had I had any idea he would have reacted that way, I certainly would have taken steps to avoid it."

Diamantha sighed faintly as she pulled out a sleeping shift for Sophie. She was pensive, subdued. "It is not the first time someone has reacted negatively to the fact that I bear de Velt bloodlines," she said nervously. "I know what atrocities the man committed, many people do. But I also know from my grandmother that marriage changed him. He became an excellent father and husband, and actually became quite a benefactor in his later years, mayhap to make up for all of the pain and suffering he had caused. He donated heavily to the church and also donated quite heavily to the university at Oxford. But... he wasn't perfect, even with all of that benevolence."

Cortez cocked his head. "What do you mean?"

Diamantha's gaze was on her daughter as the little girl poured water over her head from a small wooden cup that had been floating around in the tub.

"My great-grandfather conquered many castles," she said quietly. "He did it just the way your father said. He impaled men on poles and left them to die. He killed women and children. In the end, he kept many of those castles he conquered simply because he had killed all of the families they belonged to. There was no one left, at least no one close enough to assume the properties, so he simply kept and maintained them. He gave them to his children, or to the men who served him. Do you happen to know where your great-grandfather was killed?"

Cortez thought a moment. He had heard tale of the location, once. As he pondered her question, the answer came to him. "Comyn Castle, I believe," he said. "My father's mother was born there. It was their family seat."

Diamantha lifted her eyebrows ironically. "And she survived the siege by the great Jax de Velt?"

Cortez shook his head. "I do not believe she was there at the time," he said. "I seem to remember my father saying that his mother fostered for most of her childhood. The fact that she was sent away to foster probably saved her life. In fact, had she been there and your great-grandfather had killed her, then I would not be here today. Quite fortuitous, I would say."

213

He was smiling at her as he said it and she smiled weakly in return. But the smile soon faded. "Did you know your great-grandfather had been killed by my great-grandfather?"

He shook his head, his smile fading as well. "In truth, I did not," he said. "I knew he had been killed in a siege but I did not know the details until tonight."

"It was a rather terrible way to find out."

"Indeed it was."

Diamantha sighed, so much emotion roiling in her breast. "I feel so terrible about this, Cortez," she said miserably. "Do you think it would do any good for me to apologize to your father? I will if you think it would help."

Cortez could only shake his head. "It probably won't," he said. "I told you that my father is very family oriented and speaks of his ancestors as if they are still living, breathing relatives. The fact that his grandfather was murdered... it is a very real event to him, even these years passed."

Diamantha was gazing up at him earnestly. "Then what do we do?" she asked. "I do not want to be a wedge between you and your father. I could not bear it. And what of Andres? He will be forced to choose sides if you and your father are at odds."

Cortez didn't have all the answers. He kissed her cheek, trying to comfort her, trying to comfort them both. It was an unexpected twist in the situation and one that could have easily torn them apart. They'd had such a turbulent beginning and this was just another blow. But he was coming to realize, with great joy, that rather than run from him or fight with him about it, Diamantha was turning to him for comfort. She trusted him. She viewed him as her defender in all of this, which is exactly how he wanted it. Rather than tear them apart, they were instead drawing closer together. He could feel it.

"Finish bathing Sophie and get her into bed," he finally said. "I believe I shall go and see my father and try to talk some sense into him. Mayhap he is calmer now and will listen."

Diamantha cast him a long glance. "You will not fight him again, will you?"

Cortez shook his head. "Nay, I swear it. I only want to talk to him."

Diamantha wasn't so sure but she wouldn't refute him. Instead, she nodded her head and moved off in the direction of the bathtub where her daughter was splashing water all over the floor. She was about halfway across the room when she suddenly came to a halt and retraced her steps. Cortez was just opening the chamber door when she called to him.

Cortez paused, his hand on the door latch, as Diamantha approached. She didn't say a word. She simply stood on her toes and kissed him, on the cheek, a sweeter kiss he had never received. Then, with a faint smile, she turned around and returned to the tub where Sophie was having a marvelous time.

Cortez stood there a moment, watching her as she walked away. He could still feel the heat from her lips against his flesh. It was enough to make his giddy heart start thumping again.

"Bolt this door when I leave," he told her. "You will only open it for me. Is that clear?"

Diamantha was on her knees beside the tub now. She nodded obediently. "It is," she said. Then, she called after him one more time. "Cortez?"

He was almost through the door now but came to a halt. "Aye?"

Diamantha instinctively put her hand to her throat. "The necklace you gave me," she ventured hesitantly. "The one that belonged to your mother. Your father... well, it broke. Do you think you can go to the hall and find the pieces? Mayhap we can have it repaired."

He nodded, thinking of the sight of his father ripping the necklace from Diamantha's neck. Given how his father valued that necklace, the moment of violence was positively surreal. "I will see if I can find it," he said gently.

"Thank you."

Cortez winked at her as he finally quit the chamber and shut the door behind him. He was halfway down the dark, narrow stairs when he heard her throw the bolt. Descending all the way to the ground floor of the keep, his giddiness faded and his battle-hewn mind began to focus. Something very bad had happened this evening and he intended to rectify it, however he could. He was either going to help his father see reason or put him out of his life and mind forever.

Although Gorsedd was his father, and he loved the man, he couldn't condone his terrible and unreasonable behavior. It was shocking and horrifying, all of it, but Cortez wouldn't allow his father to rule, or ruin, his life. Not now, not just when he'd found some measure of happiness again. It was foolish to choose his new wife over his father and he knew it, but in a sense, he wasn't making the choice at all. Gorsedd was. It would be Gorsedd's choice as to whether or not he could accept Diamantha, a distant de Velt, into the family. If he couldn't then Gorsedd would lose much more than his son's respect.

He would lose his son.

Near dawn, Andres found Cortez in the great hall of Coven.

At first, Andres nearly missed him, seated in their father's chair at the great feasting table, partially hidden by the shadows of the room. The hearth was dark and the great hall was very cold at this time of the morning. Andres made his way over to him.

"What are you doing here?" he asked.

Cortez was looking at the tabletop in front of him. He was fidgeting with pieces of the great silver collar he had found on the floor, at least twelve or more pieces, and he wasn't even sure he had all of them. The break had been by the clasp so the main part of the collar was thankfully intact, but the damage had been done. He couldn't fathom the rage his father must have had in order to have done such a thing. As Cortez sat in his father's seat at his father's table, holding the necklace that had once belonged to his mother, his heart was breaking into a thousand pieces of sorrow.

"I came here to find this necklace," he finally muttered. Then, he glanced up at his brother. "Are the men getting ready to leave?"

Andres looked at him with concern. "They are," he said. "What about you? Are you ready?"

Cortez sighed heavily. Then, he sat back in the chair and dragged his hands over his face wearily. "I am, for the most part," he said. "My wife should be ready as well. I was just going to go and get her."

Andres sat down next to his brother. "What is wrong?" he demanded. "Did you speak with Father?"

Cortez looked at him again. "Aye," he said. "Did you?"

Andres wriggled his eyebrows in a resigned gesture. "I did," he said. "I am sure he told you everything he told me."

Cortez shook his head sadly. "It is as if I do not even know the man any longer," he said hoarsely. "I sat in the vault with him most of the night. I listened to him weep and shout and accuse Diamantha of terrible things, or at least accuse her of being responsible for what Jax de Velt did. It is as if the man doesn't want to listen to reason. Nothing I could say could sway him."

Andres was feeling very bad about everything, made worse by a dull throb in his head from too much drink the night before. In fact, he wasn't feeling altogether well, about anything.

"I know," he muttered. "I tried to talk to him a little while ago. He thinks you have betrayed the entire family by marrying her."

"I know."

Andres scratched his cheek wearily. "I will tell you something else," he said, lowering his voice. "Father's majordomo says that Father's behavior has been very erratic over the past year. He cannot make clear decisions sometimes, he becomes enraged quite easily, as we have seen, and he is very forgetful. That may explain why the situation with your wife has set him off so badly. The majordomo thinks there is something wrong with his mind."

Cortez looked at him, an expression of distress on his face. After a moment, he shook his head in disbelief. "That would explain quite a lot, actually," he said, "for the man in the vault is not the father I know. I do not know who that is."

Andres watched his brother for a moment. "Cortez," he began slowly. "I have been thinking... mayhap I should remain here with him, at least for a little while. You have many excellent knights at your disposal and father has no one. I think he needs me. You do not."

Cortez gazed at his brother, seeing the logic of his request. "I think it is a very good idea for you to stay with him," he agreed. "If, for no other reason, than to keep the man from getting himself into trouble. If his mind is truly going, then mayhap he needs a minder."

Andres nodded in agreement although it was clear he wasn't too keen on the idea. "Believe me when I tell you that remaining here does not make me happy, but I believe it is for the best," he said. "At least I can keep the man from charging after you and trying to kill your wife."

"That is true."

"Will you see him before you leave?"

Cortez simply nodded, rising to his feet wearily and collecting the pieces of the necklace to hold in one hand. Then, he looked at it, the jumble of silver, and put it back down on the table.

"I cannot even look at this," he muttered. "When I see it, all I can envision is father ripping it from Diamantha's neck. It doesn't mean the same thing to me as on the day I gave it to her. Now I only see anger."

Andres eyed the necklace pieces on the table before looking to his brother. "Did you sleep at all last night?"

Cortez shook his head. "Nay," he replied, taking a deep breath to bolster himself. "It is going to be a very long day ahead."

Andres was forced to agree, following his brother out into the pre-dawn morning, very cold and very damp, as the sky turned shades of blue and gray with the approaching sun. Cortez's party was very busy tending horses and hitching up the wagons, and the quartermaster was discussing additional provisions with Coven's majordomo.

Everyone seemed to be focused on their tasks as Cortez and Andres crossed the bailey to the gatehouse where the vault was located. Entering the gatehouse on the right side, they traveled down a very narrow set of stairs that led them to the vault below.

It was very damp and very cold in the hole, surrounded by moist stone and with a single torch illuminating the dark. There were two cells, and very small ones at that. Gorsedd was in the cell on the left, a bigger cell, and he had plenty of fresh straw and blankets to keep him warm. He was also snoring quite loudly when his sons approached.

Cortez and Andres stood outside of the iron grate and watched the man for a moment as he slept the sleep of the dead. When

Andres went to rattle the bars and wake him, Cortez stopped the man.

"Nay," he said softly. "Let him sleep. Mayhap it is best, after all. I do not want my last memory of my father to be that of anguish and rage. I would rather have it be one of him sleeping peacefully. That is how I would wish to remember him."

Andres understood. He put a hand on his brother's arm. "You will send me word when you arrive in Falkirk, will you not?" he asked. "I would like to know what you find once you get there."

Cortez nodded. "I will," he said. "Mayhap... mayhap in time you can join me at Sherborne. It would not be the same without you."

Andres forced a smile. "You would miss pulling me out of gutters and paying off fathers whose daughters I have compromised?"

Cortez snorted. "I will not miss *that* part," he said. He sobered, gazing steadily at his younger brother. "But I will miss you. Take care of yourself, Andres. It is important that my future children know their uncle."

In the cell, Gorsedd snored loudly and rolled around in his straw. The brothers watched to see if he was waking up, but he was not. He slept through their conversation. Cortez turned back to Andres.

"I must go now," he said with some trepidation. "As for you, be well as you watch over Father. And if the majordomo is correct and his mind really is going, keep all weapons away from him. I do not want him hurting himself or others."

Andres nodded, feeling a great sense of disappointment that Cortez was continuing the great quest for Robert Edlington without him. But he understood.

"Safe travels, brother," he wished. "Send me word when you can."

Cortez hugged his brother tightly before letting him go and swiftly taking the steps up to the bailey. He realized there was a lump in his throat at the thought of leaving Andres behind, but he was convinced it was the right thing to do. It was with a very heavy heart, however, that he left his father with such a painful situation between them. Mayhap someday it could be rectified. He fervently hoped so. He never blamed Diamantha for it, not in the least. The thought never even crossed his mind.

Diamantha and Sophie were ready to depart on time. Both of them were bundled up in their traveling clothes as Cortez put them into the wagon. He told Diamantha that his brother was remaining behind to take care of their father, which saddened her somewhat, but she understood. She also knew that Cortez had spent the entire night in the vault with his father, trying to talk some sense into the man. She didn't ask him about it, though. From the expression on his face, she assumed all did not go well and the thought distressed her greatly. She did, however, ask about the necklace and was told it was unsalvageable.

The news upset her but she didn't dwell on it, focusing instead on her daughter and on their day ahead. Cortez, in charge of the pet cage, couldn't help but notice a fifth pet had been slipped in with the others, one of the little puppies that he had seen in the hall the night before. When he questioned Diamantha about it, she simply shook her head wearily and pointed to Merlin. It seemed that Sophie's begging had broken the man down and he had brought her one. Cortez didn't know whether to scold the man or laugh at him. The puppy ended up in Diamantha's lap as the party from Sherborne left the small bailey of Coven Castle and out into the great countryside beyond.

The great Questing continued.

CHAPTER SIXTEEN

Trentham, Warrington, Euxton, Garstang, Carnforth, Kendal.
The towns were becoming an endless parade of colorless, shaggy villages without much difference between one to the next. Seventeen days on the road had left Diamantha with a different perspective about England in general. It was a brutal and unfriendly place for the most part. The people were ignorant and cold, or they were starving, or they were trying to kill each other. England, as a whole, was nothing like her beloved Corfe, which seemed to be a heavenly little enclave in this country that appeared mostly full of sorrow and strife. This journey, so far, had opened her eyes to a lot of things, and not all of it good.

They were north of Kendal this day, heading for the major city of Carlisle and the Scots border. Even though it was late November, the weather was surprisingly mild and the sun was bright overhead. It as such good weather, in fact, that Sophie had been allowed to ride General with the faithful Merlin walking alongside her. She had ridden the pony most of the day. Diamantha didn't feel much like riding her mare so she sat on the wagon bench beside the quartermaster as he drove the wagon along the road, soaking up the sunshine. It was a glorious day.

The land this far north was a deep and rich green as they moved through the wide, rolling hills and heavy foliage that comprised Cumbria. There were birds all about and on more than one occasion they had sighted fallow deer. A few of the foot soldiers had the bright idea to hunt a mother and her two fawns, but Cortez called them off because he didn't want to upset Sophie, who had full view of the white-tailed fawns. When she turned to Merlin and asked for one, he wisely told her to ask Cortez, who had spent about an hour trying to explain to her why she couldn't have one. Diamantha was in earshot, and she grinned the entire time.

Since leaving Coven, the relationship between the two had been quite different. They were more relaxed with each other and Diamantha had felt much more trusting in the man. Beneath the arrogance, the seriousness, and the resolute behavior that had comprised the man, she was coming to discover he was very humorous and very witty. Moreover, he had defended her staunchly to his father, actions which told her he was indeed a sincere and honorable man. He was polite, humorous, kind, and wildly protective of her and Sophie, all qualities of a truly respectable man. Every day saw her heart belong to him just a little bit more.

Even now, as he tried to explain to Sophie why she couldn't have a fawn, it was a very sweet and funny conversation. Sophie simply didn't understand why she couldn't have the little deer and Cortez did his best to give her the reasons why it was not a good idea. As rational as he sounded, he was losing ground against a three year old.

Finally, Diamantha stepped in to save him. She climbed off the moving wagon and went to walk beside her daughter, taking General's lead from Merlin. When the weather had been good along their journey, Diamantha had tried to walk some of the way simply because she felt better when she did. Riding all of the time cramped her legs up and walking made her feel much better on the whole. Sometimes she made Sophie walk, too, but that usually resulted in them lagging behind because her daughter had to stop every few feet to pick any flowers that might be popping up this late in the season.

"Sophie, stop begging for a fawn," she told her daughter. "Cortez has told you that the little deer needs to stay with his mother. You have several pets already, you do not need more."

Sophie was serious with her mother. "But I can be his mama," she told Diamantha. "I can feed him and put him to bed."

Diamantha shook her head. "You do not need another pet," she reiterated. "In fact, when we stop for the night, we must clean your pet cage. The animals need fresh grass and bedding."

Sophie was never much interested in cleaning out her pet cage, so she turned her attention to the doe and fawns that were not far off in the distance. Diamantha, seeing that her conversation with her child was at an end, turned to look at Cortez to make sure he hadn't suffered too much in the losing battle against Sophie. Truth be told, she simply wanted to steal a glance at him. She was doing that quite a bit these days, watching him when his attention was elsewhere. She found it fascinating to simply watch the way he moved.

This time, however, he was looking at her rather dreamily and when their gazes locked, he smiled sweetly. Diamantha returned the smile without hesitation. The warmth and attraction that had developed between them had never been instant. It had taken time to cultivate, but now it seemed to be at the forefront of everything between them, especially since the incident with his father. Cortez dipped his head politely at her.

"My lady," he greeted happily. "You are looking particularly lovely today."

Diamantha's smile turned modest as she looked down at herself. "I have been wearing this same dress since we left Corfe," she said, brushing at the dusty blue wool. "How can you possibly say I am lovely?"

He laughed knowingly. "Because you are," he assured her, his focus moving to the road ahead. "We will stop for the night in a little while. There is a town not far ahead. Can you last a little while longer?"

Diamantha nodded, shading her eyes against the sun as she looked up into the sky. "Of course," she said. "It is such a lovely day. I wish all of our travel days had been like this."

Cortez lifted his eyebrows in agreement. As the group trudged along the somewhat rocky and uneven road, Cortez began to hum in his smooth baritone. Diamantha had heard him hum before as they were traveling, more than likely to stave off boredom, and he had quite a beautiful voice.

"What is that song you are singing?" she asked. "I have heard you hum it before."

Cortez turned to look at her, a grin on his lips as he began to sing the words to the song:

"A young man came to Tilly Nodden,
    His heart so full and pure.
Upon the step of Tilly Nodden,
    His wants would find no cure."

It was a sweet little song, delivered in his beautiful baritone, but the moment he hit the chorus, the entire troop chimed in and the song went from a delightful tune to a rather bawdy song that was better suited to a tavern. Diamantha's smile fled as she looked around her, at every man singing at the top of their lungs.

"Aye! Tilly, Tilly, my goddess near,
    Can ye spare me a glance from those eyes?
My Tilly, sweet Tilly, be my lover so dear,
    I'm a-wantin' a slap of those thighs!"

Half of the men burst out laughing as others started another verse on the song. Diamantha was rather shocked at first but she had to admit the words were very humorous and they sang it with great exaggeration. She started to laugh because the men were, because Cortez was, and it really *was* rather naughty. Even Sophie started giggling loudly, only because everyone else was and she didn't want to be left out. She was having a fine time.

Cortez climbed off his charger and turned the reins over to the nearest soldier. He made his way to Diamantha, who was now grinning at her silly daughter, and took General's lead out of her hand. As he passed it over to Merlin, walking behind the pony, he took his wife in his arms as if to dance with her. He was trying to appear romantic but it ended up coming off as comical as he twirled her about even as they walked. His rich voice filled the air once more.

"Then our young man, his life less grand,
  Since the day he met our Tilly.
His love for her nearly drove him daft,
  When he discovered not a puss, but a shaft."

The men began to laugh uproariously as Diamantha, realizing what he meant, tried to spank him. Cortez had her tightly and, as she squealed with both delight and outrage, took her on a wild galloping dance up to the front of the column and then back again, straight to the wagon. All the while, the men were singing the chorus of *Tilly Nodden*, thinking it rather funny that Cortez had let his guard down. He didn't usually do that, but they were all coming to see that Lady Diamantha was bringing out a side of Cortez that no one really knew existed. He was calm with her, exceedingly considerate, and it was evident to all of them just how much he adored her and the little girl. To be truthful, not even those closest to him knew he was capable of it. It was a fine thing to see, indeed.

As Cortez came to a halt at the wagon, grinning at his giggling, breathless wife, Drake, who had been at the head of the column watching all of the fun, reined his charger back to Cortez.

"My lord," he addressed him. "Penrith is just over the ridge. Do you want me to ride ahead and secure lodgings or do you want to camp outside of town?"

Cortez looked at Diamantha, thinking that she might like a roof over her head tonight. He turned back to Drake.

"Lodgings," he said. "For my wife and I, for Lady Sophie, and rooms for the knights. The men can sleep in the livery or they can camp. It is their choice, but if we find a tavern big enough, order a meal for everyone."

"The foot soldiers, too?"

"Aye."

It was rare when Cortez wanted to pay outright for a cooked meal for all of his men, so Drake nodded shortly and was gone, informing James and Oliver what Cortez had just told him. When Drake and James took off together towards Penrith, Cortez took Diamantha's hand and kissed it gently.

"A bath and a hot meal for my lady?" he asked.

She smiled gratefully. "That would be most welcome."

He winked at her and let her hand go. "Good," he said. "Now, let me help you and Sophie back into the wagon so we can secure the pony."

Diamantha lifted Sophie off of her pony and carried the little girl to the wagon, where Cortez lifted her up and put her in the bed. Then he put his hands around Diamantha's waist and lifted her up nearly as easily as he had lifted the child, setting her on the back of the wagon as well. With a wink, one that Diamantha was becoming so familiar with, he went to collect his charger and mounted effortlessly. She watched him as he spurred the beast forward and took point at the head of the column.

Diamantha realized, as she settled down into the wagon bed with her daughter on her lap, that she was actually happy again. She hadn't been happy in so long that when it finally did come, it had been like a gentle and gradual breeze, not a slap in the face. As the wagon bumped along the road, she started to think about the point in time when she really did become happy again. She couldn't seem to remember the rough beginning with Cortez or the resentment and bitterness she had felt. All she could feel now was the thrill of his smile and the allure of his embrace. Her heart would race at the sound of his voice and melt at the sight of his interaction with Sophie. All of those symptoms pointed to one thing.

... could it be *love*?

She wondered.

It was called The Bloody Cross and it was the biggest tavern in Penrith. Situated close to the church, it sat in a very busy section of the town, near the street of the Merchants, which was just starting to close up for the night when Cortez brought his party through. They passed by dry goods sellers, spice vendors, and one merchant who had all manner of pre-made dresses hanging from the front of the store. Cortez happened to glance at Diamantha's face when she saw the garments and, noting her very interested expression, sent his men on ahead to the tavern as he took his wife and daughter to the merchant with the ready-made clothing.

Diamantha had resisted at first, saying she didn't have any trunks to pack new things in, but Cortez sent Oliver to buy a trunk or more satchels somewhere while he practically forced Diamantha to pick out some new clothing. Even Sophie was able to receive new clothing, as the merchant, a very tall man and his toothless wife, presented them with loosely-sewn clothing for young children. It was really a rather novel idea, this pre-made clothing, and Diamantha knew she could easily finish the garments for her daughter, so she selected four little tunics for Sophie as well as selecting no less than five new garments for herself.

In fact, it was Cortez who had selected them. Everything she looked at, he would come up behind her and tell the merchant that they would purchase it. Diamantha soon got wise to his game and stopped looking, telling him that she had more than enough things. But he didn't think so. He was rather enjoying purchasing things for her so along with the pre-made dresses that were slightly too large for her figure, he purchased two linen shifts, a beautiful, heavy leather robe with exquisite embroidery and fur cuffs on the sleeves, two bars of hard white soap that smelled of lemon rind, and a very pretty tortoise shell comb for her hair.

It was a big booty and Diamantha was rather astonished that he had spent so much money on her and Sophie, but Cortez didn't seemed troubled by it at all. When Oliver returned with a barrel he had purchased from the spice vendor, he and Cortez carefully packed all of the newly bought items into the barrel that smelled of cinnamon and proceeded to roll it down the avenue towards The Bloody Cross.

As night fell, it was very loud and crowded inside the tavern that smelled strongly of unwashed bodies and roasting meat. People were eating and laughing, and Cortez was met at the door by James and Drake. It seemed that people liked to eat at the place but no one had money enough for the expensive rooms, so Drake had procured all four of the tavern's sleeping rooms at a rather costly price. Cortez was in a spending mood and paid it without question.

With his knights picking up the big barrel and following him to a narrow staircase in the corner that led to the upper floor, Cortez took Diamantha and Sophie to the rooms upstairs, inspecting each room until settling on the biggest one. He escorted his wife and child into the airy, well-furnished room and his knights brought in the barrel, plus Diamantha's two other satchels, the cage containing the pets, and Cortez's saddlebags. As the knights left to get themselves and the men settled, Cortez shut the door behind them, shutting out the noise and smoke from the common room below.

It was suddenly very quiet in the big room and Cortez looked around. There was an enormous bed, another smaller bed in an alcove that was more than likely meant for a servant, and then back behind the master's bed was a sectioned off area with a painted wooden screen that shielded a half-barrel bathtub and a chamber pot. In truth, it was quite luxurious and he grunted with satisfaction.

"Well," he said, "it 'tis a better chamber than we have had this entire trip. In fact, it is very nice."

Diamantha agreed. "It seems clean," she noted, inspecting the bed and the coverlet and not finding the usual vermin on it. "I would hope it is for the price you paid."

Cortez began removing his gloves, setting them on a table near the door. "It is of little matter," he said. "You have put up with enough hardship on this trip. I will provide you with comfort when it is available."

Diamantha smiled at him as she went to the big window in the chamber and opened the wooden panels, revealing a lovely view of the cathedral across the street with the fading sunset as a backdrop. Meanwhile, Sophie had opened her pet cage and a puppy, two kittens, and a fox kit had emerged. The puppy, excited to be out, wriggled his tail furiously as he jumped on Sophie, trying to lick her face. Both the kittens and the fox kit were curiously poking around,

228

while the rabbit seemed content to stay inside the cage. Diamantha watched her daughter as she played with the puppy.

"That cage is too small for all of those animals," she said, observing the group. "We will have to find something bigger or we will have to let the rabbit and fox go."

Sophie heard her and turned around, her young face distressed. "No, Mama!" she insisted. "They are my friends!"

Diamantha sighed. "I know they are, sweetheart," she said. "But they will soon grow big and will want to go find other animals of their own kind to live with. You cannot keep them forever."

Sophie's lips molded to a pout. "But they are *mine*," she insisted.

Diamantha wasn't going to argue with her. She went over to Cortez, who had a big booted foot up on the chair next to the table, fussing with a strap on his left boot that had broken.

"Is it possible to find a bigger cage before we leave on the morrow?" she asked. "Those poor animals are very crowded. Or, we could simply set the fox and rabbit free tonight after she goes to sleep."

He glanced up at her, his fingers still toying with the boot. "I shall find a bigger cage."

Diamantha had a feeling that would be his answer. He'd rather hunt all night for a cage than see Sophie disappointed. She sighed faintly, putting a gentle hand on his dark head.

"You do not have to," she said. "She will not hold you responsible if I let two of her pets go. They are wild animals, anyway. She cannot keep them forever."

He finished messing with the strap and stood up. He was preparing to say something to her but, as he gazed into her sweet face, he ended up taking her into his arms instead. She was so soft and warm and compliant against him, that supple body, the memories of which made him shudder.

"I will find a bigger cage," he assured her again, a twinkle in his black eyes. "For now, however, I am famished and I am sure you are, too. Shall we go down into the common room to eat?"

Diamantha shook her head. "Nay," she replied. "It was so loud down there and I do not want to take Sophie into that atmosphere. It

is not someplace she needs to be. May we eat in our room? It would
be much better, I think. I can put her down to sleep early."

Cortez nodded, kissing her on the nose, then the mouth, and
utterly losing himself in her musk. Her taste was delicious and
sweet, but before he lost himself too much, he pulled back with a
groan.

"Another kiss like that and I shall not leave this room for the rest
of the night," he muttered, rubbing his nose against hers. "I shall
bring something back up to you. Do you want hot water for a bath,
too?"

Diamantha was collapsed against him, basking in his strength.
She'd come to crave it. "That would be nice," she said. "But please eat
with your men if you want to. Sophie and I will eat here and then go
to bed. I am sure you would like to spend some time with your men."

He shrugged. "I see them every day."

She grinned. "You see *me* every day," she said, laughing when he
made a face at her. "Please spend some time with your men. I am
sure there is much you wish to discuss with them and you will not
do it if I am sitting next to you. I do not need to hear all of your
business. Rest assured that I will be here when you return."

She was more astute than he had given her credit for. It was true
that there were things to discuss with his men that he would not
discuss around her, things such as their approach to Falkirk and
how to recover Edlington's body once they arrived. Things she didn't
need to, and probably didn't want to, hear. But he had been so
consumed with her the entire trip that he'd hardly had any
conversations with his men other than those that pertained directly
to their daily activities.

"Do you swear you will be here when I return?" he asked.

"I do."

"You will not trick me and sleep elsewhere?"

She grinned. "I will not, I promise."

He opened his mouth to reply but a squeal from Sophie cut him
off. The rabbit had bolted out of the cage and Sophie was now in
mad pursuit. With a grin, he watched the little girl chase the rabbit
around the room as he shook out his gloves and put them back on

again. Sophie was having a marvelous time chasing the rabbit, but the little bunny was terrified so Diamantha put a stop to it.

"Sweetheart, you frighten the rabbit when you chase it," she said to her daughter, taking the girl by the hand and leading her over to the cage where the other animals were. She put the bunny back in the cage and sat her daughter on the floor. "Please play with them without chasing them. Be kind to little creatures."

Sophie was undeterred as she took a piece of straw from the cage and teased the kittens with it. The puppy was wandering around beside her, sniffing the floor and looking for scraps. Cortez headed for the door as Diamantha bent over her daughter and the menagerie of pets. He was thinking it was all quite sweet; the running rabbit, the jumping dog, the squealing little girl, and his beautiful wife. It was the most wonderful thing he'd ever known.

"I shall return as soon as I can," he told her. "I will have a meal sent up to you and something for the animals, too."

Diamantha straightened up and looked at him. "That would be quite kind of you, my lord."

There went that familiar wink again as he opened the door and shut it softly behind him. Diamantha went over to lock it, her thoughts lingering on the tall, handsome husband that was now hers.

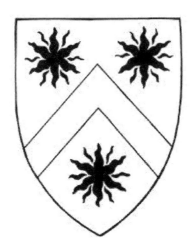

CHAPTER SEVENTEEN

Coven Castle

Four days after Cortez's departure, Andres was still keeping his father in the vault of Coven, although the cell was considerably more luxurious than any vault in the country outside of the Tower of London. Most prisoners did not sleep on comfortable beds with servants to tend their every wish, but Gorsedd had just that. He lived like a king.

Andres was with him daily, sitting with his father for hours on end and listening to his father talk about family history. He kept relieving the death of his grandfather, over and over, pounding the horrible end into Andres' brain and then cursing Diamantha for her family ties.

It was an exhausting experience for Andres, who was growing increasingly resentful that he had to remain with his father while everyone else continued on to Scotland. By the end of the fourth day of listening to his father rant, he'd finally had enough. Gorsedd was in the process of describing his mother's torment with the de Velt raid on her ancestral home when Andres finally exploded.

"Enough!" he shouted, startling his father. "Great Bleeding Jesus, do you have any idea how foolish you sound? You are living in the past, old man. You are living the horrors that your family has already lived. When does it stop? Tell me that, Father – when does all of this horror and hatred stop?"

Gorsedd looked at Andres with a mixture of hurt and anger. "Your great-grandfather was impaled on a stake, alive, and...."

"I know!" Andres roared, putting his hands on his head in anguish. "I know he was impaled alive. That is all I have heard for days and days. But he is dead. The man who did that to him is dead. And you have had the gall to blame a woman who never knew her ancestor and who has probably never done a terrible thing in her life? That makes you a beast, do you hear? You are a foolish old beast living in the past and you do not care who you hurt with old hatreds. When are you doing to stop this? Don't you realize what it is doing to you? Or me or Cortez?"

Gorsedd wasn't used to Andres yelling back at him. The man had sat and listened to him rant for days and hardly said a word about it other than pleading for calm. Now, Andres' irritation was unleashed and Gorsedd was offended by it.

"Your family is everything," he pointed out angrily. "We have an obligation...."

"The family you speak of is dead!" Andres yelled, interrupting him. "Everyone you are speaking of is dead and no amount of talk can bring them back. But your family is *alive*. Your boys are alive. Cortez and I are your family and all you have done is hurt Cortez by blaming his wife for something she had no control over. Is that what you want? To hurt Cortez? The man adores you, Father. See what damage you have done to him with your hate mongering. What do you think Mother would have said to that?"

Andres' words gave Gorsedd pause. He fell back to regroup, trying not to think on Allegria de Bretagne's reaction to his behavior but he couldn't quite ignore it. Even in death, Allegria was a very strong personality and he could just hear her yelling at him in Spanish, and then in a language he could understand when he would plead with her. He could hear her yelling even now. Nay, she would not have been pleased with his behavior at all. She adored Cortez, her eldest son, and had been fiercely protective over him.

"You'll not bring your mother's memory into this," he said to Andres.

But Andres would not be stopped. "I can and I will," he said. "You know that what you did was wrong. You hurt Cortez and you hurt his wife. If Mother was alive, she would make you beg forgiveness. Well? What are you going to do about it?"

Gorsedd looked away, he had to. He could no longer face Andres because the man was correct, he was absolutely correct.

"Your mother is not here, so your question has no meaning," he grumbled.

Andres pulled something out of his tunic and slapped it down onto the table next to Gorsedd. When the man looked over, he saw the pieces of the silver collar he had torn from Diamantha's neck, the collar that had once belonged to Allegria. The woman had worn the necklace constantly, as much a part of her as anything else was. The sight of the collar had Gorsedd slipping into deep uncertainty.

"Mother is here now," Andres said, pointing to the collar. "Look at this and tell her why you hurt Cortez and his wife. Let her tell you what a fool you have been."

With that, Andres quit the cell, locking it before heading up the stairs to the ground level above. Gorsedd sat long after his son had gone, gazing at the pieces of the silver collar, seeing it around the neck of his wife and hearing her words in his head. That necklace embodied all that Allegria de Bretagne had been; strong, shiny, and beautiful. She was the love of his life, much as Cortez and Andres were. Family was everything. *His* family. Perhaps it was time to let the past die, after all.

Collecting the pieces of the collar, he held them to his chest and wept.

Penrith

It was like old times that evening at The Bloody Cross, minus Andres, whose presence was sorely missed. Cortez sat with James, Oliver, and Drake at a table that was wedged up against the front of the tavern, near the front door, and angled so that they could see everyone coming in through the front door before those entrants saw them. After having food and copious amounts of hot water sent up to Diamantha, Cortez sat in the common room with his men and enjoyed the meal and conversation.

The room was even more packed now than it had been when he'd arrived, full of travelers, merchants, whores, a few soldiers that belonged to him, and other soldiers that did not. He thought he saw a few men bearing colors he recognized, the colors of Baron Coverdale who controlled a good deal of land in the area, but he couldn't really tell and he didn't want to stare because staring was often taken as a challenge. So he listened to Drake tell stories about his wild brothers, laughing appropriately when Drake's humor harangued out of control. He knew for a fact that Drake was the wild brother although the man managed to hide it well.

"Will Andres be joining us at some point, Cortez?"

It was a question from James. In private, Cortez permitted his knights to address him by his given name because that was the level of trust they had between them. These men were as close to him as Andres ever was, men who had been with him through both good and bad times. He took a long drink from his cup of wine that was heavy and tart, and smacked his lips.

"Hopefully," he said. He eyed his men a moment before continuing. "I have not spoken to you about my father's behavior since it all happened. I suppose I can tell you that I do not know much more about it than you do. You heard what my father said and even when I tried to speak with him afterwards, he still adhered to those views. Andres remained behind at Coven Castle not to be my father's jailer but to be his caretaker. According to my father's majordomo, it would seem my father's mind has been failing him as of late, which possibly explains his behavior. In any case, Andres is there to see for himself. It is his intention to catch up to us in a week or two, but I suppose time will tell."

The knights digested the information. It was Drake who finally spoke. "I knew Rob Edlington for years and I never heard that Lady de Bretagne was related to Jax de Velt," he said what they were all thinking. "A fearsome and dark heritage she bears."

Cortez nodded. "One hundred years later, one would hope that people have forgotten about his atrocities but evidently that is not the case," he said. "Seeing how my father reacted, that is more than likely knowledge we should not speak of outside of this circle."

The knights agreed, sipping their wine in silence, until James suddenly snorted into his cup. The other three looked at him curiously.

"What do you find humorous about that?" Cortez asked.

James shook his blond head. "It is not the fact that she is related to de Velt that I find funny," he said. "I was thinking of my great-grandfather, Christopher de Lohr, and how the man must have bargained with de Velt for the marriage contract. Can you imagine being in the room when England's two greatest warlords face off on the subject of their children? A marriage, no less? By God's Bloody Rood! Oh, but to have listened in on that conversation!"

Cortez's lips twitched. "De Lohr must have faced the man in full armor, even for a contract negotiation," he said. "I cannot imagine I would have sat in a room with de Velt and not have had every bloody weapon I owned strapped to my body."

The knights snickered. "I would have done it from the other side of a closed portcullis," Oliver muttered. "It is common knowledge that my parents came from two families that hated each other for generations, and their marriage was shocking enough. But marrying into the House of de Velt... I cannot imagine what de Lohr was thinking."

"Mayhap their children were in love," Drake said. "Wasn't it his daughter who married de Velt's son?" When Cortez nodded, Drake continued. "Then that settles it. The man probably had no choice. How could he deny his daughter if she loved a de Velt offspring?"

"Easily," James said. "He could have sent the woman to a convent or beat the foolish notion out of her. One way or the other, marrying into the House of de Velt, especially back in their generation, must have been an appalling prospect."

No one could disagree. As Cortez opened his mouth to continue, the front door to the tavern opened and two very large, very well armed knights entered. In fact, they were knights of the highest order, bearing Coverdale tunics and weighed down with a myriad of war implements. One was very tall and one was very broad about the shoulders. They looked rather out of place in the filth and levity of the tavern, with people eating and laughing around them. They looked like they were about to step onto a battlefield. The pair stood by the door as they evidently scouted out a place to sit.

Cortez and his knights noticed the duo right away. Cortez's gaze lingered on them for a moment until, suddenly, a light of recognition came to his eye. He appeared rather surprised. Abruptly, he stood up and made his way over to the knights. Back at his table, Drake, James, and Oliver stood up, hands on the hilt of their swords. If there was going to be trouble, then they would be ready.

But trouble wasn't what Cortez intended. Standing a few feet away from the pair, he spoke rather loudly.

"Who let you two into this town?" he said, rather menacingly. "There are laws against your kind, you know."

The knights whirled around, features full of suspicion, but when they saw Cortez standing there, big smiles became evident. The shorter man even laughed aloud, a happy sort of crow. They rushed the man, grabbing Cortez's outstretched hand in greeting.

"De Bretagne!" Keir St. Héver, the shortest of the pair, gasped. "God's Teeth, is it really you? I can hardly believe my eyes!"

Cortez was so happy to see his old friend that he embraced him. Next to St. Héver, Michael of Pembury, an enormous mountain of a man, clapped Cortez on the shoulder so hard that he nearly knocked him over.

"As gentle and tender as always, Pembury," Cortez grunted, eyeing the man with the bright blue eyes. "I thought it was you two when you entered because no one is as ugly as St. Héver and no one is as tall as Pembury. What are you doing here?"

Keir was still grinning like a fool, very happy to see the man he had fostered with many years ago. A very handsome man in spite of Cortez's comment, and very blond, Keir had been Cortez's closest friend, once, until time and separation had cooled those bonds. But the link was still there, unbreakable as always. The last time he had seen him had been at Helene's funeral. He continued to hold on to Cortez's hand as he spoke.

"We are on business for Coverdale," he told him. "I have two hundred men camping on the outskirts of town but I wanted a roof over my head tonight. I see that this place is crowded, unfortunately. Where are you staying?"

Cortez was leading them back over to his table. "Here," he said. "I have all four rooms but you and Pembury can surely have one. My knights can double up."

Keir was grateful. "My thanks, my friend," he said. "You have saved me a good deal of effort."

They reached the table as Drake stole two chairs from another table and pulled them up for Keir and Michael. Keir thanked the man, acknowledging the others around the table.

"So you still travel with this motley crew, do you?" he teased. "De Winter, St. John, and de Lohr. Christ, Cortez, haven't you learned to keep better company?"

Cortez grinned as everyone sat down and more cups for wine were produced. "Evidently not," he said, eyeing St. Héver as the man poured himself a healthy measure of wine. "I kept company with you, didn't I?"

Everyone snorted at St. Héver's expense, but Keir didn't mind in the least. He clapped Cortez on the back.

"Tell me what you are doing in Penrith, Cortez," he said. "Will you have time to come to Pendragon Castle and meet my wife? I would like you to."

Cortez's eyes glimmered warmly. "You have taken a wife?" he asked with satisfaction. "I am thrilled to hear that, my friend, truly."

He didn't touch on the reasons why he was thrilled, the dark reasons that all men in this tight circle knew. Keir's first wife and two children had been murdered in a siege a few years ago and the man had been emotionally destroyed as a result. Upon hearing of the tragedy, Helene had encouraged Cortez to travel north to comfort the man, to Pendragon Castle where Keir was the garrison commander for Baron Coverdale, which he had. He had stayed for two months, watching St. Héver slowly die inside. It had been terrible to watch. Now, to hear that he had married again was something of a massive relief.

Keir wasn't totally oblivious to what Cortez was thinking. He sighed happily, gazing upon his friend with more joy than Cortez had ever seen in him.

"I married a couple of years ago," he told him. "I have a son who is a little over a year old and my wife is expecting again. Chloe is a remarkable woman, Cortez. I should like you to meet her."

Cortez nodded, truly delighted for his friend. "As I would like to meet her also," he replied. "But not this trip. I am traveling with my wife and we are simply passing through Penrith on our journey north."

Keir's smile faded and he took on a rather startled expression. In fact, he glanced and Pembury to see that the man mirrored his surprise.

"Your *wife*?" Keir repeated. "You have married again?"

Cortez nodded, seeing the stunned look in Keir's eyes. He reached out and gave the man's arm a squeeze.

"You and I both suffered great losses, my friend," he said quietly. "You lost your wife and I lost Helene. But, like you, I have married again and I could not be happier. She is with me, in fact. She is upstairs with her daughter as we speak."

Keir's eyebrows lifted. "You are traveling with a child?"

Cortez nodded and poured himself more wine. "Let me explain, since I see that I have only succeeded in confusing you with my ramblings," he grinned. "You remember Rob Edlington, of course."

Keir nodded. "Of course," he said. "Rob fought with us at Falkirk. He also fell there. We lost many good men that day."

Cortez continued. "I never told anyone this because there was really no need, but I was with Rob when he was injured," he said, lowering his voice. "Edlington knew he was dying and asked me to take care of his wife. I fulfilled his wish. I married Edlington's widow. But you also recall that we were unable to recover Edlington's body. This is something that has haunted his wife so she asked me to return to Falkirk to bring Edlington back for a proper burial. Because it means so much to her, I have complied. We are therefore on a great quest to find Rob Edlington and bring him back to Corfe Castle so he can be properly buried. That is why I cannot take the time to go out of our way to meet your wife. It would throw us off our time schedule and it is my hope to find Edlington's body before winter sets in. If it does before we can get to it, we will have to wait for the spring thaw and I do not wish to remain in Scotland that long. Time is of the essence."

It was quite an amazing story, as evidenced by St. Héver and Pembury's expressions. The two Coverdale knights looked at each other, perhaps in disbelief, before returning their attention to Cortez.

"You are going to *find* his corpse?" Keir repeated. Then, he shook his head. "Cortez, you know as well as I do that it will be an impossible task. We lost many men under the mud of that field. It was horrible stuff. How in God's name do you expect to locate Edlington's corpse?"

Cortez tried not to become defensive at the question. "I was the last person to see Edlington," he said. "I know where I left him. We have brought shovels with us and we will dig test holes in the area until we find something."

Keir wasn't trying to be critical, or talk him out of it, but it was truly an outlandish quest. "It will be very difficult," he said. "What if you do not find him?"

Cortez shrugged, toying with his wine cup. "My wife is aware that we may not," he said, then looked at Keir again. The black eyes were serious and sad at the same time. "It means so much to her. I cannot let her suffer this angst without doing something about it. Besides, if I had dragged Edlington's body out of the battlefield, we would not be on this quest in the first place. She would have had something to bury and all would be well. So, you see, it is my fault that we are here in the first place."

Keir studied him a moment. "You are blaming yourself for something that could not be helped at the time."

Cortez lifted his big shoulders in a vague gesture. "Mayhap," he said. "But I intend to rectify it. So now you know why we are here."

Keir glanced at the knights around the table, knights that were loyal to Cortez no matter what. All the while, his mind was mulling over what he'd been told. He glanced at Pembury to see if he could discern the man's thoughts but he could not. Taking a deep drink of his wine, he smacked his lips.

"How many men have you brought with you?" he asked.

Cortez threw a thumb in the direction of the street outside, the last place he had seen most of his men. "Twenty-five foot soldiers and five knights," he said. "I did not want to bring too many men because that often attracts trouble, so I brought a small party. So far, it has worked out well."

"Five knights?" Keir looked around, only counting four. "Where is the fifth?"

"I left Andres at Coven Castle with my father when we stopped there a few days ago."

Keir's grin was back. "I have missed Andres," he said. "I am deeply saddened that he is not here. I owe that man a slug to the jaw, you know. The last time I saw him, he got me involved in a terrible tavern fight. He was dead-drunk and refused to pay his bill, and the tavern keeper's son did not take too kindly to that. I think we fairly destroyed the place when it was all said and done."

Cortez laughed softly. "He has a talent for such things."

Keir agreed, draining the last of his cup. "Aye, he certainly does," he said. "But enough of Andres and his foolishness. Let us continue to speak of your quest. Falkirk is at least a seven or eight day journey from here."

"I realize that."

"The Scots are not so friendly these days."

Cortez looked at him. "Have you had trouble?"

Keir shook his head. "Not this far south, but I have heard rumor that there has been trouble on the border. The Ferguson and the Armstrong clans have been rather busy, I'm told. I believe Carlisle has suffered raids." He looked seriously at Cortez. "Do you really intend to take your wife and child into Scotland?"

Cortez struggled not to feel as if he was doing something foolish. "I have no choice," he muttered. "I promised her. She wants to bury Edlington and I must do all I can to ensure that she is at peace."

Keir could see that Cortez was starting to feel defensive. He put his hand on the man's shoulder. "I am not judging you, my friend," he said quietly. "It is simply that the situation in Scotland is not at all calm. There could be trouble. Why not leave your wife and child at

Pendragon while you continue on to Falkirk? At least they would be safe."

Cortez immediately shook his head. "Although I appreciate your offer, Diamantha would never agree to it," he said. "She is tenacious. If I left her behind, she would find a way to follow me and that I could not stomach. Nay, my friend, where I go, she goes. This is more her quest than it is mine."

Keir understood what it was to have a tenacious wife, he had one of his own. He sighed knowingly as he poured himself more wine, glancing up to see the expressions on the faces of the knights around the table. He knew they would go to hell and back for de Bretagne. Their loyalty was without question. But he feared for them. He feared for all of them. More than that, this wasn't a quest Cortez should have to face alone. He knew that without a doubt. He took a long drink of wine and set the cup back down onto the table with a rather forceful slam.

"Then you leave me no choice," he said firmly. "I was at Falkirk, too, and Rob Edlington was also my friend. It could very easily have been me with the man as he breathed his last. Only by fate was it you. Rob was a good man and he did not deserve to be left behind."

Cortez nodded slowly. "And I agree," he said quietly, "which is why I am going back."

Keir was firm. "You misunderstand," he said. "I mean to say that I cannot allow you to travel to Falkirk without me. I feel somewhat responsible for this as well. Every man who took part in that bloody day shares some of this responsibility. I could not live with myself, knowing you are facing danger to retrieve a fallen comrade and quite possibly undermanned with only twenty-five men and four knights. I will therefore go with you and if you deny me, know that I am much like your wife. I am tenacious, and I will follow you. I will follow you whether or not you like it, so the matter is settled. Pembury? Are you with me?"

The big knight lifted his dark eyebrows. Michael tended to be the quieter of the pair, but when he did have cause to speak, it was usually of great meaning.

"I cannot let you go alone," he said in his ridiculously deep voice. "You are correct when you say that every man who fought upon those hallowed fields shares the responsibility of a fallen comrade, and since I was there, the burden too is mine. Besides, who would keep you out of trouble?"

Keir grinned at his companion. "Then it is settled," he said. "Tomorrow, we ride for Scotland with de Bretagne. I will hire a boy to take a message to Coverdale regarding our immediate plans and have him send word to my wife. She will not be entirely happy, but she will understand. She understands something about loyalty and friendship."

Cortez didn't know what to say. He looked at Keir and Michael with some astonishment. "You are coming *with* me?" he repeated, somewhat awed. "Surely Coverdale cannot spare you."

Keir waved him off. "We have finished our business for him," he said. "Besides, my knights are in charge of Pendragon and the garrison is safe. De Velt is in charge, and no man has ever bested a de Velt."

All of Cortez's knights, and Cortez himself, looked at Keir with some shock. "De Velt?" Cortez repeated. "You have a de Velt in your service?"

Keir could see the myriad of astonished expressions and he grinned. "I do," he replied. "You haven't met the man, Cortez. He's several years younger and came up through Coverdale's ranks. Now, I know the history of the House of de Velt in the north. Hell, everyone does, but I assure you that he is not a blood-thirsty monster as his forefathers were. Lorcan is an excellent knight and I trust him implicitly."

Cortez's knights looked at him to see his reaction, but Cortez, over his initial surprise, ended up chuckling.

"Another de Velt," he groaned, looking over at his knights. "Be sure not to tell my father."

His knights were grinning but Keir wasn't in on the joke. "What do you mean?" he asked. "What does your father have to do with the House of de Velt?"

Ordering two more pitchers of wine, Cortez launched into the story of his father, the House of de Velt, his first meeting with Diamantha, and other things. It ended up being a very long night that saw Cortez and his men going to sleep just a few hours before dawn. But it didn't matter. It had been one of the best nights he'd spent in a very long time, reliving old times and discussing the future with men he shared an unbreakable bond with. He considered himself an extremely fortunate man.

At one point in the evening, as he listened to Drake launch into one of his many humorous tales, he briefly reflected on the life he lost three years ago. When Helene had died and the baby with her, he was sure he was dead, too. Even when he went to Corfe those few weeks ago to marry Diamantha, he still wasn't sure if their union would bring any of the joy back into his life. But he was coming to realize that this quest had bonded them together as nothing else ever could have. It wasn't so much that they were joined by the mutual quest for Robert. It was the fact that they had shared so much together along the journey, perhaps more than most married couples ever do, and in that adventure Diamantha's character, heart, and soul was revealed. Perhaps his was, too.

As he watched the men around the table, men he loved like brothers, he realized how deeply content and utterly happy he was for the first time in his life. It was more than he had ever shared with Helene. It was as if he had reached for the stars and had finally managed to grasp one. Helene had been like a warm autumn breeze, gentle and comforting. Diamantha was like the scorching summer sun, searing him until he was blinded by her. He couldn't describe in words how he felt about the woman.

All he knew was that he loved her.

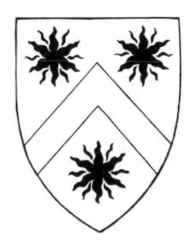

CHAPTER EIGHTEEN

Carlisle, Lockerbie, Moffatt.

Scottish towns didn't look much different from English towns, or so Diamantha thought. Scotland's topography wasn't too much different from England's except there seemed to be a lot of mountains and a lot of lakes, or lochs as the Scottish called them. They had stopped in the Scottish towns at night to eat and sleep, and for the most part they had been met with hospitable people. Not that Diamantha had expected otherwise, but Cortez hadn't been so sure.

All of the knights had been on alert since the moment the party had passed over the border. Diamantha and Sophie had been forced to ride in the wagon, even in the excellent mild weather they had been experiencing, which had made Sophie somewhat restless, even with her pets to keep her busy. Diamantha, meanwhile, had passed the time sewing on the little tunics they had purchased for Sophie in Penrith. She was an excellent seamstress and the garments were turning out beautifully. Distracted with her sewing and also with her restless daughter, she could still feel the edginess of the knights as they traveled deeper and deeper into Scots territory.

The two new knights they had picked up in Penrith, St. Héver and Pembury, had brought a good deal of power to reinforce Cortez's ranks. When Cortez had explained their reasoning for joining the quest, Diamantha had been very touched. It would seem that Robert had many men who were fond of him and their loyalty to her dead husband pleased her immensely. Now, it seemed to be more than just a widow trying to find her husband's remains. It was a host of his friends that would join her. Diamantha was coming to learn a good deal about loyalty from these knights who had fought and died together. The great Questing was taking on more dimensions, now with added friends who would see Robert returned for a proper burial, too.

So the days passed too slowly and the nights too quickly. The days were full of quiet travel because Cortez was fearful of noise, fearful it would draw a horde of Scots to their doorstep. Nothing was worse in Scotland than hearing a Sassenach accent on Scots soil. Therefore, the men traveled silently and heavily armed, making their way along the dirt roads in brittle silence. The last time most of them had been in Scotland, it had been to fight a great and terrible battle. It was therefore reasonable to expect that they would be conditioned to be in battle mode every time they walked upon Scots earth. Diamantha could see it in everything about them. They were an enemy in enemy lands.

On their third day into Scotland, they stopped for the night in a small town called Moffatt. It was a charming town nestled in the rolling lowland hills, with a rather large town square that was surrounded by homes and businesses.

As the group moved into the town close to sunset, the merchants were beginning to close their shops for the night but Diamantha needed more thread for her sewing, so Cortez and Keir found a merchant with all manner of fabric and threads, and convinced the man to stay open long enough for Diamantha to do some shopping. She did, with Sophie on her hip as she perused the dry goods.

As dark clouds began to roll in overhead and a chill wind picked up, Cortez and Keir stood watch over Diamantha while the rest of the knights took the horses over to the enormous trough in the town square to allow the animals to drink. Cortez's men fanned out around the square, exhausted from a day's journey and taking a few moments to rest as Lady de Bretagne shopped for thread.

But it was more than thread she found, she also found gorgeous bolts of Ferguson tartan, with blues and greens and reds, and she very much wanted some. They were in Ferguson country, after all, so the merchant carried a good deal of the fabric which was made locally by old Ferguson widows from Ferguson sheep. The merchant was thrilled to sell her a hefty measure of the tartan, which was very warm, and Diamantha happily bought it along with several spools of red, blue, and white thread. She also added to her sewing case by purchasing a new thimble, needles made of iron, and a pair of new shears also made from iron.

As she bartered for the price, Sophie grew restless and she put the little girl down, calling to Cortez to watch out for the child as the she wandered in his direction. Cortez and Keir turned to watch the little girl, who strolled out of the merchant's stall and promptly squatted down to pick some small yellow flowers that were growing at the base of a spindly tree nearby. Keir's gaze lingered on the lass, bundled up against the cold weather.

"My son celebrated his first year of life back in July," he said, almost wistfully. "In fact, he celebrated it when I was fighting at Falkirk. He is very curious about everything, much like your little Sophie is, except he is curious about any manner of bug that crosses his path. He frightens his mother with them constantly."

Cortez grinned as he watched Sophie yank up the weeds. "With Sophie, it is animals," he said. "You have seen her collection, of course."

Keir nodded. "You have quite a menagerie of fat and happy animals," he said. "Children *should* have pets. I think it teaches them about the value of life. My son already has a pony."

Cortez glanced at him. "Does he ride it?"

Keir nodded firmly. "Indeed he does," he insisted. "And he does not fall off. The same cannot be said for many children his age."

Cortez laughed at Keir's proud boasting. He was about to say something when Diamantha caught his attention. She was evidently finished shopping and needed him to pay the bill. He excused himself, leaving Keir to watch over Sophie. As Cortez and Diamantha paid for the booty, the big knight with the white-blond hair made his way over to the little girl as she fussed with her posies.

"Those are very nice flowers," he commented.

Sophie looked up at him and Keir noticed what Cortez had noticed also. She was the image of her father with her big blue eyes and dark blond hair.

"I am going to feed them to my rabbit," she said.

Keir pretended to be very interested. "Is that so?" he said. "Does your rabbit have a name?"

Sophie nodded. "His name is Clover," she said. Then, she reached up and took his hand. "I have a pony. Would you like to see him?"

Before Keir could answer, he found himself being dragged across the road to the cluster of de Bretagne men and their wagons. Sophie pulled him between the wagons, coming to a very fat black and white pony who was chewing happily on the thick grass that was sprouting up in spots around the square. She went right to pony's head and shoved the flowers into its mouth, which it hungrily crunched on.

Keir stood over the pair, watching with a smile on his face. He found that he missed his son, remembering the boy and his little blond pony. He missed his wife, too. As he stood over the nuzzling pair, hands on his hips, he heard a shout from behind.

Looking up, he saw Cortez and Diamantha heading in his direction. Cortez was carrying his wife's load of loot, putting it into the wagon bed as he eyed Keir.

"So she lured you into seeing her pony, too, did she?" he asked, brushing off his hands after depositing the load. "That is her usual path. I hadn't known her five minutes before she was dragging me off to the stables to see General."

Keir grinned, watching the little girl pet the pony's velvety nose and laughing when he nibbled at her. "He is a handsome beast," he said.

Cortez nodded, watching Sophie and the pony for a moment longer before stroking his chin and looking about the town. His manner was thoughtful.

"Speaking of handsome beasts, I plan to get myself into a bath tonight before my wife refuses to come near me because I smell too badly," he said. "The fabric merchant said that there is a traveler's inn on the opposite side of the square called The White Star. There should be a board with a star painted on it somewhere but I do not seem to see it."

Keir was looking around, too, spying the structure across the square. "There it is," he said, pointing. "Is that our destination tonight?"

Cortez squinted at the building in the distance. Like his brother, his eyesight at a distance wasn't too keen. "For the knights it is," he said. "I will make the arrangements. Make sure the men bed down somewhere in close range. They may camp if they wish but not too far away. I want to be moving out by sunrise. Will you please see to it?"

Keir nodded, moving away from Cortez to carry out the man's orders as Cortez pried Sophie away from her pony. The dark clouds overhead were growing darker and the wind was picking up. Random drops of rain began falling as a storm began to settle. Cortez took Sophie and Diamantha carrying the animal cage, with Merlin trailing along behind them carrying all of their bags, and crossed the square to The White Star inn on the other side.

The structure stood by itself, not crowded by other buildings, and was a very long, very slender three-storied establishment. The construction was waddle and daub, with exposed external beams for additional support, and they passed into the entrance, right beneath a massive board upon which a white star was painted.

Inside, there was a long, slender room, nearly the length of the building, and back in the rear of the room, he could see a kitchen complete with a giant, smoking hearth. Cooking smells wafted in the room, the scent of roasting meat and heavy smoke. It also smelled like dogs and nearly as soon as they entered, a pack of mutts came rushing out at them. Sophie screamed when one growled and nearly launched herself into Cortez's arms. He kicked the growling dog in the throat, and the dog yelped as it turned tail and scampered off.

"Dunna kick me dogs, mon," the innkeeper said as he emerged from the kitchen. He was a fat man with a crown of wild red hair and a long pipe hanging from his lips. "They willna hurt ye."

Cortez cocked a dark eyebrow. "That dog growled at my daughter and frightened her," he said evenly. "If it does it again, I will kill it and reimburse you the cost for a new one that will be friendlier towards children."

The innkeeper stared at him a moment before breaking into a grin, revealing crooked and green teeth. "Where are ye from, *sassenach*?"

Cortez couldn't tell if the man was trying to be friendly or trying to figure out just how much of an enemy he was. Upon hearing Cortez's speech pattern, it was clear that he was instantly suspicious.

"We have come to visit kin," Cortez didn't answer him directly. He lied, in fact. "We require at least four rooms, more if you can spare them."

The innkeeper puffed on his pipe. The smoke that emerged smelled strongly of animal dung. As he puffed away, deciding whether or not he wanted to rent a room to the Sassenach knight and his family, his round wife came waddling in from the kitchen, took one look at Sophie, and crowed with delight.

"Oooch!" she exclaimed, clapping her hands. "What have we here? A bonny lass with the face of an angel!"

Sophie looked at the woman with the loud voice and turned her head away, laying it on Cortez's shoulder. From the growling dog to the loud woman, she wasn't entire comfortable with these unfamiliar surroundings so she buried her face in Cortez's shoulder. The old woman, however, was not deterred. She went up to Cortez and patted Sophie gently on the back.

"Do ye know what it is I have fer ye, lass?" she said, trying to get the girl to look at her. "I have a sweet treat fer ye with honey and apricots and fermented milk. Would ye like some?"

Diamantha had been standing silently by, watching the woman try to warm Sophie up, but it was clear her daughter wasn't willing to respond at the moment. She was tired from travel, so Diamantha interrupted the woman's attempts.

"We are very tired," she said politely. "Mayhap she will accept your treat once she has had a chance to rest. May we go to our rooms now?"

Even though the husband hadn't yet decided if he wanted English guests, the wife took charge of the situation. She didn't care if they were English or not. She had guests and she would provide for them.

"Of course ye can," she said, moving towards the narrow staircase built against the side of the wall. It disappeared into the darkened floor above and she mounted the steps, turning to wave her guests along. "Come with me. I'll get ye settled. Would ye be wantin' a bath?"

Diamantha was already following the woman with Cortez, Sophie, and Merlin close behind. "That would be lovely, thank you," she said.

The woman gathered her dirty skirts as she took the stairs. "I'll have one brought to ye," she said. "I'll also bring up some food fer the little lass."

"We have more in our party," Cortez said as he carried Sophie up the stairs. "Five more knights who will require rooms. I shall pay handsomely for the privilege."

The woman nodded vigorously. "We have enough room fer them," she said. "There was a big market here a couple of days ago and we were all full, but everyone has left. We have lots o'room now."

Diamantha turned to glance at Cortez, who winked at her as they followed the loud, enthusiastic woman up the stairs. Once they mounted the top of the steps, she turned left and took them down a short, dark corridor that ended at a rather heavy oak door. The woman threw the latch and an enormous room came into view.

The chamber was at the front of the inn, overlooking the square. There were two good-sized beds, strung with rope with clean straw mattresses, a table and chairs near a sooty hearth, and back in the corner behind a wooden screen was an in-room privy. It was nothing more than a seat placed over the bottom half of a barrel, but Diamantha was rather surprised to see it in their room. The old woman threw open the window at the front of the chamber and let some of the damp, cool wind inside.

"There, now," she said. "This will air it out a bit. I'll send me lad up with peat fer the fire. And I'll be back with food!"

She bustled out, leaving Cortez and Diamantha to settle in. As Merlin carried the bags in and set them down near the window, Cortez set Sophie down on one of the beds and Diamantha set the animal cage onto the floor. Then she went over to her daughter and began removing the heavy outer layer of clothing that had kept her warm throughout her travels. She looked over at Cortez as the man inspected the other bed.

"Can you please bring in all of my sewing?" she asked. "It is still in the wagon where I was sitting. The barrel with our new clothing is there, too. Can you have someone bring it all up?"

Cortez nodded, finished with the bed inspection and then moving over to the in-room privy. He lifted his eyebrows and shook his head as if he'd never seen such a thing in his life. "I will go and have them bring it in right now," he said, his gaze lingering on the privy a moment longer before heading for the chamber door. "Do you require anything else while I am at the wagon?"

Diamantha pulled Sophie's arms out of the woolen coat and set it aside. "Nay," she said pensively. "But I have been thinking... well, that is to say, I have been wondering how far we are from Norham Castle."

Cortez paused at the door. "Norham?" he repeated. "What has brought that about?"

Diamantha shrugged as she began untying Sophie's little boots. "I am not entirely sure," she said. "I suppose I have simply been thinking about my father since we are so far north. He has never seen Sophie, you know. I was wondering how far away we are from Norham Castle and, if we are not too far, mayhap we can visit my mother and father for a day or two, as we did your father. I... I miss my papa, Cortez. I have not seen him in a very long time."

Cortez stood at the door a moment before coming back into the room and shutting the door. He seemed to be mulling over her request as he sat on the other bed in the chamber. The ropes creaked under his weight.

"Norham is, at the very least, several days from here," he said. "It would mean traveling through a good deal of hostile country to get there."

Diamantha pulled off one of Sophie's boots and set it down on the floor. "But we have several knights traveling with us," she said. "That should make it somewhat safer."

He wriggled his eyebrows. "Not if we are attacked by a thousand angry Scots," he said. "Moreover, it would mean delaying our arrival at Falkirk by several days at least and we want to have the chance to look for Rob's remains while the ground is still soft. If there is one snow or one freezing rain storm, the ground will harden up and there is no telling how long it will take it to soften again."

Diamantha's expression was downcast. "I know," she muttered. "It was just a thought. I do not want to delay what we have set out to do. But I thought... if we were close enough... then mayhap I could see my father and he could meet Sophie."

Cortez stood up from the bed. He went over to her and kissed her cheek as Sophie, with one shoeless foot, began playfully kicking at her mother.

"There will be another time," he told her. "But I do not believe this is the right time."

Diamantha simply nodded as he turned for the door once again. His hand was on the latch when she called after him.

"Cortez?"

He paused by the panel, hand on the latch. "Aye, sweet?"

Diamantha was in the process of fending off Sophie's playful feet as she tried to remove the other boot. "You only recently saw my father, did you not?" she asked. "When you went to Norham to ask for permission to marry me."

Cortez didn't move from his position by the door, but his expression flickered. There was something odd in his face, perhaps a flicker of fear that crossed his features but was just as quickly gone.

"Why do you ask?" he wanted to know, his tone steady.

She managed to remove Sophie's second boot. "Because I never asked you how he was," she said. "Was he healthy? How did he look?"

Cortez just looked at her. Slowly, he came back into the room as Sophie, seeing her mother distracted, bolted off the bed with her shoeless feet and, giggling, ran to play with her animals. Diamantha turned to follow her so she could finish undressing the child but Cortez reached out and grasped her by the hand.

"Wait," he said gently. "Come over here with me. I must speak with you."

Diamantha allowed him to lead her over to the bed. He sat down and pulled her down next to him, his hands gripping hers. All the while, he seemed very thoughtful, which in turn spurred Diamantha's imagination a bit. At first his manner was curious to her but now she was starting to become frightened. When he lifted his head so speak, she interrupted him.

"Something is wrong," she blurted, fear in her eyes. "What is wrong? Is it my father?"

He shushed her softly, putting a gentle finger over her lips to keep her from chattering nervously. "Listen to me, please," he murmured. "I went to Norham Castle on my way home from Falkirk those months ago. It is the stronghold of de Longley, the Earl of Teviot, and a more fortified place I have never seen. I asked for your father but it was your mother who met me. You look a lot like her, actually. I also met your brother's children. Your mother was minding them. Your brother, Corbin, lives at Norham, too, although he was not at the castle the day I was there."

The expression of fear on Diamantha's face was increasing. "Cortez," she said, her throat tight with tears. "What about my father?"

He sighed heavily, bringing her hands to his lips and kissing them tenderly. "I informed your mother of Rob's death and told her my business," he explained. "Because of Rob's passing, she did not want me to tell you what had happened. About your father. She thought it would be too much for you to take in addition to the death of your husband and I promised her that I would not tell you, at least not right away. But I find I can no longer keep it from you, not when you are asking me direct questions about your father. I will not lie to you. Sweetheart, your father passed away a week before Robert met his death at Falkirk. Your mother said he died in his sleep and that it was very peaceful. He did not suffer."

Diamantha stared at him. As he watched, her eyes grew wider and wider and suddenly she gasped as if she had been struck in the gut. Her hands flew to her mouth to hold back the scream of anguish.

"Nay!" she shrieked. "It cannot be!"

Cortez felt so very badly for her. He put his arms around her, trying to pull her close. "I am so very sorry, my love," he consoled. "I am so sorry to be the bearer of bad tidings. Your mother assured me that your father had spoken of you very recently, musing over the granddaughter he had not yet seen. She wanted you to be comforted in the fact that your father loved you dearly and that he is now at peace."

Diamantha broke into gut-busting sobs, her face buried in her hands as she wept her grief. Over by the animal cage, Sophie heard her mother crying and she stood up with a kitten in her arms, looking at her mother with great concern.

"My Papa," Diamantha wept. "I want my Papa."

Cortez could feel a lump in his throat as he rocked her gently, his eyes on Sophie as the little girl padded over to the bed, her attention on her weeping mother. Sophie tugged on her mother's skirt.

"Mama?" she asked. "Are you sad?"

Diamantha was nearly hysterical. She pulled away from Cortez, sharply, and swept her daughter into her arms, weeping all over the girl. Her grief was a palpable thing, bleeding over onto everything she touched.

"My papa is dead," she sobbed. "Just like your papa is dead, Sophie. Now we are the same. Neither of us has a father."

She sailed into gales of sobs and Cortez stood up, pulling Sophie from her arms. At this point, Sophie was more confused than anything. As Diamantha threw herself on the bed and wept her heart out, Sophie turned her confused little face to Cortez.

"Papa is dead?" she asked, cocking her head.

Cortez was in damage control mode at this point. He could feel everything tumbling down around him and he was struggling to stop it. He knew that Diamantha had not told her daughter of Robert's passing but in her grief, she had confessed his death to her bewildered daughter. Sophie was trying to understand all of it. He tried to sound comforting.

"Do you remember when I told you that your father was with the angels?" he asked calmly. "I told you that he was in a place of light and if you are a very good girl, you will get to see him someday. We all go to live with the angels when we die. It is a wonderful place."

Sophie remembered that conversation. She was a very sharp little girl. She continued to stare at him with her big, bottomless eyes for a few moments before squirming in his arms, trying to get down. Cortez put her on her feet, gently, and the child toddled over to her mother, who was sobbing on the bed.

Sophie may have only been three years old, but she was remarkably intuitive. She knew something was very wrong with her mother and only marginally understood what it was. It had something to with living with the angels, with people they could no longer see or speak with. She reached out and put a hand on her mother's trembling head.

"Mama?" she asked softly. "Mama, do not cry. Papa is living with the angels and if you are a very good girl, you can see him again someday."

Diamantha's eyes popped open at the sweet, comforting words coming from her child. Sophie was trying to ease her pain the only way she knew how. Cortez had given her words of hope and she, in turn, was giving them to her troubled mother. Though no longer openly weeping, tears still poured from Diamantha's eyes as she reached out and stroked her child's cheek.

"Shall I tell you about my papa?" she asked, sniffling. "You have never met him, but he was a wonderful man. He was very tall, the tallest man you have ever seen and he was a very great knight. He was a great knight like your papa and like Cortez."

Sophie grinned and she started jumping up and down with the kitten in her arms flapping about. "My papa is very tall," she said, holding up her arm to emphasize her point. "He is as tall as the clouds."

Diamantha couldn't help but grin through her tears. She reached out and took the kitten out of Sophie's grip because it was getting whiplash the way her daughter was jerking it around. The kitten immediately cuddled up next to Diamantha as the woman lay down on her side, reaching out to toy with her daughter's hair as the little girl stood next to the bed.

"Aye, your papa was very tall," she murmured, tears still spilling from her eyes. "But my papa was even taller. He was your grandfather. He loved you very much even though he had never seen you. God, he would have loved to have known you."

She closed her eyes and the tears fell with a vengeance. Cortez, who had stood by silently through the exchanged, moved forward to pick Sophie up. He gave her a gentle hug as he took her back to her pets.

"Play with your animals for a while," he told her. "I will go and get them some food, and you can stay here with your mother."

Sophie reached into the cage and pulled the puppy out, who immediately started licking her face. "I want to go and get food, too," she told him.

Cortez shook his head. "Not this time, sweetheart," he said. "You have no shoes on. Stay and play with your animals and I will return shortly."

Sophie didn't argue with him. She was happy remaining with her animals. Cortez moved away from the child and returned to the bed where Diamantha lay, weeping softly. He knelt down beside the bed and clutched one of her hands.

"I will just be a minute, I swear," he said. "I want to make sure that food and bath are being sent up. I will bring you some wine myself. Will you be well enough until I return?"

Diamantha's eyes were closed as she squeezed his hand. A sob bubbled up from her chest but was quickly silenced. It was clear that she was fighting to stay lucid, fighting off the pangs of grief. Hysteria was not normally in her nature but she had been through much where it pertained to the death of loved ones. She was pushed beyond her endurance and her emotions were brittle.

"I think my father must have been waiting for Robert when he arrived in heaven," she whispered. "They are together now, I am sure. I wonder if my father knows how much I have missed him."

Cortez kissed her hand. "He knows," he confirmed. "By now, he knows everything. He knows that I did not ask him for your hand but I asked your mother instead. I wonder if he will be angry with me about it."

Diamantha opened her eyes, a smile breaking through the tears. "More than likely, he will be angry with my mother," she said. "But he could never stay angry at her for long. I think you are safe."

His dark eyes glimmered at her as he kissed her hand again. "I promise that I will take you to see your mother very soon," he said quietly. "We will make sure that Sophie meets her."

Diamantha was back to weeping again. She clutched his hand by her face, her cheek against his flesh as the tears fell. "God has taken Robert away and now he has taken my father," she sobbed quietly. "But He has given me you, and for that I am grateful. Thank you for barging into George's solar and demanding that I marry you, Cortez. You were so maddening but now I see God's plan. He meant for you to be there and to be forceful with me. Had you not come, I would still be wallowing in grief for Robert's loss. I still feel grief, now more so with my father's passing, but I thank God that you are here to comfort me. I thank God that He has brought you into my life."

Cortez kissed her temple, her hands, squeezing her fingers tightly. "You are my angel," he whispered. "You have made me feel more love than I have ever known to exist. Know that I will never leave you, not ever. You have all of me, Diamantha, forever."

Diamantha stopped in mid-sob, lifting her head to look at him with an incredulous expression. "Love?" she breathed. "You feel love?"

He was an inch from her face, smiling sweetly into her wet, watery eyes. Gently, he stroked her silken cheek. "Of course I do," he whispered. "I cannot remember when I have not loved you."

Diamantha, emotional and spent, burst into tears again but this time, they were tears of joy. "I love you also," she wept, wrapping her arms around his neck as he kissed her face furiously. "Sophie and I... we are so thankful to have you."

Cortez kissed her salty cheeks, her chin, and finally her sweet lips. It wasn't a kiss infused with lust as it usually was when he touched her. It was something more than just physical. It was emotional at the deepest level, joy that bubbled up from the soul. He'd been the bearer of terrible news twice in her life; once with the death of her husband and now with the death of her father. Instead of hating him for it, which he had deeply feared, she was thanking him for his comfort. God was good, indeed.

When the frenzied kissing eased, he looked into her eyes, stroking her cheeks with his thumbs as he cradled her face. "The quest we have embarked upon has done more to draw us together than anything ever could," he surmised. Then, he held up her left hand, the one that had the Posey ring on it. He kissed the ring, grinning. "My quest is you. I think it has always been you."

Diamantha smiled in return, reaching out to gently touch his face as he kissed her fingers tenderly. She was so emotionally overwrought at the moment that it was difficult for her to speak, so he kissed her one last time and pushed her down gently on the bed.

"You remain here and rest," he told her. "I will check on our meal and a bath and return as soon as I can with some wine. Will you be well enough while I am gone?"

Tears subsiding, all Diamantha could manage to feel at the moment was exhausted. She nodded her head. "Aye," she replied. "I will be well. Go about your business and we will be fine."

Cortez quit the chamber, but not without a lingering glance at his wife, lying still and pale upon the bed. He went about his business hurriedly, working the innkeeper and his staff into a frenzy in his quest to make his wife comfortable. Soon enough, wine and bath water and food appeared in their chamber. Once Sophie was bathed and fed and put to bed, Cortez did the same with his wife.

But the sadness of the news of Diamantha's father's death lingered. It wasn't something she would be soon or easily resigned to, the pain of a daughter in losing the man she had adored her entire life. That night, Michael de Bocage filled his daughter's thoughts as her exhausted sleep brought dreams of home.

The old innkeeper thought he was doing a good turn. He was a patriot, after all, and Sassenach in his place of business sullied the very walls of an establishment that lived and breathed Scottish freedom. His wife had invited the bloody English to stay but, alas, he had not. He intended to do something about it.

When the English knights had retired and most of the foot soldiers were camping about a quarter of a mile north of the town, the innkeeper had sent one of his servants to the Widow Graham's home, which was a half mile to the west. Widow Graham had a daughter who was set to marry one of the local chieftain's sons, and it was this daughter who ran from her mother's house in the dead of night to her lover's abode, whereupon she informed him of the Sassenach knights staying in town.

The lover, infuriated with the English invasion into his town, sent word to some of his friends and in the wee hours before dawn, right before men would rise and begin to prepare for the day, twelve Scots warriors moved in on The White Star with murder on their minds. Sassenach men were going to die that night. They would make sure of it.

The innkeeper let them into the structure, unfastening the big iron lock on the back door and allowing the men to creep in. He had been watching the stairs at the front of the house, watching for any signs that the six English knights were up and about, but so far everything had been dark and still. He gave the Scotsmen directions to the rooms bearing Sassenach guests. Then, he slipped into his own chamber and locked the door. He didn't want to see what happened next. His duty was done.

Unfortunately for the innkeeper, he missed seeing Peter Merlin as the man approached the inn with the intent of waking Cortez to see what the man's orders for the day were. Merlin saw the Scotsmen moving around in the dark and he spied swords and clubs in their hands. Being that he was without a weapon, or any means of alerting Cortez's army, he did the only thing he could do: he spurred his horse forward and charged through the bolted front door of the inn, creating such bedlam that on the floor above, Cortez and the other knights were instantly awake. That few moments of preparation saved their lives.

The Scotsmen, realizing their cover had been blown, charged up the stairs and were met by English knights pouring out of the doors. The English met the Scots as most of them were still on the stairs and Drake, perhaps the most aggressive knight of the group, launched himself at the Scotsmen on the stairs, landing on top of at least four of them, and sending all four rolling back down the stairs and crashing at the bottom.

Seeing that Drake had landed at the bottom of the steps in a heap with a cluster of Scotsmen, James ran down after him. James had the legendary de Lohr skill and, much like his great-uncle David de Lohr, he was faster with a broadsword than any man alive. He managed to kill two of the Scotsmen before the others were able to engage him, and the battle spilled out into the common room of the inn. Now, it was Drake and James against three very angry Scotsmen. Merlin, once he'd taken his horse back outside and tethered the animal, rushed back into the room and began swinging a broken chair leg around. The room, already, was in shambles and blood was on the floor.

Upstairs, it was more of a battle. There were seven Scotsmen against Cortez, Keir, Michael, and Oliver, and to make matters worse, it was so dark that it was difficult for anyone to see who they were fighting. Cortez had managed to make it out of his chamber, bellowing at Diamantha to lock the door as he ran. She did, throwing the old iron bolt and listening to the sounds of battle in the corridor outside. Terrified, she had grabbed her sleeping daughter and slithered under the bed, hoping it would provide some protection should the door be breached. In her arms, Sophie hardly woke up.

Out in the corridor, however, the situation was bad indeed. Cortez was only in his breeches, with his massive broadsword sailing through the darkness. None of the English had been given time to don their armor much less clothing, and Keir was actually fighting in the nude. It was so dark that no one really noticed, but the fact that they were fighting against deadly weapons without protection made the situation extremely dicey.

Cortez was able to take care of one of the Scots by tossing the man over the railing and sending him crashing down the stairs to the floor below. After that, he went to help Oliver dispatch two men who were intent on doing the young knight serious harm. Two strokes from his broadsword, a punch, and massive kick to the torso sent another Scot over the railing and down the stairs while Oliver eventually dispatched his opponent by driving his sword into the man's ribcage. As the Scot collapsed on the floor, Keir and Michael managed to dispatch the remaining four.

"Drake?" Cortez bellowed down the stairwell. "All clear!"

Drake's head suddenly appeared at the bottom of the steps. "All clear down here," he told him. "I do not see any more Scots, at least not yet."

Cortez looked at the knights around him. They were winded but whole. "We must leave immediately," he told them. "There could be an entire bloody army coming for us and this was just the advance party. Get dressed and let us go now."

The knights scattered, rushing to get dressed and collect their belongings, as Cortez went to his chamber door and pounded on it.

"Diamantha?" he called. "Open the door, sweetheart. Let me in."

It took several moments before the bolt was disengaged and the door swung open. Diamantha was standing there in her sleeping shift with Sophie slumbering on her shoulder. She looked terrified.

"What happened?" she demanded. "Were we attacked?"

Cortez blew into the room, hunting around until he found a flint. He sparked it, lighting the nearest taper, and a soft white glow filled the room.

"Aye," he told her, hurried. "We must get dressed and leave immediately. There could be more of them to come."

With gasp of fright, Diamantha carefully lay Sophie back onto her bed and began flying around the room, gathering things and either shoving them into her satchel or throwing them into the big barrel that held all of her new clothing. As Cortez quickly donned his clothing and his mail coat, Diamantha pulled her blue traveling gown over her sleeping shift and tossed the exquisite leather robe with the fur-lined sleeves on over that. Quickly, she ran a comb through her hair and braided it, if only to keep it out of the way, while she picked up the cage with the animals in it and set it on the bed next to Sophie. She watched, breathless, as Cortez strapped on his broadsword.

"We are ready," she informed him, her voice quivering with fright.

Cortez nodded shortly and went out into the corridor, yelling down the stairwell. "Who is down there?"

Merlin appeared at the bottom. "I am, my lord."

"Where are the rest of my men?"

"Still in camp, my lord."

Cortez motioned the man up the stairs. "Come and help us vacate."

Merlin rushed up the stairs, gathering the baggage as Diamantha collected her child with one arm and picked up the animal cage with the other. Keir and Michael were vacating their rooms at the same time, fully dressed now, and helped get Diamantha's bags and barrel down the stairs. Once on the first floor where several Scotsmen were bleeding out on the dirt floor, Cortez didn't even bother to summon the innkeeper or his wife to let them know they were departing. He had feeling they already knew.

As they began to head out of town in the cold, dark morning, heading for the area where Cortez's men were camped, they could hear the town around them beginning to stir and they were increasingly anxious to leave. Cortez's encampment was already nearly packed and ready to depart, and Cortez's knights worked the men into a frenzy. They were terrified that more Scots were to come, especially since they had killed or badly injured the twelve that had come in an advanced party, so soon enough, they were all fleeing up the road, bouncing along in the early morning hours.

For Diamantha, tucked into the wagon with her daughter clutched in her arms, it was a frightening experience. The more distance they put between them and Moffatt, the better they were coming to feel, but Cortez knew the worst was not yet over. They could be in for quite a bit of trouble if the kin of those who attacked them decided to follow. Therefore, he had Keir and Michael covering their retreat, hanging back to make sure they were not followed. As the morning progressed, it seemed less and less likely, and eventually, they slowed their pace so the men could catch their breath.

But Cortez couldn't breathe easy, not yet. They were in Scotland, after all. For all he knew, this was only the beginning of worse hardships yet to come.

He prayed he was wrong.

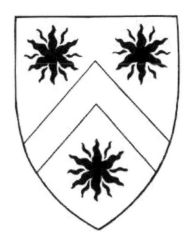

CHAPTER NINETEEN

Kirkmuirhill, Hamilton, Cumbernauld... Falkirk
Fortunately, whatever happened in Moffatt seemed to be isolated because they had been traveling for four days and no one had followed them. But the rain that had started when they were in Moffatt had indeed followed them, and the four days of travel to the outskirts of Falkirk had been wrought with some of the worst weather any of them had ever seen. It had been positively hellish.

The wind had been vicious, blowing from every direction, consequently, most everything was soaked, even in the wagon bed where Diamantha and Sophie huddled together with the animals and tried to stay dry. Cortez had fortunately been able to find shelter every night so they could at least sleep beneath a roof and with bedding that wasn't soaked, but the days of never-ending rain, mud-slicked roads, and misery weighed heavily upon them. It made for wretched travel.

On the fifth day since departing Moffatt, the party finally arrived on the outskirts of Falkirk. There was a small settlement to the northwest of the battlefield, a three-street town with many crudely constructed homes and a stretch of road that contained several businesses including a one-storied tavern. It was raining in buckets when they finally arrived in the sodden village and Cortez made no secret about the fact that he intended to take over the tavern to house his men. In fact, the entire column came to a halt in front of the tavern and Cortez sent his knights in to roust whoever was inside, clearing the way for he and his men. He didn't care if it was bad manners, either. He was tired of being wet.

Fortunately for all concerned, there was hardly anyone in the tavern and Cortez allowed those few patrons to remain as all of his men poured into the structure to get out of the elements. Cortez carried Sophie inside while Drake helped Diamantha. The tavern's common room was rather small, but it was warm and dry, and twenty-five men, six knights, a little girl and her mother quickly filled it up while the stable boys in charge of the mounts of tavern visitors took the horses away to be sheltered in the livery across the street. The wagons went with them.

The tavern keeper was a short, bald man who was surprisingly handsome and clean-appearing. He had been in the rear of the tavern, making an inventory of the ale barrels, when Cortez and his men had taken over the place. He came out into the room of drenched, weary men, and was directed towards Cortez by one of the soldiers. The man approached Cortez, seated with Diamantha and Sophie, and introduced himself.

"Me name is MacInnis, m'laird," he said. "Am I to assume ye want me tae feed the lot of ye?"

Cortez was cold and wet. He looked at the man. "An excellent assumption," he said digging into the purse in his tunic and pulling out six gold crowns. He slapped them on the table. "This should pay for the meal."

MacInnis scooped the coinage off the table quickly, eager to be of service with a good price paid. Unlike the innkeeper in Moffatt, MacInnis didn't care if these men were English. As long as they were paying a handsome price, he didn't care who they were or why they were there. He had been present during the battle of Falkirk those months ago and he found that the English were much more respectful than the Scots had been during those difficult days. The Scots had stolen from him while the English, although they had absconded with items, too, had at least paid for what they had confiscated. Therefore, he held no issue with the Sassenach crowd.

"Indeed, m'laird," he said. "I have a good mutton stew and enough bread fer all."

Cortez nodded wearily, waving the man on. "Bring it to everyone," he said. "Fill them full of it. And all the ale they can drink."

The tavern keeper nodded. "Aye, m'laird."

"And my wife and I require a room if you have one available."

MacInnis nodded his head eagerly. "I have two rooms," he told him. "They're both small, but they're clean."

"I will take them both."

The tavern keeper fled into the rear of the tavern and Cortez could hear the man shouting instructions to his staff. Soon enough, two women and a boy were scrambling, and pitchers and cups soon began to appear on the tables. The boy went to stoke the hearth, producing a rather bold blaze that launched live embers into the room and onto some of the soldiers. They were so wet and cold that they hardly cared.

At the sight of the big blaze, Diamantha began pulling off Sophie's little cloak, drenched, as well as her own.

"I am going to hang these by the fire to dry them off," she said as she stood up from her seat. "You should probably have your men do the same. They will all catch their death as wet as they are."

Cortez nodded wearily, watching her walk over to the blazing hearth and hang her cloak on a peg next to it. She did the same with Sophie's. Sophie, meanwhile, was sticking her fingers in the animal cage, which was resting upon the table and covered in a big oiled cloth to keep the creatures dry. The kittens, the puppy, the rabbit, and the fox were perhaps the driest travelers out of the entire group.

As Cortez watched his wife, warming her hands by the fire, his knights, most of whom had been either scattered around the room or out in the back where the privy was, headed to his table and began to sit down around him. A pitcher of ale and several cups appeared on their table and Cortez asked for watered-down ale or milk for the child from the wench who brought the pitcher. As the woman scurried away, Cortez turned to his men.

"Great Bleeding Jesus," he exclaimed gruffly. "Get out of those wet clothes before you rust. At least go try to dry off near the fire."

Keir and Michael were already reaching for the ale. "'Tis too late," Keir said. "My armor is already rusted shut. Your squire is going to have his hands full tonight cleaning all of our armor."

Cortez glanced over at the table where young Peter Summerlin was. The lad had been a mounted soldier on this journey and a sometimes-squire, a silent operator who kept himself out of trouble. Along with Merlin and the knights, the lad was never out of the sight of Cortez. He was a fixture. Cortez accepted a full cup from Keir, snorting softly before he drank.

"No doubt," he said. "But he's young and strong. It will be a simple task for him."

Drake pulled off his helm, setting on the bench next to Sophie, who found great interest in it.

"I will clean my own," he announced, watching the little girl play with the visor. "I do not want my armor away from me for too long, given what happened in Moffatt. That was a lesson learned."

Keir looked over at him, cup at his lips. "What lesson is that?" he asked. "To sleep in full armor? That could have been the only possible lesson learned."

Drake scratched his face casually. "You of all people should have learned the lesson," he joked. "A man fighting nude could get something quite valuable hacked off if he is not careful. Then your wife would have to find a new husband. It would be of little pleasure to her to be married to a eunuch."

Michael and James began to laugh while Keir simply made a face. "Any man that seeks to hack my manroot from my body had better get the biggest sword he can find," he said. "It will take a sword the size of a tree to cut my manhood off."

"That's not what I saw," Michael teased.

Now the entire table was laughing at Keir's expense, who was halted from delivering a stinging retribution on Michael by the simple fact that there was a child sitting across the table from him. But he was going to give it his best try, anyway, when Diamantha suddenly appeared and sat down next to her daughter.

"What is so funny?" she asked innocently.

The knights looked at each other knowingly as Cortez shook his head. "It would not interest you," he told her, quick to change the subject. "Why not take the cage over to the fire and warm the animals? They are probably quite cold."

Successfully diverted, Diamantha peered in at the little animals in the wooden cage. "They are huddled together so I am sure they are warm for now," she said, accepting the cup of ale that Cortez handed her. "Moreover, I simply want to sit on something that is not moving for a few moments. I know it is far more difficult for you men to travel and my complaints seem foolish, but my backside is sore from being bumped around in that wagon. It feels good to sit on something still."

Cortez reached out and collected her hand, holding it on the tabletop. "We are finally at our destination," he said, "so there will not be much travel in the foreseeable future, I hope."

Diamantha squeezed his big hand. "How close are we to the location of the battle?"

Cortez's gaze was warm on her but in the back of his mind he was trying to gauge her mood. Finally, they were at Falkirk, the site of the great battle where her husband had lost his life. Knowing how grief stricken she had been with Robert's death, he wondered if finally being at the location where the man met his end would bring about fits of sorrow again. So far, her demeanor didn't seem to be affected and he was grateful. He had hoped that these weeks of travel, and the weeks of bonding between them, had helped her heal somewhat. That was his hope, anyway. He prayed it held true.

"We are north of the battle site by a mile or two," he said quietly. "There is a great wooded area to the southeast and the battle took place to the south side of those woods."

Diamantha was listening closely. "Did the battle spread out over a large area?" she asked. "Surely there were thousands of men."

Cortez glanced at the men around the table who had been at that battle with him. They all knew the horrors and triumphs of it. He'd hardly spoken of it since it had happened but now that they were in a calm setting, and Diamantha was asking for answers, he thought perhaps it was time to share the details of it and pray it didn't throw her back into another cloud of grief. Therefore, he was careful in how he replied.

"There were indeed thousands of men," he told her. "Nearly six thousand Scots and fifteen thousand English, all fighting in a relatively small area south of the woods. The Scots were led by William Wallace and although some of his tactics were somewhat successful, once Edward arrived to the battle, Wallace was smashed and his forces scattered. It was an impressive and terrible day."

Diamantha had expected something more by way of information but Cortez seemed to be summing it up as a general happening. That was not what she wanted to hear. She wanted to know what *happened*.

"Did you fight with Edward?" she asked, looking around the table. "Were you all in the king's army?"

The knights let Cortez handle the answer. She was his wife, after all. "I was with Edward's army," he replied, "and so were Robert, Drake, James, Oliver, and Andres. Keir and Michael fought with the Bishop of Durham, I believe. Is that not correct?"

Keir nodded his head. "Our liege, Baron Coverdale, is allied with the Anthony Bek, the Bishop of Durham," he replied. "When the call for men came, we were committed to the bishop's army. On the day of battle, the king was late to the field while fighting had already started. Norfolk and Lincoln were already in the heat of battle but Durham was trying to hold off and wait for the king. There were some very foolish knights serving Durham and they disobeyed the man and started into the fracas. Michael and I held back with some of Durham's troops until Edward arrived, and when he finally came, we were able to destroy the Scottish archers and beat down the pikemen. Say what you will about the king, but he is a brilliant military tactician. He overwhelmed Wallace with both manpower and skill. It was a glorious English victory."

The knights at the table nodded in agreement, all of them thinking on that chaotic day. Diamantha was thinking about it also, but in a different context. She was thinking on Robert and his last moments. It wasn't such a glorious day for him. She looked at Cortez.

"You told me that you were near Robert when he fell," she said quietly. "When did he fall? Was it near the beginning or the end of the battle?"

Cortez met her gaze steadily. "Towards the end," he replied. "We were in the process of destroying groups of foot soldiers and Robert was hit by a Scottish longbow. There weren't many Scottish archers left at that point but there was at least one because his aim took out a strong English knight. When he fell, I went to him and stayed with him as long as I could, but the fighting was moving to the west and my sword was needed."

Diamantha knew the rest. She simply nodded her head and looked at her lap, sadness filling her. The abject grief she had experienced those months after her husband's death was no longer present, but she still felt great sorrow. It was a terrible way for a man so loved to die but she took comfort in the fact that they were here to finally bring him home. He would not be alone much longer. After a moment's reflection, she took a deep breath for courage and lifted her head.

"Will you take me to the spot?" she asked. "I would like to see it. The spot where he fell, I mean. It is important to me."

Cortez nodded faintly, squeezing her hand again. "If that is your wish," he said, "but not today. Let us eat and sleep well, and then we will set out tomorrow to find the location. Is that acceptable?"

Diamantha nodded and he lifted one of her hands to kiss it. He was pleased that she seemed in control, bravely facing what she must. To focus on the positive aspect, the recovery of Robert, seemed the best thing to do. He didn't want to focus on what could not be helped, the death of the man.

As Cortez sat there and watched Diamantha struggle with her sadness, the serving wench came around again with a big iron pot and a collection of wooden bowls. The bowls were placed before everyone and she began spooning out a great, hearty stew with carrots, peas, and beans, and another wench came around and put hot loaves of brown bread and bowls of butter on the table. She even brought something special for Sophie, a cup with juice from apples mixed with a bit of honey. In all, it was a tremendous feast and everyone dug in with gusto. Warm stew on a cold day was about the best thing possible.

As the rain pounded and the lightning flashed, the Sassenach army settled in for a bit of food, rest, and relaxation, for tomorrow, the real work would begin.

The recovery of a comrade, father, husband, and friend. Robert Edlington would no longer be one of the forgotten.

CHAPTER TWENTY

Close to dawn, Diamantha was awakened from a deep sleep by powerful arms pulling her close. She smiled, half-asleep, as Cortez pulled her against his naked body and rubbed his full erection against her buttocks. His hands began to rove, snaking up her sleeping shift and finding her soft, warm flesh beneath. As she groaned softly with pleasure, his fingers moved to her breasts, fondling them gently before moving to the fluff of dark curls between her legs. He stroked her and inserted his big fingers into her, preparing her body for his rigid manhood. Lifting up her right leg, he wedged his body between her legs and thrust into her.

Diamantha was all wrapped up in his big arms as he made love to her, her nose and mouth against the flesh of his muscular bicep, inhaling his sensual musk with every breath. She could feel his face against the back of her head, the heat from his body enveloping her as he whispered words of lust and passion into her ear. He told her how wonderful she felt against him and how delicious her body was, in every way. His hot breath on her ear was driving her mad with desire as he repeatedly drove into her quivering flesh.

Diamantha was so highly aroused that she climaxed quickly, biting off her gasps against his arm as Cortez released himself deep into her body. The opportunities to make love on this journey, to bond as only a man and wife can, had been extremely limited, but at this moment, they were relatively alone except for Sophie sleeping on a small bed next to them. The opportunity had been so rare that

Cortez rolled Diamantha onto her back, lifted up her shift, and thrust into her again, repeatedly, before his stiff manhood died down completely. He didn't want it to end.

He simply loved the feel of her, nuzzling her neck and acquainting himself with her delicate female scent. Perhaps he should have felt strange about making love to her with Robert Edlington's remains nearby, but he didn't. Robert was dead and had no need for the woman who had become Cortez's wife. Cortez, however, needed her a great deal. Every day saw him need her more.

When he was finished touching and tasting her, Cortez lay back down beside Diamantha, arms wrapped around her slender body, and closed his eyes in the hope that he could doze a few more minutes before he was finally forced to rise. Diamantha, too, had closed her eyes in the hopes of a few more peaceful moments, but no sooner had they relaxed than Sophie began to weep.

Diamantha was instantly up, straightening her shift as she hopped across the cold floor to her daughter's bed. It was very dark in the room since the fire was reduced to a few glowing embers, and Cortez was dozing to the sounds of the soft whispers of a mother to her daughter when Diamantha was suddenly in his face.

"Cortez," she hissed. "Sophie is ill. I need your help."

The man sat bolt upright, nearly smashing Diamantha in the jaw with his sudden movement. "What do you mean she is ill?" he demanded softly, tossing off the covers and revealing his naked body to the room. "What is wrong?"

Diamantha whispered at him. "She has soiled her entire bed," she said. "Not only has she vomited, but the bed is soiled with waste. I think she may have a fever. I need warm water so I can bathe her."

Cortez was already putting on his breeches, banging around in the dark room until he lit a taper, which cast some light across the small room. Concerned, he went over to Sophie's bed as he pulled on a heavy tunic.

The little girl was sitting up as her mother gently tried to pull her soiled sleeping shift off, and he could see a big dark stain on the bed where she had soiled herself. He sighed sadly, putting a gentle hand on the child's head.

"I will have them bring hot water at once," he said. "Do you need anything else?"

Diamantha was trying not to get the mess on herself as she stripped off Sophie's clothes. "Mayhap something to help settle her belly," she said, tossing the soiled shift to the floor. "Bread would be good. And watered wine if they have it. My mother used to give us watered wine when we had stomach troubles and it seemed to help."

Cortez yanked his boots on and quit the room. The common room of the tavern was filled with his soldiers who had slept all over the room, on tables and in chairs, and they were starting to stir at this early hour. Men were snoring, farting, coughing, and mumbling as they began to wake. Cortez found MacInnis already back in the kitchen, lighting the fires to start the day, and he told the man what had happened. The tavern keeper quickly left the kitchen, crossing the muddy yard outside to a small house where he lived with his wife and their servants. He roused the entire house and soon, people were quickly moving in order to help the sick little girl.

As MacInnis and his servants put water on to boil and began to prepare bread dough, Cortez crossed back through the common room and noticed that Oliver was already up and dressed for the day. The tall, young knight was walking among the soldiers, making sure they were waking up and when he noticed Cortez, he headed in the man's direction.

"Good news," Oliver said. "The rain seems to have vanished. It is a clear and cold morning."

Cortez grunted, running his hand through his dark hair. "Cold enough to freeze the ground?"

Oliver shook his head. "Nay," he replied. "None of the mud puddles outside the door are frozen. I doubt the field south of Callendar Wood will be frozen, either."

Cortez wriggled his eyebrows in a hopeful gesture. "We shall see," he said. "Make sure the men eat as soon as they awaken. Where are the rest of the knights?"

Oliver pointed in the direction of the livery. "James and Drake have gone to check on the horses," he said. "I've not yet seen Keir or Michael."

Cortez digested the information. "We may have a small issue this morning," he said. "It would seem that little Sophie had taken ill. Let the others know. I know my wife will not leave her and I am not entirely sure about leaving my wife if that is the case. Tell the knights I will wish to speak with them in a few minutes. Meet me back here in the common room."

Oliver appeared concerned. "I hope her illness is not too serious."

Cortez shrugged. "As do I," he said as he turned for the traveler rooms. "I will return in a few moments."

Oliver went to hunt down the rest of the knights while Cortez returned to the room he shared with Diamantha and Sophie. He was deeply concerned about the child and struggling not to let it show. He didn't want to upset Diamantha more than she already was, but a sick child scared him. Knocking on the door lightly, he let himself in.

Sophie was standing next to her bed, naked, as Diamantha mopped up more excrement on the floor around her from Sophie's most recent accident. Sophie was shivering and crying, as pale as the linens on the bed. It was evident that she was a very sick little girl. When Diamantha heard Cortez enter, her head popped up.

"Where is the hot water?" she asked.

Cortez could see that the situation was worse than when he had left it. He threw the door open and headed out.

"I will find out," he said. "I will hurry back."

He slammed the door behind him and moved quickly out to the kitchens, where he began demanding things like chamber pots and any rags they could spare. The tavern keeper thrust a wooden bucket at him to use as a chamber pot and sent a servant girl scurrying for cloth of any kind. She returned with linens for the bed, which Cortez took gratefully. He also took a second bucket filled with very warm water while the tavern keeper followed him with some food.

Returning to the room, Diamantha had the floor cleaned up but she was very anxious to clean Sophie up, who was crying steadily. Seeing the state of the room, and that of the child, the tavern keeper went back and summoned his wife, who came to help. As Cortez stood by nervously, MacInnis' wife stripped and cleaned Sophie's bed, cleaned up the floor with a combination of water, ashes and mashed pine needles, which cleaned thoroughly and left behind the fragrance of the pine to help combat the odor of the vomit and feces. She was very helpful to Diamantha, helping her bathe the girl and get her into swaddling, wrapped around her waist and between her legs, to prevent her from soiling herself again. Diamantha finally put Sophie into a clean shift and wrapped her up in a soft wool blanket she had brought with them from Corfe.

It had been quite a production and Sophie had wept steadily through it. She was miserable and unhappy, unusual for the little girl who had traveled so well for hundreds of miles. Cortez felt as badly as he possibly could as Diamantha sat on the bed and tried to coax her daughter into eating a bit of soft, warm bread.

"Is there anything more I can do?" he asked comfortingly, sitting on the bed beside Diamantha and putting his big hand on Sophie's head. "Anything at all?"

Diamantha put a tiny piece of bread in her daughter's mouth, watching the child chew miserably. "Aye, there is," she said, looking up at him. "It is evident that I cannot go with you today to the battlefield. I must remain with Sophie. When you go, will you at least send me word about what you find and of your progress?"

He kissed her on the temple. "Of course I will," he said. "Is that all? Should I send for a physic?"

Diamantha turned to look at her pale daughter. "No physic," she said. "At least, not right now. Let us see how she does through the day and then we will decide. But if she is not better tonight, Cortez, I do not want you to stay in the room with us."

His brow furrowed. "Why not?"

She looked at him with some fear in her expression. "I do not want her to make you sick as well," she said. "She may have something catching."

He shrugged. "If that is the case, then I have already been exposed," he said. "Staying away tonight will not prevent me from becoming ill if it is already destined that I should be."

Diamantha was struggling not to let her fear and disappointment swamp her. "God's Bones," she hissed angrily. "We have come all this way and now this."

Cortez kissed her again and stood up. "Not to worry," he said. "I am sure she will be fine by tonight. It was probably something she ate, a bit of stew that did not agree with her. She is a healthy child and she will quickly overcome this."

Diamantha sighed, looking down at her sick baby. "I hope so," she said. "We will remain here today. Mayhap she simply needs to rest."

She sounded as if she were trying to convince herself that the illness would quickly pass. To think of anything else would cause her to panic. Cortez glanced over at the cage stuffed with the puppy, the kittens, the fox, and the rabbit. At this hour of the morning, they were all sleeping in a big, happy, and warm pile.

"I will make sure MacInnis brings the menagerie some food," he said. "I believe I will also leave some men behind as protection."

"You will not be too far away, will you?" Diamantha put a soft hand on his arm, fearfully.

He shook his head, patting her hand. "Nay," he said. "If you screamed, I could probably hear you, but I believe you will be safe here."

Diamantha felt marginally better as she returned her focus to her daughter, who was now starting to doze off. Cortez watched the pair a moment, feeling saddened that they would not be able to join them now that they had reached their destination, but as he thought on it, maybe it was for the best. They were going digging for a corpse and he was fairly certain that Diamantha didn't want to see what was left of her husband. True, she had come along to identify him, but there were other ways of doing that; a ring, a sword, perhaps familiar clothing. He was fairly certain she didn't want to look at the face of a man who had been in the ground for four months.

"I will send you word later today of our progress," he said, kissing her on the head. "Meanwhile, you and Lady Sophie will have a restful day. That is what I prefer, anyway. You will stay here while the men do the work."

Diamantha didn't have much to say to that. She seemed more focused on her child, as she should be. Cortez would finish dressing out in the common room, as he had given young Peter his mail coat to clean, so he kissed Diamantha farewell and quit the room, moving into the greater room where his men were dressed and eating their breakfast. A big day lay ahead for all of them and he was anxious to get started.

Anxious to disturb the dead.

Cortez recognized the area immediately. Not that he had expected it to change much in four months, but the battlefield literally looked exactly the same as it did the last time he saw it.

The Battle of Falkirk had been fought in a relatively small area, all things considered. William Wallace had hid with his men in Callendar Wood and had engaged the English to the south side of forest. There were three brooks that converged there and upon a vast meadow of gently rolling hills, the Scots and the English had clashed together most violently. The Scots were heavily outmanned by the English and their defeat, under Edward's heavy hand, had been inevitable. As Cortez stood on the outskirts of the battlefield, he could still hear the fighting going on.

Scots archers were being crushed under the weaponry of the mounted English knights. He could see the knights swarming them, beating them down, as the ground began to run with blood. He could hear the sights and smells of the battle and, judging from the expressions on the knights around him, he was fairly certain they could see and smell the same thing. They were all remembering their fortune upon the field of battle. It had been a brutal day.

But Cortez shook himself away from the memories and took his men, with a single provisions wagon carrying a collection of spades and other digging instruments, around to the southeast side of the battlefield to the last place he had seen Robert Edlington alive. The mud was fairly heavy on the small path that skirted the battlefield and the wagon became stuck, twice, and the soldiers had been forced to use sheer manpower to rock the wagon until it was able to roll forward again. It made for slow going.

As they moved around the perimeter of the battlefield, to the northeast along the path of a brook, Cortez came to a halt and gazed off towards the northwest. There was a hill in the near distance, without trees on it, and it had a rather flat top. Cortez recognized it.

He moved off the path and into the field itself, with its thick mud and intermittent green patches.

There were several heavy lines of foliage to plow through, but Cortez realized he was very close to the place he had last seen Rob Edlington. Here, on the outskirts of the battle, which at that point in time had been dwindling off to the west, he had dragged Edlington out of the fighting and had leaned the man against a tree. It had been a big oak with a split trunk, and part of it had been stripped for firewood. As his horse plodded through the mud, through the heavy greenery, Cortez happened to glance over to his right and was struck with the vision of the split-trunked oak.

"There!"

He shouted the word, almost triumphantly, as he spurred his charger over to the tree, kicking up mud and clods of earth as he went. The other knights were behind him, dismounting their horses quickly because Cortez had. In his excitement, he ran his hands all over the tree before scrutinizing the ground around it.

"I left him here," he said, pointing to the ground. "I pulled him over to this tree. I remember it clearly because of the distinct split trunk. See it? And see how part of it has been stripped for firewood? This is where I left the man. He is here, somewhere, and we will find him."

Immediately, the knights began looking around, as did the soldiers who had accompanied them. It was like a reflexive action, everyone eager to search, eager to find. Everyone was hunting for a sign that Rob Edlington was somewhere beneath them. Cortez finally ordered the men to break out the spades and he stood back with his knights to gain a better view of the area so they could choose where to place their test holes.

Overhead, dark clouds began to blow in, great puffy mounds that occasionally blocked the sun out. Cortez turned his gaze upward more than once, wondering when the rain was going to return. For now, they had damp, soft soil, not mud, and he wanted to dig while the conditions were good. But the fact remained that he truly had no idea where to start. As his men stood around, shovels in hand, he began to pace around the tree.

"When I last saw Edlington, he was here," he said, indicating the south side of the tree. "I left him when Edward was making his final push against the Scots and I could not have been gone more than a half hour at the most before returning. When I did, all of this was like a swamp of mud. I sank up to my knees in it. Do you recall how terrible the mud was? It swallowed up more than one man."

The knights were nodding in remembrance of the mud of biblical proportions. Keir broke away from the pack and began pacing around just as Cortez was doing.

"You said that Edlington had no use of his legs," he said, reiterating what everyone already knew. "But he had strength in his arms. Is it possible he dragged himself away from the tree?"

Cortez looked around, at the field, at the heavy foliage. "When I returned for him and found him missing, I looked around as much as I could," he said. "The mud around the tree was particularly bad. It would not have been difficult for it to have swallowed a dead man."

Keir looked at the tree. "But so quickly?" he asked, looking at the ground again. "You said you were gone no more than half of an hour. Would Edlington's body have been swallowed so quickly?"

Cortez shrugged. "It must have been, for the man was nowhere to be found when I came looking for him," he said. Then, he motioned to the ground on the south side of the tree. "Let us begin here with our holes. We will dig from the tree trunk southward, fifteen or twenty feet. Surely he must be somewhere around here."

Drake snapped his fingers at the men standing around holding the spades, who immediately moved forward to begin digging holes in the quest to find Rob Edlington's body. Meanwhile, James, Oliver, and Michael began to walk about, looking under bushes and trying to see if they could find some trace of Edlington. If the man had crawled off, which was a possibility, then they would hunt for him.

Bushes and any growth were devoid of the body of a knight, but they were finding broken arrows and shafts as they went. Drake even came across a dagger, a lovely bejeweled one, that was sticking up through the soil. There was a shield carved into the hilt inlayed with what looked like red rubies. Drake held the dirk up into the light to see it more clearly. Oliver, standing over Drake's shoulder, pointed at the jeweled shield.

"I recognize that shield," he said. "That is the crest of William Martin. He fought for Henry."

Drake scrutinized the weapon. "Very nice," he said. "And quite expensive. Mayhap I shall ransom it back to him."

"Martin was killed," Michael said, standing off to their right. "I am sure his widow would like to have that returned without cost."

Drake made a face at the big man, conveying just what he thought of returning the valuable piece without expecting some compensation, but he tucked the dirk into his belt as he continued to search around for any sign of Edlington. Meanwhile, the soldiers continued to dig several holes near the great oak, most of which were at least three feet deep. The digging went on well into the morning.

At some point during the day, the knights also took up spades and began to dig. Cortez had a shovel and he dug around the base of the tree, hunting for any sign of Edlington. Keir, thinking that Edlington must have dragged himself away from the tree and probably the opposite direction of the battle, began digging about twenty feet to the east of the tree. He managed to dig several smaller holes and one big one, turning up nothing. The other knights, thinking Keir might have a point about Edlington dragging himself away, dug in various spaces around him.

By the time the sun was setting overhead and more clouds were blowing in from the east, they had dug sixty-three holes, had pulled up pieces of shields, more weapons including four big and extremely valuable broadswords, and pieces of leather that they thought were either parts of shoes or saddles. No one seemed certain. But in their search, they never came across any piece of a corpse or even a hint of one nearby.

Cortez hated to return to Diamantha empty-handed, but the day had not been productive. Trudging back to the tavern as the sun set, he tried to remain optimistic about what the morrow would bring.

CHAPTER TWENTY-ONE

It was dark by the time Cortez and his men returned to the MacInnis' tavern. He had the soldiers take care of the horses and wagon while he and the knights wearily approached the small, stout structure. Glowing light emitted from the small windows cut into the walls, making it a rather inviting prospect as they pushed open the entry door.

Heated, smelly air hit them in the face. There were more people in the tavern this night than there had been the day before, weary travelers seeking rest and food. As the knights confiscated a table near the door and began calling over the serving wenches, Cortez headed to the rear of the structure where the two sleeping rooms were located. He was anxious to see Diamantha and tell her about the day, and he was also eager to see how Sophie was faring. But what he found upon entering their rented room was not what he had expected, not in the least.

MacInnis's wife was there along with a man he didn't recognize. They were standing next to the smaller bed in the room, the one Sophie had slept on the night before, and Cortez's gaze immediately found Diamantha seated next to the little bed. Sophie was laying on it, bundled up, until all he could see was her little face. She appeared to be sleeping and, as he entered the room, he realized that the hearth was blazing and it was very warm in the chamber. It was cloying.

Upon hearing the door open, Diamantha whirled around to see Cortez entering the room. She jumped up and flew at him before he could speak.

"Cortez," she gasped. "Thank God you have returned."

Her voice sounded terrible, frightened and strained. She also looked ragged, with circles around her lovely eyes. Cortez reached out and pulled her into an embrace simply because it seemed like the thing to do. He didn't like her tone or the look of her. Apprehension gripped him.

"What is the matter?" he asked her, eyeing the others in the room. "Who is that man?"

Diamantha's lower lip began to tremble as she pointed to the small man in the dirty brown robes. "That is a physic from St. Francis," she said, struggling not to weep. "He is a priest but he is also the physic for the town. Goodwife MacInnis sent for him. Sophie is not doing very well and he has come to help."

Cortez felt sick. He looked down at the sleeping baby, so pale and still. "God," he breathed, turning back to his wife. "What is the matter with her?"

Diamantha was wiping away tears that spilled over. "She has not been able to keep anything in her belly," she said hoarsely. "And she continually soils herself. She has no control over her innards at all. And when it comes... well, there is blood. She seems to be bleeding inside."

Cortez looked at the physic, a man with great bags under his eyes and a big nose. "What have you done for her?" he demanded. "Great Bleeding Christ, she a mere baby. Illness like this will quickly consume her. What in the hell are you doing to make her well?"

He had quickly grown irate and Diamantha grasped at him, trying to shush him. The physic, however, was unintimidated. He met Cortez's rage with a steady heart.

"I have seen this before, m'laird," he said in a very heavy Scots accent. "Things like this sometimes settle themselves in a few days, but we must keep the girl full of liquid – watered wine, watered ale, boiled fruit juice. We have been forcing her tae drink watered ale mostly because it has been known tae cure the evils that cause this terrible sickness."

Cortez wasn't satisfied with the answer. He dropped to his knees beside Sophie, his big hand on her head. Diamantha gently touched his shoulder.

"Do not wake her," she whispered. "This is the first time she has been at peace all day. Let her sleep."

Cortez was beside himself. He lifted his hand off of the child's head, wanting to kiss her but not wanting to disturb her. He was very nearly distraught as he motioned the physic to follow him out of the room. The old man did, and followed Cortez a few feet away from the chamber door so they would not be overheard. When Cortez finally turned to the man, there was great sorrow in his expression.

"Please tell me that this will pass," he hissed. "Tell me that this will not kill her."

The physic could see how worried the knight was. "As I said, I have seen this before," he said, although there wasn't much comfort in his tone. "It could pass in a few days, or it could grow worse. Only time will tell. Make her drink as much watered wine or ale as she will take. Put a little honey in it tae sweeten it. That makes it easier fer children. Feed her porridge and soft bread when she will tolerate it. Other than that, I canna do more. Her fate is consigned tae God."

That was not the answer Cortez had been seeking. He looked at the physic, astonished and horrified. "That is *all* we can do?"

"I canna work miracles, m'laird."

Cortez stared at the man a moment longer before wiping both hands over his face in a weary, distressed gesture. He didn't know what to say. He was a man unused to feeling helpless but, at the moment, he felt incredibly useless.

"Then I thank you for your time," he conceded, digging into the purse on his belt and producing a few coins for the physic. "Will you come back tomorrow?"

The physic nodded. "I will return in the morning tae see how the lass fares," he said. For a man who had seemed rather unemotional about the entire situation, he suddenly put his hand on Cortez's arm in a surprising show of compassion. "She is young and healthy, m'laird. She is no' as sickly as some I have seen, some who did no' survive. Prayer will be a good medicine tae heal her."

With that, he left the tavern and headed out into the dark night were fat raindrops were starting to fall from the sky. Cortez continued to stand there, hearing the noise from the common room around him but not really listening. All he could think about was Sophie and her illness. The anguish he felt was nearly beyond his ability to comprehend. *Dear God*, he prayed inwardly. *I cannot lose another daughter, not this time.*

"Cortez?"

A voice came from behind him and he turned to see Keir standing there with a cup in his hand. From the look on Keir's face, Cortez knew the man had more than likely been watching the interaction between him and the physic. Cortez reached out, took the cup in Keir's hand, and drained it. He smacked his lips as he handed the cup back.

"Sophie is very ill," he said, his voice hoarse with emotion. "The physic has consigned her fate to God. He says there is no medicine he can give her, so all we can do is wait."

Keir's eyes widened and his mouth popped open in horror. "God's Bones" he gasped. "She has grown worse?"

Cortez realized he was very close to weeping. His heart ached in ways he couldn't manage to describe.

"She cannot keep anything in her stomach," he said, "and she has no control over her bowels. She is losing blood and everything else inside her belly. The physic says he has seen it before and that all we can do is wait."

Keir was horrified. He put his big hand on Cortez's shoulder, squeezing in a show of support and sympathy, but the man was at a loss how to comfort his friend. "Surely there is something more the physic can do," he muttered. "There must be *something*."

Cortez shook his head. "He has no miracle to give her," he muttered. "The only miracle can come from God."

Keir's expression was full of sorrow. "Then I will go to the church and pray for her," he said. "I will go right now. I will not let you lose your daughter... oh, Christ, *another* daughter... as I lost mine. God must listen to me this time."

Cortez could not speak for the lump in his throat. Keir patted the man's cheek before turning away and heading back to the table where the other knights were sitting. After a few words were passed around the table, all four knights stood up and followed Keir from the tavern. They headed across the road, through a small field, and down another wider road that led to the church of St. Francis. The big, squat-looking house of worship accepted the Sassenach knights into the dimly-lit hall, where the five of them got down on their knees near the corner of the altar and began to pray for little Lady Sophie. Candles were lit as the prayers were intoned, intending to beg God for the gift of life that He had denied the girl's father.

Cortez would only find out the next morning that his knights had prayed all night.

After Keir had left the tavern and taken the other knights with him, Cortez struggled to compose himself before returning to the chamber. He didn't want Diamantha to see how shattered he was. He wanted to be strong for her because, God knew, the woman was going to need it. First her husband, then her father, and now this. He wondered how much more she could take without collapsing completely. He wondered just how strong she really was. He would soon find out.

Opening the chamber door smoothly, he saw that Diamantha was sitting next to the bed, leaning forward on it with her eyes closed, as Sophie slumbered quietly. Cortez shut the door softly behind him but it was enough of a noise to wake Diamantha. Her eyes popped open and she sat up, looking at him with a big, sleepy gaze. Cortez smiled gently.

"I am sorry to wake you," he whispered. "I was trying to be quiet."

She smiled faintly and yawned, rubbing at her eyes as she stood up. She went to Cortez and he swept her into an enormous embrace, squeezing her tightly. She squeezed back.

"I spoke with the physic," he explained, kissing the top of her head. "He says we should try to force her to drink watered wine or ale. He says it will help her a good deal. Has she been able to drink much today?"

Diamantha gave him one last squeeze before releasing him. "Not much," she sighed. "Everything she ate or drink either came out of the top or the bottom of her. Eventually, she did not want to eat or drink anything."

Cortez nodded sadly, turning to look at the little girl briefly before he started removing his clothing. The tunic came off but he still had the heavy mail coat beneath and, not wanting to make noise, he left Diamantha in their chamber and went out into the common room to have Peter, who was over near the hearth, remove it for him.

As the squire took the coat away to clean it before the morrow, Cortez sought out MacInnis to find out if there were any more rooms available for his knights. So far, Keir, Michael, and Drake had squeezed into the second smaller chamber in the inn, leaving James, Oliver, Merlin, and Peter to sleep in the common room along with the rest of the soldiers. As fortune would have it, MacInnis had a room attached to the stable out back, a stable where he kept his own animals as well as supplies for the tavern, but it was not a very big or very clean room. It was where the servant boys normally slept.

Cortez went out back to take a look at it and, deeming that it was better than sleeping in the common room, commandeered it for the rest of his knights. The room had three small beds plus a brazier for warmth. It was good enough for the knights, and when Cortez went back into the tavern, he told Merlin about it, who in turn ran across the street to the livery to find Peter. The two of them settled down into the small stable room as Cortez returned to Diamantha.

"Where did you go?" she asked as he entered the room and shut the door behind him. "You were gone so long."

He put his finger to his lips in a silencing gesture and took her over to the hearth, where the little animals were awake in their cage and scratching to get out. Cortez sat Diamantha down in a chair, the only one in the room, and sat himself down on the floor next to the animal cage.

Opening the cage door, he grinned wearily as the puppy ran out, jumping on his legs, and the kittens ran out after the puppy. Soon, he had two cats and a dog crawling around on his legs as the rabbit and fox kit, being a bit more cautious, sniffed around his breeches. It brought him a distinct sense of joy to watch them play because they reminded him so much of Sophie. He felt oddly comforted by them.

"I gave my mail over to Peter to clean it," he told her quietly. "I was also tending to some business with MacInnis, but I am finished for now. Have you eaten at all today, sweetheart? You look so very tired."

Diamantha was smiling faintly, watching the baby animals crawl over his big legs. "I am tired," she admitted. "As I said, this is the first time Sophie has slept all day. She has been so miserable that I have spent all of my time comforting her. I hate to see my child so ill. It simply breaks my heart."

Cortez put a big hand up and rested it on her knee comfortingly. "She is sleeping now, so that must be a good sign," he said. "At least she is comfortable enough to sleep."

"She is exhausted," Diamantha said, rubbing wearily at her temples. Then, she focused on Cortez. "Will you tell me what happened today? I assume that you did not find Robert."

He looked up at her. "Why do you say that?"

"Because you would have told me right away."

He shrugged, looking down to pet one of the kittens who was trying to climb up his tunic. "True enough," he said. "Nay, we did not find him. But I found the place where I last saw him, so that is significant. We have started digging holes around that area to locate him."

Diamantha fell silent, pondering the information. "And you found nothing?"

Cortez shook his head, petting the puppy as it tried to chew on his fingers. "We found a few items but they did not belong to him," he said. "A dirk, four broadswords, and pieces of leather that may have belonged to shoes. We will go back tomorrow and continue our search. He must be there, somewhere."

Diamantha eyed him. He didn't sound convinced. He sounded discouraged. She slithered off the chair and sat on the floor beside him, picking up the little bunny and cuddling it.

"You said that it was raining very badly during the battle," she said thoughtfully. "Is it possible that the rain might have washed him away? Would there have been anywhere for him to go?"

He knew she was grasping at straws and he took her hand, gently pulling her over onto his lap. Putting the rabbit down, Diamantha put her arms around his neck, giving in to the man's warmth and strength. Cortez wrapped her up in his muscular arms, holding her close and taking comfort in her soft body against his. It was the most satisfying feeling he'd ever known. Tenderly, he kissed her head.

"If he is there, I will find him," he assured her confidently. "Meanwhile, I do not want you to fret. I want you to keep your strength up. This journey has been very taxing for all of us."

Diamantha laid her head on his shoulder, thinking on their quest. "It seems like we left Corfe Castle a lifetime ago," she said, reflecting. "All of it... George, the arguments between you and me, the silver collar you gave me... everything seems like it happened so long ago."

Cortez was glad she saw it that way. He'd wondered if she ever would. "We have been gone twenty-six days," he said. "This is the second journey I have made to Scotland this year."

Diamantha lifted her head and looked at him. "You must be very weary."

He met her gaze. She was so close to him that he leaned forward and kissed her on the nose. "I am," he said. "But this was a necessary quest. I am glad we came."

Diamantha cocked her head. "You are?"

He grinned. "Of course I am," he said. "What was it I told you? That this quest has brought us closer together than anything else ever could have? It's true, you know."

She smiled because he was. "Are you telling me that you are glad I came?"

"Strangely enough, I am."

Diamantha giggled softly and he kissed her again, more amorously this time. But the puppy barked, the kittens scratched, and the rabbit scampered off underneath the bed, so Diamantha climbed off his lap to corral the rabbit before it escaped or got hurt. Just as she got down on her knees to hunt under the bed, Sophie began to cry softly on her bed.

Cortez was up, bending over the girl as she wept pitifully. Diamantha forgot about the rabbit and went to her child just as Cortez reached down and carefully picked her up.

"Mama," Sophie sobbed. "I want my poppet!"

Diamantha dug around in the messy bed, pulling forth Rosie and giving her to Sophie. The little girl snuggled with her poppet, nestled in Cortez's big arms. As he rocked her gently, Diamantha put a hand to her daughter's head, feeling for a fever. She seemed cool enough.

"How do you feel, sweetheart?" she asked.

Sophie wasn't comfortable in the least. "My belly hurts," she whined. "Mama, I'm thirsty."

There was watered ale on the little table next to the hearth and Diamantha poured some into a cup. Cortez continued to hold the little girl as Diamantha held the cup so she could sip down the ale. Sophie slurped gingerly, smacking her lips because it was sweet. Then she saw something on the table that interested her, small little oatcakes that Goodwife MacInnis had made.

Diamantha took one and broke it into tiny bites, feeding it to Sophie as a mother bird would feed her chick. Sophie ate about a quarter of a cake, and all seemed fine until about half hour later when she began to cry again.

Cortez still had Sophie in his arms because she had dozed off to sleep and he didn't want to risk waking her by putting her onto the bed. But she awoke groaning because her belly was cramping and within a few minutes, she was crying loudly in pain. Her little belly was so very tight, cramping viciously because of the food she had eaten, but when Cortez tried to put her back onto the bed, thinking she would be more comfortable, Sophie clung to him and wouldn't let go.

As Diamantha stood by and watched, torn with exhaustion and worry, Cortez paced around their small room with Sophie in his arms, singing softly to her while she groaned in pain.

"A young man came to Tilly Nodden,
His heart so full and pure.
Upon the step of Tilly Nodden,
His wants would find no cure.

Aye! Tilly, Tilly, my goddess near,
  Can ye spare me a glance from those eyes?
My Tilly, sweet Tilly, be my lover so dear,
  I'm a-wantin' a slap of those thighs!"

He sang the song that had made her laugh before, hoping it would make her laugh again, but it wasn't enough to distract her from the pain in her gut. After singing it twice, it was clear that Sophie wasn't finding comfort in it. When Cortez glanced up at Diamantha, sitting on the bed and watching him pace, he noticed the warmth in her eyes.

"Is that the only song you know?" she asked lightly.

He fought off a grin, rocking Sophie gently. "I know a few more, but the language is worse," he said, shaking his head slowly. "Not for the ears of the baby."

She shook her head reproachfully, though she wasn't serious. "Do you not know any children's songs?" she asked. "Songs that are not sung in a tavern common room and speak of women's body parts?"

He appeared rather embarrassed. "In truth, I do not."

Diamantha laughed in spite of her fears for her daughter. But the laughter faded quickly. "Do you want to give her to me?" she asked, her eyes on her child. "You must be growing tired."

He looked at her as if she was daft. "Nonsense, woman," he whispered. "I am a man. Men do *not* get tired."

She cocked a doubtful eyebrow. "They don't?"

"Nay, we don't," he said, eyeing her. "But I can see that you are very tired. Try and sleep now. I will take care of Sophie while you do."

Diamantha shook her head. Her sad eyes never left her daughter. "I cannot sleep," she said. "Not when my child is so ill."

Cortez understood her point but he was firm. "You will not be any good to Sophie if you allow yourself to become ill," he said. "Just sleep for a little while. I will take good care of Sophie."

Diamantha's eyes welled up but she fought it. He was right, she was exhausted. Lying back on the bed, the one she shared with Cortez, she watched the man as he paced the floor with Sophie, singing softly to her with words she could not hear until he drew closer. Then, she caught a snippet of the song:

"There once was an old whore named Rose,
with a wart on the end of her nose...."

Diamantha couldn't help but laugh to herself. They were naughty words but she didn't care. All that mattered was that Sophie, although still miserable, seemed to be calming, naughty lyrics and all.

Watching Cortez with her daughter was one of the sweetest things Diamantha had ever experienced. It was a sincere man indeed who would love a woman so much that he would treat her child as his own. It was clear how much he adored Sophie. On that tender thought, Diamantha's eyes closed and drifted off into a weary, fitful sleep.

Cortez heard the soft snoring, looking over to see that Diamantha had finally fallen asleep. He was relieved. The woman was absolutely exhausted and the emotional strain of a sick child and the physical strain of a long journey were taking their toll. As worried as he was about Sophie, he was equally worried about Diamantha. Should something happen to her, he didn't think he could take it. In fact, he knew he couldn't. He had survived Helene's death but he knew with deadly certainty that he would not survive Diamantha's. The woman had become a part of the very fabric of his being, as if he couldn't draw breath without her. Thinking of her ill was terrifying.

In his arms, Sophie moaned and he looked down at the child. She was so exhausted that her eyes were only half-open, giving her a rather corpse-like appearance. She was so very pale, too.

As Cortez gazed down at her, he felt as if some unseen dagger were stabbing him in the stomach. He had seen that countenance once before, on the face of Sophie's father as he sat dying against the split oak tree. It was a horrifying realization that hit Cortez all at once, and tears popped to his eyes. He couldn't take this; *nay, not again!* God certainly wouldn't be so cruel. With tears spilling over and running down his cheeks, he held the little girl in his arms and gazed from the small window cut high into the wall of the room. He could see the storm clouds outside, illuminated by a full moon. He could see God looking back at him.

"Not her," he hissed, praying to a God who had ignored him more often than he had listened. "You'll not take her. I held this child's father in my arms as he died and now history is repeating itself. How much more do you expect me to take? Are you testing me? I held Helene as she breathed her last and I held my daughter after she was already dead, and now this? Why are you doing this to me? For once in my life, listen to my prayers and save something that I adore. Save this child. Her mother could not suffer her loss and neither could I. You are supposed to be a merciful God but you have never been merciful to me. For once, listen to me, O God. For once, spare this child's life and restore her. You already have my daughter at your side. Leave this one for me."

He was weeping by the time he was finished, so heartbroken over things in life he'd had no control over, things that had devastated him emotionally. Wiping at his eyes, he struggled with his composure and resumed singing the only songs he knew, his voice cracking under the strain. It had been such a difficult day for him and, much like Diamantha, he was weary both physically and spiritually. But he kept walking the floor with the child, trying to comfort her, and he continued the pacing long into the night.

Morning saw a weakening child and a distraught mother.

CHAPTER TWENTY-TWO

The rain had been merciless for two more days of digging, slogging through swamps of mud that were reminiscent of the mud puddles back in July. There was so much muck that it was as if the entire world was full of it.

It was cold, too, and as Cortez and his men dug more holes and swept away more mud, his hands were frozen most of the time. Two days of heavy rains and two days of digging had not turned up anything belonging to, or about the person of, Robert Edlington, and Cortez had finally had enough. On noon of the third day since their arrival at Falkirk, Cortez called a halt to the search and sent his men back to the tavern. Weary, and grateful, they retreated to warm their bones and get out of the rain.

But for Cortez, his return to the tavern was not one of warmth and pleasure. It was one of sorrow. Sophie was growing steadily worse and the physic had suggested last rites for the child, but Diamantha had violently disagreed. In fact, Cortez actually had to pull her off of the physic when the suggestion was made. She had screamed at the man and told him never to come back, but Cortez had spoken to the physic in private and assured the man he was needed, now more than ever.

After things had quieted down, Diamantha sat on the bed with Sophie in her arms. The woman looked as if she hadn't slept in days. There were dark circles beneath her lovely eyes and her luscious hair was unbrushed and messy. She simply sat on the bed, humming softly to her child and rocking her gently. She didn't stop humming when Cortez returned to the room from having escorted the physic out and she didn't look up. She was staring off into space. Only when Cortez put himself in front of her line of sight did she notice him. Her gaze was hollow.

"Did you find Robert?" she asked dully.

She hadn't asked the question when he'd first returned, as she had been more concerned with the physic at that point. Now, her focus was shifting, and Cortez shook his head sadly.

"Nay, love," he replied. "The weather is too fierce. We will return tomorrow and look again, but my men needed to dry out and warm up. 'Tis starting to grow cold."

Diamantha's gaze lingered on him for a few moments before looking away again. She was seemingly dazed, her heart and soul and mind shattered by the condition of her child. Cortez watched her for a few moments, feeling so desperately sad, before turning to remove his wet tunic. The fire in the small hearth was blazing brightly, making the room very warm. In the corner near the hearth, he noticed that the animal cage was open and the puppy and both kittens were sleeping in a pile outside of the cage. He didn't see the rabbit or the fox but assumed they were somewhere, sleeping under the bed. That seemed to be their favorite place.

"Has Sophie eaten anything today?" he asked, peeling off his wet tunic.

It was a few moments before Diamantha answered. "She managed a bit of porridge this morning," she said. "But she has been sleeping all day."

Cortez glanced over at the pair as he bent and started to remove his heavy mail coat. "And you?" he asked. "Have you eaten?"

Again, there was a long pause before she spoke. When she finally did, it was not to answer his question. "I have been thinking, Cortez," she said. "I have been thinking that I want to bury Sophie with Robert, so it is imperative that you find him. You must try harder."

He jerked his head around, looking at her with some dismay. "*Bury* her?" he repeated. "She is not dead, nor will she die. I will not hear that out of your mouth again, do you hear me?"

Diamantha nodded. Then, she burst into tears and hung her head. Cortez ripped the mail coat off and went to her, wet and all, and threw his arms around her. He buried his face in the side of her messy head, trying desperately to comfort her.

"I am sorry," he whispered fiercely. "I did not mean to snap. I am so sorry, sweetheart. Forgive me."

Diamantha was wracked with sobs. "She will not awaken and she will not talk to me," she wept. "If she passes, I want her to be buried with her father. Please? He would want that. He would want her with him."

Cortez was nodding eagerly, tears stinging his eyes as he kissed her repeatedly. "Of course, my love, anything you want," he said, struggling not to weep along with her. "I will try harder to find Robert, I swear it."

Diamantha continued to weep, clutching Sophie against her breast. Cortez sat next to her, his arms wrapped around them both, losing the fight against tears. He let them come. The situation was so heartbreaking in so many ways, and the pain was overwhelming them both.

For quite some time, he sat with Diamantha and Sophie, cursing God for not listening to his prayers. He hated God, he had decided, because God surely hated him. There was no point in praying when God dismissed his pleas. As he sat there wondering what he could do to demonstrated his hatred towards God, perhaps by burning a church or two, Sophie suddenly opened her eyes.

"Mama?" she asked weakly.

Startled, Diamantha gazed down into the face of her baby. "I am here, sweetheart," she murmured. "You slept a long time."

Sophie, her pallor as white as snow, looked up at her mother. "Mama, I want mush."

Diamantha felt a spark of hope in that little request. "Are you hungry?" she asked. "Do you think you could eat some mush?"

Sophie's hand wormed its way out of the blanket and she yawned, rubbing her eye with the free hand. "I want *mush*," she repeated.

Cortez, his arms still around Diamantha and Sophie, bent over to kiss the little girl on the forehead. "I will go get your mush," he told her, releasing the pair from his embrace and standing up from the bed. "Mayhap Mama would like something to eat, too."

Diamantha had to admit that her child's request for food had a dramatic effect on her outlook. Asking for food was a sign from God as far as she was concerned, a sign that all would be well. Gazing up at Cortez with the first hopeful expression he'd seen in days, she nodded to his statement.

"I believe I would," she said. "Thank you kindly, good sir."

Cortez winked at her and left the chamber, closing the door quietly behind him. Out in the common room, his soldiers were eating a thick stew and the knights were in the corner by the front door, their usual place. Cortez made his way back to the kitchen where MacInnis and his wife were doing their chores. Everyone was very busy in the kitchen, especially the wife who was hacking away at a goose. The tavern keeper finally looked up and saw Cortez lingering a few feet away.

"M'laird," he greeted, wiping his hands off on his leather apron. "How is the lassie?"

Cortez nodded. "She has awoken and asked for mush," he said. "Can you provide some?"

MacInnis nodded eagerly. "Of course we can," he replied. "And yer wife? She's not yet eaten today."

Cortez nodded, sighing with some manner of relief. "Aye," he said. "Something for her, as well."

As MacInnis and his wife began to bustle around, Cortez turned around to head back to the room but the tavern keeper stopped him.

"M'laird," he called. When Cortez came to a halt, the tavern keeper closed the gap between them. "And fer yerself? Surely ye've had a hard day, digging as ye have been."

Cortez peered at the man curiously. "How do you know what I have been doing?"

MacInnis waved him off, as if he meant no harm. "I've heard yer men talking," he said, lowering his voice. "They said ye're looking fer something south of Callendar Wood. I've heard the townsfolk talking about it, too. People have seen ye digging. That is where the great battle happened this summer, ye know."

Cortez nodded slowly. "I know."

"Were ye part of the battle?"

Since MacInnis didn't seem distressed over the question, and there wasn't any use in denying his activities. He answered.

"Aye," he replied.

"Did ye lose something?"

"A friend," Cortez said softly. "A friend of mine died in the battle and was left behind. We have come to bring him home to give him a proper burial."

MacInnis scratched his head thoughtfully. Then, he looked around, as if fearful someone would overhear what he was about to say. Cortez looked around curiously, too, wondering why the tavern keeper suddenly seemed rather edgy. Or awkward. Cortez couldn't tell which, even when the man motioned for him to follow.

"May I have a word with ye, m'laird?" he asked quietly.

Cortez followed purely out of curiosity. MacInnis took him outside, across the yard, and into the stable, which was vacant except for a cow and her calf. As the rain trickled in overhead, he turned to Cortez.

"I didna want yer men tae hear," he said quietly.

Cortez's curiosity was growing. He crossed his big arms as he faced the tavern keeper. "Hear *what*?"

MacInnis scratched his head again. "The battle left many dead and wounded," he said. "The priests from St. Francis gathered some of the townsfolk and together, we went across the field tae bury the dead and gather the wounded. There are Hamilton and Livingstone clans around here and we wanted tae get tae the bodies before their women did. They steal from the dead, ye know, and they would have killed any Sassenach that was still living. We collected the dead and tended the wounded. There was no one left on the field."

Cortez was listening seriously. "Are you telling me that you collected *all* of the dead?"

MacInnis nodded firmly. "Every one of them," he said. "We couldna leave them fer the women, ye see."

"What did you do with them?"

MacInnis pointed in the direction of St. Francis church. "We buried the dead in a big grave outside of the church yard," he told him. "There were so many, ye see. The church yard wouldna hold them all."

Cortez stared at the man before unwinding his arms and rubbing a weary hand over his face. The circumstance that MacInnis was relaying to him was really quite staggering. It was quite possible that Robert had been found by the priests and buried. It would explain why they hadn't been able to find any trace of him. But something still didn't make sense.

"My friend was left to die on the outskirts of the battle," he said. "As the battle was dwindling, I dragged him over to the eastern side of the battlefield. I had to leave him for a short while and when I returned, he was gone. There was so much mud that I naturally assumed he was sucked in by it. *When* did the priests start collecting bodies, MacInnis? Did they even wait until the battle was over?"

MacInnis shook his head. "Nay," he replied. "The priests were collecting the dead and wounded while Edward was still waging war."

God's Bones! Cortez thought as he stared at the man. As if a bolt from heaven had burst down upon him, suddenly, Robert's disappearance was starting to make a good deal of sense. He could hardly believe it.

"But the mud," he said again, still having a difficult time comprehending what he'd been told. "It could have easily swallowed up a man."

MacInnis nodded. "'Tis possible, m'laird," he said. "The only way tae find out is tae come tae the church. The priests saved all of the Sassenach armor and weapons. We dinna bury the men with their regalia. Mayhap yer friend's armor is there."

Cortez was so electrified by the prospect that he was literally shaking. "Will you take me?"

MacInnis nodded and together, they headed back into the tavern where MacInnis told his wife of their plans. Cortez, however, had moved into the common room, his mind whirling with possibilities. *Was* it actually possible that the priests had collected Robert's body and buried him? Was *that* why they had been unable to find him? He was staggered by the prospect and as MacInnis led him towards the front entry of the tavern. Cortez passed the table of his knights and he called out to them.

"All of you," he snapped. "With me *now*."

The men got up from the table without question, following Cortez out into the stormy afternoon. Together, the group of them followed Cortez and the tavern keeper across the road, across a small field, and then down a larger road that led to the church of St. Francis. It was a march of sorts, a determined pace set by Cortez, and they could all feel the seriousness of it. Curiosity was turning to concern. Keir, who had been walking with the perplexed group of knights, finally caught up to Cortez.

"Where are we going?" he asked quietly. "What has happened?"

Cortez could only shake his head. He didn't dare want to hope they'd come to the end of their journey, but on the other hand, it was difficult not to pray for that possibility. The hope that their quest would finally come to an end was heavy on his mind. He glanced at his friend, now getting soaked again as the rain fell and the thunder rolled.

"We are going to the church," he said. "I'll tell you when we get there."

Keir had to be satisfied with that answer which was, in fact, no answer at all. But he kept his mouth shut, walking next to Cortez as they marched down the road to the church of St. Francis, a squat parish that Keir and the others had spent a good deal of time in, praying for little Sophie.

Soon enough, the big, brown-stoned building loomed in front of them and the group shook off the rain as they entered the dark, musty-smelling sanctuary. Banks of candles illuminated the cavernous space, a weak defense against the darkness of the storm that cast gloom over everything. Once inside, MacInnis turned to Cortez.

"Wait here, please," he said. "I will go get the priest."

Cortez nodded as the man disappeared into the shadows in search of a priest. When he was out of sight, Cortez turned to his men. Seeing all of the curious, if not worried, faces around him, he shook his head with all of the astonishment he was feeling. He struggled a moment to put his thoughts into words.

"I have just been told by the tavern keeper that before the battle was even over, and in order to prevent the women from Clan Hamilton and Clan Livingstone from looting the dead, the priests of St. Francis began removing the dead and wounded from the battlefield." He looked around at the faces that were now nearly as astonished as his. "It is quite possible that is why we have not been able to find Edlington. The priests may have already removed him. That is why we are here, to find out the truth. The tavern keeper tells me that they kept the armor and regalia from the men they buried and I have asked to see it. Mayhap Edlington's is among it."

For a moment, no one spoke. They were all digesting the astounding information. Finally, Michael hissed.

"God's Bloody Teeth," he said. "That would make a good deal of sense. No wonder we were not finding any bodies as we dug. None were there. The priests had taken them all!"

Cortez nodded. "Exactly," he agreed. "Had I been smarter about this, I would have come to the church first, but it did not occur to me that the priests would have taken an active interest in burying English dead."

"And if they have, in fact, buried him, what will you do?" Drake wanted to know. "Lady de Bretagne must be told. With her daughter so ill, it will be a difficult thing for her to know Edlington is already buried."

Cortez shook his head. "I think it will ease her mind," he said. "To know he has already been taken care of should ease her. At least, I hope it will."

"What if she wants him back?"

"I will deal with that situation if, or when, it comes."

No one had anything more to say to that. At this point, with no hard evidence, it would do no good to speculate on the future. They stood around for several long minutes in a tense little group until MacInnis and a priest suddenly appeared out of the darkness. The knights moved forward to greet them, unable to wait, anxious to discover truths. They closed in on the priest and the tavern keeper, surrounding them.

"This is Father Lewis," MacInnis said. "He helped collect the dead and wounded that day. I told him that ye were here looking fer yer friend and he has agreed tae show ye where they put all of the possessions confiscated from the English."

Cortez addressed the small, brown-eyed priest. "Thank you, Father," he said. "We are grateful for the mercy you showed the English after the battle and we are further grateful for your assistance. I would like to know the fate of our friend."

Father Lewis was a fairly young man with bad skin and a hooked nose. He eyed the big English knights around him. They appeared rather anxious. He seemed rather wary of them but pushed it aside. MacInnis had assured him they were honorable English, if such a thing was possible, and MacInnis was a man to be trusted. Moreover, they were here in search of a friend, a noble quest. His initial reluctance faded.

"No weapons are permitted," he told them.

Instantly, swords began to drop and smaller daggers also kept on the body were removed as well. Drake even pulled one out of his boot. No one argued in the least, and no one seemed to be worried that their valuable weapons were in a pile near the front entry of a church. They were more concerned with gaining access to the church itself. Everyone except Cortez, that is. He wasn't going to part with his weapons so the most he did was release his broadsword. Everything else, including a dagger in full view at his waist, remained on his body. The priest eyed him but didn't press. They'd mostly complied, anyway. He was willing to let it go at that.

"Come with me," he said.

The group followed. Cortez in particular walked right behind the priest, his eagerness nearly overwhelming him. He was starting to feel less astonishment and more hope, hope that they could finally discover what had become of Robert Edlington and hope for closure for Diamantha. She had suffered so very much through all of this and he began to pray that finally, they would know the truth. But then he remembered he hated God so he stopped praying, only to start up again when they reached the cloisters. He was so torn that he didn't know what to do. The next few moments would more than likely tell. If Edlington's items were among those kept by the priest, then he would definitely give thanks. If not, then he would curse God once again. He didn't want to face the fact that they might never know what happened to Edlington. He had to have hope.

The cloister of St. Francis was a long, dormitory-like building. There were two floors to it, novices on the bottom floor and priests on the top. There was a room called the Warming Room, which was really just a smaller room with a hearth in it. It was on the bottom floor, near the entry door, and it was into that room that Father Lewis led them.

Cortez couldn't describe the impression he had when Father Lewis opened the door to the Warming Room. It wasn't what he had expected but once he saw it, he was nearly overcome by the sight. From floor to ceiling, it was stacked with English regalia: plate armor, chain mail, swords, pole axes, shields, personal baggage, tunics, and any number of other things. The sight was both astonishing and depressing. Each item represented a life lost, a man killed, and all Cortez could see were dead English. He saw grieving families, sad children, and sorrowful wives. He saw war.

He stood at the open door, speechless, as Keir and Michael pushed their way in, followed by Drake and the others. All of them were flooding in, searching for regalia they recognized, as Cortez stood in the doorway with the priest.

"Is this all there is?" he asked hoarsely. "This is the only room with English possessions?"

The priest nodded. "This is from both the dead and the wounded."

Cortez turned to look at him. "What did you do with the wounded?"

The priest looked at him. "Most went home," he said. "We sent word tae their families, but a few remain, those who cannot remember who their families are or those who simply want tae remain here until they die."

"Where are they?"

The priest pointed to the ceiling. "Upstairs," he said. "We have them in a small dormitory."

Cortez didn't say anything more after that. He turned his sad gaze to his knights, now going through all of the armor and shields, calling out the names of men they recognized. *De Warenne, de Berkele, Poyns, de Grundon, de Mond, Martin, Deincourt...* so many names that Cortez knew. It could have just as easily been his name, shut off in here with no one to mourn him or miss him. No one to care that he'd been killed. It was a horrendously sobering sight, this room with ownerless armor. It was a shrine to death.

"Edlington's standard was blue and white," he reminded the group of what they were looking for. "His shield is white with a blue chevron and three sunbursts on it, and he was wearing a tunic of blue and white when I last saw him."

"Was it this?"

The question came from Drake, who was back in the corner of the room. He held up a tattered blue and white tunic, barely recognizable through the dim light and battle damage. Cortez entered the room and took the tunic from Drake, holding it up for all to see. There was a massive, stained hole in the center of it and a smaller hole with an equal stain on the back.

He knew this tunic.

"Aye," he said, feeling as if they had just reached the conclusive end of their long and arduous journey. The relief, the sorrow, was indescribable. "This belonged to him. These holes are where he was wounded. Is there more in that pile? The man had a shield, a broadsword, and other items. See if there is more in that pile."

With the knowledge that they had found Edlington's tunic, both sadness and acceptance descended on the room. It filled every man, every heart. But the knights dutifully converged on the stack of armor in the corner where the tunic had been found, searching for more Edlington possessions.

His attention on the shredded tunic, Cortez wandered out of the room, wondering if he should bring this relic, this testament of Robert's death, to Diamantha. It was a rather brutal bit of reality. He paused in the open doorway, staring at it.

"Was that what ye were looking fer?" the priest asked.

Still staring at the tunic, Cortez nodded faintly. "Aye," he said morosely. Then, he unfurled the tunic and held it up again so the priest could see it. "Do you remember the man who wore this? I would not be surprised if you did not, for there were many dead that day. But mayhap you can remember him and tell me where you buried him. On that day, you would have found him to the extreme east of the battlefield, propped up against an oak tree."

The priest reached out to finger the tunic. "There were many men that day, m'laird."

"I know," Cortez said patiently. "But think hard, if you will. As you can see, he was struck by an arrow in the torso and it went all the way through him. He was a tall man with short blond hair. He always liked to wear a bit of a mustache, too. Do you remember him?"

The priest's brow furrowed as he continued to finger the tunic. He went back to that day, such a terrible day, when he led an ox cart around the east side of the battlefield to collect the dead and wounded with. So much rain and mud, death and destruction. *East side of the battlefield*.... After a moment, a light of recognition came to his eyes.

"Is *this* the man ye are looking fer?" he asked, incredulous. "He had a mustache!"

Cortez caught the priest's excitement. "Aye, I told you that," he agreed quickly. "Do you remember him now?"

The priest nodded eagerly. "Aye, m'laird," he said. "We did no' bury this man."

Cortez looked at him strangely. "What... what do you mean you did not bury him?" he asked, now gravely concerned. "What did you do with his body?"

The priest lifted his shoulders. "But he is no' dead!"

Cortez had no idea what the man was talking about and he began to grow agitated. "Of course this man is dead," he said. "He had a gaping chest wound. It would have killed him. What did you do with him?"

The priest shook his head and grabbed him by the wrist. "The man who wore this tunic is no' dead," he insisted. "He is upstairs with the rest of the wounded."

Cortez had never run so fast in his entire life.

CHAPTER TWENTY-THREE

The priest was calling after him. In fact, most of his men were calling after him, but Cortez ignored them. He mounted the stairs to the second floor faster than he had ever moved in his life, ignoring the sounds of running boots behind him as his men overtook the priest and practically shoved the man down the stairs in their haste to get to Cortez. They thought he had gone mad and were desperate to get to him. They hadn't heard what Cortez had heard. All they knew was that he was running like the devil.

The dormitories on the second floor were divided into a bigger dormitory and a smaller one. The smaller dormitory was directly to the right at the top of the stairs and it was the first room Cortez burst into. Immediately, he could see several beds in the room, shoved close together so they could get as many men as possible in the room, and he could see that the beds had occupants. As the priest came in behind him, Cortez turned to the priest and barked.

"Where in the name of God is he?" he roared.

Frightened, the priest pointed to the bed in the corner, back by an alcove that had a big drape across it. Cortez turned in the direction of the bed. All he could see was a body in it but not much else. Rushing to the bed, he threw back the rough linen coverlet only to be confronted with something he'd never thought he'd ever see again.

Robert Edlington in the flesh.

With a cry, one of anguish and utter, complete astonishment, Cortez fell to his knees next to the bed. He stared at Robert, who didn't look like the man he knew. He was sporting a massive growth of beard and his dark blond hair was long and unkempt. The mustache he had taken such pride in was blending in with the rest of the hair on his face. His eyes were sunk deep into his skull and he was at least one hundred pounds lighter than the last time Cortez had seen him. He didn't look like himself at all, little and shriveled and skeletal, but as Cortez's knights came up behind him, he could hear each one of them gasping in turn. *Edlington! Christ, it's Edlington!*

Cortez didn't know what to say. He sat there on his knees, staring at the man who was just starting to come around. He was feeling so much anguish that it was eating him alive. He was so selfish, he knew, to think that Edlington's life meant death for his marriage to Diamantha. If the man wasn't dead, then Diamantha was still married to him. *His* Diamantha. As he sat on his knees, watching Robert's eyes flutter open, he began to openly weep. It was the worst day of his life.

Robert's vision wasn't what it used to be and neither were his reflexes, but when he opened his eyes and saw Cortez next to his bed with tears streaming down his face, he stared at the man for a full minute before reacting, and he only reacted at that point because he saw Keir St. Héver kneel down next to Cortez. Up until that moment in time, he wasn't entire sure he hadn't been dreaming. But now, he was coming to realize that it was no dream at all.

"Cortez?" he asked weakly. "My God, is it you?"

Cortez nodded, tears rolling down his cheeks as Keir put an arm around his shoulders to comfort him. Cortez didn't seem to be able to speak so Keir answered softly.

"Robert," he whispered. "We thought you were dead, man, and here we find you alive? 'Tis a miracle!"

Robert looked at Keir, blinking his eyes rapidly. "St. Héver?" he groaned. "What... what are you doing here?"

Keir reached out and grasped Robert's fleshy arm. "We came to bring you home for burial," he said, his pale blue eyes glittering. "We thought you were dead and we came to find your corpse and bring you home for burial."

"Diamantha wanted you to come home," Cortez found his voice, feeling so much grief that he was having difficulty functioning. "I came here to bring you home because she wanted it."

Robert just stared at him, growing more lucid as he began to realize what was going on. "Diamantha?" he whispered. "My wife… she has sent you?"

Cortez couldn't help it. It was an emotional rage like nothing he had ever known. "*My* wife," he hissed through clenched teeth as tears and spittle when flying. "You asked me to marry her, remember? You begged me to do it and I did. She is *my* wife."

Keir had hold of Cortez, eyeing his friend with great concern. "Cortez," he whispered, his heart breaking for the man. "You cannot blame him. He did not plan it this way."

As Cortez struggled, Robert's hand shot out and he grabbed Cortez by the arm. "You married her?" he breathed.

Cortez nodded, so very miserable. "I did," he whispered. "I married her. I love her. She is *my* wife."

As Keir tried to quiet him, Robert yanked on his arm with as much strength as he could muster.

"Good!" Robert cried, his voice sounding strange and weak. "You married her and for that I am glad. Glad, do you hear? I am half a man, Cortez; look at me. The priests were miraculously able to save my life but at what cost? I cannot walk or move. I lay in this bed day after day, praying for death. Diamantha does not deserve what I have become and I could not bear to be such a burden to her. You must not tell her that you found me, do you hear? *You will not tell her!*"

Cortez burst into sobs. "How can you ask me not to tell her?" he wept. "You are her husband and she has mourned you deeply. You are her rightful husband, not I. *It is you!*"

"Nay!" Robert rasped, trying to grab on to Cortez with two hands now. He was desperate. "You will not tell her! She cannot see what I have become, a wasted shell of a man! She must remember me how I was! It is the only chance I have to know peace, knowing she remembers me as her strong husband and not as a crippled invalid. *Please*, Cortez. Grant me this mercy. You must not tell her!"

It was a gut-wrenching situation to all concerned. Cortez's knights watched the scene with tremendous anguish; Robert, for not wanting Diamantha to see him as a cripple, and Cortez for understanding that Robert was her rightful husband. Both men were weeping, filling the air with their utter and complete torment. The pain in the room was a palpable thing, cutting through them like the blades of a thousand knives. No one was immune. Suffering was everywhere.

Drake watched the scene with his hands on his head in agony while James stood there and wept. Oliver, who had once been a good friend of Robert's, had to go to the other end of the room. He slumped against the wall, heartbroken and crushed. There wasn't a dry eye in the chamber as Cortez and Robert vented their mutual anguish. Keir, next to Cortez, reached out and grasped Robert's hand.

"No matter what you want, Diamantha is still legally your wife," he said, a lump in his throat. "She has every right to know you are still alive."

Robert squeezed Keir's hand. "What if you were lying on this bed, Keir?" he rasped. "You cannot feed yourself. The priests must clean your mess constantly because you have no control over yourself. I am not a man. I am a thing, a *thing* to be tended. Would you want your wife to take care of you like this for the rest of your life? How fair is that to her?"

Keir didn't have an answer to that. He understood what Robert was saying. He understood very well. He understood the pride of a man in *being* a man, not a cripple who couldn't do for himself. But this wasn't his battle. He couldn't make a decision that would affect Cortez or Robert, so he stood up and moved away from them, afraid he would be overwhelmed by the emotion surrounding the two of them.

When Keir walked away, Robert returned his attention to Cortez. He was struggling to calm himself, realizing that, in all likelihood, Cortez was going to tell Diamantha that he was, in fact, alive. No amount of begging was going to stop the man from doing what he believed he had to do, no matter what the cost. He couldn't let that happen. Somehow, someway, he couldn't let it happen.

"Cortez," he begged quietly. "I purposely did not send word to Diamantha that I was alive. No matter how much the priests begged me to tell them of my kin, I would not do it. I do not want her seeing me like this. Do you understand?"

Cortez had his head down, staring at the ground. When he lifted it, it was covered with tears but he wasn't openly sobbing as he had been earlier. Now, he simply felt numb.

"I do," he said softly. "But I cannot keep this from her. No matter how much I want to, you know that I cannot. She *must* know."

Robert fell silent a moment, contemplating his next move. He had to do what was best for him and what was best for Diamantha. What was best for Diamantha was not living her life with a shadow of the man that she used to love. It would ruin her.

"You said that you love her," he said to Cortez. "Does she love you, too?"

"Aye," he muttered. "She loves me and I love her. We have been very happy."

"And Sophie?" Robert asked. "How is Sophie?"

Cortez thought of the very sick little girl back at the tavern. He wasn't sure he wanted to tell Robert of the child's illness. It would only upset him further. It was one of those mercies Robert had spoken of. *Grant me this mercy, Cortez.* He didn't need to know.

"She has a lot of animals," he finally said. "And I think she would sleep with that pony if we let her."

A smile came to Robert's pale lips. "General," he remembered. "I think she loves that pony more than she loves anyone else. And my father? Is he well?"

"George is well."

Robert seemed to calm a great deal with that knowledge. Diamantha was loved, Sophie had her pets, and George was well. Those were the only people in the world he cared about. He was a content man.

"Thank you, Cortez," he said. "Thank you for taking care of my family. I am at peace knowing they are well cared for. You have given me the greatest gift of all and I am more grateful than you will ever know."

Cortez couldn't respond. He was too overwrought to show any measure of generosity towards the man. He was crushed. Still, he knew it wasn't Robert's fault, any of it. He sighed heavily.

"Mayhap you should let Diamantha decide what she wants to do with her life," he finally said. "This is her choice, after all. You cannot make it for her and neither can I. She will want to see you, you know."

Robert's gaze was surprisingly steady. "Then you really are going to tell her?" he asked. "You will not change your mind?"

Cortez exhaled sharply. "I told you that I will not keep this from her," he said. "If she ever found out, she would hate me forever. It would not be fair to all concerned."

Robert didn't say anything. He simply looked at Cortez, seeing how utterly distraught the man was. It was clear that he was hurting badly. Robert was hurting badly, but not for the same reasons. It was time to finish what that Scots archer had started those months ago.

It was time to go home.

"Embrace me," Robert said, holding up his arms to Cortez. "Before you go, please... embrace me. Let me feel your strength one last time, as you held me upon the fields of Falkirk and called me Brother."

Cortez looked at the man. He didn't want to hug him but the moment he did, his guard when down and the tears came again. He could feel how weak and tired the man was simply by his embrace. He had no way of knowing it was a ruse, for the moment Cortez's guard went down and he hugged Robert tightly, Robert grabbed the small dirk had had seen nestled in the belt at Cortez's waist. Before anyone realized what had happened, Robert took the blade and plunged it deep into his chest, straight into his heart. He was dead in an instant.

Cortez realized something was wrong soon enough. He felt Robert's hand at his waist and before he could move, Robert grabbed the dagger and plunged in into his chest. Cortez screamed out in anguish, as did Keir and Michael, who had witnessed Robert grab the blade but were too far away to stop him. As Robert collapsed back onto his bed, bleeding out, Cortez stood over him and roared.

"Nay!" he cried. "Robert, no! You cannot do this! *Dear God, no!*"

Michael and Keir rushed at Robert, removing the blade and watching bright red blood run out all over him. They felt for a pulse, checked his eyes, but it was clear that the man was very dead. They looked at each other, at Cortez, with open grief on their faces. Cortez, however, stumbled back and collapsed against the wall behind him. It was too much to take.

"My dagger," he breathed. "He used my dagger to kill himself. My dagger. When I tell Diamantha we found him alive, she will think... she will think I killed him with my dagger!"

Keir went to him, falling to his knees beside him. "Nay, she will not," he assured him, "because you are not going to tell her anything. *Think,* Cortez, what good will it do her? She will have mourned for him twice! Let her remember him as he was. That is what Robert wanted, why he took your dagger to his chest. You must never tell Diamantha about this, do you hear me? She does not need to know!"

Cortez looked at Keir, hearing his words of wisdom through his overwrought mind. It made a good deal of sense. The righteous part of him was determined to tell Diamantha everything but the reasoning part, the part that was so capable of mercy, agreed with Keir. It would do Diamantha more harm than good to know what had truly happened to Robert. She had already mourned for the man and to tell her of this event would undo all of the healing. It would hurt her more than help her, and he simply couldn't do that to her. Not when he loved her so.

"Nay," he finally whispered. "I will not tell her. She does not need to know. Let her remember Robert as he was."

Vastly relieved, Keir pulled Cortez off the ground and they both stood there for a moment, gazing at Robert's body. It was a sad sight, but in a sense, it was a comforting one, for one very good reason.

"He is free now," Cortez said softly. "He is truly free."

The other knights began to gather around, their attention on Robert's corpse. Whether or not they agreed with Robert's actions, they understood why he did what he did. Not only did he do it to spare Diamantha future anguish, but he did it to save himself. The man had control of his life taken away those months ago by a Scots arrow. Today, he took control back. As Cortez said, he was finally free.

Robert Edlington's body would make the trip back to Corfe, after all.

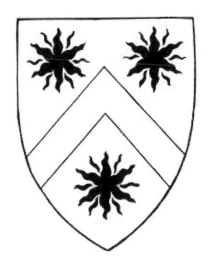

CHAPTER TWENTY-FOUR

Sophie was feeling better.

Cortez's first clue was when he felt soft baby claws digging at his belly, awakening him from a dead sleep. When he tried to move, he heard little giggles and the bark of a puppy. Opening his eyes, he saw Sophie standing next to the bed, playing with her animals as they nestled against his torso. He smiled sleepily.

"Sophie?" he asked softly. "What are you doing, sweetheart?"

Sophie looked at him and he saw the light go on in her eyes. She was pale, that was true, but her big smile and bright eyes told him that she was well on her way to mending.

"They want to play here," she told him. "They like you."

Cortez grunted when baby kitty claws dug into his ticklish middle. "And I like them," he said. "But can you please remove them now so I can get up?"

Sophie nodded, picking up the two kittens and the rabbit, and carrying them over to the other bed. Cortez picked up the puppy and the fox kit as he sat up, handing them to Sophie when she came back to collect them. She was a happy little girl and he patted her head, smiling at her as she carried the remainder of her pets over to the bed.

"There once was an old whore named Rose," Sophie sang, "with a wart on the end of her nose...."

Cortez flinched when he heard his song come out of her mouth, immediately looking around to see if Diamantha was in the room and hoping she hadn't heard. He saw her immediately, sitting over near the hearth. She was looking at him, a faint smile on her lips, and he smiled back.

"Good morn to you, sweetheart," he said, scratching his scalp and hoping he wasn't about to get a scolding for the naughty song Sophie was singing. "I must have slept long."

But Diamantha either didn't notice or she didn't care. She stood up from the chair with something in her hand and Cortez could see that it was Edlington's stained tunic.

"You were exhausted," she said as she sat down on the bed next to him, accepting a kiss on her cheek. "I am sorry that Sophie woke you."

Cortez put a big arm around her shoulders, giving her a squeeze. "It was the best thing I could wake up to," he said, eyeing the little girl as she played with her pets. "She looks much better."

Diamantha looked at her daughter, also "She is," she said, relief in her voice. "She has already eaten a big bowl of mush this morning and so far she feels fine. I cannot tell you how grateful I am."

Cortez kissed her temple. "As am I," he said, then looked to the tunic she was holding. His manner sobered. "What are you doing with that?"

Diamantha looked at the tunic, too. After a moment, she sighed faintly. "I was just looking at it," she said. "I made this for him, you know. He was quite proud of it."

Cortez wasn't sure what to say to that. She seemed sad but resigned. In fact, she had been sad and resigned since he had returned to the tavern yesterday evening with the tunic in his hand and the news that he had, indeed, found Robert Edlington.

Diamantha had taken the news better then he thought she would. There had been a rather steely resolve about her, or perhaps it had simply been the fact that she'd had months to accept his death. In any case, as she had held the tunic and wiped away tears of both sadness and relief, Cortez had been very careful in explaining that the priests had collected the dead and wounded from the battlefield, and that had included Edlington. The man had been at the church all along. He told her that he was having the priests build a box in which to place Robert's body and that they would soon be taking him home. All of it was true, of course, because the priests were indeed building a coffin for Robert, and the man was being washed and prepared that afternoon for his journey home.

Diamantha had shed tears for her late husband but they had fortunately been short-lived. They had what they had come for - the great Questing for Robert Edlington's body - and she was satisfied. Thankfully, she didn't ask to see Robert's corpse because once she saw the tunic, both she and Cortez agreed that it was better to remember Robert as he was, a big and powerful knight. Cortez, along with Keir and the other knights, assured Diamantha that the corpse was indeed Robert, so with six men identifying her husband, Diamantha saw no need to personally identify him. Their word was enough, and Cortez was deeply thankful.

As he sat and collected his thoughts, and pondered the great secret of Robert Edlington's true passing that six knights had sworn to take to their graves, the rabbit got loose from Sophie and the little girl squealed. Snapping out of his train of thought, Cortez got up and went after the rabbit, finding it hiding under the bed and delivering it back to Sophie for safe keeping.

Meanwhile, Diamantha had taken Robert's tunic and carefully rolled it up, putting it into the barrel that made anything stored in it smell like cinnamon. She stood there a moment, gazing down into the barrel.

"What did you do with the rest of Robert's possessions?" she asked Cortez.

He had made his way over to the table and the bowl of cold water. He splashed some on his face. "In addition to the tunic, we came across his sword, most of his armor, and one of his saddlebags," he said. "All of that will be stored on the wagons. I asked Drake to see to it. Why?"

She shrugged, still looking down the barrel. "I want to make sure we preserve them for Sophie," she said. "It is something of her father that she can have. I think it is important."

Cortez agreed. "We will put them away for safekeeping and she can have them when she comes of age, mayhap to give to her own son."

Diamantha liked that idea. "Thank you," she said sincerely. "When did the priests think they would be finished with Robert's coffin?"

Cortez splashed more water on his face, drying it with a piece of linen nearby that was there for that purpose. "More than likely today," he said. "I will go to the church later and check their progress. Once Robert is settled, there is no reason to delay returning home. I would like to before the heavy snows fall."

Diamantha agreed. She began rearranging the barrel as Cortez finished dressing and headed out into the common room. He wanted to meet with his knights to make preparations for the return journey. As emotionally draining as yesterday had been, he awoke this morning feeling a great sense of relief – relief that their journey had ended and relief that they had what they had come for.

Still, he couldn't help feeling some guilt and sadness over Robert's final demise. Perhaps he would always feel some guilt for it. But he, like the others, prayed that Robert was finally at peace. Perhaps God would take pity on the man and not condemn him to Purgatory for his actions. God was a man, after all. Perhaps he would understand.

His knights were at their usual table near the entry door of the tavern and he made his way over to them, listening to Keir and Michael deal him a few insults for sleeping late. Cortez grinned and slapped Keir on the shoulder, good naturedly, as he sat down to bread and warmed-over stew. As he began to eat his first real meal in days, the door swung open and young Peter appeared.

"My lord," the squire said. "You had better come."

A sense of concern shot through Cortez as he swallowed the bite in his mouth and rose to his feet. "What is it?" he demanded.

Peter merely waved him on. "Come and see, my lord."

The young lad bolted from the room, leaving the knights to follow. Everyone was wrought with curiosity and some apprehension as they made their way to the area outside of the tavern, with Peter pointing down the road to the southwest. It was clear this day with the rains having cleared out, but a touch of winter was in the air. It was very cold and breath hung in great foggy clouds

as they all tried to see what Peter was pointing at. Cortez's eyes
were no good at a distance but Keir's were. A slow smile spread
across his lips.

"Andres," he finally breathed.

Cortez wasn't surprised. "He said he would catch up with us," he
said, great satisfaction in his voice. "But do I see two riders?"

Keir nodded as Drake came up beside Cortez. "It looks like your
father," he muttered.

Cortez sighed heavily. He didn't want a battle on his hands, not
today. After yesterday, he wasn't sure if he'd ever be ready for
another emotional battle so he braced himself.

Sensing a hard change in Cortez's demeanor, Drake leaned into
him. He knew what had the man on edge.

"Andres would not have brought your father with him if the man
was still full of venom," he said in a low voice. "But to be safe, I will
go sit with your wife."

Cortez nodded faintly as Drake headed back into the tavern. As
the rest of the knights stood there, the two great chargers heading
up from the southwest drew closer and closer. Andres and Gorsedd
came clearly into view and Cortez, feeling very edgy, moved
forward.

"Stop right there," he told them. "Father, if you have come here to
further denounce my wife, know that I have no patience for it. You
can turn around and go home. Today is not the day to push me."

Andres held up a hand to signify his peaceful intentions.
"Greetings to you, too, brother," he said somewhat wryly, noting Keir
standing next to Cortez. His face lit up. "St. Héver, you ugly beast!
How did you come to be part of this ragtag group? And is that
Pembury? Good God, *two* ugly beasts in one place. I've never been so
happy in my life!"

Keir grinned, as did Michael, but neither one of them responded.
There was still the unanswered statement from Cortez. Uncertainty
filled the air as Cortez took another step towards them.

"Answer me," he said, looking mostly at his father. "What are you
doing here?"

Andres gave his brother a droll expression. "Can we at least
dismount?"

"Nay."

Andres sighed sharply. "Cortez, we came to find you," he stated the obvious. "Father and I had many serious discussions after you left and he has come to see the error of his ways. Old prejudices die hard but Father agrees that your wife should not be held responsible for the actions of her ancestor. He has come to make amends. *Now, can we dismount?*"

Cortez was looking at his father now. "Is this true?" he asked, considerably less hostile. "Did you come to apologize?"

Gorsedd looked rather ragged and pale, sporting several days' growth on his face. "All I have is my family," he said, rather simply. "You must understand that I spent my youth listening to stories of de Velt's atrocities against my grandfather. I had grown up hating the very name. Your wife... she comes from that family but she did not commit the crimes. Forgive an old man for living in the past and for letting old prejudices cloud his thinking."

Cortez couldn't help but think of what he'd been told. *Father's mind is going.* Maybe in flashes of insanity, he would forget his apology and relive the old hatred. He couldn't help but be wary.

"You are forgiven," he said quietly. "But I am not entirely sure I can trust you around my wife. She is the most important thing in the world to me, even over you."

Gorsedd appeared genuinely remorseful. "Will... you at least allow me to apologize to her?"

"Why?"

"Because I want my son back and this is the only way he will return."

That was probably very true and for that fact alone, Cortez was willing to believe that his father would behave himself. His family was the most important thing to him and he would do what was necessary to preserve it – perhaps even put aside an old hatred. Still, time would tell, but for the moment, Cortez was willing to agree. It was his father, after all, and he had missed him. He would like nothing better than for these wounds to be healed. He looked at Andres.

"Do you believe him?" he asked.

Andres nodded. "I would not be here if I did not," he said, his gaze softening on his brother. "Give the man a chance, Cortez. Please."

Cortez could feel himself relenting. "Very well," he said after a moment. "Dismount your horses and come inside. I will have Peter take your mounts to the livery."

A collective sigh of relief went up as Gorsedd and Andres dismounted their horses. As Andres went straight to Keir, who tried to punch him in the nose as he had once promised to do, Gorsedd went to Cortez.

The old man gazed up at his son. There were a thousand things he wanted to say to him but the words just wouldn't come. At this point, actions would speak louder than words and he knew it. He had much to atone for. As the cold wind blew around them and the knights began to head back into the warmth of the tavern, Gorsedd dug into the pocket of his heavy cloak.

"I have something for you wife," he said. "Mayhap... mayhap in some small way, this will emphasize my regret at my behavior. I hope it will."

Cortez was trying not to feel pity for his father but it was difficult. He loved his father very much and the rift had greatly upset him.

"What is it?"

Gorsedd pulled out a piece of cloth, carefully wrapped around something, and as he unwrapped the ends, Cortez could see flashes of silver beneath. The great silver collar suddenly appeared, whole and bright and beautiful as it had been the day it had been forged. It was magnificent beneath the cloudy, cold skies and Cortez couldn't help but reach out to touch it. So many memories in that one collar.

"The necklace," he breathed. "You had it repaired."

Gorsedd nodded. "I did indeed," he said, looking up at Cortez. "I hope your wife will accept this. Your mother would have wanted her to have it and, in some small way, mayhap this makes your mother a part of your marriage. She would have been so happy to know your wife, Cortez. With this necklace, I believe your mother is giving you her blessing. I hope your wife will wear it with honor and accept the apology of a foolish old man."

Cortez grinned. He put his hand on his father's shoulder, giving the man a squeeze. "Let us go inside and ask her."

Gorsedd nodded, broke into a smile, and then fiercely hugged his son, who returned the embrace firmly. Finally, Cortez could feel warmth again and hope. He could feel so very many things, not the least of which was his father's genuine regret and remorse. For them, so many things had come full circle and for life in general, the great Questing undertaken those weeks ago was now at a close.

Everyone had what they had come for; for Diamantha, it was Robert, and for Cortez, it was Diamantha. For Gorsedd... it was the understanding that life goes on and old family hatred should remain in the past. For Gorsedd and Cortez and Andres, it had no meaning. Life was good now and they intended to keep it that way.

The great Questing, to all concerned, meant something different to each and every one.

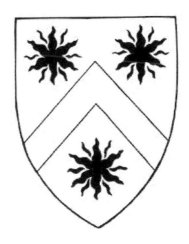

Epilogue

Sherborne Castle
1313 A.D.

"Great Bleeding Jesus," Cortez grunted. "Is everyone not ready yet? It will be a three day journey to the Marches and you know I wanted to leave on time. What on earth is the delay?"

He was standing on the landing just outside of the great bedchamber he shared with Diamantha at Sherborne, watching his children scatter past him; two small boys, aged seven and four, ran down the staircase while three girls, aged twelve, ten, and nine years, ran into the chamber across from the master's chamber and slammed the door. This level had two bedchambers, one belonging to him and his wife, and the other belonging to his daughters. But the boys had a chamber on the floor above and it seemed as if everyone was migrating in a great herd in front of him, in all different directions, and suddenly they were all gone except for one. Cortez called out to the last child remaining.

"Rhodri," he addressed his eldest. "Where is everyone going? Are all of your brothers and sisters ready to depart?"

Rhodri de Bretagne was a very big lad, handsome and well mannered, named for Gorsedd's grandfather who had lost his life at

323

the hands of Jax de Velt. He had been fostering at Blackstone Castle in Norfolk for the past four years and had only recently returned at the request of his mother, who had missed him very much. Moreover, the family was about to celebrate a milestone in their lives: the birth of Diamantha and Cortez's first grandchild, Sophie's son, and the entire family was heading to the Welsh Marches to visit Trelystan Castle, the seat of the great marcher lords, the House of de Lara. Sophie had married into the very big clan and the birth was cause for celebration for all concerned.

In fact, Diamantha had wanted all of her fostering children home for this great event, so the keep of Sherborne was full of brothers and sisters who had not seen each other in quite some time. Therefore, it was a bit chaotic. But neither Cortez nor Diamantha cared. They were simply thrilled to have all of their children home again.

"Father, the girls will not listen to me," Rhodri said, sounding as if he was defending himself. "When I told them we had to leave, they yelled at me."

Cortez looked at his son, lifting his eyebrows drolly. "They *yelled* at you?"

Rhodri nodded seriously. "Loudly," he insisted. "They were *loud*."

Cortez shook his head and rolled his eyes. "And that frightens you?"

Rhodri stood his ground. "Sometimes they throw things, too," he said. "Allegria threw a shoe at me yesterday. She is a very mean girl!"

Cortez couldn't help the wry expression. "Lad, do you realize you are quite a bit bigger than they are?" he asked, almost rhetorically. "You could have forced them to come."

Rhodri cocked his head. "Could *you* force them to come?"

Cortez backed off, but not entirely. "Aye," he said. "I can. Diamantha?"

He called out to his wife who was inside their chamber finishing with the last of the packing. From inside the room, they heard her muffled reply.

"What is it?" she called.

"Sweetheart, can you please attend me?" Cortez responded politely.

As he and Rhodri eyed each other, confident that the rebellious girls would soon be defeated, Diamantha appeared, her hands clutching a blanket for the new baby that she had been trying to pack. Her bags were nearly full, however, and it was taking a bit of effort. In the dimness of the landing, she smiled at her son first before turning to Cortez.

"What is it?" she asked.

Cortez opened his mouth to speak but Rhodri interrupted his father. "I tried to tell the girls that we must leave and they yelled at me," he said. "Papa wants you to tell them we must depart."

Diamantha lifted her eyebrows and looked at her husband, who merely nodded his head as if it were an entirely serious matter. Diamantha shook her head reproachfully.

"And you cannot do this?" she hissed, holding up the blanket. "I am not quite finished packing the baby's items."

Cortez lifted his shoulders. "They throw things."

Diamantha turned her head. She didn't want her husband or son to see that she was about to laugh. "You are both bigger and stronger than they are," she said, but she dutifully went to the door on the opposite side of the landing and rapped on it heavily. "Allegria? Isabella? Juliana? If you are not down in the wagon by the time I finish packing, and I am nearly finished, then I will take my hand to your backsides. Is that clear? Your father is coming in to collect your baggage, so you had better be prepared."

She could hear hissing and shuffling behind the door. Satisfied, she turned to her husband and eldest son. "There," she said. "I have tamed the wild beasts for you. All you have to do now is go in and collect their bags. That should not be too hard, should it?"

Rhodri looked embarrassed while Cortez merely grinned. "You are a marvel of womanhood," he said, pulling her to him and kissing her cheek. "A goddess divine. A...."

Diamantha put a hand over his mouth, grinning as she pulled away. "Enough flattery," she said, looking at Rhodri. "Go upstairs and get your brothers, Rhodri. Cruz and Mateo are already packed. I finished up their things myself last night."

Rhodri pointed down the stairwell. "They are already down in the wagon, Mother."

She reached out and patted his cheek. "Thank you, my son," she said, seeing so much of Cortez in that handsome little face. "Go to them. I will finish packing and meet you down there."

Rhodri turned obediently, heading for the stairs that led down to the ground floor of the keep and subsequently out to the massive bailey of Sherborne. Cortez stole another kiss from her and turned for his daughter's chamber but a word from his wife stopped him.

"Cortez, wait," she said. When he paused and looked at her, expectantly, she continued. "Do you recall those years ago when we returned from Falkirk with Robert's possessions? Do you recall how we discussed giving them to Sophie for her first son? Where did you store those items? I should like to bring them for her now."

Cortez nodded in both remembrance and agreement. "They are in my solar," he said. "I put them in a chest. I shall have the chest put on the wagons."

Diamantha put the blanket aside. "Let me see what is in that chest first," she said. "I never did look through everything when it was brought back. I... I suppose I did not have the strength. Did you ever look through his things?"

Cortez shook his head, trying not to think back to that time, a time that had been so wonderful yet so terrible. It was a time that had given him a secret he had kept from his wife all these years. With time, the guilt of bearing it had eased, but it had never gone away completely. Now, with the mention of Robert Edlington, it threatened to return.

"Nay," he said softly. "I suppose I did not particularly want to. I simply packed everything away."

Diamantha understood. "Then we should probably take a look now just to see what we will be giving her."

Cortez took her hand and escorted her to his solar, which was in a wing of the complex of Sherborne that was separated from the keep. The great stone buildings that made up the complex of Sherborne were cool on this day, a bright day in spring that had dawned quite cold. In fact, the entire spring had been unseasonably chilly. By the time they reached the well-appointed solar that smelled of rushes, Diamantha was rubbing her arms against the chill.

Cortez went over to a great wardrobe that was situated behind his well-used desk, a cabinet that held his writing implements, law books, and other things. It was quite cluttered. On the bottom shelf was a rather large chest, and Cortez pulled it out, setting it upon his desk. As he bent over to pull out the broadsword that had once belonged to Edlington, still in its scabbard, Diamantha opened the top of the trunk.

The first thing she saw was Robert's tunic, the one he had been wearing when he had been wounded. So many memories tumbled upon her, memories she hadn't thought of in years. Some were sad, some were not. With a sigh, she carefully pulled out the tunic and held it up, inspecting it. It was dirty and yellowed with age, but the impact of the sight of it was not any less powerful.

"Do you suppose she is going to want this?" she asked.

Cortez set the broadsword down on the table, looking at the tunic. "Has she ever seen it?"

Diamantha shook her head. "I never showed it to her. I never saw the need."

Cortez put his arm around her shoulders, his gaze on the tunic that held very heady memories for him. Once again, he could feel the sorrow of that day, a day that had changed his life forever. It was a struggle not to linger on the reflections.

"We can bring it," he said softly. "She is old enough now that she may want to see it. It will be her choice whether or not she wants to keep it."

Diamantha nodded and carefully folded it, setting it aside. The chest contained a saddlebag, one of two that Robert had owned, but the second bag had never been located. She pulled the bag out and set it on the desk next to the chest as Cortez untied the top and opened it up.

He pulled out knitted gloves, a knitted cap, and two tunics that had belonged to Robert. Diamantha took the tunics, inspecting them.

"I remember when I made these," she said, almost wistfully. "Robert had put on weight and they were too tight, but he insisted on wearing them. I told him he looked as if he were wearing a sausage casing."

She chuckled at the memory, as did Cortez. But when the laughter died, Cortez watched her expression, wondering if the humor was giving way to sorrow.

"How do you feel seeing all of this again?" he questioned.

Diamantha shrugged as she carefully refolded the tunics. "I suppose I feel sad that he never got to see Sophie marry," she said honestly. "I am sad that he will never know his grandson, his namesake. But beyond that, I do not miss him if that is what you mean. I know it sounds terrible to say this, but had he not died, I would have never married you, and you and I have had a perfect life together. I have a beautiful family and a wonderful husband... I am very thankful for my life."

Cortez smiled faintly at her, warmed by her words. He reached deeper into the saddlebag and pulled out a small dirk, a pair of hose, and a small sewing kit. He set them all upon the table as Diamantha carefully examined everything. The last few items in the saddlebags belonged to a writing kit. He pulled out an inkwell and quill, tightly wrapped in a leather pouch, a sanding phial that still had sand in the bottom of it, and a pouch containing sheets of vellum.

"Robert was keen on writing," Diamantha said, scrutinizing the sanding phial before opening up the vellum pouch. "In fact, he used to... God's Bones... Cortez, I think some of this vellum has writing on it."

Carefully, she pulled it out. There were several sheets of uneven size and width, and three of them had writing on them. As Cortez lit the taper on the desk so they could see more clearly, Diamantha held up the first sheet with dark, somewhat smeared lettering on it.

"Can you read this?" she asked Cortez.

He took the vellum, peering at it in the dim light. His eyesight had never been the greatest and over the years, it had grown steadily worse, so it took him a moment to see what had been written. After reading a few sentences, he grinned.

"It's a story," he said. "He has written about a family of rabbits. He must have written it for Sophie."

Diamantha nodded eagerly. "He loved to write little stories for her," she said happily. "What a blessing this is – now Sophie can have it for her son."

Cortez set the vellum down and picked up the next one. He read a couple of sentences. "This seems to be a letter to George," he said. "I am sorry we did not know it was here. I am sure George would have liked to have seen it."

Diamantha looked at the letters. Since she did not know how to read, it all looked like scribble to her. "How sad," she said with regret. "He never did recover from Robert's death. It was one of the last things he said before he passed away last year, do you recall? He said he was glad to die because he would see his son and wife again. What a terrible thing to be so lonely."

Cortez nodded in agreement, thinking on George Edlington and how he spent a great deal of time at Sherborne since Robert's passing. He did it to be close to Sophie, but he eventually became a grandfather to all of their children. The end of his life had been very full. As he thought on George, he took a look at the third piece of vellum. After reading the first few words, he looked at Diamantha.

"This is addressed to Sophie," he said.

Diamantha eyed the letters on the vellum, some of them smeared and dulled with age. "What does it say?" she asked.

Cortez returned his gaze to the yellowed vellum with the faded writing on it. Quietly, he began to read.

My dearest Sophie;

My days are long and my nights longer. I miss you and your mother fiercely. I know you are too young to understand why I have gone away, but please know it was not because I wanted to. It was because my king, and my country, had need of me. I pray for a swift end to this conflict so that I can return home to you and your mother. In my dreams, I can see your smile and hear your laughter. Sometimes, I see rabbits or butterflies all around, and I can imagine that in their beauty, I see a glimpse of you. You are a breath of wind, the song of a bird, or a flower petal that blows away on a breeze. You are all these things of beauty to me and if the fates are unkind and I never see your face again, then know that throughout this journey, I have been

*comforted by the life I see around me. It reminds me of you. I pray for
the day when we will be together again, my little flower, in this life or
in the next. But know that if my life ends today, I will be with you,
always. I will be in the song of a sparrow or in the patter of a gentle
rain. As you are with me now, so will I be with you until the end.*
  Your loving Papa

Cortez had tears in his eyes as he finished. He couldn't even see
the vellum anymore. He looked up at Diamantha to see tears
streaming down her face. Stifling a sob, she wrapped her arms
around Cortez's waist, her head upon his shoulder.

"He loved her so much," she whispered, wiping at her face.
"Although I am sorry we did not find this letter sooner, just as we
did not find George's letter sooner, I cannot help but be grateful that
we found it now. This will have so much more meaning to her as an
adult than it would have as a child. But I wonder why he never sent
it to her? Why did he keep it with him?"

Cortez hugged her tightly, thinking on that day so long ago when
Robert Edlington had ended his life on his own terms. He'd never
faulted the man his decision. In fact, he had always understood his
motives. *Let them remember me as I was.* Now, they had.

"I do not know," he said softly. "Mayhap it was something he
wrote right before his death and never had time to send it. Or maybe
it was a sentiment he wanted to keep with him, something to remind
him of his daughter. Whatever the reason, it does not matter, for
Sophie will soon have it and she will know how much her father
loved her. In fact, he has described how I feel about her, also. It is
how I feel about *all* of my children, but it is particularly how I feel
about you. As you are with me now, so will I be with you until the
end because my quest, always, has been you."

He quoted the last of Robert's letter with his own sentiment on
the end of it, a phrase that had been the core of their marriage.
Diamantha hugged him tightly.

"It is beautiful," she whispered. "Truly beautiful."

They remained in a tight embrace for a few moments longer,
lingering on Robert's adoring letter, until they were forced to pack

up the chest, remembering the children waiting for them. *Their* children, born from a love that had been forged in sorrow and fire, a love that was stronger than the bonds of earth, and held together by a little Posey ring that Diamantha had never taken off her finger.

It summed up everything they had ever meant to one another, the heart of their very existence, in this life or in any other.

My quest is you.

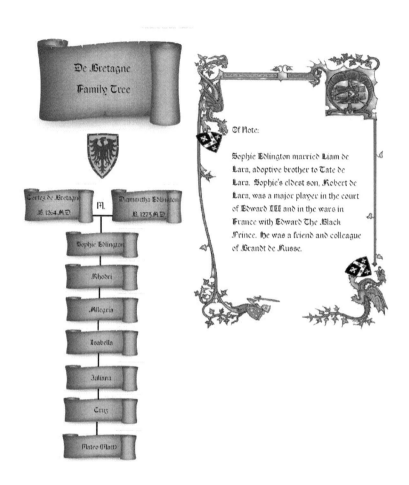

De Bretagne
Family Tree

Cortez de Bretagne
B. 1264 A.D.

M.

Diamantha Edlington
B. 1275 A.D.

Sophie Edlington

Rhodri

Allegria

Isabella

Juliana

Cruz

Mateo (Matt)

Of Note:

Sophie Edlington married Liam de Lara, adoptive brother to Tate de Lara. Sophie's eldest son, Robert de Lara, was a major player in the court of Edward III and in the wars in France with Edward The Black Prince. He was a friend and colleague of Brandt de Russe.

Now, please enjoy a bonus chapter from **THE DARK LORD**, featuring Ajax de Velt, Diamantha's great-grandfather. You can find the complete novel in Kindle format, paperback, or audiobook format on Amazon.

Enjoy!

THE DARK LORD

"Doomsman of Deeds and dreadful Lord ... Woe for that man
who in harm and hatred hales his soul to fiery embraces"
- Beowulf, Chapter II

CHAPTER ONE

May, 1180 AD
Scots Borderlands, England

He had her by the hair; strands of spun gold clutched in the dirty mailed glove. Perhaps it was because she had tried to bite him and he did not want to chance another encounter with her sharp white teeth. Or perhaps it was because he was a brute of a man, sworn to

Ajax de Velt and knowing little else but inflicting terror. Whatever the case, he had her tightly. She was trapped.

The woman and her father were on their knees in the great hall of the keep that had once belonged to them. Now it was their prison as enemy soldiers overran the place. There were memories of warmth and laughter embedded in the old stone walls, now erased by the terror that filled the room.

Pelinom Castle had been breached before midnight when de Velt's army had tunneled under the northeast tower of the wall, causing it to collapse. The woman and her father had tried to escape, along with the populace of their castle, but de Velt's men had swarmed them like locusts. It was over before it began.

Around her, the woman could hear the cries of her people as de Velt's men ensnared them. She had been captured by an enormous knight with blood splashed on his plate armor and she had understandably panicked. Even now, trapped against the floor of the great hall, she was terrified. Tales of de Velt's atrocities were well known in the north of England, for it was a dark and lawless time. She knew they were about to enter Hell.

From the corner of her eye, she could see her father on his knees. Sir Keats Coleby was a proud man and he had resisted the invasion gallantly. Why he hadn't been outright killed, as the garrison commander, was a mystery. But he was well-bloodied for his efforts. The woman couldn't see his face and she fixed her gaze back to the floor where the knight held her head. He very nearly had her nose pushed into the stone.

There was a great deal of activity around them. She could hear men shouting orders as the screams of her people eventually faded. Horror consumed her, knowing that de Velt's men were more than likely doing unspeakable things to her servants and soldiers. Tears stung her eyes but she fought them. She wondered what horrors de Velt had planned for her and her father.

She didn't have long to wait. With her face nearly pressed to the stone, she heard a deep, rumbling voice.

"Your name, knight."

The woman's father answered without hesitation. "Sir Keats Coleby."

"You are commander of Pelinom, are you not?"

"I am."

"And the girl?"

"My daughter, the Lady Kellington."

The silence that filled the air was full of anxiety. Kellington could hear boot falls all around her, though it was difficult to see just how many men were surrounding them. It felt like the entire army.

"Release her," she heard the voice say.

Immediately, the hand in her hair was removed and she stiffly lifted her head. Several unfriendly faces were glaring down at her, some from behind raised visors, some from helmless men. There were six in all, three knights and at least three soldiers. There could have been more standing behind her whom she did not see, but for now, six was enough.

Kellington's heart was pounding loudly in her ears as she looked around, waiting for the coming confrontation. The knight to her right spoke.

"How old are you, girl?"

She swallowed; her mouth was so dry that there was nothing to swallow and she ended up choking. "I have seen eighteen years, my lord."

The knight shifted on his big legs and moved in front of her; Kellington's golden-brown eyes dared to gaze up at him, noting a rather youngish warrior with a few days growth of beard and close-shorn blond hair. He didn't look as frightening as she had imagined, but she knew if the man was sworn to de Velt, then he must be horrible indeed.

"Does your husband serve Pelinom?" he asked, his deep voice somewhat quieter.

"I am not married, my lord."

The knight glanced over at Keats, who met his gaze steadily. Then he turned his back on them both, leaving them to stew in fear. Kellington watched him closely, struggling to keep her composure. She wasn't a flighty woman by nature, but panic was the only option at the moment.

"Are there any others of the ruling house here?" The knight paused and turned to look at them. "Only the garrison commander and his daughter? No sons, no husband, no brothers?"

Keats shook his head. "Just my daughter and I."

He deliberately left out "my lord." If it bothered the knight, he did not show it. Instead, he turned his focus to the gallery above, the ceiling and the walls. Pelinom was a small but rich and strategically desirable castle and he was pleased that they had managed to capture her relatively intact. The chorus of screams that had been prevalent since the army breached the bailey suddenly picked up again, but the knight pretended not to notice. He returned his focus to Keats.

"If you are lying to me, know that it will only harm you in the end," he said in a low voice. "The only class spared at this time is the ruling house. All others are put to death, so you may as well confess before we kill someone who is important to you."

Keats didn't react but Kellington's eyes widened. She had never been a prisoner before and had no idea of the etiquette or behaviors involved. Living a rather isolated existence at Pelinom for most of her life, it had left her protected for the most part. This siege, this horror, was new and raw.

"What does that mean?" she demanded before she could stop her tongue. "It is only my father and I, but my father has knights who serve him and we have servants who live here and..."

The knight flicked his eyes in her direction. "You will no longer concern yourself over them."

She leapt to her feet. "My lord, please," she breathed, her lovely face etched with anguish. "My father's knight and friend is Sir Trevan. He was with us when you captured us, but now I do not see him. Please do not harm him. He has a new infant and..."

"The weak and small are the first to be put to the blade. They are a waste of food and space within a military encampment."

Kellington's eyes grew wider, tears constricting her throat. Her hands flew to her mouth. "You cannot," she whispered. "Sir Trevan and his wife waited years for their son to be born. He is so small and helpless. Surely you cannot harm him. Please; I beseech you."

The knight lifted an eyebrow at her. Then he glanced at the other knights and soldiers standing around them; they were all de Velt men, born and bred to war. All they knew was death, destruction and greed. There was little room for compassion. He looked to Keats once more.

"Explain to your daughter the way of things." He turned away from them, seemingly pensive. "I will listen to what you tell her."

Keats sighed heavily, his gaze finding his only child. Though a woman grown she was, in fact, hardly taller than a child. But her short stature did nothing to detract from a deliciously womanly figure that had come upon her at an early age. Keats had seen man after man take a second look at his petite daughter, investigating the golden hair and face of an angel. He was frankly surprised that the de Velt men hadn't taken her for sport yet, for she was truly a gorgeous little thing. He was dreading it, knowing it was only a matter of time and there was nothing on earth he could do to stop them. The thought made him ill.

"Kelli," he said softly. "I know that you do not understand since you have never seen a battle, but this is war. There are no rules. The victor will do as he pleases and we, as his prisoners, must obey."

"He will kill a baby?" she fired back. "That is unthinkable; it's madness. Why must they kill the child? He's done nothing!"

"But he could grow up to do something." Keats tried to keep her calm. "Do you remember your Bible? Remember how the Pharaoh killed all of the first born males of Israel, afraid that one of them would grow up to be the man prophesized to overthrow him? 'Tis the same with war, lamb chop. The enemy does not see man, woman or child. He only sees a potential killer."

"You understand well the concept of destruction."

They all turned to the sound of the voice; a deep, booming tone that rattled the very walls. Keats had the first reaction all evening, his brown eyes widening for a split second before fading. Kellington stared at the man who had just entered the great hall as all of the other men around her seemed to straighten. Even the knight who had been doing the questioning moved forward quickly to greet the latest arrival.

"My lord," he said evenly. "This is Sir Keats Coleby, garrison commander of Pelinom, and his daughter the Lady Kellington. They claim that they are the only two members of the ruling house."

The man who stood in the entrance to the great hall was covered in mail, plate protection and gore. He still wore his helm, a massive thing with horns that jutted out of the crown. He was easily a head taller than even the tallest man in the room and his hands were as large as trenchers. The man's enormity was an understatement; he was colossal.

He radiated everything evil that had ever walked upon the earth. Kellington felt it from where she stood and her heart began to pound painfully. She resisted the urge to run to her father for protection, for she knew that no mortal could give protection against this. The very air of the great hall changed the moment the enormous man entered it. It pressed against her like a weight.

The great helmed head turned in the direction of the knight who had been doing the interrogation, now standing before him. Then he loosened a gauntlet enough to pull it off, raising his visor with an uncovered hand. The hand was dirty, the nails black with gore.

"I have been told the same," he replied, his voice bottomless. "We counted only four knights total, including Coleby, so this is the lot of them."

"Would you finish questioning the prisoners, my lord?"

For the first time, the helmed head turned in their direction. Kellington felt a physical impact as his eyes, the only thing visible through the helm, focused on her. Then she noticed the strangest thing; the left eye was muddy brown while the right eye, while mostly of the same muddy color, had a huge splash of bright green in it. The man had two different colored eyes. It unnerved her almost to the point of panic again.

"I heard some of what you were saying," the enormous knight said, still focused on Kellington. Then he looked at Keats. "Your explanation was true. You comprehend the rules of engagement and warfare so there will be no misunderstanding."

Keats didn't reply; he didn't have to. He knew who the man was without explanation and his heart sank. The knight continued into the room, scratching his forehead through the raised visor. Kellington followed him, noticing he passed closely next to her. She barely came up to his chest.

"I am de Velt," he said, returning his attention to both Kellington and Keats. "Pelinom Castle is now mine and you are my prisoners. If you think to plead for your lives, now would be the time."

"We must plead for our lives?" Kellington blurted. "But why?"

The massive knight looked at her but did not speak. The second knight, the one in charge of the interrogation, answered. "You are the enemy, my lady. What else are we to do with you?"

"You do not have to kill us," she insisted, looking between the men.

"Kelli," her father hissed sharply.

"Nay, Father." She waved him off, returning her golden-brown focus to de Velt. "Please, my lord, tell me why you would not spare our lives? If you were the commander of Pelinom, would you not have defended it also? That does not make us the enemy. It simply makes us the besieged. We were protecting ourselves as is our right."

De Velt's gaze lingered on her a moment. Then he flicked his eyes to the man at his side.

"Take Coleby."

"No!" Kellington screamed, throwing herself forward. She tripped on her own feet and ended up falling into de Velt. With small soft hands, she clutched his grisly mail. "Please, my lord, do not kill my father. I beg of you. I will do anything you ask, only do not kill my father. Please."

Jax gazed down at her impassively. When he spoke, it was to his men. "Do as I say. Remove the father."

The tears came, then. "Please, my lord," she begged softly. "I have heard that you are a man with no mercy and it would be easy to believe that were I to give credit to the rumors of your cruelty. But I believe there is mercy in every man, my lord, even you. Please show us your mercy. Do not do this horrible thing. My father is an honorable man. He was only defending his keep."

Jax wasn't looking at her; he was watching his men pull Keats to his feet. But the older knight's attention was on his distraught daughter.

"Kelli," he hissed at her. "Enough, lamb chop. I would have your brave face be the last thing I see as I leave this room."

Kellington ignored her father, her pleas focused on Jax. "If there is any punishment to be dealt, I will take it. If it will spare my father and our vassals, I will gladly submit. Do what you will with me, but spare the others. I beseech you, my lord."

Jax's face remained like stone. Seeing that the enormous knight was ignoring her, Kellington broke free and raced to her father, throwing herself against him as de Velt's men pulled him from the room. Keats tried to dislodge her, but his hands were bound and men were pulling on him, making it difficult.

"No, Father," she wept, her arms around his left leg. "I will not see you face the blade alone. They will have to kill me, too."

"No," Keats commanded softly, hoping the knights dragging him out would at least give him a moment with his only daughter. He lifted his bound arms and looped them around her, pulling her into an awkward embrace. "It is not your time to die. You will live and you will be strong. Know that I love you very much, little lamb. You have made me proud."

Kellington wept uncontrollably. Her father kissed her as their brief time together was harshly ended. There were many men attempting to separate them and someone grabbed her around her tiny waist and pulled her free. It was de Velt.

"Lock the girl in the vault," he commanded. "Take the father to the bailey and wait for me there."

He handed her over to the blond knight, who heaved her up over his shoulder. As he turned around to follow the father and other knights from the room, Kellington's upside down head found de Velt.

"Please spare him, my lord," she begged. "I will take all of his punishment if you wish, but do not harm him. He is all I have."

Jax watched his knight haul her away. She wasn't kicking and fighting as he had seen her do earlier when she had first been captured. She looked somewhat defeated. But the expression on her face was more powerful than any resistance. His gaze lingered on her a moment before he pulled on the loose gauntlet.

He had no time to waste on mercy. He was, after all, Jax de Velt.

THE END

Author's Notes:

I hope you enjoyed THE QUESTING (and THE DARK LORD bonus chapter!). Truly, I don't think any other novel I've written encompasses such a journey – this entire book was more about the journey than the actual destination, although the destination surely played a big part in this. The term "quest" had many different meanings for many different people in this tale. So let me highlight some things:

The execution method for the mother and her children in Gloucester was actually from Medieval law. It was very specific. Horrific, but specific. And Sophie's illness? Dysentery. She survived it because her physic was smart enough to know that the alcohol kills whatever germs cause it, so she got lucky. Alcohol was actually the only remedy they had for it in Medieval times. Finally, the names that the knights read off at the church, all of the names they recognized in that room that was stacked with English regalia, were actual names from men who fought at Falkirk.

Also, lots of Le Veque novels converge in this book – every one of Cortez's knights was a son or grandson of another Le Veque hero – Christopher de Lohr (RISE OF THE DEFENDER), Davyss de Winter (LESPADA), and Christian St. John (THE WARRIOR POET). Plus, Diamantha had the same condition of the eye that Jax de Velt (THE DARK LORD), her ancestor, had – two-tone eyes, otherwise known as heterochromia, although her case was less severe than his. Plus, her father, Michael de Bocage, was one of William de Wolfe's knights from THE WOLFE. Lots and lots of tie-ins!

I really hope you enjoyed this touching journey. Thank you for reading!

Made in the USA
Charleston, SC
01 July 2014